Saved

Krista Holly

ALSO BY KRISTA HOLLY

Wanted

For the readers.
I wouldn't be able to do this without you.
xoxo

Prologue

Kennedy

They said bad things happened in threes.

I guessed that seemed right. I mean, last year, I'd lost my grandmother and almost lost my best friend to some asshole seeking a little payback because she wouldn't put out. He'd drugged her and nearly overdosed her in the process.

After my terrible junior year, I'd thought I'd escaped that old cliché.

I couldn't have been more wrong.

Or more ill-prepared for what I'd find out.

Maybe bad things really did happen in threes.

But I believed the choices we made were usually the cause.

Chapter 1

Kennedy

Senior Year, Second Semester

This should have been the time I was preparing for my future. I should've been planning for college with my best friends. I should have been hanging out with them after school and causing mayhem on the weekends.

Not that I was one to cause mayhem. I was definitely the type to plan for my future though.

But right now? Honestly, it was the last thing on my mind. I didn't want to picture my future right now.

Instead, I was sitting next to a hospital bed, surrounded by beeping machines. I had no clue what the machines were monitoring. Some type of breathing machine was forcing air into his lungs, keeping oxygen flowing through what one might consider a lifeless form.

I held on to an extremely cold, pale hand. I could feel the callus on his thumb, caused by years and years of flipping through books—one book in particular that was resting on my lap now.

I swore, if I just kept holding on and letting my warm hand rest in his icy, rigid hand, he might wake up. I would get to see eyes that matched my own and a smile that rivaled the sun.

It'd been a week. One full painful, sleepless week.

Seven days.

One hundred sixty-eight hours since my world had blown up.

I'd been plastered to this uncomfortable plastic seat for most of that time. My back begged for mercy as I'd been hunched over for many nights of prayer since he was admitted.

When I had gotten the call that something had happened— something terrible, something probably irreversible—I'd nearly passed out. I had known for a fact that my hearing was impaired for an unmeasured amount of time before my boyfriend, Kyle's, concerned voice broke through my temporary deafness. He'd been across the room when I'd answered the call, and then he had stood in front of me, holding my face in his hands and begging me to tell him what was wrong.

"Everything, Kyle. Everything is wrong."

I had been nothing but sobs and tears for the first two days. After that, I'd become numb to all the medical talk and prognoses. The odds were not in our favor from what the doctors had told us.

If I were being honest, I didn't think he even had a chance, especially if the machines were any indicators. They were currently the only things keeping him alive. I didn't know about anyone else, but this was not how I wanted to see my dad.

The doctors had taken a scan this morning, one that would probably alter everything and confirm my deepest fears.

I'd texted Mom an hour ago, telling her that she needed to be here to hear what the doctors had to say. I had a gut feeling that today was going to be the last day I sat here.

The first two days, my mom and I'd both stayed here. After that though, we had been taking shifts with her being here during the day while I would come and sit through the night. I didn't want to go home, but Mom would insist I rest.

One of the machines beeped loudly. I jerked upright from my bent over position, and a nurse came in, hitting some buttons and stopping the noise somehow. She apologetically smiled at me and then walked back out.

At the same time, my mother walked in. "Hey, sweetie."

Her steps faltered when she saw me. I knew I wore my sadness like a neon sign. She, on the other hand, looked surprisingly well rested and put together compared to me. I didn't think I'd actually gotten any sleep that wasn't fitful and short. Her hair was done. She was wearing nice jeans with a button-up silk blouse and no makeup. Me? I was dressed in yoga pants and a baggy sweatshirt.

"Has the doctor been back?" she asked while walking over to me. She placed a kiss on my head and then moved back around to the other side to sit on the spare plastic chair.

She took my dad's hand and placed a brief kiss on his wedding band before gently setting his hand back down.

"No, but I'll go grab a coffee and find him, so you can have some time alone with Dad," I meekly said while standing and placing the worn and cherished Bible under my dad's hand.

As I walked down to the waiting room lounge, I took my phone out and saw six missed calls—four from Kyle Masters and two from Lo Grande, my best friend since seventh grade. I knew I should have clued them in on what was going on, but I was still feeling numb to everything, outside of the fear and pain consuming me.

I poured my coffee and added way too much sugar and creamer. Then, I began my journey back to the critical care wing. I made my way over to the nurses' station and asked for Dr. Cramer—supposedly the best neurosurgeon in the Midwest. Currently, I doubted his credentials, especially when I considered the condition my father was in now.

Seven days ago, Dr. Cramer had performed an emergency brain surgery for a ruptured aneurysm. The bleeding had been stopped, and everything had appeared to have gone as planned. Until two days after when the machines had started beeping like an angry virus-impaired computer. The nurses and doctors had whisked into the room and shooed my mother and me out. Dad had suffered another rupture that had then caused a stroke.

After that, everything had tumbled downhill faster than a boulder falling from the top of a mountain. When I had finally been allowed back into the room, all the machines had been in place.

After the second surgery, I'd asked the doctor what'd caused the first aneurysm. Dr. Cramer had said it could have been a number of things, but usually with cases like my father's, stress and poor eating habits had contributed to his blood pressure rising and subsequently had caused the aneurysm to burst.

While my mom had sat next to the hospital bed, softly praying, she'd briefly connected eyes with the doctor and suddenly looked away after his explanation. If I didn't know any better, I'd think I had seen shame instead of sadness. Her eyes had glazed over, and her hand had trembled when she lifted it to catch her sob.

Now, as I walked back into the hospital room that essentially had my father on his deathbed, I questioned what God's plan was.

My father, the pastor at the town's biggest Christian church, was the last person who deserved to go out like this. I knew God had his reasons, and I didn't want to question him, but I couldn't seem not to.

Why him? Why my dad? The man who never turns his back on a struggling soul. The man who follows God's word to no end, dedicating his life to the man upstairs.

I just didn't understand it.

As soon as I took my seat, the doctor walked in, holding an iPad. He wore a solemn face.

I met his eyes. "Just tell us. Don't beat around the bush, Dr. Cramer."

I could see the answers etched into his creased forehead and his downturned lips. And, even though doctors were supposed to be scientific and not emotional when it came to their cases, I could still see the glittering sadness in his eyes.

He attended our church on Wednesdays. He knew my father. He knew me. He knew his news would kill us.

I quickly glanced at my mom, and she started to open her mouth but then closed it as she nodded to the doctor.

"Well, after our scans this morning, I'm sorry to say, but your husband's brain is no longer functioning. The EEG shows no electrical activity coming from the brain. There's nothing more we can do. The second rupture was just too much for him to handle. The only things keeping him alive now are the machines."

I choked down the sob trying to escape from my throat. My head met the mattress, and I sobbed quietly.

The doctor continued, "I know this is incredibly difficult. I'm sorry there isn't more we can do." He sadly looked at me when I lifted my head back up, tears running down my face. To my mother, he said, "I'll give you some time to yourselves."

"There's nothing else you can do? No trials or medications?" My desperation mixed with anger, uncontrollable and all-consuming.

I stood to shout, but Mom hissed my name, effectively scolding me back into my place.

My chest ached. *Don't take him from me!*

I wasn't a doctor, but I couldn't accept this outcome. I couldn't accept giving up. It'd only been a little over a week since I said my last words to my father. I couldn't even remember what they were. Probably something stupid like, *I'll see you at dinner.*

"Kennedy"—the doctor looked overwhelmed with pain, like he couldn't bear the sight of me breaking down—"we've done all we can. If there were any other options, I would have exhausted them all before coming to you with these results. You can leave him on life support, but it won't change anything. I truly am sorry." With those final parting words, he moved to leave.

When the door slid back into place, I looked to my mother. No emotions were showing on her face while silent tears raced down my cheeks.

I took my father's hand again and clasped both of mine around his. Resting my head on the Bible that lay at his side, I sent up my final prayer and kissed my father's hand and then his cheek good-bye.

I choked out through my torrential tears, "I'll miss you, Daddy."

I grasped Kyle's hand so tight; my knuckles were white, and the tips of his fingers were red. My right arm draped through Lo's bent elbow while I leaned my head on her shoulder. My tears continued to fall. My eyes squeezed painfully shut while we sat in the front row at my father's funeral.

All the members of our church were in attendance, paying their respects to their deceased pastor. I couldn't count the hugs and offerings of prayers I'd received since news of him passing was announced. I should be grateful they cared, but I was finding it more and more difficult to accept their condolences with the looks of pure pity pinching their features.

My mom and I'd pulled the plug two days ago.

What a crappy thing to say—*pulled the plug*—like he was some old, obsolete computer that just needed to be unplugged and forgotten about.

I'd spent the last couple of days lying in my bed, clutching his old Bible to my chest and praying that this was all just an extremely bad dream. A nightmare that would end soon. I hadn't let out any emotions even though my body screamed at me to purge the overwhelming sorrow and fury I'd felt from the moment his lungs stopped inhaling. I was numb to my surroundings and all the people who had tried their hardest to comfort me.

Today was actually the first day I'd let any sort of human emotions show. I had woken up and finally let the tears that I'd held back for two days fall. I'd originally thought that holding the tears back would be the most painful thing I'd ever experienced.

But, now, as I let all my sorrow pour from my eyes like a waterfall, I knew I was so wrong, and this was more painful. It felt like my tears were burning trails down my cheeks. I was sure that when I looked in the mirror later, I'd see the charred, scraggly lines my tears had left behind.

The junior pastor, Clayton Young, was standing behind my father's casket that sat suspended over a six-foot hole in the ground, a fresh pile of dirt off to the side. He spoke about death and our souls moving on to heaven above where God would greet Pastor Kiblen with open arms.

I knew it was wrong, but I almost wished God had crossed his arms and said, *Sorry, buddy, but you're needed downstairs more than you are here. Go back home and see your daughter graduate high school and college. Don't forget to walk her down that aisle when she marries the man of her dreams.*

But I knew that'd never be the case.

It wasn't even the fact that he wouldn't be able to see those things. It was the fact that he wouldn't be here *at all*. He wouldn't be a phone call away or working on his sermons downstairs in his office. He wouldn't be at the church where I went to watch him inspire a roomful of people, wanting to hear God's word. *Never again.*

"And, now, as we lay to rest our dear senior pastor—a father, a husband, friend, confidante, and follower of the Lord—his daughter, Kennedy, would like to read a verse from the Bible that Pastor Kiblen always turned to in times of death and grief."

I stood slowly, dropped Kyle's hand, and turned around to face all the people who had been blessed with meeting my father and experiencing his spirit.

Death.

It was a bitter pill to swallow.

I took a deep breath and reached out to grasp Kyle's hand once more. I was desperate for an anchor. I needed his strength right now because mine wasn't enough.

He gave it a reassuring squeeze, and I closed my eyes before speaking. For some reason, it was easier—not being able to see all the people who loved my father so dearly. Besides, I didn't need to look at the paper folded in my pocket. I'd heard my father recite this dozens of times.

"Second Corinthians 1:3-4. *Praise be to the God and Father of our Lord Jesus Christ, the Father of compassion…and the God of all comfort, who comforts us…in all our troubles, so that we can comfort those in any trouble with the comfort we ourselves receive…from God.*" I gasped painfully for air after stumbling through, releasing a new round of furious tears.

Reciting something I had heard my father preach on many other occasions was too much. Many found comfort in those words. I knew I used to. But, right now, those words hurt more than they healed.

My knees shook, threatening to give out, and then Kyle was holding me up in front of a crowd of people as I burst into sobs.

This hurts.

I'd never felt something so heartbreaking before, like a knife continuously being stabbed through my heart over and over. I'm surprised there wasn't a pool of blood surrounding my feet.

My mother didn't even seem affected. Her eyes were glassy, but no tears fell. And I wasn't sure why, but that made me so angry.

Show me something, Mom.

I didn't know if anyone else could see the fiery rage burning inside me, but Kyle squeezed me like a vise before he pulled me back down to my seat.

He whispered in my ear, "It's okay. We're going to get through this, I promise."

I didn't know how those words were supposed to comfort me. They did nothing but incite more fury. Everything was not okay.

The junior pastor said the final parting words before the machine started lowering my father's casket. When it was put six feet down, I grabbed my handful of dirt and tossed it in. My prayers hadn't been answered for days, and I almost let God know what was really on my mind.

How could he take the one man who never harmed anyone, who had shared his word, who had spent more time in that church than he did at home? It's just not fair.

I couldn't help but angrily toss in the white rose I'd been clutching for the last thirty minutes. Something so beautiful shouldn't be given on such a dark day. It deserved to be six feet under as well.

I looked back to see my mother wiping at her nose before pulling her sunglasses down from her hair. Not a single tear was shed from her today. I didn't know if it was shock or what, but I would have felt more comforted if she had just shed a damn tear.

Why am I the only one losing my ever-loving mind over this?

I was so struck with pain and sadness. It felt like my heart was actually bleeding. My tears wouldn't stop flowing like the waterfall I wanted to throw myself over.

Kyle led me to the limo that the funeral home had supplied. I slid in and moved to the opposite side, and he climbed in after me. My mother followed him, shutting the door with a deep sigh.

I saw my reflection in the window and cringed. I'd never felt this broken. Surely, the cracks I was seeing in my mirror image were just a figment of my imagination and my exhausted body.

Mom's phone rang from her purse that she'd left on the floor of the limo. She bent to pick it up and silenced it. I wondered briefly who would call her on a day like today. The day of her husband's *funeral*, for God's sake.

When we finally got back to our house where guests had already begun to arrive, I quietly slipped upstairs and burrowed under my covers. I wouldn't accept any more hugs or condolences or prayers.

I was becoming enraged with God. With Mom. With everyone and everything. I couldn't handle it. I just wanted it all to go away, to stop beating me harder into the ground.

This day didn't happen.

I hoped and prayed—like I had done every day since Dad was rushed to surgery—that this would all be the worst nightmare I'd ever experienced, and I'd wake up and find Dad in the kitchen, making pancakes and frying bacon.

My dreams granted me that vision.

Too bad I couldn't stay there.

Chapter 2

Kyle

Kennedy wouldn't talk to me. I knew I should have been able to console her and make things better, but she wouldn't give me any clue as to how I was supposed to do that. She was grieving. I got that, I did, but then again, I didn't. I'd never been through this. Both my parents were alive and well.

She didn't have that anymore. And I didn't know how to fix it. If there were any way for me to help her get over this, I was drawing a blank. The best thing I could do for her was be there for her and get her anything she wanted or needed.

But she didn't want anything. I'd asked.

And, when I'd asked if she needed anything, her only answer had been, "My dad."

How am I supposed to give her that? How am I even supposed to respond to that?

"How long has she been sleeping?" Lo asked as we sat on the back porch of Kennedy's family home. It was like an old farmhouse but in the middle of town.

I looked at the time on my phone. "About five hours. But it was like this yesterday, too. When I left her house the other night, she had been sleeping for four hours already, and when I came back yesterday afternoon, her mom said she never even woke up." Looking up at the sky, I shook my head. "I don't know how to fix this, guys."

"I don't think you can, Kyle. She just needs to grieve, and she'll figure out how to cope," Lo quietly answered. She was sitting on Chase Carter's lap—her boyfriend for a little over a year and my best friend. Their hands were laced together, resting on her lap.

"Her dad was everything to her," I said painfully.

"So, it's going to take her a little longer to move on from this, man. But you can't beat yourself up about something no one had any control over," Dieter Farley, one of my best friends, said calmly, which was rare for him since there wasn't a calm bone in his body.

The guy was always fidgeting and on the move, never sitting for longer than necessary. But, today, he was different. I'd never seen him so stationary, so somber.

I straightened my head back up and looked at my group of closest friends. It felt like just yesterday when we'd all become so close, but then again, it felt like we'd been this way since we were babies. We'd become family at some point. I was just hoping Kennedy remembered that as she went through this rough time.

"I'm gonna go check on her." Standing up and shoving my phone into my back pocket, I walked over and opened the screen door to slip inside the house.

Everyone—except for the junior pastor, his wife, and their three kids—were gone.

Sandra Kiblen, Kennedy's mom, stepped out of the kitchen to stop me from going up the stairs. "She's still sleeping, Kyle." She had a sympathetic look on her face, but I didn't know how she was coping so well while Kennedy was torn to pieces. "You and your friends should probably just head home. Come and check on her tomorrow."

"Is it okay if I just go up now, and then I promise, we'll all leave?" I asked hopefully.

I'd never really talked to Mrs. Kiblen. She hadn't been around when Kennedy and I first started dating, and when she had come back from taking care of her mother in St. Louis, she was always busy. She worked for some kind of nonprofit organization, but that was all I really knew.

"Sure, Kyle, but I know she needs the rest, so please don't make it too long."

I was sure a hostile tone was hidden in there somewhere even though she masked it with her smooth drawl. After over a year of dating Kennedy, I still got the feeling her mom didn't like me. She tried to keep us separated as much as possible.

Her dad had loved me though, and I'd really looked up to David Kiblen. He'd welcomed me into his church and his home, and he'd trusted me to take care of Kennedy when he wasn't around. And I did. I loved that girl. I'd never felt so crazy about someone in my life as I did for Kennedy.

I tapped on Kennedy's door before turning the old knob. "Kennedy?" I whispered softly before going into the dark room and walking closer to her bed.

I turned on the lamp that sat on her nightstand. She didn't even stir. I was more concerned about her now than I had been yesterday, thinking that it was just all the sleepless nights at the hospital and the emotional toll it had taken on her. Now though, something seemed more off than I could pinpoint. Like a sixth sense, I could feel her sadness draining her energy.

I sat on the edge of the bed and nudged her shoulder a little. She stirred slightly but not enough to wake up.

I leaned down to place a kiss on her cheek and then moved over to her ear where I whispered, "Ken, baby, wake up."

It wasn't enough to wake her though.

And this was where my nerves settled in again. I'd read about the symptoms and side effects of depression. I knew there was a possibility of her becoming severely depressed. She had been closer to her dad than anyone in the world, but I hadn't thought his death would affect her so hard.

She was one of the strongest girls I knew. She was always the happy-go-lucky kind of girl, never letting a single bad thing in her life bring her down—at least, not for long. She was *that* girl—Miss Optimistic, glass half-full, and all those clichés—and I loved her even more for that.

But, when all of this was said and done, I didn't know if her positive attitude toward life would matter, if she'd even be the same girl. The day she had gotten the call of her dad's hospitalization scarred her deeply.

I'd love her no matter what, but it hurt me so much to see her so incredibly down.

"Kennedy, babe, come on, wake up for me. I'm getting ready to leave."

She uncurled from her little fetal position and rolled onto her back, still dressed in her clothes from the funeral—a simple long-sleeved black lace dress that hugged her curves. "That light hurts my eyes," she rasped softly.

"I'll turn it off." Reaching over, I twisted the switch, and the room was flooded with darkness. "I have to go. Your mom said I could say good night. Do you need me to do anything for you before I go?" I asked hesitantly. I already knew she was going to say there was nothing I could do.

I couldn't see them, but I knew tears were falling from the corners of her eyes. It was obvious when she subtly wiped at her cheeks while a small sniffle she'd tried to hide broke the silence.

"I want you to stay," she cried, sounding so broken.

"Do you think your mom would make an exception?" I asked cautiously, knowing her mother would say no because she always did.

Kennedy's dad never had a problem with it as long as I slept on the little couch in the corner of her room. I'd respected him enough that I never tried anything in his house. The most Kennedy and I had done in here was sneak a kiss on the lips when no one was watching.

Kennedy pushed herself up higher on her bed. She looked weak and stiff, her body tensing with the movement. "I don't give a damn what she says is okay or not. If she doesn't let you stay, then I'll leave. I'm eighteen. I can do whatever I want," she said heatedly, switching emotions like a coin toss at the beginning of a football game.

I clasped her hand to try to soothe her. I knew I should watch my next move. I didn't want to upset her any more than she was. "Hey, hey…calm down, Ken. It's okay. Let's go down and ask together, okay? You need to eat something, and I'm sure Lo and the rest of the crew would like to say good night, too. If your mom says no, I'll do whatever you want. You can stay with me, or we can all go to Lo's." I swooped down to kiss her pale cheek. "I'm sure Lo's dad wouldn't mind."

"I just want to be with you or alone, Kyle. I don't want a pity party at Lo's." Her tone switched to biting and severe so quickly that it shocked me, but I didn't let the surprise show. She'd never be able to scare me off.

"All right, babe. I understand." Standing, I offered her my hand.

She slowly climbed off her bed. The short hem of her dress scrunched up to the top of her thighs.

"Do you want to change?" I glanced around the room instead of focusing on the newly bared skin. I would not be the kind of guy who only thought of sex.

When I looked back at her she slowly shook her head from side to side, the blonde hair around her shoulders swishing with the movement.

"Everyone's still out back." I grabbed her hand and pulled her out of her room and to the stairs.

We started to walk down to the kitchen. I moved my arm around her waist, slowly guiding her. She walked so sluggish and weighed down. I didn't want her to feel anything other than happiness, but I could see the grief and sadness eating away at her.

Her mom was sitting at the dining room table, typing away at the keyboard on the laptop in front of her. Kennedy bypassed the kitchen and headed straight for the back porch, opening the old squeaky screen door and stepping out.

I heard muted laughter, and when I saw Dieter dancing to no music, grinding his ass in Lo's face while she hid behind her hands, I couldn't help my little grin. At least they were trying to lighten this unbelievably depressing day. If it was hard for me to accept the events of today, I couldn't imagine how Kennedy was feeling. I had no clue of the depths it would drag her.

"Kennedy!" Talan gasped, straightening from her hunched over laughter and standing to come hug her. "Are you hungry or thirsty? Here, sit—"

"No, Talan, but thank you," she abruptly cut her off, instead taking a seat on one of the old Adirondack patio chairs. "What's everyone doing?"

I looked over to Dieter.

He had a cautious smile on his face. He was dressed in black jeans and a black tee with his discarded black button-up placed over Talan's shoulders. "Nothing, K, just trying to talk Lo into coming to the dark side where I strip and she pimps me out. What do you say? You want to take a cookie from Santa's plate and earn yourself a spot on the naughty list with us?"

"Us? Dieter, I never said I'd be your pimp. Besides…you're not hot enough for my operation." Lo deviously smirked at him while Chase tried to withhold his laughter, burying his face in her back.

Dieter pretended to be hurt while holding his hands over his heart.

I sat next to Kennedy and grabbed her hand to squeeze it. She didn't squeeze back, but I didn't let go either. I needed to feel some kind of connection with her and reassure her that I was there, that I wasn't going anywhere.

"Do you think you'll be back at school on Monday?" Lo asked.

I looked over to my girlfriend and didn't take my eyes off her. She had missed school since the day her dad went into the hospital.

Kennedy gently bobbed her head instead of answering her best friend. When I glanced briefly at Lo, I saw the pain for her best friend glistening in her eyes. We'd been through a lot together as a group of friends. But never something like this.

I could tell Kennedy was struggling to sit here and have a normal conversation. I watched as she closed her eyes, and she kept them shut for a while. Her knee jiggled, and she fiddled with the hem of her dress.

I couldn't figure out what was bugging her the most—being here when all she wanted was to be alone, or the stares from our friends. Their stares were in sympathy and concern, but I could tell they were at a loss, too. None of us knew how to comfort her.

There was an awkward silence while we all sat there, and the only way I could think of curing it was by getting everyone to leave. She'd said she wanted to be with just me or alone. Sitting here with all our friends was probably overwhelming her more than she needed right now.

Taking initiative, I stood and pulled Kennedy up with me. She willingly came, but it was leaden, her body moving like a block of cement.

"I think we're going to crash for the night, guys. We'll call you tomorrow."

At once, everyone stood and simultaneously said, "Yeah," and, "You got it, man," and, "Catch you later."

While our friends shuffled off toward the side of the house, Lo stayed back for a beat. "Ken, I know I've said this, but I love you. And I'm really sorry for what you're going through. Call me if you need anything, okay? Dead of night, and I will be here." She took Kennedy's hand and smiled. "I just want you to know that."

They hugged briefly, but even I could see how detached Kennedy was in the moment. When they pulled apart, I smiled weakly at Lo.

I thought we both knew.

We couldn't fix this.

Not with hugs or encouraging smiles.

Not with *I love you*s.

Nothing.

Chapter 3

Kennedy

When Kyle had woken me up, I'd never felt so distant. From myself. From him. From our friends.

We walked back into the house and stopped at the dining room where my mom had been sitting when we went out back. She was still there, continuing to type on her laptop.

"Mom," I said lowly.

She glanced up from her screen.

"Can Kyle stay the night?"

"Kennedy," she sighed. "I would prefer it if he didn't. You know how I feel about this kind of stuff."

I clutched Kyle's hand harder, my bones shifting with the movement. "I understand. I'll see you in the morning."

She gave me a curt nod before focusing back on the screen. I pulled Kyle toward the front door where I slipped on my black ballet flats.

"Wait, babe. Are you sure? Maybe your mom just wants to spend tonight with you," Kyle said tentatively, dropping my hand to help me adjust the heel of my shoe. "I can come back bright and early. I—"

He started to say more, but I stopped him with a hand to his shoulder. "Just take me to your house, Kyle. *Please*. I don't think she gives a damn about this day. I don't think she gives a damn that her husband is under six feet of dirt," I growled out quietly enough so that Mom wouldn't hear me.

He opened the front door without another word and ushered me out to his new Dodge Ram—a birthday gift from his parents a week ago. Kyle helped me inside the tall truck and then shut the door.

I hadn't even grabbed clothes or my phone. But I didn't really need them either. I'd been keeping clothes stashed at Kyle's house since the third month we'd officially been together, just like he had some stashed in my closet, and I didn't really need my phone because anyone who knew me well enough knew they could get ahold of me through Kyle.

We drove through the quiet streets of Davidson, Indiana, the town I had been born and raised in, and when we pulled into the garage at his large house, a little bit of that crushing, painful weight dropped off my shoulders. My home no longer felt like home. It was empty, cold, and lonely. I'd never been at home without Dad there unless he was at church.

"Do you want to watch a movie?" Kyle asked me as we exited his truck.

We entered the house through the professionally designed huge mudroom, decorated with light-blue and yellow paints and nice white cabinetry. Everything was organized and put in specific places. It was a stark contrast to the laundry room at my house where clothes constantly sat on top of the dryer.

My mind tried to focus on everything but the pain, tripping over small and useless details of interior design. We walked down a hallway and then through a sitting room that opened up and led to the foyer. Kyle followed my slow pace. I could feel his concern and worry swell, trying to swallow me up.

Don't look at me like that, Kyle.

His pitying stare fueled my need to forget even more. Otherwise, if I focused on the events of today, the agony from missing someone so vital to my life would feel like it was going to pull me under like a riptide.

We moved through the house, unhurried. Kyle gave me time to just *be* without forcing me to talk or think.

I knew his house like the back of my hand. I knew where every family picture that hung on the walls had been taken. I knew of every childhood picture of Kyle because he was adorable, and his mom had made it a point to show me every chubby-cheeked glory there was. I knew that every figurine that rested on the entryway table had been bought in different countries where the Masters had traveled. Like the one of the Eiffel Tower and the one of the Taj Mahal. I knew that the all-white bedroom was only ever used by Kyle's grandparents because it had hypoallergenic everything in it. I knew where all the extra linens and cleaning supplies were. This house was my second home. But, right now, it felt like my only home.

"Kennedy?"

I didn't know how many times he'd said my name, but I finally heard him.

"Yeah?" I responded while self-consciously wrapping my arms around my waist. Maybe I could hold myself together better that way. Keep all the emotions threatening to explode like a bomb at bay. I didn't really know. I just knew my body was seconds from bursting into a million pieces.

He sighed. I knew I should've felt guilty—or felt at least some kind of emotion—for the way I was acting and all the effort he and everyone around me had been putting in to comfort me, but I couldn't bring myself out of my shell. I didn't know if I ever would. Even if I did find my way out of what felt like this abyss of loss and pain, I didn't know if things would be the same. If *I* would be the same.

When we walked into his room, Kyle started to talk, but his generic ringtone stopped him. He pulled out his phone from his back pocket and sighed heavily, letting all the air rush from his nose. "It's your mom."

"Just put it on speakerphone," I told him.

He slid his finger across the screen and set the phone on his desk while taking a seat in the office chair.

"Let me talk to Kennedy, Kyle," she said before he even got a chance to say hello.

I rolled my eyes. If she could see me, she'd seethe. "It is me, Mom."

"Kennedy, damn it, when you said you'd see me in the morning, I thought you meant you were going to go upstairs and go to bed. Not sneak out the front door with Kyle. Do you realize how terrifying that was?"

As terrifying as being stuck in that house.

So much heat and anger rushed through me at her tone. I could feel my cheeks flush as I tried to stay calm.

I walked over and sat on Kyle's lap. He wrapped his arms around my middle and twisted the chair from side to side, all while my mom ranted on and on about respect and how my dad would never have let me get away with this.

That told me how much she knew. My dad had already let me stay at Kyle's. My dad had let Kyle stay in my room. My dad had trusted us.

I knew what he would and would not allow, but my mother's voice tainted my thoughts. Talk of my dead father brought burning, thick tears to my eyes.

"You'd better come home right now, Kennedy Grace Kiblen. I won't tell you twice." Then, she hung up, like the command and threat could actually make me come home.

I had news for her. I was eighteen. I didn't have to come home if I didn't want to.

"I don't want this to become a thing between you and your mom," Kyle said in a soft tone.

I loved him for his effort never to become a wedge between my parents because he cared, and he wanted things to be better.

So, I told him that. "I love you. You know that, right?" I twisted my head around to look at him behind me, tears running down my eyes and all. "I love you so much, but right now...things aren't good with Mom and me. They haven't been for a few weeks. And, now, my dad is dead, Kyle." Admitting it out loud twisted my guts so tight, I had to squeeze my fists to fight off the cramping I felt all over, predominantly in my chest. A terrible fist constricted around my heart. Tears continued to rain down. "And...I don't know how I'm going to get over this. If I will *ever* get over this," I choked out, the pain strangling my throat.

He stood, effortlessly lifting me in his arms, and walked us toward his king-size bed. Not saying a word, he turned me to face his bed. He took off my simple guardian angel necklace, a gift from my dad, and carefully placed it on the nightstand, knowing how much it meant to me. Then, he gently lowered the zipper down from the base of my neck to the bottom of my spine. Then, he pushed the fitted lace off my shoulders, arms, and down my legs.

"I know, Kennedy. I know things are rough right now. Things don't make sense. But you will always make sense to me. You. Me.

Us. We're forever. I'm gonna love you through it all." He softly kissed my neck after his loving words.

The fist around my heart loosened only slightly, but it was enough for me to take a full breath without feeling like I might collapse.

Kyle stepped away for a few moments. I shivered in his absence and my lack of clothes. A drawer sliding open caught my attention, and when he approached again, he slipped a shirt over my head and then helped me slide my arms through the long sleeves. From the size and the smell of his detergent, I knew immediately it was his shirt.

He leaned around me and pulled the covers back. I climbed under the sheets and propped myself up against his black leather-upholstered headboard. Kyle walked away and stepped into his bathroom. When he came back out, he had a pair of basketball shorts on, no shirt. All defined muscles and tan skin.

As he crawled in on the other side and scooted toward me, I shifted down further and turned toward him. Taking my right hand, he played with the Claddagh ring he had given to me the first time he told me he loved me.

"I love that you never take this off." He admired the ring with a small smile gracing his lips.

"Never," I told him honestly.

A deep breath lifted his chest before he spoke, "However long it takes, no matter the amount of time you need…I'm going to be here. This is always going to be true." He swiped his finger over the ring where the heart pointed inward. "I believe that. You've always been the one to get everyone else through, Ken. So, I know you can get through this. It hurts right now; I know that, baby. But please…just please always remember the good things about your dad and family. All the good things you remember are what's going to keep him alive in here." He pressed his hand over my heart.

I breathed in deeply, shutting my eyes and letting those last few tears slip out. His words were true and so right. But none of that mattered to my broken heart.

Kyle tightly squeezed my hand. "Baby, I'm so sorry. I know you're tired of hearing that. I love you so much."

I nodded my head. I knew all of that, but for some reason, the words sat on the surface like a buoy even though I needed them to dive deeper into my ocean of grief.

As I moved closer to him, he awkwardly wrapped his arms around me and kissed my forehead. It wasn't enough though. Right now, I needed more. I needed to feel something else other than this soul-crushing pain.

I maneuvered myself so that our lips were level and then leaned forward to touch mine to his. He was hesitant. I didn't want him to be so timid around me. But, right now, I was broken, and he knew that. It made him extremely cautious with me.

And all I could think was, *No, I don't want careful at all.*

My heart pleaded for something other than pain, galloping at Kentucky Derby speeds, anticipating a win.

"Please..." I begged him.

I needed him. He gave me what I wanted.

He pursued me like he usually did. Not rough, never rough. But with more effort than what I was getting from him a second ago. He moved his hand to my hip and pulled me closer. Still kissing him, I propped myself up onto my elbow. I was moving all on muscle memory and the need to forget this day and these last two weeks.

"I need this," I whispered to him.

My hands trailed his tan skin before I had my hands shoving his shorts down, trying to free his hardness. He swiftly grabbed my hands and pinned them down as he moved to hover over me.

The slight shake of his head stabbed at my heart, his lips sliding from side to side in a feather-light touch.

"Babe—"

But I didn't give him the chance to argue before I shoved him away, and I moved on top of him.

"Kyle, *please*..."

Four a.m. came slowly. Kyle was lying on his side next to me, his mouth slightly open, while soft snores came from him. I looked him over in the dimly lit room. The only light coming from the bathroom spotlighted his ripped chest.

I'd been lying awake the entire time since he'd reluctantly let his eyes drift closed after shutting me down six hours ago. I'd cried more after he said no. I knew it was wrong to want to numb the pain with something else, but for some reason, I needed something that was going to pull me out of this slump, even for just a brief moment. Damn the consequences.

But his only response had been, "I can't enable you like that, babe. It's not healthy."

And I'd cried more. He'd held me fiercely and tried to soothe me by running his large hands up and down my back and through my hair, down my sides and to my hips, before wrapping me in a crushing hug while I just continued to cry.

I was falling apart.

I couldn't just sit there anymore. My body and mind were so restless and refused to relax. I got up off the bed and walked over to Kyle's computer desk where I opened his MacBook. I guessed now was as good a time as any to check my email.

The first thing in my Inbox was an email from the Admissions Director at Wheaton College, offering his condolences and his help and guidance if I ever should need it. He was a close friend and previous classmate of my father's. I appreciated him reaching out, but I wished everyone would just stop with the sympathy and condolences and reminders of how great of a man my father was. Deleting the email after a quick read-through, I switched to my iCloud account.

I had thousands of pictures on here, but my favorites were the ones from the last mission trip my dad and I had taken to Israel two summers ago. It was the best religious and spiritual trip we'd ever gone on. I'd never felt so in touch with my beliefs and closer to God. I'd never admired my dad's wonder and his devotion to teaching about the Lord's word as much as I did then. There were hundreds of pictures of the biblical landmarks and of us getting to know the people, experiencing their culture and day-to-day lives.

It was truly one of the best times of my life. And I had gotten to share it with my dad. But I'd never get to share that again—those moments where I finally understood why my father was so passionate or when he'd tell me all the answers to my problems were in the Bible and in my prayers.

That pain I'd felt earlier was back tenfold, rocking my body with overwhelming grief. I was trembling. I quickly exited out of the browser. The hurt that came from looking at those pictures weren't worth it anymore. I could never re-create those memories, never experience something so majestic and eye-opening again.

I slid a pair of Kyle's sweats on and stealthily left his room. Tiptoeing down the stairs, I headed for the kitchen where I grabbed a glass from the cupboard above the sink and filled it with water. I hadn't eaten more than a couple of bites for maybe two days, but hunger pains were the least of my concerns.

Even though I felt more at home here than at my own house, I still needed air, so I made my way outside to the pool. April mornings were still slightly chilly, but the Masters had a heated pool. I rolled Kyle's sweats up to my knees and sat on the edge, dipping my legs into the bath-like water. This quiet morning with no noise but whatever insects were out and the slight slosh of the water at my feet was like a warm hug to my overworked body and mind.

I'd never been the night-owl type, but the feeling I got from the calm morning was finally soothing my racing thoughts.

I heard the door open behind me and turned to see Kyle's mom slipping outside with a mug in each hand.

"Is it okay if I join you?" She tentatively approached me. "I brought tea."

I nodded, and she sat next to me, slipping her feet into the pool as well. We sat in silence for a while. I didn't know what to say. I'd come out here, so I could shelf my thoughts, but I could feel her glancing at me every now and then. The pity radiated off my boyfriend's mother in spades.

"I want you to know you're always welcome here, Kennedy."

For a tiny moment, I worried that my mom had called and complained or forbidden me from staying over.

Jennifer, being the awesome mom and woman that she was, would have said, *To hell with that.* She'd always treated me like one of her own.

"Thank you, Mrs. Masters," I said, hoping it came out genuine but knowing my voice carried no emotion.

She sighed. "You've known me for over a year, Angel. Will you ever call me Jen?" A little hopeful laugh came after.

I'd never once called Kyle's parents by anything other than Mr. and Mrs. Masters. My manners never allowed me to call them Jeff and Jennifer.

"I'm sorry."

"Kennedy, I've been through what you're going through. I know it's rough. You know I lost my mom when I was just eleven. I understand what it's like to lose a parent. I hope you always remember you have a family here, too. I promise you, things will get better."

I did remember that she'd lost her mom to cancer, but it didn't make this any easier. I didn't want to be a part of the I Have a Dead Parent Club.

Maybe it was true. Things probably would get better, but it was hard to accept a world without my father. Right now, I wasn't accepting it at all, but I nodded my head anyway.

I was pulled into an unexpected side hug. I tensed at the affection. Comfort hadn't been what I was looking for when I came out here. I didn't really know what I was looking for.

"I love you like my own daughter, Angel. You can come to me for anything, okay? Don't ever forget that." She sniffled a little and wiped at her cheeks.

I continued to feel unemotional. I knew I should feel something though because I loved her like a mother, too. She was trying to make me feel better and loved, and I'd turned to stone.

She took the mug I'd only taken a tiny sip from and stood, walking away without another word. I hoped she wasn't hurt by my lack of interest in more conversation, but she somewhat understood, too.

I slowly fell back to lie down. Staring up at the stars was something my dad and I had done every night before bed on that trip to Israel.

Anger overcame me once again. Now, even the stars were nothing but a reminder of better, brighter memories.

I'd never escape the feeling of loss and the longing for a chance to have an adventure with my dad, and the acknowledgment of his death made the pain ten times worse.

Chapter 4

Kyle

It'd been a little over a week since Kennedy's dad's funeral. Things were still...dark. That was the only way I could explain everything. I had taken her home the day after the funeral, and her mom hadn't even looked at me. Honestly, no surprise there.

Today was going to be Kennedy's first day back at Davidson High. She'd told me the day after the funeral that she just needed a break from school, so she had taken the week off.

I was supposed to be picking her up within the next fifteen minutes, but my football coach had called me at the crack of dawn to come in early to meet with a last-minute recruiter. I hadn't signed to play anywhere yet, but I had a few offers. Good ones, too, but I had been hesitating to sign. Something had told me to wait it out, and I was damn glad I had because, now, I was sitting in Coach's office in the back of the locker room with one of my dream team's recruiter a half hour before school would be starting.

I needed to make a decision, and I thought I had. I was going to stay as close as I could to Kennedy. But this new offer was one I wasn't sure I wanted to pass up. My dad was here with me, like he was at every recruitment meeting. I explicitly trusted his advice, and I needed his guidance on this.

I knew where I wanted to play, where I could play, what athletic programs would benefit me the most, and which coaches I liked best. But none of that would truly matter if Kennedy wasn't close to me.

It was terribly freaking cliché, but that girl was my world. If I couldn't be close enough to see her at least on the weekends, then everything would fall apart. I couldn't handle that. Handle letting her go. Handle her losing someone else.

The meeting came to a close, and I stood to shake the recruiter's hand. It was the first Big Twelve team to show any interest in me, and this was huge.

"It was a pleasure meeting you, Kyle. I hope you consider Texas for your academic and athletic career."

"I definitely will. Thanks for considering me, sir. It means a lot," I said respectfully.

He patted me on the shoulder and left my coach's office.

I sighed a big, heavy deep sigh. One that lifted my chest and collapsed it like a balloon.

Coach Laken sat in his chair once again and clapped his hands, loud and enthusiastic. A huge grin was plastered to his face. "Well, son, if you want my opinion, that's the offer of the year. If I were you, I'd seriously take some time and do some research of your own. Maybe schedule a visit, like he suggested, and go see the facility and meet the team. All the good stuff."

I looked to my dad. He was grinning. And I loved that. Because this was *big*. I'd invested so much time into football, and even though I knew I had a ton of room for improvement, I was still pretty damn good.

"I think he's right, Kyle. Let's schedule a visit."

Slowly nodding my head, I agreed even though a whirlwind of thoughts swept through my mind.

Kennedy. I can't leave her.

And, now, I had to figure out how to tell Kennedy.

She should be the first person I told, but she was still so fragile. I didn't want to risk shattering the tiny bit of progress she'd made with coming out of her depression by throwing this great opportunity in her face, especially if it was highly likely she'd look at it as losing someone again.

I walked with my dad out to the parking lot. "Thanks for being here, Dad."

He pulled me in for a quick hug and then stepped back. "I'm so proud of you, Kyle. You've done great for yourself, and this offer proves it."

I didn't even know how to explain the triumph and the respect received from the look in my dad's deep brown eyes.

He hopped into his truck. "We'll make travel plans," he said before slamming the door and pulling away. That was when I finally slipped my phone out of my back pocket to pull up the messages from Lo.

She'd sent me one halfway through my meeting with the coaches.

Lo: Yeah. Don't worry. I'll pick her up. Good luck!

I responded quickly.

Me: You guys on your way?

Lo: Just pulled into her driveway. I think today is going to be a good day for her.

A bit of relief shot through me with that text. It had been such a rocky road with me tiptoeing around Kennedy and trying to fix the unfixable.

I didn't respond because school would be starting soon enough, and they'd be here. I turned to walk back into the school right when Chase's Chevy Tahoe pulled into the parking lot. I walked over and waited for him to climb out.

"Dude, you totally cockblocked me when you asked Lo to go get Kennedy this morning," he said immediately, dramatically dropping his head back. "Do you know how long she makes me wait in between times? It's forever, my friend. Fucking. Forever. I'm going to have blue balls for a month."

I laughed. I didn't really feel his pain. "Well, you're going to love the reason I cockblocked you, bro."

"Doubt it," he grumbled skeptically. "Unless it involves me getting laid this weekend, I sincerely doubt it."

"I got a full-ride offer to play football at...drum roll, please..." I pounded my fists against the hood of his Tahoe. "The University of..." I paused for dramatic effect, but before I could say it, Dieter

33

pulled in like a bat out of hell and nearly hit us as we stood in front of Chase's truck.

We simultaneously jumped back, and Dieter's car came to stop an inch away from Chase's grill.

"Jesus!" Chase shouted, his hands flying into the air in a WTF motion.

Dieter slowly climbed out of his Audi with a shit-eating grin on his face.

"Were you trying to fucking kill us, man?" Chase shook his head. "Jesus, you fucker, you should slow down."

I had to admit, my knees were shaking from how close he'd actually gotten to taking us out.

"Just trying to wake you shitheads up." Dieter grinned ruefully.

I could punch the jerk.

"You scratch my freaking truck, you buy it, *shithead*," Chase fired back.

I sighed. "Guys, I'm trying to tell you something big."

"Yeah, Dieter, you ruined the climactic moment of Kyle telling me where he got his latest full-ride offer."

"You were going to tell him without me, Kyle?" Dieter held his hands over his heart in mock hurt, his favorite new gesture.

He had been spending way too much time with the theatrical Talan. She spent so much time on a stage and in front of people that it only made sense that was her personality all the time.

"How could you, baby?"

"Shut up, Dieter." I groaned. "Anyway, as I was saying…I got an offer from The University of Texas," I said nonchalantly, shrugging my shoulders, like it was seriously no big deal. But, in reality, this was huge. I was beaming on the inside, like a little boy who'd just won his first peewee football game.

"You're joking?" Chase questioned, his eyes big and hopeful.

I shook my head.

"Seriously?" He held his hand out for our bro handshake. "Dude! This is great! My two best friends and my girlfriend at the same college? I think I've hit the lottery."

Dieter pulled me in next for a bro hug. "Congratulations, man! Big Twelve is where it's at!"

"So, did you accept immediately, or are you taking some time?" Chase asked as we all started walking into the school.

The parking lot was beginning to fill up with all makes and models of cars, but I hadn't seen Lo's Chevy Camaro pull in yet.

I shook my head. "No, I'm gonna do a visit first to check out the facility and meet some of the team. Make sure they've got the major I want."

Dieter's eyebrows furrowed. "You're going to college with a full ride, no matter where you go. Why do you care about majors? You know you're gonna go pro, Mr. All-American."

I laughed at him. "The likelihood of me going pro is slim. Plus, I need a fallback. Duh, Dieter. What if I get injured?"

"Just work for your dad." He shoved my shoulder, and I stumbled a few feet to the left. "Isn't that what parents start companies for? For the next generation to take over? Legacies and all that shit."

"Dieter, do you even know what Kyle's dad does?" Chase asked the guy we'd both been friends with since third grade. He laughed.

"He installs security systems or something like that." He shrugged, and I punched his shoulder this time. "Ouch, fucker. Don't be a dick. I know what your dad does. I was just kidding. But I don't see why you need a degree to take over. Providing protection detail doesn't seem like a line of work that requires a college degree."

"My dad's company deals with a lot of stuff and a lot of important people. I'll need to either soldier up or get a degree in International Relations or Political Science or something," I offered. It was fine because International Relations was always the plan for my undergraduate degree.

After serving thirty years in the Marine's, my grandfather retired and started a private security company. As soon as my own father decided to leave the service as well, my grandfather officially retired, moved to Hawaii and signed the company over to my dad. My mom was one of their attorney's and handled new contracts. It was always the plan to work for the family business at some point, whether I played professional football or not.

We stopped at our lockers and grabbed the books we needed for the first half of the day. I had AP Chemistry and Spanish IV. Our school had switched to block scheduling when we were sophomores, so now, we only had four classes a day on Mondays through Thursdays, and we had all eight, just shorter classes, on Fridays.

Dieter was surprisingly in my first two classes of the day. I didn't think he was that smart. Sue me. And Chase had Anatomy, so we started to walk toward the Science hall on the first floor. Kennedy's and Lo's first period was Study Hall. Lucky them. I wouldn't actually get to see Ken until lunch since the first half of her day was spent on the third floor where all the Math and English classes were.

The first bell rang as Dieter and I reached the door to the Chemistry lab.

"Wait." Chase stopped us before we slipped into class. "How are you gonna tell Kennedy?" He looked at me, almost pained, like he knew how much the question meant and could potentially hurt, but he had gone for it anyway. "Don't get me wrong; I'd love to have my two best friends at college with me, but...weren't you so excited about Purdue, Loyola, and IU because of how close you'd be to her?"

Sighing deeply, I looked to my best friend. "I know. I'm going to talk to her after school. Can we just keep this news between us until then?" I pointed at both of them. "No telling Talan. And definitely no telling Lo." Sighing again, I said, "And, to answer your question, yes, that's why. But none of the offers I've gotten are Big Twelve schools. This opportunity could be huge. I've always paid more attention to Big Twelve and SEC games anyway. I'll just have to see how everything goes. Their program is legit, and the recognition is ten times higher than my local offers."

They both nodded. Then, the bell rang, and we went our separate ways.

Shit. I didn't know how I was going to tell the girl I loved that I really wanted to go to Texas.

I didn't have to go see the school or meet the team to know I wanted to be a part of that team. They had been damn near unbeatable last year with kick-ass stats and players. I could be one of them. I wanted to be a member of a team that worked their asses off for success.

Class began, and we were thrust into a lecture about assignments before we prepared for finals. I tuned the whole thing out because the only things I was able to focus on were Kennedy and Texas—and what those two things meant to me.

One meant everything. The other meant opportunity.

But the problem was, I didn't think I was willing to give either up.

"So, can we talk after school?" I asked Kennedy, resting my shoulder against the locker next to hers after lunch.

She squatted down to pick up a book from the bottom of her locker and then stood slowly. "Don't we always?" she said timidly. Her eyes grew with worry, like I was going to give her more bad news.

I knew I'd already fucked up. *Who the hell leads with,* Can we talk?

"I mean, yeah, we do. But I have some really big news, and I just wanted to make sure you'd be up for it. I know people have been trying to talk to you all day." I gripped her hip to reassure her I meant no harm.

She wrapped her arms around her World Studies textbook. "What's that supposed to mean?"

That was a little more defensive than I had expected, and I was sure my face conveyed my shock with my eyes widening and my lips parting.

Foot, meet mouth.

"What do you mean, trying?" She sounded irritated now. I reached for her arm with my other hand, but she jerked back, severing my touch completely. "I've talked to everyone who's talked to me today."

I immediately tried to soothe her. "Babe, I know. That's not what I meant."

"Well, what did you mean?"

I shrugged my shoulders before shoving my hands in my front jeans pockets. "Kennedy, I know people have been asking you how you are and how things have been since…*you know*. I know how draining that can be. I just didn't want to overwhelm you with more talking if you were all talked out."

She sighed and let her arms relax a bit, loosening the death grip she had on the textbook. "We can talk, okay? But I'm fine. And I need to get to class early, so I can turn in all my missed assignments." But her tone said she wasn't okay at all. She was just placating me.

You should know me better than that, Ken. I know you better than that.

Then, she turned on her heel and headed for the stairs. No good-bye kiss. We always kissed between classes. Call me juvenile, horny, whatever...but this was a shock to me.

"Kennedy!" I called out.

But she didn't stop or look back. She just ignored me and headed up the stairs. When she was out of sight, I quietly cursed at myself, fighting off the urge to punch and kick the locker. I was already doing a bang-up job of telling her the news.

It felt like, every time in the past week that I'd tried to be close to her and make things better, I'd only fucked it up. I didn't want things to go back to how it had been before her dad had died because it would never be the same. There was no changing that. I just wished we could move forward without all this awkwardness between us.

I was still here. I didn't want her to treat me like I wasn't. But that was kind of how I was feeling. And it wounded the shit out of me.

With her gone and me not knowing what the hell to do, I made my way to my Weights class. It would be good for me to work some of this frustration off. I was mad at myself for even feeling upset about something so little when Kennedy was going through something so monumental. I needed to be more understanding of Kennedy's situation, but I was having a hard time connecting with a lot of the emotional factors, especially since I'd never lost a parent. Also, I was close to both my parents, but Kennedy had been closest to her dad.

I forced myself to focus on training my muscles. I knew that, if I signed on with any school for an athletic scholarship, this would be just the beginning. I'd be dedicating more of my time to perfecting my physical abilities, and this was where it would begin—with strength.

I worked on my legs for the first half of class. Just as I was moving on to work on my arm rotations, Coach Laken walked over to me.

His face and posture were serious. I respected him, but his pensive face was something to be scared of. He almost always looked like he had bad news. The meeting with the Texas coach was just this morning.

Did I already screw it up by not answering immediately, and the recruiter rescinded the offer?

I leaned against one of the full racks and waited for him to tear into me for being so stupid.

"I just want to tell you how proud I am of you, Kyle. You worked your ass off this year, and even though you weren't the number one pick for recruiting, you still made them notice you. That's an accomplishment in itself," Coach said proudly, his stance stiff and wide. He always stood like a drill sergeant who was just waiting to insult your mama.

I was thankful for this man who'd coached me since seventh grade.

I shoved off the rack and moved closer to offer my hand to shake. "Thank you, Coach. It really was a shock, but I know I wouldn't have gotten here without your coaching and you using your pull with recruiters to come watch me play."

"Damn right, kid. You took us to state this year, and if it wasn't for those Blue Devils, we would have won." He shook his head.

Coach still thought the refs had picked sides. Truth was, we just hadn't played our best that game, and we'd made a lot of mistakes early on.

I thanked him again.

Then, I worked my ass off through my arm rotations before he released us all to shower up for our final classes of the day.

Wanting to make it up to the second floor before Kennedy's class got out, I showered quickly, rushing through washing and rinsing my hair and body, and then I dried off and dressed in my jeans and blue button-up.

"Where's the fire, Masters?" Max, a close friend, asked while getting dressed himself.

"Gotta make it to Kennedy's class before the bell," I murmured, shoving my phone into my back pocket and tossing my gym clothes back into my locker. I sat down to slip my Nikes on and tie them.

"How's she doing?" Max moved at a leisurely pace, not in any hurry to go to class.

I stood and slipped my backpack onto one shoulder. "She's been better, man, but thanks for asking."

I always tried to make it as light as possible while still letting people know that things weren't great. But I'd rather people asked me how she was instead of badgering her to the point of a breakdown.

He nodded, and I knew he understood that was as far as I wanted the conversation to go. There was only so much I could say about how she was. Honestly, I didn't even know how she was anymore. She'd shut me out where her emotions were concerned.

As I made my way up to the second floor and rounded the corner to her classroom, the bell rang. I heard chairs being scooted back, bags being zipped, and classmates and friends starting to converse before the doors opened, and then students poured out of the classrooms.

The door to World Studies opened, and people started to file out, but I didn't see Kennedy. When the door cleared of students, I stepped inside and looked for her. The room had emptied out, except for the teacher and a couple of stragglers, but I knew she hadn't passed me.

So, where the hell is she?

"She got called to the office halfway through class."

I turned around to see who was talking to me.

"Oh. Who are you?" I asked, confused.

The small girl with slightly blonde hair smiled brightly. "Bevin."

I ignored the way her eyes ate me up.

"Okay. Well, thanks for letting me know." I moved to walk past her.

She mumbled a quiet and almost silent, "No problem."

When I made it back to the first floor, I pulled my phone out to text Kennedy as I opened up my locker.

Me: Where are you?

She responded almost immediately.

Kennedy: In the counselor's office. I'll see you after school.

I dropped my head back. All that frustration I'd worked off came back and swarmed my veins, putting a jittery and edgy feeling in my blood. I could only imagine what the counselor was asking and prying out of Kennedy. I had known it would happen eventually, but I kind of thought the faculty would give her a few days to adjust back to school. In the back of my mind, I hoped that, whatever the counselor was saying and asking her, he would help her find a way to deal.

I made my way to my final class of the day—Composition I. It was a dual-credit course offered by the local community college and our high school—and a class I hated with a burning passion. I hated writing and everything it involved. I'd never been able to put things on paper. Research, fiction—it didn't matter what it was; I just didn't have the patience.

As soon as we were all seated and the bell rang, Mrs. Evans started to hand back papers that we'd turned in two weeks ago. When she got to my desk, she set it down and pointed to the large, bold red *D-* circled at the top. I sighed. That was definitely going to hurt my grade.

"You can do better, Mr. Masters," she said quietly.

I sighed even deeper, feeling more pressure mount on my shoulders.

She spent the first half of class going over where improvements could be made on our returned papers, and the second half, she went over our next and last assignment before finals next month.

As she moved to her desk at the back of the room, she instructed us on what to do for the rest of class. "Everyone grab a computer and try to get through the introduction and first body paragraph. Don't forget to document your online sources. You may listen to your music if you have headphones."

While everyone was pulling out the laptops provided by the school, Mrs. Evans called me to the back of the classroom. "Mind if we step in the hall to talk?"

"No, ma'am," I responded respectfully.

When I stepped through the doorway, she turned and smiled softly. "Congratulations on the latest offer, Kyle. You've been the talk of the staff."

I nodded graciously and waited for her to continue.

"Your latest paper is a bit of a concern to me though. I know you have the potential. The ideas are there. You just need to expand. Right now, you're sitting at a high D, but you know this class won't transfer to a university if you don't get at least a C. So, I'm giving you an opportunity to rewrite that paper to improve your grade. I'd hate for you to have to pay for this class twice."

"Mrs. Evans, thank you. But I don't think it's going to do me any good. I'm not a writer."

She adamantly shook her head. "Kyle, I know you are. Your research paper at the beginning of the semester was great. Much better than the work you turned in two weeks ago. I know things are rough, and you've been dealing with a lot, but that's not an excuse; it's a challenge. Do better. You have until the third."

She was giving me plenty of time for a redo, but no matter the time, it wouldn't improve my writing. That first paper she'd referred to, Kennedy had helped me write. I doubted she'd be in any mood to help my barely passing ass again.

When I sat back at my desk, I didn't even know where to begin. It didn't really matter anyway because I was in no state of mind to be thinking about writing. I had just a little time to figure out how I was going to tell Kennedy that Texas was in the cards now and how I really wanted to go.

An idea popped into my head, but even if it was the best idea I'd ever come up with, I doubted Kennedy would see it that way. But I still pulled up some links and printed off some information that could be useful. I just had to convince her they were positive. I ignored the latest assignment and continued searching until I found what I needed.

The bell rang just as I was folding the papers and slipping them into my backpack. I practically ran out of the room and down to the first floor. I immediately spotted Chase caging Lo in at her locker. Those two were so damn handsy. I didn't know why he complained about getting some.

I stopped at my locker and grabbed my keys from the top shelf.

"So, congratulations are in order!"

I knew Talan Bass' excited voice from anyone's.

I rotated around, and she instantly hugged me. I smiled so hard, my cheeks hurt because this girl was like the sister I never had, and her excitement for me rocketed my own up times ten.

"Shh…I haven't told Kennedy about it yet," I said quietly after celebrating for a brief moment.

She nodded when she stepped back. Her eyes narrowed as she glanced down the hallway to where Dieter's locker was. I followed her gaze when I saw her frown. I hated seeing my little wannabe sister upset.

Dieter had his hand on the hip of some junior girl.

When Talan noticed I was watching her frown at the scene, she quickly recovered and nodded. "Oh, okay. Well, I just wanted to tell you congrats." She smiled brightly again.

I nudged her shoulder with my fist, making her stumble just a step. "Thanks, my little wannabe sister."

Talan laughed. I loved it when she did because her laugh was contagious. It lit up her whole face.

"You only wish I were your little sister. But speaking of brotherly duties…" She dragged out her next statement and then did a little twirl on the tips of her toes. "Are you coming to my recital next weekend?"

Talan was an amazing dancer. She'd done ballet for as long as I could remember, and she had been invited to dance at prestigious programs all over Europe and the US.

"Do you even have to ask?" I sighed at her. "Seriously, you know I'd never miss it."

"Miss what?"

Kennedy's voice made me whip my head around to look behind me.

"My recital!" Talan beamed and did another fancy twirl on the tips of her toes that I'd never know the name of. Her brunette hair whipped around with her and almost hit me in the face. "You'll come, too, right?" She never stopped twirling, using Kennedy as her focal point.

I adjusted my stance, so I was facing Kennedy at an angle but could still see Talan spinning. "How was the counselor?"

Kennedy shook her head. "Can we talk about it some other time?"

I nodded once. Even though I wanted to beg for answers and know what they'd talked about, I would never force her to talk before she was ready. She'd tell me when she wanted. I hoped.

Please don't shut me out, Kennedy.

"We're gonna head out. T, I'll talk to you later."

When I placed my hand on Kennedy's shoulder, she shifted to start walking out the building. I stepped closer and put my arm around her shoulders, leaning down to place a kiss on her cheek. She turned to stare at me and smiled faintly. That impish, small smile burned me. I'd seen it too much in the past weeks.

That smile said, *I'll smile for you even though I feel like shit.*

We reached my truck, and I moved to the passenger side to open the door. She hopped in and threw her bag in the backseat. I jumped in and started the truck. Then, I turned to her and focused on her profile. My beautiful Kennedy was broken.

When she swiveled to look at me, I asked, "Do you want me to just take you home?"

She delicately shook her head. "Your house is fine, babe."

Nodding, I put the truck in drive and set off for my house.

When we got inside and upstairs to my room, she fell back on my bed and huffed out a breath. "So, what did you want to talk about?" Her eyes stayed shut, and her hands rested on her stomach.

I followed her move but lay down on my stomach. She turned her head. I couldn't help but admire her. She was so damn gorgeous without even trying. I loved that she only wore mascara and a clear lip gloss, enhancing her natural beauty. Her slightly long blonde hair was pin straight and fanned out behind her on my bed.

"I love the way you look on this bed." I grinned at her, Cheshire Cat–style.

Kennedy let a little laugh out. "Just on this bed?"

"You know what I mean."

"Yeah, I do." She leaned over and brushed her lips against mine. "And I love the way we look on this bed together."

"So about the talk…" I started to say.

But she brushed her lips against mine again, silencing me. Her eyes drifted closed, long lashes fluttering like butterfly wings.

I moved closer to her and pushed myself up onto my hands, shifting to hover but never breaking our slow kiss. She opened her mouth to me, and I followed her lead. She'd been so distant since the night of the funeral after I told her no. Told her that I didn't want to enable her like that. That I would feel like I was taking advantage of her when she was in such a vulnerable place. It'd felt wrong, but right now…this felt so right.

She moved her hand to the top button of my shirt and nimbly undid it, then the next, and the next until she was finally shoving it off my shoulders. I leaned up onto my knees to take off my white undershirt and settled myself back over her.

I loved how she always tasted like spearmint when we kissed. I loved how, when I was kissing her like my life depended on it, she always braced her hands on my shoulders, like she needed me closer and in constant reach.

"I need you so much," she panted on a breath when we broke apart.

I nodded. In this moment, I thought I needed her more. My body was aching for her touch.

She lowered her hands down to the button of my jeans, and I stopped kissing her to look down and watch. I loved her small hands and how they would flex so sensually to undo my jeans and pull the zipper down.

"I've missed this," Kennedy said quietly, reverently never taking her eyes off her hands.

I clenched my eyes shut because I felt bad for denying her last time. Some of those reservations washed over my arousal again. Somehow, I thought this might break her, make it worse.

But I pushed that away and started to undress her like she wanted.

We'd been sexually active for a while. Probably way before we should have been. But wasn't that the case most of the time? We'd stumbled through our first few times together, but now, we had the hang of it. We were much more comfortable with each other. She knew my body, and I made it a mission to know hers better every time.

When she was in nothing but her bra and panties, her milky skin beckoning me closer, I dived down to kiss her neck. She moaned. I'd missed *that*. She was so sexy when she did it, and I didn't think she even knew she made noises that made me jerk forward for more. To make her repeat that sound over and over and louder and louder.

Her hands wrapped around my forearms while I glided down her torso and kissed all over her stomach. She was so soft here, her smooth curves making her impossible to resist. And warm. God, she was warm. I loved her body heat.

When I shifted back up to her face, she placed her hands at my hips and started to shove my jeans down. "I need this," she whispered.

I kept hearing those words from her, and it made me pause.

She placed her palms on my cheeks and pulled my face back to hers. "Don't overthink this, *please*. I *want* this. I want *you*. *I love you*," she stressed.

I was about to dive back in to taste her lips, give her what she was begging for—

"Kyle, your father told me the big ne—oh my God!"

Then, my bedroom door slammed back shut.

Fuck.

Chapter 5

Kennedy

I dropped my head back down to Kyle's bed in defeat with a thump. "Tell me your mom did not just walk in on us," I groaned, frustration and sadness and shame lacing my voice. That was probably not the reaction I should've had. It was the middle of the day. I should be embarrassed. Not angry or sad.

Kyle jumped up the second the door had slammed shut and started redressing, pulling a shirt over his head and his jeans back up his hips. "She did," he said nervously, fastening the button and then zipping his fly. "Here." He handed me my shirt and shorts. "I'm gonna go talk to her. I'll be right back." Then, he cracked the door open just enough to disappear without a glance backward.

I could seriously scream. I'd needed this, *him*, for the longest time, and I was sure the grief counselor, whom the school had made me talk to today, would certainly be against this type of coping mechanism, but *damn it*, I needed some type of release.

Everything else wasn't working. Talking wasn't working. Silence wasn't working. Crying. Sleeping. I needed something else. And it seemed I was either being told no or parents were walking in.

Great.

I hastily threw my clothes back on and then walked over to where I'd dropped my bag by the door. I pulled out my cell. My mom hadn't even called me back. The counselor had asked if I'd like to call her to ask if she could join the session because Mr. Blanc, the school's senior guidance counselor, couldn't get ahold of her. Funny thing, neither could I.

Mom and I would do nothing but argue politely or sit in complete silence when we were together. I didn't know what it was really. I just felt so detached, and I got the strangest feeling when I was around her. She was always on her phone or typing away at her computer. She had gone back to work almost immediately. I got it; I did. The world continued to spin even if you were at a dead stop, trying to just hold on to anything that would anchor you to reality.

It was absolutely irritating, being around Mom, and I couldn't shake that feeling—the one that made me feel resentful.

I called her one more time just to see if she'd answer, but it went straight to voice mail. I tossed the phone back in my bag. There was no reason to keep it on me. Obviously, I wasn't that important to my mom at the moment.

At the bottom of my bag, I could see the silver glint of the flask that I'd stolen from my dad's office desk. It had been empty when I first found it. Now though, it was filled with a fiery whiskey. I pulled it out and took two tentative sips, letting the harsh liquid sit on my tongue before swallowing it down, and then I slipped it back into my bag.

No one knew. They never would. I just needed to stop thinking so much, and the alcohol numbed me enough to slow my thoughts. Gave me the reprieve I desperately needed. It wasn't like I was getting wasted and stumbling over myself. Just taking a few drinks, feeling a burn. Feeling *something*.

Moving over to Kyle's desk, I sat and pulled out a piece of paper and a pen, mindlessly doodling.

I kept replaying the conversation I'd had with Mr. Blanc and the young grief counselor he'd brought in shortly after calling me in. Miss Quill was a nice Asian girl who couldn't have had her degree for longer than five minutes. She'd asked how I was doing and how things were at home. At school. With my mom.

All questions that had the answer, "Okay." An empty answer for silly questions.

She should have known the answer to those questions. Things were bad. Things were broken. They'd never be the same, and I didn't care how childish I might have been acting. It was how I felt.

Between Mr. Blanc and Miss Quill, the questions had been all the same, and my answers never changed. I could tell they were becoming frustrated and concerned. Possibly thinking that I was becoming a ticking time bomb. And maybe I was. I was internalizing everything. The pain. The grief. The anger.

It was something my father would have hated. We'd had such an honest and open relationship. It wouldn't surprise me any if he looked down and cringed when he saw me, shaking his head in disappointment.

They had taken brief notes on their little yellow legal pads, looking back at one another after every seemingly simple question. But I could sense the unspoken questions in their eyes. They'd let me go, realizing I wasn't ready to talk but promising me they would be there for me when I was ready.

I looked down to the piece of paper I was scribbling on now, only to see multiple crosses drawn and the beginnings of angel wings.

"My mom told me to apologize for her."

I jolted around in the chair. I hadn't heard when Kyle came back in or moved to stand beside me.

"Whoa, are you okay? I didn't mean to scare you." He chuckled softly, placing his large hand on my shoulder.

I gave him a weak smile, shaking my hair out and breathing deep. "I'm fine." I tried to force a bigger smile. "So…what did you want to talk about?" Worry weighed my words down, trying to pin my tongue to the roof of my mouth. *Please, don't break me.*

He moved closer and leaned down to grip the arms of the computer chair, pulling me over to his bed where he took a seat. "I had a meeting with Coach and another recruiter today," Kyle said slowly, staring into my eyes that widened instantly at the admission.

"Oh, yeah? What school is after my quarterback now?" A cheeky grin painted my lips while I tried to hide my fear.

He laughed at that. "Well…it's far away." Then, he paused when I instantly tensed at the words *far away*. "But it's a full ride at a great school with lots of opportunities."

I tried to let myself relax, but I was still stuck on the far-away detail. "Where?" I questioned, the fear becoming real.

"Texas. The University of Texas." He sounded hesitant and scared.

I was overwhelmed and terrified. My heart hammered in my chest, but I forced it to slow, blowing out a heavy breath. "That's where Chase and Lo are going," I said faintly.

He nodded and then said, "Yeah, and Dieter, too." He put his hands on my knees. "I didn't sign anything. We just met today. But it's a really good offer, great school, really amazing athletic program."

Kyle sounded so excited even if he was holding back for my sake. He tried to keep his expression neutral, like he didn't care one way or the other.

"So, you want to go, right? I mean, that's where our friends are going to be, and you...you got an offer. Their program's way better known than what you've already been offered."

"I mean...my dad and I are planning a visit. But that's as far as it's going for now."

"For now," I repeated quietly, almost a whisper.

"Hey." He reached up to lift my chin. I hadn't even realized I had been staring down. "It's just an option right now."

I pushed away from him with my feet against the bed. Irritation won out of all the emotions that coursed through me. I should be happy for him. This was a great opportunity. He deserved it. But I was petrified. I was nervous and sad.

"But it's an option you want, Kyle." *God, could I be any more of a brat right now?* I should be happy he had been offered this great opportunity.

"I'm not just going to leave you, Kennedy, if that's what you're thinking. A lot of thought and consideration will go into whatever school I decide to sign with," he said evenly. But, underneath his softened tone, I could sense his own irritation.

I didn't want to feel like this. Like I was going to hold him back. Or worse, that I was going to lose him, too.

I stood abruptly, walking over to my bag and picking it up. "I don't think you should include me into any reason you pick a school," I said low and slowly, trying not to sound passive-aggressive.

I heard him stand and walk over to me.

"Kennedy, come on. You know I'm going to include you. I love you. I'm not leaving you. I'm not going to break up with you. I'm just considering this really good school with big opportunities."

I turned around to see him holding a few folded up papers. "What's that?" I pointed to the papers.

"Just something I looked up after my meeting."

"Okay...well...I kind of want to go home now, so can you give me a ride, or do I need to call Lo?"

"Wait, just...wait. I really don't want this to affect us. I looked up some stuff. I know you got into Wheaton, where your dad went, and it's a Christian college, but I don't want to be apart. There's a Christian university close, and it's highly recommended." He unfolded the papers and held them out to me.

Shaking my head, I pushed them away. "Take me home, Kyle."

But he ignored my command, continuing his plea for me to just listen. "It's close to UT. We can still see each other all the time. We can even get a place together."

"Kyle." I didn't want to hear any of this right now. It killed me to feel this way.

I clung to my bag harder. The urge to drown these thoughts in a hazy fog of alcohol beckoned me.

Why are you doing this to me, Kyle?

"I'm not saying you have to consider going there, but, babe, it's a Christian school, too. I know how much that means to you."

"*Kyle*," I growled.

"Don't do that, Kennedy. *Please* don't do that. Don't shut down on me again. I'm trying to talk to you about this," he pleaded. His whole body seemed to be begging me, his body language open and summoning. Arms spread out to the sides. Eyes wide and imploring me to listen to him.

"Just stop!" I shouted as I threw my arms up in front of me, palms up begging him to just stop. "Kyle, I'm not talking about this anymore today. I'm really happy for you."

He looked like he didn't believe me.

Who am I kidding? I would feel the same way as him if the roles were reversed.

"I mean it. I am *so* happy for you. But, right now, things I should be feeling, I don't." It was the first time I'd let out anything close to how I felt. Letting my shoulders drop from their tensed position, I whispered, "Just please give me some more time." I was so defeated. So worn down.

I didn't feel the tears slipping down my cheeks until he reached out and wiped them away.

Kyle nodded, stepping closer to me. He wrapped me up in a protective hug. "All the time you need, babe."

I didn't return the gesture. I just placed my hands on his hips and nodded.

"I didn't mean to push you," he confessed.

My body relaxed a fraction more, shifting toward him completely.

"Do you still want to go home?" he asked while pulling back.

But I clutched him back to me. I didn't want to feel so disconnected, and he was the only person I felt connected with. Everything and everyone else, I was so detached from. Nothing made sense, but he did.

"No."

"Okay."

"Can we just go watch a movie or something?"

"Yeah, babe. Whatever you want. Even if it's a chick flick."

I laughed because I knew how much he hated them. But he loved me, and he'd suffer an hour and a half just to make me happy.

We made our way downstairs to the living room, the cushy, oversize couch and love seat taking up the most space in front of the large TV mounted on the wall. I took a seat in the middle of the couch, directly facing the TV. I didn't even really want to watch a movie, but the suggestion had made me feel a bit more *there*, like I . was trying, and I knew Kyle liked to see that.

I'd seen the way he and our friends looked at me—with obvious pity and painful expressions when they asked a question that had anything to do with how I was doing or feeling.

I let Kyle pick the movie, just barely hearing the options he'd thrown out. He popped the DVD into the Blu-ray player and then turned the surround sound on. Taking the spot to my right, he reclined the seat and then pulled me into his side where I snuggled against him. His arm stayed around my shoulders, and he reached for one of my hands with his other. He didn't lace our fingers together or hold it but turned it over and started to trace little designs on my palm and up toward my wrist. Chills raced down my spine, and I breathed in deeply.

Out of the corner of my eye, I noticed the movie starting. I'd seen it a thousand times. It was one of my dad's favorites. Kyle's, too. *Remember the Titans* was probably one of the best movies I'd seen, and I loved it even more because my dad had loved it the most, always stopping to watch it even if it was halfway over.

I fell asleep on Kyle's shoulder, and the next thing I knew, I was being lifted from the couch, cradled in his arms. He carried me up to his room and laid me down in the middle of his bed. Then, he covered me with his gray comforter.

I drifted again, but I didn't miss the feeling of his lips pressed to my forehead or his parting words.

"I love you so much, Kennedy. I'm never going to leave you."

I knew that. Deep down... I knew he would never leave me.

But I couldn't help wanting to leave myself. My thoughts. My fears. My memories.

Chapter 6

Kyle

"So, when are we gonna celebrate?" Dieter shouted excitedly as he made his way to our usual lunch table in the middle of the cafeteria.

I shook my head. He was always ready for a party.

"Dude, let me visit the damn school before you decide to throw me a party."

Dieter was usually an ass, but when I gave a quick glare to him and a shifty glance toward my girlfriend, he let the subject drop.

"When do you leave?" Lo asked in a soft whisper, casting a glance at Kennedy to make sure she wasn't suddenly listening to us.

She was biting her lip and concentrating on her iPad with her headphones in, head bopping to the music I assumed she was listening to.

"Tonight," I answered back just as quietly. "I'll spend the day with the coach tomorrow, meet some of the team, and then fly back on Friday afternoon."

"Just in time for my party then!"

Dieter and his parties. I swore that was all he lived for. He'd throw them as often as he could, and when he wasn't throwing one, he was going to someone else's. Made me wonder what kind of future he had in mind for himself.

"Yeah, we'll see." I slightly nodded my head toward Kennedy, trying to get everyone to shut up about it.

Even if she wasn't paying any attention to us, she still knew. She'd told me this morning that she could feel everyone staring at her. She felt like she could hear their pity and apologies before anyone even voiced them. It made her retreat into herself. She was marginally better but still distant.

We finished our lunch with Dieter as the entertainment. He gave us the spiel on his latest hookups. I laughed at all the right places but mainly focused on Kennedy and her withdrawn state.

The rest of the school day slowly went by, and by the final bell, I was ready to get the hell out of there. I quickly walked out to my truck. Kennedy was leaning up against the driver's side door. She had on a pair of skintight jeans and a tight, bright pink tank top, her white cardigan laying on top of her backpack.

I walked up to her, dropped my bag at our feet, and caged her in against my truck. She sucked in her bottom lip and looked up at me with hooded eyes.

I knew what she wanted. It'd been a few days since my mom walked in on us, and Kennedy had been dropping subtle hints ever since.

"You want to come over before my dad and I leave?" I whispered against her lips.

She nodded, her eyes glazed and hopeful. She looked like she'd been crying recently. But I didn't push.

She'd talk when she was ready. I hoped.

"So, what does Kennedy think about all of this?" Dad asked as we walked out of the practice facility for the football players at The University of Texas.

We'd had a meeting with the team captains and coaches and physical therapists and trainers. I'd met so many people, and I remembered only half of the names.

It had been a whirlwind of meeting player after player and trainers, all telling me about their experiences at UT and the things they'd been able to accomplish while here. I was falling in love with the damn place, and I couldn't help but be held back by my guilt. I couldn't love a place that Kennedy wouldn't be near.

"We haven't really talked about it." I looked out to the practice field. This could be where I started my future. Where I saw what I could make of myself in a sport that I loved.

The sun relentlessly beat down on us. No clouds in the sky. I could practically smell the hard work and sweat and dreams that took place on a field like this. The stadium. The lights. It all felt so right.

"Well, Kyle, I'm not going to try and persuade you one way or the other. I know what she means to you. But I also know how hard you've worked for this."

"She means the world to me, Dad."

"I know."

"But I could make something of myself here with football."

"I know that, too. But you're going to make something of yourself wherever you are. With or without football. With or without Kennedy."

I stopped walking. I couldn't imagine my world *without* Kennedy. No matter what she was going through now, no matter how much it changed her in the end, I was going to be by her side.

That was the only thing I knew for certain.

Me: I miss you so much.

I texted Kennedy as I settled into my room in the two-bedroom suite my dad had booked for us. I was glad we had our own space. It gave me the room to be by myself and think about what I wanted.

I wanted it all. The team. This school. Kennedy by my side. I was too fucking greedy to give any of it up. But that was not how our relationship had ever worked. Never one getting more than the other. We compromised. We worked things out, so both of us would get what we wanted.

Kennedy responded a short five minutes later.

Kennedy: How'd everything go?

I lay back in some sweats, sprawled over the entire queen-size bed with a fluffy white down comforter.

> *Me: It was really great, babe. I met with the team and the coaches today. It's hot as hell here, but Austin is an awesome city. I think you'd like it.*

I had thrown in that last comment for purely selfish reasons. I needed to gauge her reaction.

She didn't respond as fast that time, and I took the opportunity to shoot Chase a text.

> *Me: Are you living in student housing or off-campus?*

He responded instantly.

> *Chase: Off-campus. Lo doesn't want to do the dorm thing. We've got a couple of houses picked out. You could definitely be our roomie. Dieter doesn't want to live with us. Said we'd cramp his style. Fucker.*

> *Me: LOL. I'll keep that in mind. Thanks, man. Did you see Kennedy at all today?*

> *Chase: Uh, I think Lo was going to talk to you about that.*

> *Me: About what?*

I instantly lifted myself up into a sitting position. *Talk to me about what? Did something happen? Fuck.* I was starting to freak out. My chest felt tight with anxiety.

My phone rang in my hand, and I rushed to answer Lo's call.

"What happened today?" I eagerly questioned her. I could feel myself clenching up with fear of the unknown.

Did Kennedy do something to herself? Fuck.

I didn't even want to consider that as an option.

Lo fucking sighed. "Calm down, okay? Today just wasn't a good day for her."

I groaned, thrusting my free hand through my hair. I wasn't there for Kennedy, and it was tearing me apart.

"What happened?" I asked again. I needed fucking answers, and I wanted them right the fuck now.

"I got called into the Mr. Blanc's office today." She stopped talking.

I was ready to strangle my friend through the damn phone. "And?"

"And, when I got there, Kennedy was curled up in a ball on the couch, crying."

"Why?" I asked angrily, teeth clenched, my grip on the phone tightened and my other hand fisted.

I shook my head. If this was what I was going to feel like every time Kennedy had a bad day and I was hundreds of miles away…I didn't think I could do it. That realization made everything a lot more complicated in regard to what I wanted.

"Everything was fine when I left," I said. "She was smiling when I dropped her off at home on my way to the airport. How could she slide back so rapidly?"

She whispered something to whom I assumed was Chase. Then, she groaned. "I don't think I should be the one to tell you this, Kyle. It's really not my place."

"Just tell me," I growled.

"I'm going to tell you, only because I know she won't. Not in the state she's been in." She stopped again and took a deep breath. "Her mom is already seeing someone."

What. The. Fuck?

Her husband had *just* died three weeks ago.

"You're joking." I jumped up from my bed and paced the room, agitated. "That can't be true. Maybe whoever it is, is just a friend?" I instantly doubted my own words. *Damn it! Of course I'm out of town when something bad happens.*

"I wish that were true, but the way Kennedy was acting and the pitiful look that Mr. Blanc gave me…it just seems really likely. He asked if I'd take her home, and she *freaked* out, Kyle. She said she wasn't going to go home to stay with her mom, that she couldn't face her, so she's staying in my room with me at Chase's. She's been laying down since we got here."

"You don't think…" I couldn't even get the words out.

"Maybe. I mean, her mom spent half a year without David while she was in St. Louis."

God, if that were true…if Kennedy's mom had cheated on her dad…I knew what kind of damage that would do to Kennedy. It would destroy her.

"I can't believe this," I said quietly. "How is she now?"

"I think she'll be better after a good night's rest."

I nodded my head, knowing full well that she couldn't see me. Then, we said our good-byes, and I told her to call me if anything else happened.

For hours, I lay there in my bed, thinking about Kennedy and what she might possibly be going through. I had to clench my fists to keep my anger in check.

How could her mom have even thought about stepping out on Pastor Kiblen?

He was the best man I'd ever met, besides my own dad.

I'd always felt this weird vibe from Mrs. Kiblen. She always just kind of struck me as a self-righteous bitch, and now that this new information was coming to light, I couldn't help but agree with my own thoughts.

Shit. Shit. Shit.

Kennedy didn't deserve more stress or heartbreak in her life. She'd been through enough in the last year. First, her grandma had passed away in a car accident that her mom was the driver in. Then, we had gone through the shit with Lo—when she was drugged by Cam, the psycho jealous cheerleader, and Brent, a guy who wouldn't take no for an answer. They'd given her such a strong dose of GHB that she had a seizure. Chase had thought it might have been laced with something even stronger. Then, David had passed away. And, now, there was this news of her mom being with another man.

When would the hits stop coming?

How much more could Kennedy possibly take before she shut down completely?

I wasn't willing to find out. From now on, I was going to be everything she needed. Do everything she asked. Protect her from everything that could hurt her. Even if she needed protection from her own mother.

Our flight was delayed for two hours because of some mechanical issue. That definitely should have worried me, but I was only worried about Kennedy and getting back to her. My knee bounced with irritation. Every annoying person surrounding us was munching on their crunchy snacks or typing roughly on their laptops. The old man behind me was hacking up a lung, and it grated on my nerves. My patience was down to nothing, pushing me toward insanity.

Lo had said Kennedy didn't go to school with her and Chase, claiming she had a headache and just needed the day to recoup.

She was going to shut everyone out again; I could feel it in my bones. It made my head hurt and temples pound, just thinking about her locking me out again. She was my breath, my sight, my life, and when she was in pain, I was dying a slow death.

Once we finally got on a fixed plane, the two-and-a-half-hour flight seemed to drag on. Dad could see me becoming twitchy, and when he asked me what was wrong, I didn't have an answer for him. Because too many things were wrong. But the anticipation of getting home and seeing Kennedy, holding her, was my first and only concern.

When our flight landed and we walked out to the carport where Dad had left his truck, he'd had enough.

"What the hell is bothering you, Kyle?" He opened the backseat door and roughly threw both our duffels inside.

Great. Even he was irritated with me now.

"And don't you dare say, *I don't know.* I know you better than that. Did something happen while we were gone? Are you worried about Texas?"

God, my dad could figure it all out with his own questions. He knew just what to ask, and I flinched at every freaking one of them because they were dead-on. Something had happened while we were gone, and I was freaking out about Texas. More specifically, I was freaking out about how I was going to tell Kennedy how badly I wanted to play for Texas.

"Both." I sighed when we were seated and buckling our seat belts. My body ached with tension and stress.

Dad turned off the radio and waited for me to speak as he drove away from the airport.

Usually, I was just like him. Cool, calm, and collected. But with all the recent changes and all the wondering about my future—and all things Kennedy—I was losing my bearings. My shoulders pressed down with an intolerable weight. But I held it up with my belief in better days. In love. In Kennedy. As long as we were together, I could withstand anything.

I caught Dad looking over at me every ten seconds before focusing back on the road.

"And?"

"Kennedy found something out about her mom, but I don't really know if it's true, so I don't want to say," I spoke softly and fast, hoping he wouldn't ask for more than I could give. It wasn't my place.

But, if her mom truly was seeing someone else, it wouldn't be long before news spread. Our town wasn't small, but it was just as rumor-filled as a small town in the middle of nowhere.

He hummed, scratching at his unshaven jaw. "Okay, so that's the first thing. What else?"

"I want it." I ground my teeth together. *Shit. Am I really admitting this?*

"Want what?"

"To go to Texas. To play football in the Big Twelve."

Fuck. I'd said it out loud. It was real now.

"Then, do it," my dad said assuredly. No wavering doubts in his command. He just continued driving, his attention solely on the road in front of us.

I shook my head. It wasn't that simple. I couldn't give up Kennedy. My heart pounded against my chest in panic from the fear of not having her.

No way.

"I know what you're thinking, Kyle. But it *is* that simple. If she loves you, then she'll let you do this. And, if you love her, like I know you do, you'll make it work."

But I didn't know that, and deep down, I was terrified that I couldn't make it work if I was hours away from her all the time.

What kind of relationship will we have if we only get to see each other during long breaks and holidays? I wasn't okay with that.

When my dad had been overseas as a Marine, my mom had had the hardest time coping. I remembered it like it was yesterday even though he'd been out of the military and home since I was ten. It had been harder for her after the short phone calls he made home between missions or during the off-chance times when he got two days to be home with us. It'd destroyed her to let him leave again. Each time, I had seen it wear her down that much more.

Even though I would just be going to play football in a different state, I knew Kennedy would feel the same. Somehow, she'd see it as losing me even if I wasn't willing to let her go. No matter the time or distance we were apart, I would *never* let her go.

We pulled up to our house an hour later, and I rushed inside to see my mom and catch her up on how everything had gone. Then, I was up the stairs and in my room, unpacking.

Chase called me shortly after.

"Hey," I said.

"You coming tonight?"

"I gotta see what Ken's plans are. I think we kind of need a night in."

"Ah, yeah, I got you. We'll see you tomorrow or something then. Ken's still at my house, so I assume you're coming to get her. Do you want me to let her know?"

"Nah, I'm getting ready to call her."

"All right, cool. Well, we're gonna head to dinner before the party. Let us know if you change your mind, and I'll make sure we have a cold one ready for you, bro."

I thanked him, and we simultaneously hung up. Then, I was back to unpacking. I called Kennedy as I threw clothes in the hamper and put my toiletries up. After six rings, it went to voice mail with her cute-as-can-be voice coming over the line. I couldn't help but smile.

"Hey, you've reached Kennedy's voice mail. I'm unable to answer but leave a message, and I'll get back to you. If this is Kyle, *I love you.*"

The tone came.

"I love you, too, baby. I'm on my way to pick you up."

Ending the call, I headed downstairs. My parents were talking quietly in the kitchen.

When I came to a stop in front of the fridge to grab a water, my mom started speaking, "Kyle, your father and I just got a business call. We've got to head to LA to meet with a client this weekend and finalize a contract. Will you be okay with everything?"

"Or you could come with us? Get out of town for a couple of more nights and think about everything," Dad chimed in.

I slowly turned around and looked at my parents. Their facial expressions were blank.

Mom put her hand out to me, and I walked closer to take it.

"Thanks, guys. I'll be fine though."

They nodded, and that was the end of the conversation. I appreciated my dad and mom trying to help me find the best path for myself and letting me do things on my own, but going away for the weekend wasn't an option. I needed to be here for Kennedy.

As I backed out of the garage and started to leave, I turned the Bluetooth on and switched to the playlist Lo had made for me. "Fader" by The Temper Trap came blaring through the speakers. I drove out of our gated community at the Plantation Estates and headed for Chase's house. It was a short ten-minute drive, and when I pulled up, Chase's parents were just backing out of their garage.

I parked on the side of the street and slowly climbed out. I didn't want to rush inside and make Chase's parents worry. Chase and Lo were already out, and with his parents leaving, it'd be a good time to talk to Kennedy and find out what had happened while I was gone.

Mr. Carter came to a stop at the end of the driveway and rolled his window down.

I stepped up and leaned down to see inside. "Hey, Mr. and Mrs. Carter. You guys heading out?" I asked politely.

Plenty of times over the years, they'd given me permission to call them by their first names, but I just hadn't been raised that way.

Mrs. Carter beamed at me. "I hear congratulations are in order, honey! Texas would be lucky to have you."

"I'd be happy to see what you could do for my team, Kyle. When are you going to sign the letter of intent?" Mr. Carter asked me.

I just shook my head, still trying to wrap it around this big opportunity. "I haven't decided yet, sir, but I have to let them know by Wednesday."

He nodded his head. "Well, whichever school you play for, you'll always have us as fans. Even if my team has to kick your ass," he joked, his voice loud, as he finished pulling out of the driveway.

I waved as they sped off down the street.

I stood there, weighing all my decisions. My brain was scrambled, warring over what to do. *What the hell is the right thing?*

I had good offers close to home, but none of them felt as right as Texas.

Hopefully, Kennedy would help bring some clarity to me. If she asked me to stay, I would. But if she told me to go? Shit, I just didn't know. I didn't want to leave her and have to conquer a long-distance relationship.

I walked inside without knocking and headed up the stairs to the guest bedroom, which was actually Lo's bedroom. She'd moved in after her mom threatened to send her back to boarding school because of the drugging incident. Jacob, Lo's dad, had gone to high school with Chase's mom, and they had come to an agreement that allowed Lo to stay here.

My phone chimed, and I pulled it out of my pocket to see who it was.

Kennedy: Sorry! I was in the shower when you called.

I laughed lightly and went to the last door in the hallway. She had the music on loud, so she had no idea that I had just walked in. She hovered over the desk up against the opposite wall, her back to me.

"How can you listen to this crap?" I shouted.

"Oh my God!" She practically jumped ten feet in the air and spun. "Don't fucking do that, Kyle! You almost gave me a heart attack."

Then, she threw her hand over her mouth, and my jaw dropped. I'd never heard her say the word *fucking* in my life, and she was just as shocked as I was.

"Um, wow. Okay." I laughed.

Then, she laughed, too.

"Don't make fun of my music." Her cheeks were bright red, but her eyes were shining.

She was still laughing and shaking her head in disbelief, and it was the cutest damn thing. My innocent angel was letting a little dark side out.

I grinned so big because she had a smile on her face, and she looked so happy. It was the best expression she had. Pure joy lit her whole face up. Bright eyes and rosy cheeks.

"I think Lo is rubbing off on you. Should I start calling you Sailor, too? I don't think I've ever heard you drop an F-bomb." My smile grew as she dramatically rolled her eyes.

"Beyoncé is not crap, by the way, and '7/11' is my favorite song right now." Kennedy grinned as she did a little sultry dance, throwing her hands up in the air, during the chorus of the song.

I threw my head back and groaned. God, she was so sexy. I loved her when she was like this—carefree and flirty. I couldn't get over how much I loved it when she was full of bliss. I hadn't seen her like this for days, weeks. It lightened the worry I had been carrying.

She danced over to me and put her hands on my chest. I brought my head back down to look at her, and she wiggled her hips and dropped low. Then, she popped back up and bit her lip. *Oh. My. Holy. Hard-on.*

I had an instant erection, and she was just dancing. But dancing provocatively.

Fuck. My mind was all over the place.

I would try so hard to be a gentleman when we got hot and heavy, but she made me carnal. Fucking obsessed. Ready to beg for more.

Kennedy acting like this seductive, wanton minx was a total turn-on. I wasn't used to it.

I put my hands on her hips and pulled her to me roughly. The song changed.

"Turn it back."

"No. I like this one, too." She grinned and sang the lyrics about being worth it.

Oh God, she's so fucking worth it.

"Am I worth it?" she taunted, grinding her hips into mine.

"Fuck," I groaned. "Yes, babe. Way more than I'm worthy of."

She turned around, so her ass was to my groin, and I slid my hands up and down her waist and back to her hips where I gripped tighter.

"Let's…" she whispered.

"What?"

How does she expect me to comprehend anything when she's doing this?

"Let's fuck."

Oh my God.

She was talking dirty.

Holy fuck!

Kennedy had *dirty*-talked. It was basically nothing compared to what some girls said, but holy shit…

She usually just said she wanted me, or we didn't use words at all. Just fell into a tangle of arms and legs and heat and sweat.

"Are you sure?" I asked hesitantly.

"Mmhmm," she hummed as she ground against me, rolling her hips.

I heard a zipper being undone, and I looked over her shoulder and down to where her hands were. She slightly pushed her jeans and panties down. Then, she moved to grab my hand off her hip and pushed it over until it was placed just above her underwear.

"Babe," I growled this time.

"Touch me," she ordered.

I did. I moved my hand lower, slipping under the fabric. I found her so wet and didn't stop. I fingered her and ground into her ass because I was fucking turned on, and she was making me so damn horny. Her knees started to buckle, and she was panting. I wrapped my other arm around her chest to keep her upright, and she grunted when I thrust two fingers into her, deep.

"Kyle, I'm so close."

Shit. I loved hearing her say that.

I moved my thumb to her clit and stroked her.

"Mmm," she moaned, her head lolling to the side.

I was so hard. "Oh my God, babe. You're turning me on so bad."

"I want you," she whispered softly, almost like she was scared to say it.

Maybe she thought I'd deny her, like a few weeks ago.

Never again.

"You've got me," I declared.

Then, I pulled my hand out of her pants and walked her forward to the bed. I pushed her jeans and panties all the way down and didn't even bother with her shirt. I pulled my wallet out of my back pocket, took a condom out, and then undid my own pants, pushing them down to my knees. I was way too turned on to even bother getting completely naked.

"Kyle." Kennedy was becoming impatient, clenching her thighs and panting harder.

"Let me put the condom on, babe." I worked faster, slipping it on, and then I pushed down on the middle of her back to flatten her chest on the bed. "Ready?" I asked, strained, just as impatient as her now.

"This is different," she murmured lowly, her hands braced on the mattress.

Fuck, I hadn't even thought about the position. I just wanted inside her. This was new for us. We weren't that adventurous, and I loved to see her face, her eyes, her pleasure. This felt wild and less attached but in the best way. Hurried and rough.

"Is this okay?" Suddenly nervous that she'd say no, I started to pull her up.

"No," she said quickly as she grabbed at my hands, placing them on her hips once again. "I want it like this. Let's try it."

"I love you," I ground out through clenched teeth.

Something had changed in her, and I wanted to question it, but fuck it, I wanted her any way I could get her.

I started to push into her. Bracing herself, she placed her hands back on the bed and leaned forward.

There was a new song on with a heavy beat, and I was getting mindfucked with the beat and the lyrics. "It's Going Down for Real." *Thank you very much, Flo Rida.*

I pushed into her harder, and she gasped.

"Am I hurting you?" I started to pull out.

"No, no." She pushed back onto me, and I watched as her hands fisted the bedspread. Then, she let out a long moan. "Oh God, Kyle."

"Fuck." I pushed back into her again, trying to control the urge to just fuck her into the bed. I wanted to make her gasp and moan again.

My world disintegrated at her quiet noises. I thrust and thrust and thrust. She pushed back onto me, and I grunted.

What in the hell has gotten into my sweet, angelic Kennedy?

This was like having sex with a completely different person.

Don't get me wrong; I wasn't complaining, but *fuck!*

My mind was in so many different places. I had no idea how I was even doing this. My body moved with basic instinct, animalistic desire, and need.

She gasped, "Kyle!"

Oh God. When she sounded like *that*…like she was desperate…I almost lost my ever-loving mind.

"Come on, Kyle."

Fuck.

That gravelly sound in her voice, that demand, was killing me. I loved when she sounded gritty. It was always there in her voice, but when we had sex, it was so much more prominent.

"Kennedy," I huffed out. *Fuck, I'm going to come.*

I looked down and saw one of her hands missing from the bed.

Fuck. No. She isn't. Is she?

"Kyle, I'm almost there."

Yep. Yeah, she is definitely touching herself.

"Ugh, Kennedy."

I thrust hard three times, and she moaned and shivered. *Yeah, she's coming.*

"*Babe. Fuck!*" I growled as she rotated her hips.

Then, I was coming and thrusting through it. My chest collapsed to her back. We were both breathless. I didn't think we'd ever worked that hard or quick. I pulled out gently, and she groaned.

"Fuck, Kennedy, don't do that."

"I can't move," she stated in a whisper after falling onto the bed.

I chuckled. "Good or bad?" My hands were still braced on her waist.

"The best."

"God, I love you."

"I love you, too. We should go get cleaned up." She grabbed a couple of tissues from the desk and handed them to me.

I disposed of the condom, and she walked out of the room with a new pair of panties and jeans held to her chest.

I sat down on the bed. *Holy shit. Did that really just happen?*

"So, how was Texas?" she asked as she walked back into the room, brushing her blonde hair.

I sighed. I kind of didn't want to talk about that right now, but I guessed it was inevitable, so we might as well get it over with.

"It was really, really great," I confessed. My eyes never wavered from hers. I needed to see her reaction.

"So, when do you sign?" she asked calmly.

Her brush slowed but never stopped running through her long strands. I could tell she was scared of what I'd say by the way she kept in her emotions, but I'd never make this decision without discussing it with her.

"I don't know if I will, but I really want us to talk about everything," I said gently. But I knew how much she was tired of talking. My elbows on my knees left me in a hunched position. I fidgeted with my watch, clasping and unclasping it.

We needed to figure this out together because there was no way I was going to let her go.

She nodded. "Can I just say something?" She moved closer to the bed, the brush discarded.

I looked down at her hand fiddling with the hairband on her wrist.

"Yeah. You don't have to ask to speak your mind."

"Go to Texas."

My head shot up. "What?"

"I want you to sign with Texas."

Chapter 7

Kennedy

I could see it in Kyle's eyes. Texas was everything he wanted.

Who the hell am I to hold him back?

He could be great. Hell, he already was great. Texas knew it. I knew it. And he deserved this.

He roughly shook his head from side to side. "There's more to it than that, Ken. I'm not just going to walk away from you, from *us*. Don't you know how much I love you?" His hand reached out and grabbed mine.

"Of course I know that, Kyle. But this is what you want. We can figure everything else out. Just sign with Texas. Now, let's go celebrate." My voice was serious, and I didn't want to talk anymore about the subject. I might change my mind if we did.

I beamed at him as I took his other hand while he sat on the edge of the bed. I tried to pull him up, but he stayed cemented to the bed.

"What?" He looked baffled, his eyebrows furrowed.

"Let's go to Dieter's bonfire," I said happily. I dropped his hands and moved to grab my things. I threw my brush into my bag and picked up the remaining clothes and things I had strewn across Lo's room at Chase's house, shoving them in my bag as I walked around. I unplugged my phone from the docking station and reached for Kyle's hand, successfully pulling him up off the bed this time.

"Wait," Kyle said quietly, confusion lingering in his voice and marring his face with scrunched eyebrows. "What's going on? I left, and you were...and then Lo called, and now you're acting like..."

"Like what? Like I'm so proud and happy for my boyfriend?" I laughed. "Come on, I want to be with our friends and tell them you're going to Texas."

"Kennedy," he scolded. Frustration painted his face. His lips pulled tight. But he was still the most gorgeous guy I'd laid eyes on. "Hold up. I know you're not telling me something."

I stopped and rolled my eyes at him. Of course he knew.

"I know you know. Because Lo told you. She's my best friend, and you're my boyfriend. I love you both so much, and that's why I'm not mad. Can we just put all the other stuff on the back burner for a hot minute? I just want to be with our friends and celebrate *you*."

I looked up at him with big puppy-dog gray eyes. He had a hard time resisting them—unless it was a serious matter.

But, when he sighed, I knew I had him. He didn't want to push me to open up. I knew he feared that I would spiral into the deepest depression. I was already there. He just didn't see it. I had been hiding my emotions too well this time.

"I think we should talk about this more." He tried once again. The concern in his eyes blistered with curiosity.

It was painful for me to keep everything inside, but it was too soul-wrenching for me to communicate. I hadn't fully processed everything. My scattered mind and shattered heart were trying to piece themselves back together and make sense of all the changes and emotions, but something in me resisted. Whether it was my heart or my fears, I was holding back.

"Later. Come on, take me out, and show me off!" I compelled my smile to stay bright and unwavering. It hurt my cheeks to force it, but for him, I'd grin and bear it.

Kyle could read me so well, but could he keep up with all my conflicting emotions?

He looked unsure but relented and took my bag from me. Then, he took my hand and guided me out to his truck. I looked at the clock. It was eight thirty, so the party should just be getting started.

Even though I'd already started my own party.

I'd asked Lo to take me to my house after school to get some more clothes, and while there, I'd snuck some Crown Royal into my stolen flask. Mom would never notice since she hadn't been into Dad's office for weeks.

I leaned back into my seat and sighed. I had no idea what had come over me when Kyle walked into the room. I'd just had to get out of my head for a moment. I hadn't known I was going to take it to sex in Lo's room, but I couldn't help myself. I'd needed that release.

And, oh my goodness, had Kyle given it to me. We'd never been that way. That rushed and crazed. I'd shocked myself with what had come out of my mouth tonight. I never cursed like that. I never acted so…I didn't even have a word for how I'd acted compared to my reserved, quiet demeanor. Tonight, I had been vocal and daring though, chasing a high to outrun my constant thoughts.

Kyle didn't know I'd already drunk half of the flask between the time I got to Chase's and right before he showed up. I'd luckily just brushed my teeth.

By the way, whiskey and toothpaste? Gross.

Then, when I'd slipped back to the bathroom to clean up, I'd finished the last few swallows and brushed my teeth again to get rid of the taste and smell. Alcohol was so new to me that I instantly felt the effects. Warmth and light-headedness. But finally finding a bit of peace.

I knew what I was doing was wrong. That my father would have been so disappointed. But I liked the burning sensation and the slight numbness I got from just a few sips.

As we drove in silence, Kyle reached over for my hand and weaved our fingers together on the console. Something he always did when we drove somewhere. From the very first date.

He was playing "Simple Desire" by All Mankind, a band we listened to all the time. Kyle was like Lo in the music world. He listened to a little bit of everything, but he also listened to artists no one else had ever heard of.

Kyle tapped the steering wheel with his other hand and hummed along to the song. I didn't take my eyes off him. I couldn't take my eyes off him. Somehow, I'd landed this amazing, loving, talented godsend, and I was suddenly terrified of losing him. I was so unbelievably proud of and excited for him because he'd been offered this scholarship, but I didn't know where that would leave us.

Leave *me*.

I had to drag my eyes away from him. Glancing out my window at the pitch-black night, I gazed at the stars scattered across the dark sky. The darkness depressed me more. Making me think of the past and the future. The memories and the unknown.

Everything had fallen apart this year, and it hadn't seemed to stop. I'd lost my dad, and I was still in this unmoving fog. Stuck in my head, in my heart, not breaking out of it. Just trying to cover it up.

That was what I was doing. I was covering up my emotions, my pain, my sadness. Because I didn't want anyone to ask if I was okay anymore. I was *not* okay. Saying no wasn't going to help me though. No one really wanted to hear how well I wasn't doing. And, even if I did tell them, I didn't want their sympathy or the pity.

I knew I had to talk about it—what I'd found out two nights ago after Kyle and his dad dropped me off on their way to the airport.

I should have known something was up when I saw that slightly familiar siren-red Mercedes. I mean, I'd only seen it every other weekend for months while I was in St. Louis, helping my mom with Grandma. Why it hadn't registered until after I walked into the house was beyond me.

But then again, why would my grandmother's forty-two-year-old neighbor, Cole, be at my house in a completely different state than where he lived?

The laughter was what had caught me off guard. I hadn't heard my mom laugh in weeks, but there she had been, laughing up a storm with some guy who used to be my grandmother's neighbor. Either I had been drunk or dreaming because that reality was impossible.

I'd peeked in on them from the hallway. Her hand had been placed on his arm, his hand on her thigh. Neither caressing the other, just simply touching. But it had still been repulsive and infuriating. I couldn't even bear to watch it anymore as they'd acted like they weren't sitting in my father's house, cozied up to one another.

I'd rushed upstairs and slammed my door. As I'd slid down to the floor, pressing my cold hands to my teary eyes, I'd heard their hushed whispers, telling each other they'd talk later and that things would work out how they were supposed to.

What bullshit.

Kyle turned off the main road and drove us through an open gate and into a huge cleared field. The bumps pulled me back to the now. This was the backside of the Millers' farm, where Dieter had all his bonfires. His godparents let him get away with everything, and his dad worked a lot. I wasn't even sure if his dad or godparents knew what actually went on down here. Dieter was smart though. He made sure everyone had DDs, and while he couldn't prevent some people from lying, there hadn't been any accidents.

We drove farther onto the land on a worn path, caused by the many parties that Dieter had had. After we went down a slight hill and curved around a bank of trees, all the cars of people attending came into view.

I immediately recognized Chase's Chevy Tahoe at the end of the pack. I knew Lo always made Chase park far enough out, so they wouldn't be blocked in by anyone and could easily leave. She still wasn't much of a partier. I used to have to drag her out to them. I just liked to see and be around people, happy and having fun. Sometimes, I'd step in to be a designated driver or even just help clean up.

Now though, I was just here to unwind and to take the focus off me.

"Are you sure you want to be here? I was thinking we'd just stay in and have the night to ourselves," Kyle questioned me after parking and turning off his truck.

His face was shadowed in the dark field, but I could still make out his chiseled features and frowning lips, thanks to the moon.

"It's a little late for that, don't you think?" I put on a cheery smile and leaned over the console to give him a kiss on the lips. "Come on, let's go tell everyone about Texas." I opened the door, jumped down from the high truck, and ran off toward the bonfire.

I heard Kyle's door slam, and I turned around to skip backward down the path. "Catch me!" I shouted.

"Kennedy!" he yelled.

I turned and skipped faster.

I could see the fire down the hill. I slowed and surveyed who was here. I immediately spotted Dieter. His hand was around the waist of a girl I didn't recognize. Come to think of it, I never recognized the girls he'd had with him this past year.

"Kennedy!" Dieter shouted.

He nodded his head toward me, so I walked over to him.

"Hey!" I smiled.

The girl he was with bristled at me, her glare instant but harmless.

"Who's this?" I asked.

She laughed and then buried her head into Dieter's chest.

All right then. Weird.

"Sorry. This is Shay. She's from Rivers." He squeezed her waist and then took his arm off her.

Her face stayed on his chest. I wondered if she was extra drunk or super high.

"Is Kyle here?" He took a swig of his Miller Lite can.

"Yeah, he should be walking down any second." I looked to his drink as he took another gulp.

He laughed. "Looks like you're wanting one of these, Ken."

I kept my face clear of any craving, but maybe I did. I just didn't want to be judged or questioned. I'd keep my desire to numb and quiet the racing thoughts to myself.

"Kyle! My man! How was Texas?" Dieter shouted to my boyfriend, seeming to forget my perusal of his beer.

Kyle came up behind me and wrapped his arms around my waist, pulling me back into him. He whispered, "You're in trouble. Just wait until we're alone again." Then, he chuckled and bit at my neck. Raising his voice, he answered Dieter, "It was good, man. Where's everyone else?"

He looked around the fire before answering, "Um...I'm not really sure. Last I checked, they were sitting at Beckon's truck."

Beckon was a friend of Lo's. Or I should say, he was one of the many guys who had wanted in her pants before she fell hopelessly in love with Chase. After Chase and Lo had made things official, Beckon had finally realized that anything other than a friendship with Lo would never happen. He had taken on a big brother role instead—and not just over Lo, but all of us. He was twenty-one and worked as a mechanic at his father's garage. Chase and Kyle had been more than welcoming after they knew Beckon wasn't after us girls and could get discounted services on their vehicles.

"Ah, okay. Well, you wanna come with us to find them? I've got some big news." Kyle grinned down at me.

I plastered on my fake enthusiasm for what was about to happen. This was it. His future was about to be sealed. I couldn't take back what I'd said when I saw how happy it made him.

Dieter nodded, completely forgetting about the girl who was awkwardly standing beside him, and he started to walk with us. I saw the back of Lo's head when we moved around the fire. She was laughing and pushing at Chase's hands that were trying to grab at her butt.

I let go of Kyle's hand to rush up behind her and covered her eyes with my hands.

She froze. "I'm gonna kick whoever's motherfuck—"

"Hey!" I shouted. "That's no way to talk to your best friend!"

Then, I laughed, and she did, too.

"Oh my God. Don't do that. You know how I get with that stuff." Her posture tensed, but I could see that she wasn't mad. Just nervous.

Sometimes, I forgot all of the trauma she'd gone through with crazy Cam and Brent. They'd sneakily slipped GHB into her drink, and she'd started to have trouble seeing. She'd even stopped breathing and had a seizure in the ambulance on the way to the hospital. It'd scared the crap out of all of us. The doctor had said she was lucky Chase had called 911 when he did.

She'd really come out of her shell since she and Chase became an official couple. But there were still moments when she felt that fear. Like when she would see Cam and Brent whispering in the hallways at school. She'd track their movements whenever they were near, just in case they tried to pull something shady.

Once word had gotten out about what Cam and Brent had done to Lo, everyone had shied away from them, and they kept to themselves. Rumor was, they were dating now. A match made in heaven, if you asked me. They stayed away from the local parties, which was a smart move.

I hugged Lo to me. "I've missed you," I whispered to her.

She pulled back to grin at me, but I could see the worry and questions in her eyes—*Are you okay? Is there anything I can do? I'm still worried about you.*

"I've missed you, too."

I gave her the best smile I could, letting it tug my lips upward. My teeth clenched, and my cheeks ached with the effort.

"So? Texas? What'd you think?" Chase asked Kyle.

Kyle smiled, shook his head, and then looked at me. I nodded, encouraging him once again to take what he wanted.

"Why are you shaking your head?" Chase asked cautiously.

"I think…" Kyle paused, hesitating. Then, he took my hand again, waiting for my squeeze of affirmation that this was okay.

We would be fine. I had to believe that.

"I think, if I don't have to live in the athletes' dorms, you'd better get a big enough house for me to room with you."

The smiles that overtook everyone's faces were contagious. I smiled up at my loving boyfriend, knowing this was what he wanted and what he deserved.

Everyone shouted their congratulations and cheered for him. I focused solely on him. I took in his dark-wash jeans that seemed to cling and hang perfectly on him. His T-shirt hugged his biceps, and underneath, I knew the sculpted and chiseled muscles never disappeared. He was an athlete. And, while he was gone in Texas, playing football, and I was here…I'd miss him excruciatingly so. Just the thought of it caused fissures in my already fragile heart.

"Wait…" Lo said slowly. "What do you mean, a big enough house to room with Chase?" Her glare zeroed in on her boyfriend like a hawk. "Chase?" she prompted.

She was dwarfed in a black hoodie that reached her thighs. Her super-long brunette hair flowed everywhere.

"I, uh, was going to tell you." He sheepishly looked to his angry-looking girlfriend.

Her blue eyes narrowed fiercely. I laughed. He looked ready to run. Or drop to his knees for forgiveness. Probably the latter. I couldn't see him ever leaving her.

"You offered me a room at your shared house, and you didn't even ask her?" Kyle ribbed, full of humor, as he shook his head. "You're so dead."

"I didn't think you'd care! You said you didn't want your dad buying a house, so I figured we could get a big house and split the rent!" Chase explained with his hands up in self-defense, looking so scared about what she was going to do next. His expression was nervous, his eyes trying to silently communicate with her.

"You're lucky I love you." She laughed, shaking her head at Chase. Then, she looked to my boyfriend. "Yes, Kyle, you can room with us in one of the houses we decide on."

Then, she walked over to Chase and jumped on him, wrapping her legs around his waist. He effortlessly caught her and kept her up with his hands on her butt.

"You're not getting laid for a very long time!" she told him, her tone not totally teasing. That was another thing about Lo; she wasn't afraid of rumors getting started anymore, so she spoke more freely.

"Hey! What does that have to do with anything? You *like* Kyle!" he whined.

Everyone laughed. He shot us all with laser eyes, obviously not happy with the outcome.

After scanning the group, I realized one of our pack was missing. "Where's Talan?" I asked.

"She's got a performance tomorrow, so she didn't want to be out late," Dieter chimed in.

I looked at him with curiosity and amusement. He always knew the whereabouts of Talan. I didn't know if they had anything more than a friendship. I had a feeling that, if it ever went beyond that, there'd be explosions and car chases happening with those two. They were too wild and volatile, never standing still for longer than necessary.

I looked around the group of people who were my closest friends, and I couldn't help but still feel down. Everything that I was pushing away and trying to keep buried deep down inside was constantly gnawing at my psyche, trying to get me to focus on it, fix it, something other than just sweep it under the rug.

Chase placed Lo back on her feet.

She immediately looked to me and walked over. "What's wrong?" she asked quietly.

"Nothing." I continued to look around at everyone.

Everybody had a drink in their hand but me, Kyle, and Lo.

I wanted my own, but I knew what kind of reactions everyone would have.

Good little Kennedy never drinks. She was raised better than that. She isn't pressured to fall into the high school norm. She doesn't let things alter her mind. She's the pastor's daughter.

Well, screw that. My mind was already altered.

I looked to my best friend with what I was sure was a weird face. "I kind of want a drink," I said low enough, so no one would overhear.

"Really?" She looked stunned. Her blue eyes widened, unblinking.

"Yeah."

"Here?" Lo now looked confused. She scrutinized me with narrowed eyebrows and pursed lips. Her mouth was slightly parted.

I know, Lo. I'm just as shocked as you.

I stood my ground, not retracting my statement. I understood everyone's concern. I did. But I could be just like every other teenager, trying things for the first time and just wanting to have a good time. Even though I knew deep down that was not the case.

"Why not? It's a party, isn't it?"

"Maybe we should head back to Kyle's, and we can drink where you'll be more comfortable," she suggested.

I shook my head at her. *What difference does it truly make? Here. There. It doesn't matter.*

"Dieter!" I shouted, ignoring her proposal completely.

His head shot up. "Yeah?"

With the crook of my finger, I motioned for him to come toward us. Nothing seductive. Just summoning my friend who always had a beer in his hand. He walked over to Lo and me and wrapped an arm around each of our shoulders, bearing down more weight than I was used to carrying. A longneck bottle of beer was clutched in his hand over Lo's shoulder.

I grunted, adjusting the position of his arm, and then quietly asked him, "Can you get me a beer?"

He coughed and then laughed. "Yeah, okay," he said sarcastically, his eyes rolling dramatically.

"I'm serious."

"No, you're not!"

"Actually, I am," I deadpanned. I tried to prepare myself for all the questions and worry that were bound to surface.

"Hands off our girls!" Chase shouted from a few feet away.

Dieter flinched from the abrupt command and pulled his arms away. He held them up in a fending-off motion. "Kyle! Your girl wants a beer!"

Way to sell me down the river, dear Dieter.

And, like a bad harmony, everyone at once said, "What?"

Lo punched Dieter in the gut. Her glare was fierce. I never wanted to be on the other side of that glare.

"Look what you did now, you dumbass!" she hissed.

"Hey!" he growled back at her. "That's not fucking fair! Kyle would beat my ass if he thought *I* was trying to get Kennedy drunk. No way am I taking the heat for that one." He shook his head and chugged his own beer, eyes wide and focused on us—me mainly.

Kyle slowly walked over to us. "Hey"—he took my elbow and pulled me away from everyone—"if you want to drink, you can. I have no problem with it," he said sheepishly.

His deep brown eyes scanned my face. I gave him a sweet smile. His features hardened for only a brief moment. I barely caught it.

"Lo said we should go back to your house, so I'd feel more comfortable, but honestly"—I looked around—"I feel fine here."

"Well then, let me get you a beer. But, if I'm being honest, you'll probably like what Talan usually drinks more—you know, those fruity little wine coolers."

"Then, I'll take one of those. Thank you, babe."

He leaned in for a kiss, and I gave it to him. When he pulled away, I could see the brief hesitation in his eyes. He hadn't expected this. At least, that was what I assumed.

I'd never wanted to drink before. Not until I'd lost my father, so I'd sought comfort in my dad's home office. I'd found the key to the liquor cabinet and an empty flask, and I'd wondered how alcohol made some people feel better.

My dad would probably want to kill me right now if he saw me. He'd definitely give me a long lecture about the danger I was putting myself in and the consequences of my choices. I could almost picture his narrowed eyes as he sat across from me at his desk. He'd prop his elbows up and steeple his hands together in front of his mouth.

Why can't you be here to watch me screw up, Dad?

But none of that mattered anymore.

He was dead.

And I had already been sampling my parents' small alcohol collection.

Warmth. That was what I felt. I felt really warm. My cheeks were red. That was what Kyle kept on telling me.

He whispered in my ear, telling me how flushed I looked. How it reminded him of how I looked during…other activities.

And I had to pee. Like really bad. These sugary things made me more light-headed than the harder, more bitter sips of alcohol I'd been taking. But that could be because I'd had five within the last hour. I didn't feel drunk. But my never-ending thoughts were quieted, and my body finally felt loose and free. Not frigid and tense or overwhelmed.

Kyle was sitting on the back of Beckon's tailgate. I was standing between his legs while he massaged my shoulders. I relaxed back into him, feeling my eyes drift shut.

Is this what happens when you drink a lot?

I mean, I knew I was going to be a lightweight, but dang, I felt like I was going to fall asleep, and that was all. I didn't feel like dancing or taking my clothes off, something some girls around us were well on their way toward. Sugary alcohol didn't really do much of anything for me.

I slowly turned around and looked up at Kyle.

"Hey," he whispered while lowering his forehead to mine, our noses touching.

I breathed him in deeply. The bonfire smoke clung to our clothes, but I could still smell his expensive cologne. I wrapped my arms around his waist and closed my eyes. I took another deep breath and then sighed.

"What's wrong?" he asked.

I shook my head, keeping my eyes closed. Nothing was at this point. I was in limbo.

People were talking, shouting, and laughing all around us. They had been for hours. It felt like it'd been hours. I honestly wasn't sure. I'd been in my own head, thinking about not thinking, trying to fight my thoughts, trying to stop feeling. The alcohol had helped.

"Ken?" Kyle nuzzled my nose.

I slowly let my eyes flutter open to connect with his.

"Are you all right?" he asked quietly.

Dark chocolate eyes penetrated my stormy grays.

"I'm fine," I said meekly.

He knew it was a lie, but he didn't say anything. No one ever did when you said that.

A semi-effort squeeze of my arms around his waist would hopefully give him some reassurance.

"I have to pee."

"Oh, thank God! Me, too!" Lo shouted, startling me for a moment.

It had felt like Kyle and I were alone in our own little world. I kind of wished we were.

He laughed and kissed my nose. "Okay. Do you want me to come with you, or do you want Lo to go?"

"We'll be fine. Lo will protect me." I smiled brightly at him, and he bought my forced merriness.

When I started to step away, Kyle jumped down and grabbed my hand to swing me back to him. He softly kissed my lips, and I responded in kind. Then, his hands wrapped around my back, and he yanked me flush against him. The lack of oxygen made me dizzy, but I didn't shy away. This was what took my mind off things, as unlike me as it was. A physical connection broke my emotional madness, making me forget my depressing thoughts. It was instant and gratifying.

"I love you," he whispered against my lips.

Nodding my head up and down with my eyes tightly shut, I whispered back, "I love you, too. To heaven and back."

Then, he let me go, and I slowly walked away because I was still feeling the dizzy rush he'd given me. I went up the path to where Lo was standing. I cast glances behind me to Kyle. His eyes seared into me, following my steps, until I knew he couldn't see me anymore.

We walked toward Chase's Chevy Tahoe, and Lo unlocked it with the remote key.

"What are you doing?" I asked, confused.

"Grabbing toilet paper." When she popped back out, she laughed. "I always come prepared." Then, she opened up the back passenger door and held up a towel. "You first."

I laughed. *What the hell?*

I'd never peed outside before, and usually my I was full of sugary alcoholic drinks so I could hold off till I got home, but Lo was apparently a pro. And I appreciated her effort to protect our modesty.

When I was finished, we switched places. I awkwardly told her not to step in my pee, and she laughed it off. She probably knew better, being a pro and all.

"So, how are those wine coolers treating you?" Lo asked while zipping up her jeans and grabbing the towel from me.

"At first, I was kind of woozy, and then I was really hot, but now, I'm just really tired. Is that weird?"

She didn't know I'd had a full flask of whiskey earlier. I'd almost blurted it out.

She shut the door and then locked the truck up. "Nope. Not weird. Makes sense, and it's probably better to start off light. Wouldn't want you to get wasted on hard liquor first and then regret it."

If only you knew, Lo.

We started to walk back down to the bonfire.

My phone beeped, distracting me. I pulled it out of my back pocket to see a text from my mom. My heart thrashed at the message. Revolted, I even started to feel slightly ill from it.

I stopped walking and froze. My whole body locked up. Muscles tight. Brain deserting me.

Mom: Are you ever going to come home?

Lo was a couple of feet in front of me when she turned to see me cemented to the ground like a statue, clutching my phone with white knuckles.

That's not my home anymore.

"Are you okay?" She rushed back to me.

At first, I started to shake my head, but then I nodded, not wanting her to see me break. I was tired of being this weak, fragile girl. I was used to being the one who comforted others.

"Yeah, I'm fine." *Lie again.* "I have to call someone. Can you tell Kyle I'll be right down? I'll be by his truck."

"You want me to wait?" she asked hesitantly. She reached out to touch me, but she stopped short, her arm hanging midair between us.

I shook my head. I just needed space from everyone. When she started to walk away, I turned back around and walked to his truck.

My chest felt tight with sudden anxiety, and I had to take a deep breath, but it didn't ease any of the restless panic that had started to settle in.

Mom…Jesus, what is wrong with her? How can she expect me to be okay with her basically having some random guy in our house? In my father's house? Acting like nothing is wrong with that situation.

I leaned back against the passenger door and let my head crash against the window. She'd already moved on. I just knew it. God, I couldn't believe her. She didn't have to say it for me to know it. I'd suspected it as soon as she tried to explain that man's presence in our family home.

There had been so many signs pointing to her seeing someone—all the secret phone calls, emails, and texts—but I'd missed them all. Suddenly, I wondered if it was more than her just moving on, if she'd started seeing him before Dad passed.

My God, did he know? Could the stress of finding out his wife of nineteen years had been cheating on him kill him?

I'd heard what the doctor said about his condition. It could have been brought on by anything, but stress was a major factor.

I squeezed my eyes shut to the point of pain, trying to stanch my inevitable tears from falling. But there was no stopping them. The acid-like liquid burned down my cheeks and dripped off my chin and to my jacket. Even when my throat ached from holding back as much as I could, tears still gushed to the surface.

Feeling this way was what scared me the most. This unbelievable pain and confusion took over my whole mind, and I couldn't stop it. I just wanted my dad. I wanted my family back to the way I remembered it. I wanted laughter and family game nights. I wanted Sundays and Wednesdays spent at church.

I wanted the past. Because this present was slowly shattering me, grinding me down from glass to dust.

"Hey, are you okay?"

A deep voice startled me, and I jumped and quickly turned around to face the passenger mirror, wiping at my tears and runny mascara.

"I'm fine." I took a deep breath and tried to steady my breathing.

"Are you sure?" the voice asked again.

I turned to smile brightly and act like nothing was wrong, but that smile faded swiftly when I realized who was asking. My shock was evident on my face, and he backed away a couple of feet.

"You shouldn't be here," I warned.

"I'm just here to pick up my stepsister. She called me," Bryan Endears explained.

I quickly looked away from him, hoping no one was around to see him.

"If Kyle, Chase, or Dieter sees you, they're going to lose their minds. You'd better get her fast and leave."

He smiled. "You think I don't know that, Angel? I can't go down there, but now, she's not answering her phone. Mind helping me out?"

I cringed at his use of endearment.

I couldn't decipher his smile from his request. He seemed so genuine in his words, but his smile was sinister.

"Sure. Who's your sister?" I looked over the hood of the truck to make sure no one was coming up the path.

"Bevin."

"I don't think I know her. Do you have a picture, so I know who I'm looking for?" I didn't think I'd ever heard of a Bevin in our school.

Bryan pulled his phone out and scrolled through some photos. When he picked one, he turned the phone to me, and I scanned her face. Yeah, I'd never seen her either.

"She hangs out with that Casey chick, who has dyed red hair and always wears dark lipstick," he tried to explain.

I knew who Casey was. Her parents attended my dad's church.

I nodded and started to walk down the path. "I'll send her this way," I softly replied.

Why I was protecting him, I had no idea. He'd almost killed my best friend a year ago. He was the one who had given the GHB to Cam and Brent. I should've been terrified of him and his capabilities. He was a womanizing jerk with nothing but self-serving qualities. And that was just the surface of him. I didn't want to ever know anything more than that.

I walked around the bonfire, and when I spotted Casey, I walked over. "Hey, um…is Bevin around?"

She looked confused. Her face pinched in a disturbed expression. Like she couldn't understand why I was asking. I'd be skeptical, too. Especially since I'd never even talked to Casey before now.

She looked around her group of friends before answering, "She left with another friend from her old school. Some guy." Her eyes rolled, and she pursed her lips. Effectively dismissing me, she turned her back to me.

None of my friends had noticed me walking down or back up the path. If they had, they didn't stop me.

When I got back to where I'd left Bryan, he wasn't there. I walked farther up, and when I didn't see him, I started to turn and go back to my friends, but Bryan was suddenly there, in my face, scaring the living crap out of me.

I yelped and then slapped his chest. "What the hell is wrong with you?" I growled roughly, too pissed off to care if I sounded crazy. "You don't just sneak up on someone like that!"

His sinister smirk appeared again, and I shoved him out of the way to go back to the safety of my friends.

I shouted over my shoulder, "Your sister left with a friend from a different school." I left out the part about her leaving with a guy. Somehow, I didn't think her brother would be too happy to find that little nugget out.

"You're joking, right?" Bryan scoffed. "That stupid little bitch."

Anger raced through me, and I didn't hold back. I turned abruptly at his blatant disrespect for his sister. "That's rude. And you're an asshole. How could you even talk about your sister like that?"

"She's my stepsister, and we've known each other for only two months."

"So? That doesn't mean you can call her names."

I swiveled to leave again. He had already gotten enough of my time.

"Wait!" he yelled out.

I felt him come up behind me. I held my breath.

"You were upset earlier. Are you sure you're okay?" The sincerity in his voice didn't match his personality at all.

I turned around to glare at him. "Like you would even care." *How could he go from disrespecting his sister to checking about my well-being? What made me more important than finding his sister?*

"*Sooo*, you're holding a grudge for something that happened over a year ago? What would your daddy think?"

"He wouldn't think anything about it because he's dead." I flinched at my own brashness.

It shocked him enough to where he stumbled back a step. I took a deep breath at my quick and careless response.

"Kennedy, I'm sorry. I had no idea." His eyes widened with apology.

"Well, it just proves that your asshole capabilities never cease to amaze me."

I started to leave again, but he grabbed my shoulder and twisted me back around.

"Are you joking? Why would you even think it's okay to put your hands on me?" I shoved his hand away.

He rolled his eyes. "My mom loves your church. I know how much he meant to you."

I wasn't aware his mom attended. I didn't think I'd ever met his mom.

Tears started to brim in my eyes.

Bryan was basically a stranger to me.

How could he possibly know how much my father meant to me?

The tears no longer lined my eyes, that damn burning feeling returned as they raced along my cheeks. I thrust my hands over my eyes, trying to shield my sorrow.

"Hey, hey," Bryan consoled as he reached for my hand. "It's okay." His voice was soft but edged.

I rapidly shook my head. It wasn't okay. *How could he say that?* If he knew how much my dad meant to me, then he knew everything was *not* okay.

"Kennedy?"

My name was shouted from down the path, and Bryan's hand squeezed mine tightly.

"That's my cue to get the fuck out of here, but let me see your phone."

He reached for my phone in my pocket, and I flinched back. I pulled it out of my pocket myself, swiping at the screen and unlocking it. I handed it over, thinking I was stupid to even do this. He typed in his first name and left the last-name slot blank.

"This is my number. Text me if you need to." Then, he shoved it into my hand and weaved through the cars to disappear from sight.

I swiped at my eyes and took a deep breath. I didn't want Kyle to see me losing it. It was bad enough that Bryan had.

"Ken? Babe?" Kyle was closer now.

I turned and tried to flash a bright smile for him. His shoulders tensed in a slight cringe. I saw it in the way his shirt gripped his muscles. He knew me so well; there was no doubt he could see the distress in my eyes.

"Are you okay? You've been up here forever."

"I'm fine." *My new motto.* "I just…I got a text from my mom."

"What'd she say?"

I shrugged. "She wants to know when I'm coming home."

Kyle wrapped his arms around me in a crushing embrace that I welcomed and relished. "You don't have to go back there. You can stay with me. You know you're always welcome at my house. My parents love you."

I nodded my head and pulled back to give him a small smile. "I love you."

He leaned down to softly kiss my lips, only putting the slightest pressure down.

"To heaven and back," he whispered.

I heard a car start and turned to see a two-door black car pulling away from all the others.

"Who's that?" Kyle watched over my shoulder as the car drove off.

I never even saw which car Bryan had gotten into, but I knew it was him.

"I don't know," I lied in a quiet whisper.

Chapter 8

Kyle

I looked up to the crowd standing in front of me. Then, I leaned over the table in the middle of the school gym, pen in my hand. Bright flashes from cameras went off as I signed my name at the bottom of the letter of intent. I was sealing my fate to play football as a Longhorn.

You couldn't wipe the smile off my face as I was making one of my dreams come true on this awesome day.

My parents stood behind me while pictures continued to be snapped. That was when I noticed Kennedy. She was standing off to the side with our friends. I could see happiness, but deep down, I knew there was something else she felt. Something that I couldn't quite put my finger on.

But I knew at least one thing she felt was fear. She'd opened up a little for me even though I knew she wanted to hold everything in. We'd talked during lunch while sitting in my truck. I'd wanted to get her honest thoughts on everything that was going on and what she was encouraging me to do. And, although she was happy, she was scared. Scared she was going to lose me forever. Scared that her heart wasn't ever going to heal after losing her father. But I'd assured her that she would never lose me and that her heart would heal. She just needed time.

Now, as I'd signed my name to a future, she put on a happy face and smiled lovingly at me. A glassy sheen made her eyes flicker in the light gym.

I pointed at her and then curled my finger in a come-hither gesture. She slowly walked up to me with a hesitant smile, and I grabbed her hands and pulled her to my body, our hips and torsos plastered against each other. Then, I leaned down and kissed her, smashing our lips together. Her surprised gasp made me grin, my lips no longer flush with hers. She almost chased me with her own, but then her eyes fluttered open, as she must have remembered where we were when a camera brightly flashed, directed right at us. As I pulled away and she shifted to face the camera, I placed my arm over her shoulders while the local newspaper representative directed the photographer to continue snapping photos.

"Everything's going to work out, babe. I promise," I whispered in her ear before kissing her cheek.

Her skin was hot to my lips. I grinned wider. I'd made her blush, and I would take that victory every time.

Her head nodded in acceptance of my promise. Fear still swirled in her irises though. I could almost hear her uncertain thoughts trying to take over her mind. They blared and reached into my own.

As everyone started to clear out of the gym, I wrapped her up in a hug where she burrowed into my chest with her arms snuggled up between us while my parents and I chatted over her.

"We're so happy for you, Kyle," my mom said lovingly.

My dad hugged her to his side. "Absolutely," he said proudly.

Their smiles took over their faces. They looked cautiously toward Kennedy. It wasn't just me who was worried. My parents were as in love with Kennedy as I was. It was hard not to fall for her. And, when she was fragile and hurting…you couldn't help but want to mend the hurt and protect her.

"Where's Leighton? I thought he was coming," I asked, sad that my older brother and role model wasn't here to see this all go down.

My mom sighed. "He had a project that he had to complete and present this week. And he needed to stay and study for exams as well."

"Oh." Well, I couldn't really be mad about that. He always was the studious type.

"What, what! Texas, here we come!" Dieter was such a jackass.

School was done for the day, so when the signing ceremony was over, the stands emptied quickly. Just my parents, our friends, and a few of the other guys from the team standing around in the gym remained.

Jake Ferrando, the football team representative the Longhorns had sent, snapped his briefcase closed and walked over to shake my hand. "Congratulations again, Kyle. We can't wait to see what you accomplish with the team. We'll be in touch with training camp information soon, okay?"

I squeezed Kennedy tighter when she tensed at the mention of training camp.

"I've got a flight to catch. Reach out if you need anything." He pulled a business card from the inside of his navy sport coat.

I nodded and looked at the glossy card with The University of Texas logo emblazoned across the front and his contact info on the back before pocketing it. "Thank you, sir. I'm excited to start training. I look forward to it. Have a safe flight."

We shook hands before he hustled out of the gym.

I looked over to see my dad hugging my mom tightly. When he released her, Mom clapped her hands together and beamed with pride. "Okay, okay. One of you is going to get hurt." Mom's authoritative voice was a notch louder.

I turned to what she was glaring at. Chase, who was keeping Dieter in a headlock. His hands pulled at Chase's arms, and his face burned with frustration.

"How about we do a barbeque tonight at our house?" Mom offered with a bright smile. She loved having everyone over and loved celebrating even more.

I remembered when she had thrown a party after Leighton broke his arm and when I didn't get into the All-Stars Summer Football Camp. Now that I thought about it, I realized how much better those parties had made us feel.

Well played, Mom. Well played.

At that, Chase let go of Dieter.

"Yes!" Lo shouted. "Mr. Masters makes the best food. Oh my God, my stomach is so happy you said that."

"Mom is totally going to take that as an insult if she ever finds out you like someone else's cooking more than hers." Chase wrapped his arm around her neck and reached up to tangle it in her hair.

"Tell her and die," she deadpanned while swiftly smacking his hand away from her head.

Everyone laughed at Lo. She totally had him whipped.

We made plans to meet at my house in an hour.

I walked out of the gym, following my friends and family, with my arm slung over Kennedy's shoulders. "You okay with everyone coming over?" I quietly asked her, my lips close to her ear.

"Absolutely." She grinned up at me.

I swooped down and kissed her lips, getting a brief taste of her strawberry lip gloss.

When we arrived at the house, Kennedy and I went to my room to slip into our swimsuits. The summer heat was coming, and the pool was the perfect temperature. We changed in silence, and when she was ready, she placed her hand in mine, and we walked down to the back patio.

Dad was already firing up the grill, and Mom was chopping up some vegetables and making a dip on the outside bar.

"Anything I can help you with, Jennifer?" Kennedy asked politely.

Mom beamed. It'd taken over a year for Kennedy to call my mom by anything but Mrs. Masters or ma'am, which Mom hated.

Still grinning, Mom shook her head and told us to go have fun and relax in the pool.

I pulled Kennedy behind me and over to the steps where we walked into the pool until we were both waist deep. Kennedy's swimsuit was one of those tank-top kinds. A royal-blue crochet-style covered most of her torso. She was always modest when we were around my parents.

Mom finished up the dip and sat on one of the loungers close to us. She propped her feet up while we waded around, and Dad kept on prepping the food for the grill.

"So, Kennedy, have you talked to your mom yet?"

I whipped my head to the side and glared at my mom's abrupt question.

Kennedy had been staying with us for the past few days. She'd refused to go home. I couldn't get her to talk about what had happened or how she'd found out her mom was actually seeing another man, but all I knew was some guy from St. Louis was in town, and he'd been at Kennedy's house the afternoon I left to go to Texas.

I swiftly pulled Kennedy to me and wrapped my arms around her from behind, crushing her to me. The water sloshed and swirled around us.

She let out a deep breath, and her whole body shrank in on herself. "No."

"Honey, I really think you should call her," Mom encouraged softly.

She didn't want to force Kennedy to do anything, but I knew her maternal instinct was kicking in. If the situation were reversed, I knew she'd want Kennedy's mom to encourage me to speak with her.

I slightly shook my head while shooting daggers at Mom. Kennedy didn't want to talk to her mom, and if I were being honest, I didn't want her to talk to her mom either.

"I might," was all Kennedy said while skimming her hands lightly across the water.

I squeezed her tighter.

The back door opened, and our friends poured out—Lo and Chase, Dieter and Max, Talan and her new puppy. He was a little tyrant named Ripper. It was such a fitting name since he shredded everything in his sight.

"You brought the little devil?" I laughed and splashed water at Chase and Lo as they edged closer to the pool.

"Hey!" Lo shouted.

"Of course I brought my little Ripper. He needs my undying love and attention while he's young, so he knows his mama loves him *so* much! Isn't that right, my little Ripper?" Talan used her adorably annoying mama voice and bent over to place him in the grass.

Lo sniffed the air. "Do you smell that?" She whirled around. "Mr. Masters, are those burgers ready?" she shouted over to my dad.

He just laughed and shook his head. Lo was always hungry.

As everyone settled in or around the pool, we started laughing, joking, and preparing for prom next weekend. We'd all decided to forgo the limo and just drive ourselves. Now, we had to decide if we were all driving separately or taking one car. Mom was offering up her Escalade, encouraging all of us to go together. She also wanted group pictures at the man-made lake in our gated community.

The girls would be getting ready at Chase's. Chase's mom had told Lo she wanted to help her and the girls with their hair and makeup. Since Lo had moved in with the Carters, Mrs. Carter and Lo had become extremely close.

The guys came to the conclusion that we'd get ready at my house. Now, the only things we had to decide on were the driving situation and dinner.

"I vote your dad just cooks dinner!" Lo shouted as she headed over to the bar to grab some snacks. Kennedy hopped out of the pool to follow her. My eyes stayed glued to her until she took a seat.

I looked at the others, and they were all nodding their heads in agreement. We always got invitations to be a part of larger groups but we always kept to ourselves for the most part.

"You okay with that, Dad?" I asked as he flipped burgers and steaks on the grill.

"I'd love to," he responded with a grin, the smoke distorting his face when he flipped the meat over.

I knew he loved getting to spend the extra time with me and my friends, especially with Leighton gone and me leaving soon. We were a close family. We'd always been that way, even more so since Dad had gotten out of the military.

My parents' jobs were demanding and had them constantly leaving town, but they never missed the important stuff. They'd always been there for Leighton and me, like every academic thing for Leighton and every football game for me. I never had to ask if they'd be there; they just were.

My mom stood to go over and help my dad. She stretched up on her tiptoes to give him a peck on the cheek. "You're so sweet, honey."

I loved seeing their love for each other expressed so clearly after twenty-five years of marriage. I knew I would have that with

Kennedy someday. No matter what, my parents had overcome distance, war, and loss, so I knew Kennedy and I could overcome our challenges.

"So, that's settled, and thank God because I really didn't want to go to a restaurant in a tux," Dieter murmured.

Everyone laughed.

"What?" he shouted out. "I hate these formal things." He splashed water at Talan. "And my date is driving me nuts with what kind of corsage I *have* to get her because she has fucking allergies. What's the damn point of having something that's just going to wilt anyway?"

Such a whiner.

"Oh! That reminds me, Talan! My mom said not to worry about the boutonniere. She's going to make them both," Max exclaimed.

I didn't miss the glare Dieter shot toward him.

Talan smiled brightly at Max and laughed. "Great! I actually forgot all about those things." She shyly swam away from everyone and got out to go sit with Lo. She played with her barking tyrant that was under the table at Lo's feet, begging for scraps of food.

Max got out to sit with the girls and bent down to pick up the tyrant. Ripper growled at him and snapped his little razor-sharp puppy teeth at him until he set him on his paws below the table.

Dieter swam over to where I was standing in the pool, next to where Chase had his legs dangling over the edge of the pool.

"So, remind me again…who are you bringing to prom?" I asked Dieter.

He shook his head, seeming annoyed or angry or something, and looked back over to the table where Talan, Lo, Kennedy, and Max were sitting. "I'm bringing Shay from Rivers. She was at my party last weekend."

"Right, right! That girl was so quiet. I'm surprised she's your type, D." Chase laughed and kick-splashed him. "Is it just weird to me, or is anyone else wondering how Max swung Talan from right under D's nose?"

I smirked over to my best friends. We all knew Talan and Dieter had a thing for each other. I'd told Dieter last summer not to hurt her if he was going to try something. I didn't think anything had happened yet, but those two had a relationship I would never understand. And, as outgoing as Talan seemed, she kept her personal life under lock and key.

"Shut the fuck up, Chase. It's not like that with us." Dieter tried not to make eye contact with either of us and then sighed, "It doesn't matter anyway."

Holding up his hands in surrender, Chase let the conversation go.

We knew not to push the topic. I'd fought with Dieter about Talan before. We'd neared physical altercation before Chase intervened.

Kennedy's cell rang on the lounger that was closest to Chase. I hopped up onto the ledge of the pool and leaned over to grab it, my hips holding me half out of the water. Her caller ID flashed *Mom*.

"Hey, Ken, babe, your mom's calling!" I shouted over to her.

Her head swiveled to me leaning out of the pool. She stood and slowly walked over. Taking the phone out of my hand, she immediately silenced the call and then sat down on the lounger.

I looked to the guys. "Give us a minute, would ya?"

They nodded and made their way out of the pool to go sit at the patio table.

"Babe?" I prompted.

She shut her eyes.

I got out of the pool and straddled the lounger. "How many times has she called today?"

"Four." She sat up and leaned in to softly kiss my lips. "Come on, I'm starving." She grinned and then stood.

As she walked away, I grabbed the towel next to me and started to dry off. I noticed her phone still sitting on the lounger, and as I started to walk away, it pinged.

I'd never been the nosy type. I trusted Kennedy so implicitly; I knew I'd never have to question her actions. She loved me, and I loved her.

Even so, I leaned over to see the lit-up screen.

Bryan: You still holding up, Angel?

But the message wasn't what made me pause. It was the sender.

Bryan.

I racked my brain for mutual Bryans we knew but only came up with one. But, if it were someone I didn't know, the possibilities could be endless.

I shook off my paranoia and walked over to our crew. Mom came out the French doors with a bottle of champagne, and Dad followed with the glasses.

"So, since it's a special occasion and I'm so proud of Kyle for chasing big dreams and obtaining them, I thought we could do a toast," she announced.

She popped the cork and started to fill the glasses Dad held out for her. A foam fountain filled the first glass. When everyone had a glass, Mom held hers up, and we all followed suit.

"To my baby boy, the toughest and most stubborn thing to ever grace my world, who has made me so proud and happy and adored. I hope this next journey is all you've dreamed of and more. I love you, honey. Congratulations."

The absolute love and honor she radiated when she looked at me warmed my heart. Her chin dipped, and glistening tears shone in her eyes. But all I could see was pride and happiness in my mom's smile. Those two emotions filled my whole being.

Everyone cheered.

Dieter threw out a, "Damn right! Texas is gonna be the shit with my boy tearing up the field!"

Everyone laughed because we always laughed at Dieter.

The night progressed as it usually did with our group, cracking jokes at each other's expense and reminiscing about all the dumb stuff we'd done.

In a month, we were going to be high school graduates. We'd be moving on from the safety of a place we'd known since forever. It was a scary thought.

As soon as my parents went inside, we cranked up the music, cracked open some beers for the guys and wine coolers for the girls, and resumed our lazy night by the pool. There was a party at some junior's house, but we were content with just our circle of friends.

Talan splashed at everyone with her arm swooping around as she spun and then pouted. "I can't believe *all* you guys are leaving me."

She was only a junior and didn't hang out with any of the people in her class. She'd moved here last year from overseas, so she hadn't had the benefit of growing up with her classmates, like I had with Chase and Dieter. Before my dad had retired from the service, he had been her dad's commanding officer, and they'd stayed friends since then. When Talan's dad had decided to retire as well, my dad had been the first to offer him a job.

I'd known Talan for a long time, but when she'd moved here, I'd seen how the guys reacted—all with greedy eyes and grabby hands, including Dieter—and I'd immediately had the urge to protect her. Now, I was her assumed big bro, and I wouldn't have it any other way.

So, here she was, with us, and knowing we only had a few weeks left together must really be depressing her.

"Oh, come on, T! You're going to be fine. Besides, you'll always have a place to stay when you come to Austin to see us." Lo swam over to hug her, and when Talan splashed water at her, she cursed and ducked under the water.

When Lo popped up, Talan continued, "It's not the same. I'm not friends with anyone else."

"Well, I'm only going to be, like, three hours away, T. I'll come visit you, and you can come see me," Max tried to console her.

I cast a glance over to Dieter and noticed his eyes roll.

He jumped out of the pool and swiped up his phone. "I'll see you guys later. I'm gonna head out."

"Where are you going?" Lo asked him.

"Shay's. She wants to hang." He started to towel himself off and then grabbed his T-shirt off one of the tables.

As he slipped on his shoes, Talan hopped out of the pool, too. Shivering instantly, she reached for a towel and wrapped it tightly around herself.

"I thought you said she was out of town," she quietly said to him but still loud enough for us all to hear.

"I guess she didn't go," he responded sharply. Then, with an angry glint in his eye, he challenged, "Why do you care?"

Her shoulders tensed, and I raised a brow at him.

"I don't. But do you really think you should be driving? You just had five beers."

He smirked and snickered condescendingly at her. "So, you're counting my beers? What are you? My *mommy*?"

"You're such an asshole. I'm just looking out for you."

"And you're sticking your nose where it doesn't belong. But, to appease your hovering tendencies, I'm not driving. She's out front." He bent to pick up his flat-billed Longhorns hat and slipped it on.

As he walked around the side of the house, we all said confused good-byes. He waved nonchalantly to us over his shoulder as he went out the gate.

I hadn't even noticed Kennedy had slipped out of the pool and was back on her lounger. She had her phone in her lap, and the screen was lighting up her face as she hunched over it. I hopped out, too, and walked over to her.

I moved in behind her and pulled her back against my chest. As I rested my chin on her shoulder, she darkened the screen of her phone and tossed it down. I could feel her taking deep breaths. Her entire body was tense for a few moments.

"Wanna go watch some movies?" I faintly asked her.

She slightly turned her head and kissed my lips—softly, slowly, and with determination. I slid my hands up her thighs and to her hips where I held her firmly. She moaned, and I gripped tighter.

"Is that a yes?" I grinned as I hesitantly pulled away.

I never wanted to stop. I never wanted to give up this moment or this girl. She was in my mind. My heart. Twenty-four/seven.

"Get a room, you two!" Chase shouted, breaking our moment.

Laughing, I got up from the lounger, pulled my girlfriend with me, and did exactly that. Fuck watching movies with our friends. They knew where the guest rooms were. They could handle themselves.

I just wanted to be with Kennedy and forget everything else but us.

Chapter 9

Kennedy

I should've felt bad for what I'd done. I should've felt bad for shutting my mother out. Shutting Kyle out. I should have probably felt a lot of things that I just didn't.

So, as Kyle lay asleep next to me, I silenced my phone and responded to the text.

I'd never planned on using the number. I wasn't entirely too sure how Bryan had gotten my number in the first place, but it didn't matter now. He'd texted me first. And I was six shots of whiskey in, courtesy of Kyle's closet bar—aka the alcohol he hid from his parents—and not caring about much of anything.

Even though I should've felt guilty for texting another guy behind my boyfriend's back, I didn't. It was a foreign feeling for me. I was used to being the good girl, but I didn't care. Not right in this moment. I was sure the regret would come later.

My phone lit up with his instant response.

> Bryan: *I didn't think I'd hear back from you tonight, Angel.*

I didn't like that he called me that. The only people ever to call me Angel were my dad, Kyle, and Kyle's mom. Hearing Bryan say it or even reading it from him made me cringe.

But that didn't stop me from replying. It'd been days since I saw him, and in those days, he'd tracked down my number and texted me at least once a day.

> *Me: Kyle is sleeping. I've got too much on my mind.*

> *Bryan: Like?*

> *Me: Like...you shouldn't be texting me. And I shouldn't be texting you back.*

> *Bryan: I knew I'd never hear from you if I didn't. And you could have just not responded. Besides, we're not doing anything wrong.*

But we are, aren't we?

He'd almost killed my best friend with his stupid drug. I knew he had been a dealer when he was in high school. Only marijuana, from what I'd heard. But that was a long time ago. If last year was any indication, I'd say he was dealing a little bit more since graduating three years ago with Beckon and going off to college.

Slipping out of the bed, I walked over to my bag. Checking over my shoulder to ensure Kyle was still fast asleep, I squatted and pulled out the flask I'd recently filled with more whiskey from the same stash in my father's home office. I'd only go home to grab clothes when I knew my mom was at work, and while I was there, I'd refill my little flask of rebellion. A sort of *screw you* to my mom. She obviously hadn't been in there since he passed; otherwise, I was sure she'd have noticed more and more missing from the various bottles. I didn't want to worry Kyle if he noticed too much missing from the bottle hidden in his closet, so it was best if I switched back to my own.

I took a few swigs and let the fire spread through my body, keeping my thoughts quiet and my heart numb. Then I slipped into the bathroom and swished some mouthwash to hide the evidence.

I placed my phone on the nightstand beside Kyle's king-size bed and crawled back under the covers, moving closer to him. Snuggling into his side, I draped my leg over both of his and placed my arm over his waist. He jolted slightly and then relaxed as he wrapped an arm around me.

"You okay, Ken?" he asked sleepily.

I softly murmured back, "Just getting comfortable."

"I love you, Ken," he slurred in his sleepy state.

I whispered my forever response, "To heaven and back."

Kyle's phone was ringing loudly and nonstop. I burrowed into him, and the sheets twisted around us as I tried to block out the sound. It felt like I'd just fallen asleep only minutes ago. My mind was trying to force me to think about things I wasn't willing to let surface. Memories and fears.

His phone rang and rang until whoever was calling gave up. I groaned in relief.

Ten minutes later, the incessant buzzing and ringing began again, and I pushed away from Kyle to get as far away from that noise as I could without getting out of bed. I pulled a pillow over my head to block it out.

Kyle finally started to stir and blindly reached for his phone. I maneuvered the pillow to my chest and clutched it tight. In his attempt to grab his phone, he managed to knock off a candle, some random receipts and change, an empty water bottle, and his phone to the floor.

"Damn it." He leaned over the edge of the bed to search for his phone.

His toned back peeked out from the sheets. My fingers itched to trace the deep line of his spine.

The phone stopped ringing, and he sighed. "Someone had better have won the freaking lottery to be calling at whatever time it is."

Leaving the phone wherever it had fallen, he scooted across the bed and reached for me. Kyle pulled me back to him and snuggled his face into my neck. I tried to stifle my giggle as his morning stubble tickled and scratched at my sensitive flesh.

"Morning, babe. You want breakfast?"

His phone started to ring once again.

"You should probably check to see who that is," I suggested quietly.

"Jesus. If it's Dieter, I'm gonna beat his ass."

We both laughed, and he hopped out of bed and grabbed his phone off the floor.

"Ken, it's your mom."

I rolled my eyes at his hesitant tone.

"Do you want me to answer it?" he asked.

"No."

But he had already accepted the call.

"Hi, Mrs. Kiblen."

I rolled my eyes again. She didn't deserve his respect after the way she'd treated him.

"She's right here, Mrs. Kiblen." He paused to listen. Then, he muted the phone and put it on speaker, placing it on the bed beside my head.

"I want to see my daughter, Kyle, and you've been influencing her to avoid me and her home. It is really starting to grate on my nerves. I've tolerated your disrespect for my wishes about your and Kennedy's relationship long enough. David might have let her get away with this, but I will not allow it."

I unmuted the call. "He's not influencing anything," I said with annoyance.

She couldn't be more off base. The Masters had only encouraged me to call her, to go see her, and to make nice.

But I had nothing nice to say to her, and I didn't want to hear anything she had to say either.

My mother sucked in a breath and then sighed. "Kennedy Grace, come home now." The authoritative tone she took on was like an annoying parrot repeating its owner's sentences over and over again.

Kyle reached for my hand and threaded our fingers together.

"Why should I? That's not a home. You let our home become something else when you invited *him* in."

"Kennedy, please come home. I just want to talk to you. We *need* to talk. You can't keep avoiding me. I want to explain and make this right. Maybe you'll understand then." She sounded upset and helpless.

I could almost picture her pacing in the kitchen, back and forth from the sink to the back door that led to the patio.

I tightly closed my eyes and breathed in deep. I wanted the truth, but I didn't think my psyche was ready for it. Her version of the truth would be all I could get though.

"I'll be home this afternoon."

"Good. Great! I'll make lunch. Just the two of us, okay?" Her instant cheeriness made me wonder if she was remorseful at all.

Of course she had made sure to exclude Kyle, my one safety. She couldn't stand Kyle or our relationship, always trying to find a way to push him out of my life. At first, it had been threats, and then it was blatant disregard. She ignored him and refused to let me invite him to family events. Dad had usually persuaded her otherwise, but it had been a constant battle in our family. Maybe she feared that we'd gotten together so young and that we said we loved each other.

But I was never just *saying* it. I cherished the love. I'd never experienced something so strong with anyone else.

"I'll see you in a few hours," she said happily before hanging up.

I sighed and threw my head back into the pillows. "How can she even begin to make this right, Kyle?"

"Babe...come on." He jostled my arm to get me to look at him. "Hear her out, and if it's not working, come home." His eyes shone with honesty and truth.

I loved that about him so much. He never let me feel unwelcome, and since my dad's funeral, his house was more of a home to me than mine.

I nodded my head in agreement and then snuggled closer to him, wrapping my arms around his neck and burying my face in his chest. "Thank you." I placed a timid kiss on his pec.

He pushed my hair off my shoulder and skimmed his soft lips against my skin. Our mouths seemed to pull together. Automatic attraction. It never failed when our bodies were within reaching distance.

In this room, still shrouded in darkness from his blackout curtains, we kissed lightly and slowly, memorizing each other's touches and embracing each sensation.

As our lips warmed and brushed together, a slight growl came from my stomach.

Kyle laughed, breaking our moment. "Come on, let's get you some food and wake the others. Then, we can work on some homework before I take you over to your mom's."

While he went downstairs, I jumped in the shower and got ready quickly. After blowing out my hair and doing minimal makeup, I dressed into a sky-blue spaghetti-strap lace-eyelet dress. With jeweled silver sandals on, I slipped on the small pendant necklace Kyle had given to me for my birthday. The charms, all bunched up, hung low between my breasts. The charms were the earth, angel wings, his initials with mine, a star, and a heart.

I'd loved it from the second my eyes landed on it. I loved wearing it but was afraid of the fragility of it, so I only did so when I needed the reminder of him and our love for each other the most. I needed the reminder now more than ever.

Dressed and ready, I walked down the stairs and toward the noises of whisking, scraping, and laughing in the kitchen. Our friends were still here, dressed and showered as well. While they all sat at the large kitchen bar, chatting away, Kyle and his dad manned the stove and the griddle.

Jennifer strolled in from the foyer, dressed in a pair of designer jeans with an Army-green polo and perfectly white tennis shoes. Even casual, she still looked like a million bucks.

"Angel, you look so beautiful. What's the occasion?" she asked sweetly with observant wide eyes.

I shook my head, not ever the one to seek compliments. "My mom wants me to have lunch with her."

She nodded her head and smiled softly. "I think that's great, Kennedy. I don't think I have to remind you, honey, that you are always welcome here, but I hope you and your mom can get back to a better place." Then, she gracefully walked away and went to her husband to help with the breakfast prep.

I loved Jennifer like my own mother. She was family, and I hoped it would never be any other way.

Guilt for feeling such a connection to someone else as a mother swarmed me for a brief moment. But all the anger and confusion trumped that guilt. I was just grateful I had someone who watched out for me. I had more love coming from this family than my own. And the hurt from that fact ate at my heart and soul.

We all sat at the bar and ate our breakfast around laughs and jokes. I'd forgotten how blissful these moments were. I had always found an amazing sense of joy from being here with my friends. They'd become so much more than that over the last couple of years. With all that had been happening, I realized that they were closer than that though. The only way we could get closer was by blood. They were my family.

As breakfast wound down and our friends left, Kyle and I made our way to his dad's office. It was easy to work in there and not get distracted. The forest-green walls and the wall-to-wall bookshelves full of all kinds of books—classics, biographies, and some of Jennifer's smut—made this place feel warm and inviting, like an old library. Two leather wingback chairs that were hardly used faced each other at the furthest end of the room. They still held the stiff, uncomfortable shapes they'd always had.

Kyle and I settled on opposite sides of the large, traditional oak desk. I pulled out my World Studies book and began working through the last assignment before we graduated.

Kyle had his laptop open and would type for a long minute. Then, he'd groan as he pressed what I assumed was the backspace button before starting the process all over again. I tried not to smile at his frustration. But, come on, he was just too darn adorable. I could see the struggle and irritation in his eyes and the way his mouth scowled at the screen, like the laptop was threatening physical harm.

After half an hour of hearing him struggle, I shut my book and walked around the desk to his side. "What assignment are you doing?" I asked, glancing at the screen.

He handed me a paper from his Composition class, and I immediately saw the circled, bold red *D* at the top.

"Mrs. Evans is giving me a second chance to fix this stupid thing, and it's due on Wednesday. I've had a couple of weeks to correct it, but every time I try, I just get major writer's block." He pushed his laptop and papers away from himself and stood.

I hovered by the desk and continued to read his graded work. "Why didn't you ask me for help?" I was fairly good at writing. I'd taken Composition I the semester before, and I was currently taking Composition II.

Kyle walked across the room to sit on one of the wingbacks. "I didn't want to add anything else to your plate. You were already dealing with enough."

He placed his chin in his left hand that was propped up by his elbow on his knee. When he slightly cocked his head toward me, I walked over and sat in the chair in front of him.

I tucked my hair behind my ears, and quietly, I said, "You could have told me. I don't want my issues to be bigger than yours. Ever."

I shifted forward and took his free hand. He followed the action by taking my other hand and angled forward as well.

"Let's get the body paragraphs fixed. Then, on Monday, we can have lunch in the library and finish the intro and conclusion. Easy fixes. You've got the information. You just need to word it better," I said.

And that was how we spent the next two hours.

We'd successfully tweaked his paper, and now, I was sitting in the passenger seat of his truck, parked on the side of the street in front of my house.

"Text me when you think you'll be ready, okay?"

I nodded and leaned over the center console to kiss his cheek. As I rotated to open the door, Kyle pulled my hand, and I spun back right before he planted his lips on mine. I smiled wide while I jumped down from the lifted Dodge Ram.

He was my heart, keeping me alive and in the moment. And what a good job he did.

I skipped on the stepping-stones that led to the front porch.

Kyle rolled his window down and shouted, "I love you! Don't forget to text me."

I twisted around and blew him a kiss, feeling flirty and girlie and forgetting my troubles for just a moment.

I watched as he slowly drove away. Then, I took a deep breath, filling my lungs with fresh air, before I stepped into my grief-saturated home.

Before I even took a step onto the porch, Mom opened the door with a bright smile. "Kennedy Grace, honey, you look beautiful."

She didn't look bad herself. She actually looked great. Her light-blonde hair had been highlighted, and she wore a navy shift dress I'd never seen before. A diamond heart necklace—the one my father had given her on their fifth anniversary—hung low, just like my pendant necklace from Kyle. She had on nude Mary Jane heels—also new.

After I took the final step onto the porch, she leaned in for a hug, and I accepted stiffly. I could smell the sweet perfume she'd always worn when I was younger. Dad had given it to her every year for their wedding anniversary. She loved it so much and always commented on how light it was.

"Come on then, let's eat. I made those croque monsieurs you like so much."

I followed her into the house I'd lived in my entire life. On the walls were family pictures and cheap artwork my mom had collected over the years. Shelves were built into the side of the staircase that housed Dad's favorite novels and biographies, Mom's little trinkets, and family photo albums.

We walked past all of that and into the kitchen at the back of the house. At the little breakfast table, she had the little French ham and cheese sandwiches, some cut fruit, and a salad bowl placed in the center.

I sat and started to fill my plate with food, not saying a word. I kept eye contact to a minimum, finding it hard to look her in the eyes.

"School is still going okay?" she asked.

I nodded.

"You got your prom dress tailored, right?"

I nodded again and then took a small bite of the sandwich. We ate in silence for a short while before she sighed loudly.

"You haven't ever acted like this. I'm not sure how to go about it."

"I've never lost a parent before. I'm not even sure how to go about my own feelings," I snapped at her.

Her eyes widened with alarm. Scooting her chair closer to me, she took my hand. "Sweetie, I get it; I do. But you can't shut me out. I'm your mother, and I miss him just as much as you do."

I wanted to scream, *Do you? Because it doesn't feel or look like it.*

"Then, what was *he* doing here?" I demanded. I pushed away from her and the table to stand. "I don't understand how you couldn't wait longer than two damn weeks before you invited someone else into our home. You were *laughing* with him!" I marched to the back door and threw it open to walk out onto the patio, ignoring her calls to come back and calm down.

I couldn't calm down. My heart was racing with fury, fueled by hurt and confusion.

I sat down in one of the weathered iron chairs that had come from my grandmother's house in St. Louis after she passed. Pulling out my phone, I started to text Kyle to come and get me when Mom came out to sit across from me.

"He was in town on business, Kennedy. He called to see if I was available for lunch. That's all it was. He wanted to catch up and see how I was doing. He'd had no idea your father passed away."

I looked into her green eyes, and I saw it. That brief flicker of guilt. That fleeting moment when she let her lie show.

She studied my face. I was sure I looked unrecognizable. Anger seemed to scrunch my face and darken my eyes.

Pushing up from the chair, I turned to go back into the house. I couldn't listen to it anymore.

"Your dad knew, Kennedy!" she shouted after me.

I froze by the back door. "Knew what?" I asked with all the reluctance in the world. *Please, please don't make me hate you, Mom.* I didn't want to know even if I recognized that, deep down, I already had the knowledge she was about to impart on me.

"He knew I'd had an affair while I was away." Her voice broke, and I could hear the regret and pain in my mother's tone.

My entire world crashed to the floor. My stomach felt like it was trying to claw its way up my burning, dry throat.

I opened the back door and slammed it as hard as I could. Once I was inside, I rushed up the stairs and into my room where I grabbed my large suitcase from my closet. Throwing in all my clothes and pictures full of memories that I wanted to keep, I kept filling it until it was overflowing with my things.

"I was in a weird place, Kennedy. I was away from your father and constantly taking care of Grams. Cole was there, and when I needed someone's help, he never hesitated." Her voice was like nails on a chalkboard to me.

I scoffed, "Dad would have been there the second after you called, and you know it." I shut one of my dresser drawers harder than I'd meant to, and a picture of my parents and me crashed and shattered on the old, scuffed hardwood floor. Turning slowly, I crossed my arms over my chest. "Do you even realize how much worse that is?" The tears I was trying so hard to fight welled thickly in my eyes.

"We worked through it, Kennedy. It was over a year ago."

As she started to walk closer to me, I threw my hands up.

Is that supposed to make it okay? Is that supposed to make it all disappear?

The force of me shaking my head, warning her off, gave the tears the momentum they needed to fall.

I gave in to the only reality my mind would accept. With my voice quaking, I said, "You killed him, you know that? You broke his heart, and you let me lose my father. Because of your *selfishness* and *betrayal.*" So much venom laced my tone. I didn't even recognize my own voice. The words were harsh and like glass spewing from my lips. I choked on my resentment and sorrow.

"You don't think I don't feel the guilt, Kennedy? I feel it every day, but your father was sick. We couldn't do anything about the aneurism. I wished, and I prayed. But I have to accept it. We were in a good place when I got back. We worked through it." Her eyes glistened with her own tears.

Sure, *now* she could cry. But when the funeral directors had lowered the man she was supposed to love and honor six feet under…nothing.

"Just get out of my room," I said severely, leveling her with a fierce glare that I hoped crushed her bones. I hoped it gnawed at her soul.

She gave me a frustrated look and sighed. "I want you home. I don't want you running away to your boyfriend's. We need to work through this as a family."

Stepping further away from her, I responded, "I'm not staying here. And you can't make me. I'm eighteen."

"You're staying. End of discussion. I've been lenient enough. Your father wouldn't have appreciated you acting this way." Her command and insult, all in one breath, stabbed me in the chest.

She walked out of my room and quietly shut the door. I'd figured she'd slam it with finality.

I sat on the edge of my bed and stared at the destroyed frame holding a picture of the three of us at the lake on my sixteenth birthday. I couldn't remember a happier time with them. The love and devotion they had shown me on my birthday was never greater on any other day. They loved me like a blessing every single day.

That love felt dimmed now.

I heard the back door creak open and shut as I lowered myself to the floor by the foot of my bed. Mom's muffled voice crept back in through the house.

I was ready to tear this room apart. Tear this house apart. But, instead, I slipped down the stairs and into the office. I opened the cabinet that held an escape. Slipping out the bottle of Crown Royal that was three-fourths full, I charged back upstairs without a second thought.

With the picture of my sixteenth birthday clutched in one hand and the glass cup from my bathroom now filled with whiskey, I took my first sip. Then, my first mouthful. Then, I tossed the remainder back and filled the cup again.

The picture taunted me with happy memories.

The bitter liquid taunted me with a numb mind.

I tossed the picture as far away from myself as I could.

I clutched the cup closer, tighter.

I couldn't remember falling asleep or crawling into bed, but I woke up to my phone ringing "Sugar" by Maroon 5.

Kyle had set that as his personal ringtone one night when we were cuddled in his bed after we made out for what seemed like hours. I'd had to be home in twenty minutes, and he'd kept pulling me closer every time I'd slip away. I'd ended up missing curfew, and when Kyle had dropped me off and tried to apologize a million times, Dad had just shaken his head, trying to fight a grin.

I reached for my phone on the other side of the bed and answered, "Kyle?"

"Ken, I've been calling for hours." I could hear the anxiety in his voice. "I didn't know if she took your phone or something."

"I'm fine. The afternoon was a little more emotional than I would have liked. I must have fallen asleep after I packed up my bags."

"I'm coming to get you, babe."

I heard a dinging noise in the background.

"No, wait…" I quickly sat up. My head felt like I just had a five-hour ride on the Tilt-A-Whirl. My brain was sloshing, and my vision was blurry. I tried to shake the fog clear, but that just made my head ache something fierce.

Jesus, I couldn't believe I was even going to say this, but I didn't want him to see me like this. And, somewhere deep down, I had taken my mom's command to heart and was compelled to stay. "I'm going to stay here for the rest of the weekend."

Kyle breathed deeply. "Are you sure, Ken? You don't sound like you are."

"I'm sure," I whispered, most likely counteracting my words. But loud noises made my temples throb.

I heard keys jingling, hopefully him turning the ignition off.

"Okay. I'll talk to you tomorrow then?"

"Yeah, I'm just going to go grab something to eat and lie back down."

"You don't want me to bring you anything? Mom made lasagna."

"No, thank you. But I love you for offering."

I could hear his smile in his own, "I love you," before we said our good-byes.

When I swung my legs over the side of the bed, my head rushed with dizziness. My mouth was dry with the lingering taste of whiskey coating my lips.

As I wandered down to the kitchen, all the lights in the house were off. I grabbed the bowl of chopped fruit out of the fridge to snack on.

Not wanting to stay in this house, I walked out the front door and sat on the porch swing. My dad had installed it for my mom when she said she needed somewhere to watch me from while I played in the front yard. He had always been doing something for her—making her life easier, adorning her with nice but simple jewelry and gorgeous dresses, fixing anything she'd asked him to.

I missed that.

Before he had gone into the hospital, the garage door had started acting weird and wouldn't close all the way. I couldn't help but think it'd already be fixed if he were still here, but instead, we just didn't use it anymore. Mom's car stayed parked in the driveway, and Dad's old Ford F-150 was locked away in the garage.

"Is that you, Angel?"

I whipped my head up from the bowl of fruit I had been absently picking through to see Bryan walking up the sidewalk from the right side of my house.

"What are you doing here?"

He laughed a raspy, throaty laugh. A cigarette pinched between his fingers glowed as he took one last drag before he flicked it into the street. "My new stepdad lives over here," was his only explanation.

"Oh, well, welcome to the neighborhood then."

Bryan came closer and closer until he was walking through my yard and up to the porch steps. "Well, that's an enthusiastic welcome wagon. What are you doing out here this late? Don't you know the freaks come out at night?"

I didn't miss that sinister glint in his eye. He always had this edge to him, and it always showed in his eyes.

"I take it you're a freak then?" I resumed picking through the fruit and plucked out a strawberry.

He let a little growl out. "You wouldn't even be able to handle it, Angel. I walk on the other side of the tracks that you're used to."

"Is that so?" I looked up at him standing in front of me. He was at least six feet and maybe a couple of inches, but it was hard to tell from my vantage point. "Are you the devil to my angel then?"

"Only if you'll let me be." He smirked a smirk I was sure Lucifer himself had adorned. Running his hands through his short dark brown hair, he expectantly looked down at me.

I laughed softly. "You know, Bryan…I bet you're a madness I don't want to get lost in."

"What if you don't get lost? What if you find yourself?" he countered.

I glanced back to my front door. I was lost in those walls already. *What if he's right?*

"Do you want to get out of here for a bit?" he asked. I could just hear that devil tempting me. "Come on, I'm not gonna hurt you. Let's just go for a drive."

I hesitated. But, deep down, I wanted to get away from this house. It didn't hold the same comforting feelings anymore. "Okay," I offered tentatively.

What the heck else am I doing?

The more intelligent part of my brain though was screaming at me, *Why are you doing this, Kennedy? If Kyle, or Lo finds*—

I stopped the thought before I could let it change my mind.

I slid the lid on the fruit, stood up, and stepped inside the house. I went and put the bowl in the fridge and grabbed a water. As I was walking back out the front door, I slipped on a pair of black flip-flops.

We walked an arm's length apart in silence. Turning right to go around the block and then two blocks up, we stopped at a nice two-story home with a light coming from what I assumed was a second-story bedroom.

He went through the front door without an invitation for me to join. The light from upstairs flipped off, and a few seconds later, Bryan came back out in a new red T-shirt with his wallet, phone, and keys in hand. The lights on the black BMW sitting in the driveway flashed, and he walked to the driver's side.

"Get in."

Before sliding in, I second-guessed myself and started to back away from the door I'd already opened. *Seriously, what the heck am I doing?*

"It's just a drive, Kennedy."

I knew though, once I was seated in his car, it wasn't going to be *just a drive*. With a guy like Bryan, there was bound to be all sorts of misrepresentations. He could play the nice guy all he wanted, but I knew what he was like, what he was capable of.

Bryan hopped out of the driver's seat and walked around to where I was standing. I turned slowly, and he braced his hand on the open door.

"I promise to take you home whenever you're ready. You can trust me." Behind the sinister look was softness but only a fraction compared to his wickedness.

"Fine." I ducked into the car, and once I was seated, I adjusted my sky-blue dress over my knees. I pulled the seat belt across my chest and blew out a deep breath. *At least I'm taking one precaution tonight.*

We drove to the outskirts of town, and then he jumped on the freeway. "Ride" by Twenty One Pilots was playing through his fancy stereo with more bass than I was used to in a car. He cracked the window and pulled out a pack of cigarettes. Before lighting his own, he offered one to me. I shook my head and looked back out the passenger window.

I didn't even realize thirty minutes had passed until he turned off on the exit for Fielding City. We drove through the main part of what was more like a small town than a city. The private Christian school was here. Wealthier families who didn't want to live in the city usually settled their families here and commuted.

We turned down the road that led to the school and then parked in the student parking lot behind the large building.

"Should we be here?" I asked, feeling paranoid about the possibilities of trouble.

He chuckled. "Calm down, Angel. We're waiting for someone."

I whipped my head back toward him and shoved his shoulder. "Tell me you did *not* bring me to a drug deal!" I started to pull on the handle to the door to escape his car and his criminal activities. What the hell had been going through my mind when I got in his car, I'd never know, but now, I was freaking out.

"Kennedy! Wait!"

But I was already out of the car and walking back toward the road. *How could I be so stupid?*

Bryan moved so stealth-like, I never even heard him get out of his car and run up behind me. He grabbed me around the waist, pinning my arms down as well. I bucked, trying to break free of his hold.

"I swear to God, if you don't get off me, I'm going to scream rape."

As I struggled in his hold, he grunted out, "That's not very nice, Angel. You're not supposed to swear to God or falsely accuse someone of rape."

A light chuckle grazed my ear as he kept me in his clutch. He turned us, and lifting me, he walked me back toward the car door I'd left open. When he set me down in front of it, I spun around and shoved him back, but he didn't even move an inch.

"I'm not doing a drug deal here. We're waiting for a friend of mine to get back into town, then we'll head to his house."

I snorted. "Oh, right, so you can do a drug deal there. Even better, Bryan. Just take me home," I demanded.

He crossed his arms over his chest. The move was so brute and full of defiance for what I wanted. I couldn't do anything but huff out hot air like a petulant child.

As I started to step away from him and the car once again, an even fancier car pulled into the parking lot and stopped in front of the BMW.

Some guy rolled down the window and asked, "You ready?"

"Give us a minute, Dylan." Bryan stepped closer to me, bringing his face down to make us eye-level. "Just come hang out with us, Kennedy. If you want to leave after twenty minutes, we will."

His dark, enticing eyes would be the downfall of some poor girl's soul. Heck, who was I kidding? They most likely already were.

I pushed him further away from me and exhaled.

Tell him to take you home, Kennedy. This time, it was Kyle's voice trying to be my voice of reason.

Instead, I slid back into the car. "You said we were just going for a drive," I mumbled loud enough for him to hear.

"We did, didn't we?" He leaned down into the space and chuckled. "You're hot when you're mad, you know that?"

Then, he shut the car door and jogged over to the other car. He and Dylan exchanged a few words and then laughed. I caught Dylan staring at me from below his flat-billed hat. He winked at me as Bryan walked to the driver's side. When Bryan started to roll forward, he gave me a cocky smirk that I ignored.

As we followed the guy to a gated community, I checked my phone. I had only one message. Guilt swarmed me as I read it.

Kyle: I love you to heaven and back, babe. Good night.

My love for the only person who understood me and stood by me when I just wanted to be alone begged me to send a response. But my guilt for where I was, who I was with, talked me out of it.

"How do you know this guy?" I asked, keeping my eyes fixed out the windshield, making sure they weren't taking me to an empty house to do terrifying things. Lo had made me watch too many scary movies, and all the slasher-movie scenarios were flashing wildly in my brain.

"We were roommates our freshman year at Northwestern." He didn't elaborate anymore.

We pulled into a large half-circle driveway with cars lined up and down on the street.

I turned to Bryan as he switched the car off. "I didn't think this would be a huge party."

"Afraid your boyfriend might find out?" he teased.

I rolled my eyes at his childishness.

"Kyle trusts me." I pushed out of the car and slammed his door.

Bryan hissed behind me, "Jesus, Kennedy. Could you be a little nicer to my car? If you're gonna get rough, I'd rather you do it to *me*."

I didn't even bother responding to his gross comment.

Dylan walked over to us, and a guy, whom I'd had no idea was in the car, climbed out and joined us as well.

"Ready to party, Bry?" the guy who'd yet to be introduced asked.

"I'm taking it easy tonight, Shawn. Got precious cargo with me."

He started to wrap his arm around my shoulders, and I backhanded his stomach and stepped away from him.

Dylan looked me up and down, and I rolled my eyes. Guys were so obvious.

"Well, let's get inside and get her a drink." Dylan smugly smiled, like he knew something I didn't.

My guard immediately lifted.

I followed the three guys up the driveway and into the large mansion, walking through fancy wrought-iron and glass doors, stepping on to the marbled foyer. It reminded me of Kyle's and Lo's houses. This one was bigger though. The furniture all looked antique, and there were all kinds of artwork hanging on the walls. A crystal chandelier, too big to even comprehend, hung overhead, and I looked up and twirled around as they continued into the house.

"Shiny stuff catching your eye, Angel?" Bryan whispered by my ear, frightening me, as he grabbed my hand. "Come on. We're going downstairs where it's quieter."

It was only then I registered the crazy loud music. Rihanna's latest single, "Bitch Better Have My Money," was blasting so loud, and there were girls everywhere, trying to dance and grind on guys and other girls. Nothing different than what other parties had.

I roughly pulled my hand from Bryan's but continued to follow him. We walked through the kitchen and down a hallway. When we rounded a corner, Dylan was waiting with the door open. I followed Bryan halfway down the stairs and then turned back to see Dylan flicking a deadbolt lock on the door.

My eyebrows furrowed at the action.

He laughed, catching my confused expression. "I don't let too many people in the basement. My dad's office is down here, and he'd flip out." He did a mock freak-out impression of what I assumed his dad would do.

I hadn't asked for an explanation, and I was surprised he'd even given me one.

When I reached the bottom of the stairs, I took in the large open room with oversize couches and chairs spread out, all facing a huge projection screen. Different music than upstairs was playing at a much quieter volume. I could actually hear and think down here.

There were a handful of people, mostly guys and a few girls. I instantly felt weird and moved instinctually closer to Bryan.

Our arms touched, and he looked over and smiled. "Don't worry. None of the guys bite. I'd look out for those girls though." As he laughed at my wide-eyed expression, he took my elbow and guided me over to the couch.

Dylan walked over behind a bar in the far corner and poured some drinks. I meticulously watched his hands. As nice as Bryan and he had been so far, I still couldn't trust them.

Dylan walked over and held two cups out. "Vodka and Sprite? Or whiskey and Coke?"

I took the Coke and sniffed. For what, I didn't know. I had no clue what kind of guy Dylan was. I watched their faces as I took a tentative sip. It wasn't like I'd know if there was anything in it other than whiskey and Coke until it was too late, but I was hoping, if something was wrong, their facial expressions would give them away.

"You don't have to drink anything," Bryan whispered in my ear.

Scowling at him, I asked, "You think I don't know that? I'm a big girl, *Bry*. I can handle myself."

As a chorus of oohs rang out, I rolled my eyes and took a larger swallow.

"You bring it?" Shawn asked.

If you asked me, he seemed kind of twitchy.

I looked at him and tried to decipher whom he was asking. No one answered, and then I glanced to the side at Bryan, who was nodding.

"Bring what?" I asked.

The guy laughed, and I expectantly looked at Bryan.

He shook his head and then gave a reluctant laugh. "You don't want to know, Angel." His dismissive tone made me bristle with annoyance.

Who was he to tell me what I did or did not want to know?

Dylan started messing with an iPad sitting on the couch, and the projection screen displayed the song changing to "I Mean It" by G-Eazy. Dieter liked this artist, but I still didn't know much about rap. I usually just listened to Top 40 even though it drove Kyle and Lo insane.

"So, come on, man." Shawn gestured with wide arms.

"Fuck, man, chill. I just got here." Bryan looked at me.

I caught the nervous vibe he was giving off. He tried to play it off with a devilish smirk.

"Hey, Angel, what school do you go to?" Dylan asked.

I rolled my eyes. "My name is Kennedy. Not *Angel*. And I go to Davidson High."

"No shit? So, you know Kyle Masters?" He smirked, and I tensed. He took notice and laughed. "Sorry. Sore subject?"

"Kyle's my boyfriend. How do you know him?" I could feel everyone's eyes on me, burning my skin up with their heated stares.

Shawn snorted.

Dylan chuckled darkly. "I thought I recognized you."

"If you knew who I was and who my boyfriend was, why'd you ask?" I squared my shoulders and took a large gulp of the mixed drink.

"It's just interesting. You being here with our boy Bryan and all. I played football against Kyle a couple of years ago."

I glanced away from him, suddenly realizing just how stupid I was. I was here with another guy, and Kyle didn't even know. This situation could become way more than I'd know how to handle.

"Come on, guys, get off her case. She's just getting away from home for the night," Bryan bit out.

Everyone seemed to shut up. He appeared to have an authority over the others.

But Shawn wasn't really into being silent. "Let's light up, Bry. I ain't got all fucking night. Or give me what I called you for, so I can get out of here."

"In the other room, you fuckface." Bryan stood, and I went to follow him. "Stay here, Kennedy."

Rolling my eyes, I sat back down and drank from the cup again. "Whatever." Why I was following his command was beyond me. I probably didn't want to know what he was up to anyway. Accomplices and all that.

Laughing, Dylan stood and came to sit by me. "So, you're really dating Masters, and you're here with Endears?"

He stretched his arm out behind me, and I scooted forward on the couch, adjusting and straightening out my dress as I moved.

"Why do you care?" I glanced back at his relaxed state on the couch.

He was attractive and way too confident.

He grinned, a lot like Bryan did, with too-white teeth and mischief in his eyes. "Why do you want to get away from home? Trouble with Masters in paradise?"

I snorted. "That's the best you've got?"

"You want me to try harder?" His leer grew darker, and I suddenly felt extremely uncomfortable.

Taking a sip from the cup, I peered at him over the rim. When I pulled it away, I slowly licked my lips. The buzz of alcohol swarmed my veins, warming my skin up once again.

He pulled in a deep breath and scooted closer. In a silent stare-off, we watched each other. I waited for him to make another move or try a pick-up line. Before he could, we were interrupted. He looked highly disappointed but smirked anyway.

"Dylan!" Shawn shouted as he and Bryan came out of a door off to the side of the projection screen. "You've gotta fucking try this shit."

He walked over, and I took notice of the skinny cigar, glowing red on the end, pinched between his thumb and index finger.

"Hey, Dylan," I whispered.

He tilted over and placed his ear in front of my lips.

I leaned closer, and my lips brushed his ear as I whispered, "You wouldn't stand a damn chance against Kyle. I'd never stray, especially with you."

He jerked back, and his face pulled down into a disbelieving expression with a snarl curling his lip as if he couldn't believe someone was better than him. I smirked and tossed the rest of my drink back. Just because my mom was unfaithful didn't mean I would follow in her footsteps.

Bryan sat on my other side, and I gave him a small smile when he took on a quizzical expression.

"You good?" he asked.

"Sure." I shrugged my shoulders. "I thought you weren't bringing me to any drug deals?" I point-blank asked him.

He ignored my question and took my cup to refill it. I followed him to the bar and watched his every move.

"How is Lo?"

I looked at him and shook my head at his smirk. He knew exactly what I was thinking. The way I observed his hands, noting where they were and what they grabbed, was a dead giveaway of my acute observation of what he was or wasn't putting in my drink.

Sitting back on the couch, I paced myself with this new drink. I didn't need to get drunk in front of people I didn't fully trust or even really know. The music was on continuous play while the small handful of people down here passed around various cigars, heavy smoke surrounding us.

"Is that weed?" I turned to ask Bryan. I was becoming lightheaded as I drank more and as the room filled with more smoke.

His grin was enough to answer my question. He pointed to Shawn. "Only that one. The rest are just Swisher Sweets. The girls think it makes them look cool."

I pushed up from the couch, sighing. "I should probably go home."

He stood, too, and as I was walking toward the stairs, I turned to see Bryan toss down a small baggy of what looked like little blue pills and then another with something I couldn't really make out.

Dylan stood and followed us up the stairs to walk us out. When we got to Bryan's car, I climbed in and shut the door. I stared out the windshield, but out of the corner of my eye, I watched as Dylan pulled out his wallet and slipped some cash into Bryan's hand.

As Bryan took the driver's seat, I turned my head away from him and leaned it against the window.

What am I doing? This wasn't me. I didn't hang out with other guys, especially with a guy who had almost killed my best friend or guys who dealt drugs and didn't even try to hide it.

When I collapsed onto my bed half an hour later, I finally texted Kyle back.

    Me: I love you.

But what it really needed to say was, *I need you.*

Chapter 10

Kyle

I spent Sunday with my parents. Kennedy and I texted a few times, but she'd said she was just trying to come to terms with everything in her house. That she needed some space.

I had been nervous about her going back home and confronting her mom about seeing the new guy. I'd gotten little to no details from her about the situation. I'd tried bringing it up in our text conversation, and she'd said she didn't want to talk about it.

That was how she'd been about everything.

I couldn't say she hadn't improved because, the past couple of weeks, she'd been more like her old self than the weeks after David had passed. But there was still something off or missing. I just hadn't figured it out yet.

It was the moments when she was alone that scared me the most.

I'd walked into my room one night after a gym session and caught her sitting on the floor at the bottom of my bed, staring off into space, with tears falling slowly down her cheeks. When I'd asked her what was wrong, she'd said she just needed to hear his voice. I'd noticed her phone clutched in her hand. I'd assumed she'd called his phone and gotten his voice mail.

I hated that she tortured herself that way, but I couldn't fault her for wanting to hear her dad's voice. I'd be the same way if it were one of my parents.

Now, here I was, trying to figure out these opening and closing paragraphs for my paper, sitting on my bed and just staring at the stupid words on the screen. But my mind was completely preoccupied with Kennedy.

Just as I began to shut my laptop, completely giving up, a FaceTime call started to come through. I lifted the screen back up and saw Leighton's picture. I accepted the call and adjusted the screen.

"What's up, big bro? How are your finals going?"

He had his thick black-framed glasses on and was holding a Longhorns hat up to the screen. "Mom sent me this." He grinned and laughed. "Congrats again, man. I'm so proud of you. Finals are good. I'm almost done. Can't wait to be home for the summer." He flipped the hat backward and slid it on.

I swore, the nerd could pull off anything.

"I haven't even figured out when I have to be at training camp, but I hope I get to spend at least half the summer here."

The recruiting guy had said I'd get the email soon, but I'd yet to see that shit.

As I looked back up to the screen, I watched a girl pass behind Leighton. I pointed. "She yours?" I laughed, kind of impressed. She was wearing the tiniest shorts I'd ever seen and a tight neon pink tank.

He glanced behind himself and then rotated back to me. "Nah, she's Logan's, not that she's property. But, yeah, not my type."

"I'm everyone's type!" the girl shouted from wherever she had disappeared to.

Laughing, I shook my head. "Always the ladies' man, huh, bro?"

Scoffing, he rolled his eyes. "I've got all the time in the world to settle down. But, speaking of ladies, how's Kennedy?"

Glancing at my phone sitting next to me on the bed, I clenched my teeth to keep from cursing out. She hadn't responded to my good-night text yet. "Honestly, man, I'm worried. She started drinking with us. Granted, it's just with us, and she doesn't do it up excessively, but I mean…the timing just feels wrong."

"No shit?" He looked incredulous. "Didn't you say something about her mom the last time we talked?"

"God, dude, don't even get me started. Let's just say she's already moved on, from what everyone is guessing."

His eyes bugged out and then squinted. "Seriously? How do you know?"

I explained everything I knew and gave him the rundown. Honestly, I didn't know diddly-squat about it, but shit, I didn't think Kennedy even knew. She'd caught the guy in her house, but I hadn't heard a single thing more than that one incident. He could have been just a friend, but she was so devastated, so it was hard to hope otherwise.

"You think that's why she's suddenly taking an interest in drinking? You're keeping an eye on her, right? She's not drinking to avoid shit and bury her feelings? She was really close to her dad, and losing him—"

"I know, I know." Ever the knowledgeable one, my brother. "I don't think I've got too much to worry about. She's at her mom's now though, which does kind of make me concerned. I don't like when she's alone. When she's with me, I can at least *see* that she's okay. Even if she is silent and in her own head most of the time."

Nodding his head, he picked up some papers and started sorting them. His eyes sporadically glanced back to the screen, like he was uncomfortable with this conversation. "You just have to keep an eye on her, Kyle. I'd hate to see that girl turn off the lights, ya know?"

I bobbed my head, understanding exactly what he meant. Kennedy in a dark place was…it just wasn't right.

"All right, little brother, I've gotta get back to the books. You've got prom this weekend, right?"

"Yeah, man."

He went on with a little lecture, grinning, "Be safe, dude. No drinking and driving. And, for the simple pleasure of laughing at Dieter's expense, please send me pictures and/or videos of that douche bag dancing."

I laughed and promised him I would.

"I can't wait for your nerdy ass to come home, man. Hasn't been the same without you here, big bro."

"Yeah, I can't wait either. I'm just about over these exams and projects. See you in a couple of weeks, all right? Don't forget my pictures and videos."

"Yeah, yeah. Later, nerd."

The last thing I saw before he hung up was his middle finger. I laughed out loud.

We'd always had this crazy easy relationship. We had been so different all our lives that we never really clashed. He was so freaking smart, evident by his full academic scholarship to Princeton. But that never stopped him from working out and training with me when I needed it. I had always been the sporty kid, coming home with scraped up knees and elbows, while he buried his nose in a book. When he'd needed someone to help quiz him for a test or academic decathlon, I had been there even though I hated the subjects, especially the language and literature ones.

As I started to work on some other homework assignments, my mom popped her head into my room to say good night. I worked for a couple of hours more before everything was done, except for that damn paper.

I got up to put all my stuff back into my backpack. I continually glanced at my phone on the bed even though I knew it was on loud. Every single thing I was doing was all in an attempt not to blow Kennedy's phone up. She'd text me when she wasn't busy. At least, that was what I kept telling myself.

It'd been hours since her last text.

After my nightly ritual of showering and brushing my teeth, I lay in bed with my phone sitting on my chest. As an hour passed, I finally decided to say fuck it and text her a good-night message again.

Expecting her to respond with our little saying, I waited and waited until I drifted off to sleep.

After being asleep for what felt like hours, I was jolted awake by the slight movement of my blankets and the bed dipping. I rushed to turn on the lamp on my nightstand and sighed in relief when I saw Kennedy. My relief quickly vanished when I saw the redness in her eyes and the mascara streaks down her cheeks. Her blonde hair was hiding some of her face, but I could see the sadness in her tightly closed lips and furiously blinking eyes as more tears welled and fell in a steady stream till they dripped off her chin.

"Kennedy, what's wrong?" I asked, quickly crawling closer to her and placing my hand on the side of her face, my thumb running back and forth under her eye.

She lightly shook her head and then clenched her eyes shut so tightly that I thought she might be in pain.

"Are you hurt? Do I need to take you to the doctor? How'd you even get here?" I rapidly fired questions at her. My pulse spiked in fear.

Noticing her hands clenched into fists pressing against her stomach, I immediately tried to pry them away and lift her shirt, thinking that maybe something was wrong there. She let me move her hands away, and when I lifted her shirt, nothing seemed wrong. No bruises or anything.

I placed my hand on her face again and pleaded with her to tell me what was wrong, "I can't fix it if you don't tell me what's wrong."

She opened her mouth to say something, but only a soft whimper slipped out.

"Just tell me if you're hurt, Kennedy. Please…I'm freaking out here."

She shook her head.

"No, you're not hurt?"

She nodded faintly.

"Babe…" I whispered worriedly.

She was scaring me, and I didn't like it. Feeling so helpless really made me lose my mind.

I gave her some time and just stroked her cheek with my thumb. Glancing over my shoulder at the alarm clock, I took notice of the time. I'd only fallen asleep for an hour and a half.

Kennedy took a strained deep breath and sniffled. "She invited him to dinner tonight without telling me," she said quietly, but her voice was laced with anger. "I had to sit there and listen to them reminisce and laugh. In my *father's* house. I just sat there and listened to her sound so freaking happy without a care in the world." Her tears were thick drops. "And he was *so sorry* about my loss. *My loss.* Not *our* loss. But *mine.* Like my mother hadn't just lost her husband of nineteen years."

My mind was still trying to play catch-up with what she was telling me, but she heatedly continued on, "He offered his lake house to us for a weekend getaway, and my mom accepted. Said she'd *love* to spend a weekend away from everything." Her voice pitched, and then she started to cry harder. "I couldn't imagine a world where my parents weren't...happy and together...and...and now, I'm seeing it fir-firsthand." She stumbled through her words before she blew out a deep breath.

I maneuvered us to where I was back against the headboard, and I pulled her up into my lap. She wrapped her arms around my neck and uncontrollably cried into my chest for what felt like hours.

"Shh, babe. Calm down." I tried to coax her into relaxing with my hand rubbing wide circles on her back.

She took strained but deep breaths, trying to get ahold of herself.

When her tears stopped and her breathing slowed, I thought she'd fallen asleep. I continuously stroked her back, trying to fight off the anger for what her mother was doing.

Is she that oblivious to the pain she's causing Kennedy?

I still couldn't believe it. I wanted to shout. I wanted to force Kennedy to never go back. It was only causing her more pain.

My eyes widened when she whispered, "She had an affair with him, Kyle. She cheated on my dad, and now, he's gone. She wants me to get to know this *stranger* whom she's going to play house with. It's like she never loved my dad."

I pulled her as close as I could get her and squeezed, trying to hold her together and keep my rage at bay. Her mother was wrecking her and didn't even give a damn about what kind of emotional turmoil she was putting Kennedy through after everything she'd already gone through.

She kissed my neck, something I hadn't expected. Her lips slid over my skin, and she sighed. "I can't be around her. Every time I see her face, I see my dad dying in a hospital bed. She did this, Kyle. He couldn't handle the stress. It was too much to know his wife had chosen someone else."

Kennedy was never the pessimist in any situation. Hearing these darker thoughts coming out of her mouth with such conviction was so jarring. I couldn't even respond. Whether her theory was true or not, we would never know. Pastor Kiblen had a history of high blood pressure, so it could have just been a health thing, but if it were stress-related, then, yeah, her mom could have played a hand in pushing him too far. But I wasn't a doctor, and Kennedy was upset. It was fueling her.

"What else did she say, Ken? Baby, I'm trying to understand."

Kennedy shook her head from side to side, making her hair swish across my hand that was held firmly against her back.

Trying to coax information out of her lately had been like that splinter in your hand that you just couldn't quite reach without some frustration and pain. The longer it was there, the more irritating it would get. She was embedding the information deep inside of herself and letting it irritate her, refusing to just remove it. I could still see it sitting on the surface.

"How'd you get here, Ken?" I changed the topic to something lighter, hoping it would let her cool down and maybe allow her to open up to me a little later.

"I took my dad's truck," she said defiantly. "It's mine anyway. He left it to me."

"I thought the garage was broken. How'd you get it out?"

"I pulled that emergency-string thing and manually lifted it," she said with a slight smirk on her face.

I watched her with my own amusement mirrored back at her. "Rebel."

"Absolutely," Kennedy adjusted herself to straddle my thighs. "She probably doesn't even know I'm gone."

She started to pull her little green tank top up and over her head before tossing it to the floor.

"What are you doing?" I whisper-groaned.

She lifted up onto her knees.

"Babe…hold on a sec." I tried to grab her hands, but I caught bare hips as she shoved her shorts down her thighs and then awkwardly stood to get herself out of them. "What are you doing?"

Kennedy smiled devilishly as she knelt back down. The soft, gentle touch I was used to with her wasn't there. She was rushing, being a little more forceful. Completely out of character and such a fucking turn-on.

I wasn't prepared for her acting this way, but my dick certainly wasn't complaining.

She helped me push my shorts and boxers off, lightly scratching her nails down my thighs and back up to my abdomen.

"I love you," she whispered, her voice still laced with a bit of sadness.

I ran my hands up and down her sides, just barely grazing her skin. Her silky skin formed goose bumps, and she shuddered. After I'd touched her a thousand times like this before, she still felt new, like unchartered territory.

She reached over to my nightstand and opened the drawer, pulling out a condom and ripping it open. Her hands were moving swiftly as she slid it over my erection. Not even hesitating a second, she immediately lifted up and slid down onto me. I ground my teeth together to keep from grunting.

She immediately started working me. Fast...hard...and all for her own pleasure, I realized.

"Slow down," I whispered harshly, grasping her hips to take over the pace.

Still propped up against the headboard, I let my head fall back and moved her at a pace that let her catch her breath and kept me from exploding too quickly.

Kennedy had her arms wrapped loosely around my neck. She slightly leaned back and looked down to where we were connected, her blonde hair falling over her shoulders and covering her breasts. When she glanced back up and our eyes locked, her gray eyes were blissfully glossed over with her lust.

She was fighting my pace though, trying to speed up when I forced her to move slower.

Grunting, she slid a hand to grasp where my neck met my shoulder. She ground down harder since I hadn't let her go faster, making sure to rub her most sensitive spot against my pelvic bone.

Not close to being satisfied, she moved her other hand to grip the top of the headboard. As she leaned forward to rub her breasts against my chest, her lips pressed right below my ear. She breathed heavily, panting her need.

"I need it," she pleaded.

Fuck.

I thrust up harder. It was a challenging thing to do with our position, but I managed to make her gasp.

She vetoed my slow movements and moved faster. She was working me to the point where she was glistening with sweat. Her body rolled and curved. I could feel my own sweat forming on my brow, but she was slick to the touch. My hands glided up and down her hips and waist with such ease.

Her hand on my neck tensed. Biting her lip to keep quiet, she couldn't seem to let go. She half-growled, half-sighed in frustration.

"Kennedy," I groaned, "baby, I'm there."

"Yeah?"

"I can feel you; you're almost there."

She nodded her head against the side of mine.

I was on the brink of explosion when she moaned, "Get me there, Kyle."

Fuck, fuck, fuck.

I roughly rolled us, her back thudding to the mattress, and then I slid in between her open thighs, going deep back into her heat and thrusting harder. It didn't take long in this position. Every single time, this was the position I could hit the spot that made her pant and squirm.

She braced her hands on my biceps and smiled up at me.

She loves it. She loves me. I love her.

Then, she let go. Her thighs twitched and squeezed, making me lose myself in my thrusts. She tightly wrapped her arms around my back and pulled me down until I collapsed on top of her. My weight surely made it harder for her to breathe, but I could tell it spurred her on. I continued to piston my hips into her until I released with a muffled groan into her neck. I could feel the clenching and twitching, wrapping snuggly around me.

I kept myself raised off her, just enough not to entirely crush her. My chest rose and fell in quick succession, and my muscles felt sore. I usually didn't hold back, but all the delayed gratification seemed to exhaust me in the best fucking way.

Not wanting to break the moment we'd just had but feeling the exhaustion starting to set in, I raised myself up further on my hands and knees. Her hands slid from my sweat-slicked skin.

"Shower?" I asked.

Her head bobbed up and down, and I helped her up from the bed.

After showering, I slipped into some boxers while she slipped one of my T-shirts on. We lay down—me on my back, her on her side. I wrapped my arm around her and had my other hand braced behind my head.

I could tell Kennedy was tired, so I kept silent. She fell asleep almost instantly. I sighed when I heard the small breaths she inhaled through her barely open pink lips, the bottom lip bruised slightly from her biting it to keep from crying out. My movements were minimal, so I wouldn't rouse her.

That feeling of something being off came back tenfold as I thought longer.

Her words kept playing in my head as I watched her sleep.

"I need it."

She'd said it more than once since her dad passed away. She needed intimacy and sex. I didn't want to take advantage of her. In the back of my mind, I knew she was using it as a way to get out of her head, to cope with all the things she'd been going through lately.

That was why I'd been caving since the day I left for my Texas visit. I was letting her get away with it. I was giving into this unhealthy use of distraction. Depending on a different emotion to get over another was going to cause more problems than it solved.

I knew, deep down, that we were headed down a rocky, dark road.

I just couldn't figure out how to stop it.

And I didn't want to stop it. If this was her way of coping…fine. I just didn't want her using something else or letting her sorrow and anger stew inside herself.

She needed an outlet, and if I was it, I could deal.

Chapter 11

Kennedy

"Hey." Kyle's voice boomed and startled me when he pulled one of my earbuds out to get my attention.

I'd been in the library for a short ten minutes, waiting on him to come and join me for our lunch hour.

He leaned down and kissed my cheek while sliding a salad and a fruit cup in front of me. "I tried texting you to see what you wanted."

As he sat down, I turned my phone over from its facedown position. Seeing the text, I apologized, "I'm sorry. I've had it on silent all day. I've been fielding texts and calls from my mom."

"Is she mad?" He opened up his laptop and started to browse the Internet.

I rolled my eyes as he pulled up ESPN.com.

"Livid actually."

I didn't tell him why—that she had called and asked me to give Cole a chance, and instead of me being Miss Manners, I'd turned into a little brat and called him a homewrecker.

I reached over and moved his hand out of the way to exit the browser and open his paper. "We should finish this first." I sent him a stern but flirty scowl with fluttering lashes.

His hand fell onto my chair, and his thumb teasingly grazed my back. "Whatever you say, boss."

"I can see you tried to work on it." I laughed at his opening paragraph.

His writing wasn't bad. He just couldn't get his ideas in order. I suspected his only issue with writing was his attention span. He couldn't focus on an idea long enough to finish it out. With a little guidance though, he could manage.

Over the next thirty-five minutes, we successfully got the introduction and conclusion in order. He printed it off and tucked it away in a folder.

"You ready? I'll walk you to class." He offered his hand to me.

I took it and grabbed my bag. "You can walk me to the counselor's office."

Kyle's head turned fractionally toward me, his brows furrowed and eyes probing. "For what?"

"Mr. Blanc asked to see me after lunch. I'm not entirely sure what for." I shrugged. I honestly didn't know. I was just glad he hadn't asked Miss Quill, the grief counselor, back to probe my feelings.

I'd received the note from the office in my last class before lunch. I'd been called to see the counselor so many times since my father passed that I didn't really ask why until I got there. Mr. Blanc was constantly checking on me. For all I knew, instead of dealing with me herself, my mother had called him with mock concern.

Kyle sighed. "All right, let's go." His hand tightly squeezed mine and tugged me along until I matched his long-legged pace.

He pulled me into a hug when we stopped at the door. As he backed away, he spoke, "I'll see you after school. You're coming home with me, right?"

I nodded just as the door to Mr. Blanc's office swung open. Kyle quickly kissed my cheek before walking away.

"Ready?" Mr. Blanc asked.

My body would go on alert for devastating news every time I came in here. Walking into his office always made me tense up. Today was no different.

"How are things at home, Kennedy?" Mr. Blanc asked as he sat behind his generic wooden desk. He gave no hints away about why I was in here.

Taking my seat on the uncomfortable and scratchy fabric-covered chair angled off to the side, I dropped my bag and responded with my standard answer, "Fine." I stared down at my hands in my lap. Noticing the chipped Radical Red nail polish, I scratched and dug to remove the rest of it.

I didn't look up when he began talking about the call he'd received from my mom this morning, confirming my suspicions. How she was *so* worried about me. How she felt I needed to talk about things with someone, if not her. How I should try to hear her out. And how he understood my frustrations and my pain. While I was sure he did to some point, nothing anyone had said made me feel differently. I was either numb or angry.

I zoned out, thinking of all the times I'd missed the signs of my mom having an affair. I'd spent every other weekend with her at my grandmother's and never suspected a thing. She'd hidden it so well. Never even mentioned Cole, except for in passing or when she'd ask me to go and borrow some type of tool or something from next door. I wondered how it'd even come to be. How he'd tricked her into cheating on my dad, who had been so dedicated to her, their marriage, and our family. It hurt to think about it, so I tried to block it out. Though that was easier said than done because, every time I thought about my dad—which was every day—it would bring me back to the fact that she'd *cheated*.

"Kennedy, did you hear what I asked?"

My eyes immediately went to the counselor's and then to the clock. Forty-five minutes had passed.

"Kennedy?" Mr. Blanc prompted again.

"I'm sorry. No, I didn't."

He sighed and then braced his hands on his desk as he pushed up from his chair. As he came around to the front of the desk and sat on the corner, I watched the deep frown lines encasing his lips hollow even more.

"I know a lot of things might feel out of control, and you're still trying to figure out how to move on. I'm sure things at home aren't like they used to be, but after talking to your mom, I think she's having similar feelings. Maybe you would feel better if you talked to her about all the things going on in your head that you won't let me or Miss Quill in on."

"No offense, Mr. Blanc, but whatever crap lies my mom has been feeding to you, she doesn't feel the same. I'm sure she'd benefit much more from her weekend getaway with her *new boyfriend* than she would from talking things out with me."

I stood and grabbed my bag from the floor, exiting his office without so much as a backward glance.

Walking toward my third-period Anatomy class, I pulled my phone out and scrolled through my texts. Lo and Talan wanted to go shopping for jewelry after school.

We'd all gotten our prom dresses weeks ago, courtesy of Lo's mom sending us to a designer boutique in the city. None of us had had the energy to shop for jewelry after four hours of nonstop changing, posing, switching dresses, groaning, and then finally finding *the one.*

After sending my text, agreeing to the shopping trip, I walked into class and moved silently to my table as Mrs. Biel continued going over her PowerPoint. I pulled out a notebook and flipped to a blank page, mindlessly taking notes on the last portion of the lecture. Before I knew it, the bell was ringing, and she was telling us to review all our previous notes to prepare for the final.

As I shoved my notebook into my bag, Mrs. Biel called out, "Could you please stay for a minute, Kennedy?"

I sat back down as the rest of the class filed out into the hallway. When everyone had exited the classroom, she walked over to shut the door, and then she came and sat on the table in front of me.

"I gave back the tests at the beginning of class, and I wanted to return yours." She held out a packet that had my name on it and a circled red *C-* sitting next to it. "Your average for the class is great, so I don't see the need for a retake, but I wanted to see how things were going with you. I know you took a couple of weeks off for very important and life-changing reasons. And, if this grade is an indication of anything, I know it's affecting your studies."

I kept my head down while I rolled my eyes. The sympathy and the questions just never ended.

When I looked back up, I gave her a blasé shoulder raise. "Everything's been okay. I've just been a little distracted. I'll try harder."

With a nod and unflinching eyes, she let me leave.

There was no escaping people's questions or counseling, I realized.

"So, what about this?" Lo held up a necklace with different-sized ruby-colored stones surrounded by diamonds, all linked together beautifully. It was perfect for her prom dress.

Talan and I nodded our heads in absolute agreement.

As Lo pursed her lips at it, she asked, "You don't think it'll be too much? I mean, my dress is extravagant enough."

Scoffing, Talan rolled her eyes, her hands wrapping around her own throat in mock asphyxiation. She was bored with this jewelry store. "Lo, your dress is dramatic because it's backless. This will really set off the front. I think it's perfect. And ruby is totally your color."

"I don't know. I think I'm just going to do the ruby teardrop earrings with the diamonds." She turned back to the jeweler and handed over the extravagant necklace. "Besides, the neckline is really high on the dress."

"You know, for having all the money your family does, you do not act like it," Talan commented on Lo's financially fortunate family.

Lo quickly clenched her teeth before handing over her credit card to the jeweler. "I'll just get the earrings. Thank you." She waited patiently as the man in a fancy suit moved over to the cash register. "I just don't have those kinds of needs. This is a stretch for me as it is. But I'm trying to get along with my mom, and money and things are what she likes. She'll love the fact that I'm spending so much on these."

Putting on a smile, I suggested our next stop, "So, can we get out of here and go somewhere I can afford?" I laughed while saying it because, honestly, there was no way I was going to even look at anything in here.

I knew Lo's mom's taste, and it wasn't cheap.

The jewelers were all dressed in suits and designer dresses. At first, they'd looked at us with disdain until the manager stepped out from the back and recognized Lo. Only then had they all fallen over themselves for their next commission.

Talan tugged on my arm as Lo signed the receipt. Then, she grabbed the black bag with red tissue paper sticking up that held the expensive jewelry she'd just paid for.

"To Claire's?" Talan joked. We all laughed. "Just kidding. My mom said we should go to Macy's or something."

"Sounds perfect," I said.

"You guys are mean." Lo pouted.

"We're just teasing you, Lo!" Talan wrapped her arm around Lo's neck and pulled her down. "We know you're a closet spoiled brat."

Swatting at Talan, Lo got loose and huffed. "I should go back and buy that necklace then. It only had the price tag of a small car."

"Yeah, actually, you should because it was stunning. And I bet Chase would love to see you in *just* that necklace."

We climbed into Lo's Chevy Camaro and set off for the mall. As I sat in the backseat, it didn't take long for me to lose myself in my thoughts again as we drove across the city. I couldn't stop thinking about Kyle and him leaving for Texas soon and about my own college decisions. About what my dad would have wanted me to do. About my mom. The Cole guy who'd swept in and changed everything. And I couldn't stop thinking about just forgetting it all.

The flask sat in my purse. Full and tempting. But there was still that little voice in my head, telling me I could do without. That it was wrong to forget in that way.

How contradicting could I get?

I was confusing myself with the constant back and forth between clinging to the fog and figuring things out with a clear mind.

I had never acted like this in my life. It was a foreign feeling— caught up in my own head and not being able to turn to the one person who was always there to guide me. I was severed from my faith. From God. I felt like I couldn't be saved.

And, in all honesty, I didn't even want to be saved. Because being saved meant forgiving God for what he'd taken away from me.

That was the hardest part for me because I knew my dad would have been so heartbroken to see I couldn't turn to my faith, to God, to get me through this fear and grief. He'd have been upset that I was letting my anger with his absence and the way he had been taken away from me blind me from the only thing he knew was a sure thing.

With my rebellion and the disappointment I knew Dad would have felt, I was suddenly submerged under so much guilt. Guilt for so many things that I couldn't even cope with, which brought me back to trying to forget. To just let it all go.

"Kennedy? Are you going to get out of the car?" Talan was holding the passenger seat forward, waiting for me to climb out of the backseat.

It hadn't registered to me that the car had come to a stop. I unfolded myself from the small backseat and apologized.

My two best friends traded nervous glances that I didn't miss. I couldn't blame them though. Sometimes, it was like I was coming out of a zombie state.

We walked in and headed to the jewelry department in the less fancy chain store. I still didn't know what kind of jewelry I wanted, but it took Talan no time at all to pick out a black pearl chandelier set of earrings and a black onyx bracelet.

"What about this one, Ken?" Lo pointed to a collared gold necklace behind the glass. "It's just like the one you showed me in that picture."

I glanced at the price tag below it and shook my head. "It's over my budget. My mom would kill me."

"So, I'll pay for half," Lo offered. "It's exactly what you want. You're getting it. And, if you don't buy it, I will, and we'll call it a late birthday gift."

Sighing and rolling my eyes at my best friend, I relented easily and let her pay for half. I knew she would have just bought it the second I turned my back anyway. And it would go perfectly with my dress and the bracelet I planned on wearing.

"Let's go look at shoes!" Talan squealed as she left us for the shoe section.

Lo and I finished paying for the necklace and then followed our shoe-crazed friend to a place she did not need to be in. The girl had an addiction.

I looked up and saw the sign for the restrooms, and I decided I just needed a minute to myself. "Hey, I'll be right back. I'm just gonna go use the restroom."

Lo nodded her head but was distracted by her phone. I slipped down the path to the right and walked by the handbags section.

I'd almost made it to the restrooms when a hand reached out for my arm and yanked me roughly to the left, behind a large pillar.

"Bryan!" I shouted. Then, I lowered my voice to a whisper. "What the hell? Are you stalking me now?"

He laughed and wiped his hand down and over his mouth. "Easy, killer. I saw you walk in and didn't want to talk to you in front of Lo."

"That doesn't explain why you're here." I realized his hand was still wrapped around my arm, and I shrugged him off, crossing my arms over my chest.

Tsking, he rolled his eyes. "My mom is the manager of the women's department here. I was bringing her dinner."

"Oh."

"Yeah. Oh. So, no, I'm not stalking you. But you haven't responded to my texts since I dropped you off on Saturday. That kind of torture might make me stalk you, Angel." He winked, and that damn smirk of his appeared instantly.

I took a step back to create some distance. "I have a boyfriend, Bryan. And you're not the best company to keep."

"Oh, come on." His blue eyes glared, focused right on me. "You liked hanging out. You didn't really have a problem with what I did on Saturday; otherwise, you would have called the cops or that *boyfriend* of yours. Don't play so innocent with me, Kennedy."

"You're bad news, Bryan."

I moved to walk away from him and all his rebel-without-a-cause attitude. He was even sporting a leather jacket today. He came up behind me and grabbed my arm, twisting me back around. With his eyes boring into mine, I couldn't look away.

"I know you're just itching to not feel or think for a while. I have no doubts, you'll call me when you're ready." He was hinting at more; I was sure of it. "Until then, there's a party on Saturday night; you should come."

"Prom is Saturday," I declared. *Seriously, Kennedy? That's the best excuse you've got?*

He rolled his eyes. "Yeah, yeah. Whatever. Look, I have something for you." His eyes glowed with mischief.

He was such a devil. He scared me and confused me and made me forget all the things I needed to remember.

"I don't want it," I whisper-growled.

"Whatever you say, *Angel.* Have a good night." He patted my shoulder, giving me a devious look. Then, he walked away.

I pivoted and finally made it to the restroom. After I peed, I stared at my reflection and cursed myself for letting him get into my head. No amount of alone time was going to give me the reprieve I so desperately wanted.

I left the restroom with more weight on my shoulders thanks to Bryan.

Make up your mind, Kennedy.

"I'm trying, brain."

Oh God. Now, I was talking to myself.

I spotted Talan on a bench, trying on a pair of Calvin Klein heeled sandals.

"What do you think?" she asked, lifting her foot to model her dancer leg strapped into a stunning black shoe.

"Perfect. Where's Lo?" Turning in a circle, I looked for my best friend. Talan didn't respond, so I nudged her foot. "Hey. Lo? Where is she?"

"She went outside to make a call," she said while slipping the shoe off and placing it back into the box. "I'm definitely getting these. You want to look around?"

"No. I already bought my shoes," I said, a slight nervousness noticeable in my voice.

Lo might've run into Bryan—or worse, she might have seen *me* talking to him. I tried not to fidget.

Talan took her time with paying for the shoes, and then we walked out toward the main entrance. I could see Lo on the phone with one arm wrapped tightly around her waist. I wondered whom she might be talking to, but my fear of her seeing me with Bryan outweighed that wonder.

Lo was my best friend. Bryan had almost killed her last year with Brent and Cam. I knew, deep down, that even just having brief words with Bryan would mean a world of betrayal to her.

Walking out the doors, we paused, and she turned to us.

Still talking on the phone, she said, "I know. It just freaked me out, seeing him again since Dieter's party last year. It was like déjà vu, and my brain just short-circuited. I couldn't breathe, and I needed to talk to you." Her blue eyes were glistening. "Love you, too." Then, she pocketed her phone.

She eyed Talan's bag and then chuckled, a brief smile painting her lips. "Seriously, T? More shoes?"

Shrugging, Talan said, "What? They were ten percent off. I couldn't pass them up."

"Ready?" Lo asked us as she turned for the parking lot.

She never made eye contact with me.

Chapter 12

Kyle

I threw the ball one last time, hitting Chase right where his hands were positioned over his chest. Then, I jogged toward him, halfway down the field.

"I think that's enough for the day." He panted and sighed.

When he'd called and asked to work out with me after school, I didn't think he'd realized just how hard I trained. I'd planned on studying, but a workout had sounded way more appealing, so I'd told him to come get me at my house, and we'd hit the school gym and field.

After making him go through my stretches, running, throwing, some weights, and then some more throwing, I gave him a nod, knowing he'd had enough and we moved to walk back toward his Tahoe.

"I have a feeling, I'm not going to be able to walk tomorrow." He half-laughed, half-cringed when he lifted himself up into his seat.

Smirking at him as I jumped up into the passenger seat, I called him out, "Pussy."

"Fuck off. I don't play sports like you do. I don't have to train like a beast. I was gifted with an insane body by the grace of God." He drove out of the school's parking lot and then smirked over at me. "Think the girls are done shopping?"

"Definitely no—" I was cut off by the music being replaced with the hands-free ringing. "And I'm mistaken." Glancing at the dash told me that Lo was calling.

"Hey, what's up? You headed back to—"

"Chase?"

I looked over to Chase, hearing the distress in Lo's voice.

"What's wrong?" he asked as he quickly pulled over to the side of the road so that he could focus on just her.

Through the speaker, I heard her take a panicked short breath. In turn, it made me panic because my girlfriend was supposed to still be with her. An accident flashed through my mind, but Lo was one of the best drivers I'd ever met even if she was a little reckless sometimes.

"I saw him, and I just…it just…I freaked out. I feel like I can't breathe."

"Saw who, baby? Tell me who."

I quickly glanced at Chase when his voice softened for her.

"He was here, Chase. Bryan. I'd thought I saw him when we first walked in, and I blew it off. But then I *actually* saw him. He was talking to Kennedy! Why would she even talk to—"

This time, I cut them both off, "What do you fucking mean, he was talking to Kennedy? Where is she now?" I yelled. I didn't mean to, but I couldn't stop myself either. My entire body tensed with a mix of fury and despair.

"Kyle?" she questioned in a shrill voice. "I'm sorry. I…I just know what I saw."

Chase eyed me with a don't-fuck-with-me-right-now look that actually made me pause.

"Where are you? I'll come get you." Chase put the Tahoe back in drive and started to head for the highway.

"No. Don't. I just needed to talk to you." Her voice was full of anxiety, an emotion that I never would have associated with Lo Grande. She was too fierce to fear anything.

Chase's hands clenched the steering wheel tighter. "Did he say anything to you?"

"No, he didn't. He was just…I…I think we should talk about this later." She sighed, her breath rough through the speaker.

I knew she was saying that because she knew I was in the car. Something felt majorly off, and anger, panic, and confusion were building inside me at a rapid speed, flooding my brain with irrational thoughts. I could kill a motherfucker for even coming close to Kennedy, especially one as vindictive and fucking useless as Bryan fucking Endears.

"You're okay to drive?" Chase asked her.

Her response was quiet. "Yeah, I just want to go home now."

"Baby, everything's going to be fine. Just breathe, okay? Go drop the girls off, and come home. I'll meet you there."

"Okay."

I'd never heard her sound so defeated. The events of last year really had done more damage than she'd ever let on.

I stayed silent during their exchange, finding my control slipping.

"I love you, baby, okay? Don't let him get to you."

"I know. It just freaked me out, seeing him again since Dieter's party last year. It was like déjà vu, and my brain just short-circuited. I couldn't breathe, and I needed to talk to you."

I turned to Chase and watched him clench his jaw and tighten his fists.

"I'm glad you called. Come home, okay? I love you."

"Love you, too."

Then, the phone cut off, and the music started playing through the speakers again. Chase reached over to turn the volume off.

"I'm going to kill that bastard," he said.

That was all he said for a few moments. Then, he abruptly raised his hand and slammed it onto the steering wheel three times, shouting, "Fuck! Fuck! Fuck!" with each quick beat.

The thing with Chase...ever since he and Lo had become an official couple and stopped dancing around their feelings, making us all nauseous and annoyed with the push-pull thing they did— and especially after what Bryan, Brent, and Cam had done to her last year—his protectiveness and possessiveness had grown. Maybe to an unhealthy level, if I were being honest. But I couldn't see myself reacting any differently if it were me in that situation.

Now, I had the same fuckwit messing with my relationship. With *my* girl.

But my anger wasn't ever visible like his. I bottled it up. I tried to always give the benefit of the doubt.

So, while Chase showed his frustration and cursed and sped back to my place to drop me off, I stewed. I told myself I was *not* going to snap. I was going to ask Kennedy why Bryan would be talking to her, what he could possibly have to say to her, and I was going to do it calmly. Even though there was absolutely nothing calm about me.

My fists were clenching just as hard as Chase's were.

My jaw was so tight, I was scared I was going to crack a tooth.

My nostrils flared.

My pulse raced.

I was about to lose it.

Then, something occurred to me.

"Motherfucker," I said under my breath.

But Chase still heard me because there was nothing but the quiet hum of the wheels on the road and our breathing.

"What?" he questioned, cautiously looking over at me. "Before you decide to beat Bryan's ass, let me talk to Lo. She might have heard what he said to Kennedy, or maybe he was just saying hi. Who knows?"

I must have looked ready to kill for him to interject so quickly. His sudden need to pacify me was unnecessary though. I just felt duped.

And how the fuck did he switch off his anger so quickly when mine is rapidly building within me like a fucking volcano?

I already fucking knew Bryan had had more to say than hi, and it was *not* the first time they'd spoken.

"I can't believe this," I said aloud, but it was meant for only me again.

Chase probed back, "What?"

"It was right in front of my fucking face. I had a gut instinct, and I let it go. I'm a fucking idiot."

"What are you talking about?"

I shoved my hands through my too-long hair, fisting them at the back of my head. "He texted her the night I signed my letter of intent. I brushed it off. Thought it was someone else. Someone from her church maybe."

Chase gave me a swift glance. "What did it say?"

"He asked how she was holding up. He called her Angel," I growled out that last part in disgust.

"Maybe you're right. Maybe it was a different Bryan."

"Fuck that, Chase. Why would she talk to him today? Why would she even have his number, let alone be texting that psycho? He almost fucking killed her best friend. And, now, he's suddenly talking to her in public, knowing who she's dating? Who her best fucking friend is? Who her boyfriend's fucking best friend is? I was there when you kicked his ass."

Pulling into the gated community I lived in, he looked out the windshield with a contemplative expression. His eyes squinted, and his jaw worked back and forth.

Trying to find some sort of explanation or different answer, he said, "You just said you thought it could be someone else…"

"Yeah, maybe. But what if it wasn't?" I rotated to look at him.

"Then, we'll take care of it."

I rolled my eyes at him. He acted like we were some sort of high school mafia.

He pulled into my driveway and parked. "Whatever it ends up being, she loves you, man. You can't forget that."

I climbed out of the truck and then turned back. Bracing my hand on the roof, I let my head hang. Sighing, I glanced back at him and then out toward the road. "You know…a month ago, I would have said that'd be enough. But ever since her dad died…she's been different. It's like she's dependent on other things, and when she's not getting that, she's distant and quiet, retreating into her head and thoughts and shutting me out."

"You're not worried about her cheating on you, are you?" His hesitancy to ask that question said more than the actual question. I wasn't sure if he realized what *things* I was talking about, but the cheating question certainly hit home. "She's, like, the most loyal person I've ever met. It's just not in her nature."

"Does cheating have to be physical? Even if it is just some type of weird emotional thing, I would still feel cheated on. We've never had a problem with talking about stuff. I think it would hurt more if she were using him as an emotional outlet than her touching him. But, either way…I'm going to kill him if I see him."

Shaking his head, he looked over at me. "I don't think it'll come to that, Kyle. And, if it starts to…I've got your back. You and Dieter were there for me when I needed you."

I briskly nodded my head. I knew he'd have my back.

As I started to shut the door, his hands-free phone rang once again.

"It's Lo," he stated. Then, he hit Answer on the dash and turned the volume up on the speakers. "Hey, I'm just dropping off Kyle. You almost home?"

Her voice came over the speakers once again. "I just dropped Kennedy off. I've got to drive T to her house now."

"Where? I thought she was staying with you, Kyle." Chase glanced over to see my frustration.

She *was* staying with me. Other than the night she'd had dinner with her mom, she'd been with me, in my bed, every night, whether she had to sneak over or just ignored her mom, she was always in my bed at the end of the day.

Lo sighed, sounding reluctant to answer. "No. Her mom called, and they had an argument, I think. She told me to drop her off at her house."

I turned away from Chase's Tahoe, scared that my anger would cause me to kick in his door. I hurled my gym bag off my shoulder and across the driveway. My hands tugged at my hair as I paced.

What the fuck is going on with her? With us?

I barely registered Lo saying she'd see Chase tomorrow.

I walked over to where I'd launched my bag and sat down on the driveway beside it. I unzipped it and dug around my stuff for my phone. When I pulled it out and saw zero missed calls or messages, I dropped it back into the bag, pissed that Kennedy hadn't called or even left a simple fucking text message.

Chase shut the engine off and climbed out. He tucked his phone in the waistband of his athletic shorts and then sat in front of me with his arms braced on his knees, just like mine were.

My jaw worked back and forth, trying to expel some of my tension.

This day fucking sucked. I had known shit was going to hit the fan. I'd tried to ignore it. But I *never* thought it would come in the form of Bryan fucking Endears. His name just made me want to punch something.

"Dieter's on his way. We're gonna chill tonight. Forget our girl problems, school shit, and family stuff." Chase tried to sound excited.

I knew that he wanted to be at home with his girl, making sure that seeing that fucking douche bag hadn't caused even more damage than he'd already done.

I threw my head back and looked up at the sky. "You don't have to do that. Go home. Be with Lo. I'll figure this shit out."

"Not alone, you won't. And not tonight. Not fucking taking no for an answer." He stood and tossed his phone to the grass. "Come on. Let's shoot some hoops till D gets here with the beer."

Laughing, I stood and walked over to the garage, typing in the code to open it. "Getting your ass kicked in every sport by me in middle school wasn't enough? Now, you want to take a trip down loser's lane?"

As I grabbed a basketball from one of the shelves, he bent down to retie his laces. "Still the cockiest bastard I've ever had the pleasure of knowing, I can see." He laughed as I chucked him the ball.

Chapter 13

Kennedy

Mom looked mad. Not worried. Not concerned. Mad.

As soon as I walked through the door, she sat me down and glared until I asked what was wrong.

That was when she pulled the bottle from beside her seat and placed it on the coffee table.

An empty bottle of Crown Royal sat between us, and instead of us talking, we both just stared at the bottle.

"Don't even try to tell me it's not yours, Kennedy. I found it in your room, under your bed. Is this why you've been acting out?"

I rolled my eyes at her.

"Where'd you get this?"

My eyes rounded and shot to hers. *She doesn't know where it came from? What? She's been so torn up with grief that she still can't step foot in Dad's office to notice the missing bottle? But she had the nerve to cheat on him and move on almost instantly after his death? When she swore they'd reconciled and worked through her epic fuckup?*

How convenient and sad for me.

My shoulders drooped, and I almost called her out. On how pathetic she was. How disconnected she was. How ignorantly bliss she was.

"Did you get this from Kyle?" she snarled, her distaste for him so obvious.

She would try to paint him as a bad influence.

"Is this what you've been doing, Kennedy? Drinking and disregarding the law? You're just a kid. This can cause serious harm."

Because it could never be about something much bigger. Something even I didn't want to admit. Something that terrified me. Because if I did, then it would be real. It would be a problem. And right now? I wanted to live in the same ignorant bliss she'd so easily fallen into.

"You're one to talk," I mumbled under my breath.

She stewed across from me. I took in her sleek ponytail and a dress I'd seen her wear a handful of times. Modest and classy. Not a hint of cleavage showing, and the length ran down to the bottom of her knees. A simple white cardigan was layered over the deep plum-colored dress. She looked so put together and just like I remembered her from before. Before everything had changed, and I'd learned of her misdeeds.

She picked the bottle up from the table and placed it back on the floor beside her chair. "I think you need a break, Kennedy. Away from your friends and this town. Come with me to Cole's lake house. It'll be good for you. We'll make it for next weekend instead. That way, we don't interfere with prom."

"You can't be serious," I sneered as I stood. "Go on vacation with your *boyfriend* and *disgrace* my dad's memory, but leave me the fuck out of it."

I heard her breath catch as my spiteful words lashed out at her. But I wouldn't console her for her own choices, and I sure as hell wouldn't let her try to play the happy little family with someone I knew nothing about other than he was a home-wrecking piece of shit.

God, it felt so good to let those feelings take hold.

I walked up the stairs with anger I'd never really felt, carrying me away from her sniffles. I only felt the slightest bit of pain for what I'd said and how I'd acted, but that pain was overshadowed with loathing and bitterness.

I swiftly opened my bedroom door and then shut it with a jarring slam. The sound cracked through the stiff and tense air from my dramatic exit. I sat on my bed and felt my blood heat with all these emotions I wasn't used to. I turned my stereo on to drown out her mumbled conversation with whomever she'd immediately called.

Probably Cole.

It hurt to feel all this anger and grief. It pushed and tugged at me. Begging me to let it out. But I worried about the consequences and the damage I'd ultimately cause if I did. *Would it be some multiplying virus, spreading further and further, infecting me and bringing me down deeper?* I didn't know the science of it all, if it were possible...but it certainly felt like a monster was ready to consume me.

So, instead, I numbed it. I blanketed it. Tried to smother the hate and the resentment. The burning fire. With a cupful of expensive vodka this time, courtesy of the cabinet my mom so carelessly hadn't checked. I drank the smooth liquid like it would solve all my problems. Instead of smothering, it stoked. Making the licking flames rise higher and fiercer. So, I took larger sips until I couldn't feel my tongue, finally snuffing out the anger just enough.

And I knew what everyone would think.

She's becoming an alcoholic.

She's being so naive and stupid.

She has no idea how good she has it.

She's a fool.

Drinking doesn't fix anything.

How could she fall so far from grace?

What would her father have said?

He wouldn't have said anything. Because he couldn't.

And I wasn't becoming an alcoholic. I could stop whenever I wanted. And it wasn't even like I was getting wasted or blackout drunk.

I was simply taking the edge off from the overwhelming thoughts, the emotions, the grief...just for a little while.

Chapter 14

Kyle

Dieter was passed out on the couch in my room with a beer next to his hand on the floor. Chase was in a similar position on the air mattress he'd found in the back of my closet and aired up. It was just like middle school—minus the beers. Back then, we had been trying to hide all the candy my mom had told us not to take up to my room and the rated R movies my dad always said were for grown-ups. No, not porn. Just the action-filled, heavy-cursing films that would make your heart pound with adrenaline and your eyes widen with shock. Like *Die Hard* and *Bad Boys II*. Bruce Willis was the motherfucking man. And who didn't love Will Smith and Martin Lawrence?

Bad Boys II was playing the credits on the flat screen I had mounted on my bedroom wall.

I was sitting against the headboard of my bed, scrolling through Facebook, when my email pinged. Switching tabs on the browser, I noticed right away that it was from the assistant coach for the Longhorns. The email was finally confirming the dates for training camp. I read through the entire thing twice, making sure that I didn't miss anything. I'd be leaving July 5 and not returning before school started. Training would lead straight into preseason games and then classes.

I wondered how I was going to tell Kennedy I'd be gone for the majority of summer and that I wouldn't be coming back.

I was still so unbelievably furious with everything that'd been going on.

At first, I'd tried to be the understanding boyfriend, the one who would do anything for her, but now, I was so pissed off and had been speculating everything since her dad passed away that I couldn't find it in myself to feel bad about leaving for that long.

I flipped back over to my Facebook page and started looking through random people's pages that I didn't really know. Some guys from football camps and other schools. Girls I didn't even remember friending. My grandma, who still had no idea you couldn't command Facebook to do something in a status post.

Show me pictures of my grandkids, was her current status.

Funny enough, my mom posted a picture of me and Leighton from this past New Year's.

When I found myself typing in Kennedy's name into the search bar, I berated myself and then slammed the laptop closed.

If she couldn't find the time to text me or call me to tell me why she'd suddenly changed her mind about staying here and going back to her mom's, then I'd have to find some other sort of distraction. I couldn't let myself get caught up on the rejection because that was what it felt like. Blatant disregard for my feelings. It would only make me angrier to keep focusing on it and torturing myself.

Setting the laptop on the nightstand, I hunkered down into my sheets and put my hands behind my head. Staring up at the ceiling proved to be even more infuriating.

My phone buzzed on the pillow next to me.

I ignored it.

After twenty more minutes of mind-numbing staring at the ceiling, it started to buzz continually. I glanced over to see Kennedy's face lighting up the screen. She was finally calling me.

But did I have the calm nerve to even speak with her right now? No, not really. But I loved her, and I really fucking needed her to explain this shit in a light that wouldn't make her out to be a cold-hearted zombie, like I'd been relating her to all night.

I sighed, and giving in to my only temptation, I swiped across the screen to answer.

I didn't say anything, just pressed the phone to my ear.

She didn't talk at first.

A good thirty seconds of tense silence passed.

Then...

"Kyle?"

But still...I said nothing.

Then, the sound that was like a sword that always slayed my heart like it was a dragon came.

Kennedy sniffled.

I took a deep breath. At this moment, I hated myself for allowing her to own me and ruin me so completely. I'd done nothing but love her. But this silence reeked of secrets.

"Just tell me," I commanded softly. My eyes squeezed shut to keep this moment from blinding me.

My chest tightened in fear. If she confessed to anything but casual conversation in passing, my heart might just fail.

She didn't say anything, but I could still hear her sniffling. That meant something was wrong. And it was going to ruin me.

I couldn't take the silence anymore. So, I asked what I needed to know, "Are you cheating on me?" It came out as a heated whisper, so my friends wouldn't wake, but I couldn't hide my anger or disgust.

"Kyle!" she wailed. "No. *God, no.* I would never cheat on you. I love you."

"I don't want to feel like this, Kennedy...like I'm losing you." *It will kill me.*

"You're not."

Promise me.

I was too stubborn to say all the things I wanted to and too scared to ask everything I needed to.

Her raspy voice became even rougher and scratchier as her crying strained her throat. "I'm just...a little lost right now, Kyle. But the only thing I know for sure is that I love you, and no one and nothing is going to change that. *I need you.*"

I noticed a slight slur to her words but chalked it up to her crying.

"Okay." All emotion was lacking in my response. A bland answer was all I could give, and I knew it was like a dagger to her heart when she continued to cry.

She asked me to stay on the phone with her till she fell asleep. So, I did until her soft sniffles turned into deep breaths.

I whispered, "I love you," and then I pressed End on the screen.

I wanted to go to her. I wanted her to come to me. I wanted her to need me.

Not anyone else. Not anything else.

Just me.

I tossed and turned for the rest of the night. When morning came and all of the alarm clocks on our phones blared through the silence, we groaned like upset bears, refusing to come out of hibernation.

"Let's just skip," Dieter groaned out, rolling onto his stomach and burying his face in his pillow.

Throwing his arm up in the air, Chase agreed, "I second that."

I threw my covers off and got up to take a much-needed shower. I smelled like shit since I hadn't showered after working out yesterday and then drinking beer all night.

I took a short shower, trying to keep my mind constantly moving and not focusing on anything long enough to piss me off. Stepping out of the shower, I wrapped a towel around my waist and headed back into my bedroom to grab some clothes. Dieter and Chase had fallen back asleep.

When I was dressed in jeans and a tee and had my shoes on, I placed my foot on the air mattress and jostled it around until Chase stirred. "Dude, you staying here all day or what?"

"Shit," he whispered. Then, louder, he said, "Fuck. No. I want to, but I need to see Lo."

"Yeah, I get that. I'll be downstairs, making breakfast. Wake up D after you shower."

After he nodded, I grabbed my backpack and headed to the kitchen. I could hear my mom and dad talking about flight plans and rental cars in his office down the hall. They were scheduled to head to DC for work.

I grabbed some eggs and bread to make the guys and me some breakfast before heading out. I was doing anything to keep my mind off Kennedy.

Honestly though, I just wanted to beat Bryan's ass and put all this shit behind us. I wanted Kennedy to go back to the optimistic and cheery girlfriend I'd had a month ago.

I was being selfish. But I didn't fucking care. Things had been perfect before her dad passed. I just wanted us back to the way we had been.

There was a knock at the door while I cooked. Mom shouted that she'd get it and breezed past the kitchen to the foyer. I barely heard her happily greet Lo, and then they were both walking into the kitchen as I scrambled eggs on the skillet.

"Should I make more?" I asked while I stirred the eggs in the pan and pushed the bread down in the toaster.

Lo shook her head and took a seat on one of the barstools.

"What brings you here this early, Lo?" Mom asked as she grabbed plates and silverware.

Slowly moving her gaze to me, Lo looked hesitant. "I just needed to talk to Kyle before school," she explained. She accepted the glass of orange juice Mom held out for her.

Mom suspiciously eyed me, and with a raised eyebrow, she said, "Oh. Well, I'll excuse myself then, so you two can chat." She walked out of the room and back toward Dad's office.

"What's up?" I asked cautiously.

"Did you talk to her?"

I didn't miss the slight edge to her voice.

I never took my eyes off the skillet when I responded, "Yeah."

"And what did she say they talked about?" Lo was all business this morning.

Not saying anything at first, I finished scrambling the eggs and divvied them up on the plates I'd set out. The toaster popped, so I grabbed the four slices and placed them on the plates. I put two more in just as Chase and Dieter walked through the archway.

"We didn't really talk in detail. I didn't want to say anything I'd regret, and she was really upset when she called." Those were lame excuses and even lamer attempts for Kennedy and me to figure our shit out, but it was the truth.

"Fuck that," Lo sneered with a scrunched up face.

"What?" I asked, totally confused for her disregard of Kennedy's feelings.

"I'm not okay with this." So much anger was in her tone.

Chase walked up behind her and placed his hands on her shoulders, trying to knead away the tension. She was coiled like a snake. I just didn't want her to strike at me.

The final pieces of toast popped out, and I tossed them on my plate. "I get it," I said as I spread some butter on the toast. "I do, Lo. I hate that fucking guy as much as you do. But I love Kennedy more than I hate him."

She viciously shook her head. "I think I'm going to be sick." She launched off the barstool and ran out of the kitchen.

Chase ran to follow her to the guest bathroom down the hall, past my dad's office.

I stared after them, frustrated and sad. I loved Lo like a sister, and to see her so frustrated and scared hurt me, too.

Dieter stayed silent as he ate his scrambled eggs and toast.

Chase and I had clued him in on everything last night. He had been just as pissed as the two of us. But, now, he sat quietly, not saying a damn word. It freaked me out even more because he was usually the most vocal out of all of us.

Chase slowly sauntered back into the kitchen.

"She all right?" Dieter asked, his concern evident in his tone.

Ever since last year and all the drama, with Lo and her hospitalization and the three of us guys making sure Brent, Cam, and Bryan stayed far away from her, he was always protective over her. He'd taken a brotherly role with her. If he wasn't such good friends with Chase and played the field so much, I'd wonder if there was more to it.

"Yeah." But Chase didn't elaborate any more than that. He just picked up his fork and stabbed at the eggs I'd made him.

We finished our breakfast, and as I was loading the dishwasher, I heard the front door open and close.

"Was that Lo?" I turned to Chase, who had a solemn look on his face.

He nodded as he stood and then grabbed his bag that had been resting at his feet. "She's still upset. She didn't want you to see her like that."

"This guy is causing more fucking problems for my family. Just let me do what we threatened last year, Chase. It will solve this whole fucking mess and get him out of our hair for good," Dieter ranted angrily, finally speaking more than a few words. His face was turning a little red even.

I studied his tense facial expression. Locked jaw, furrowed eyebrows, pursed lips.

Last year, we'd threatened Bryan and Brent with Dieter's dad. Mr. Farley was a detective. He'd put some seriously dangerous guys behind bars. But, last year, he'd been promoted to the head of the Drug and Gang Unit. And even though that option was tempting, I didn't want this all to go too far.

I tried to take control of the situation in front of us and calm Dieter down. "He's not going to bother us anymore. And Kennedy wouldn't jeopardize her friendship with Lo."

I knew Kennedy better than anyone. Lo was like a sister to her.

"She already has," Chase said quietly as he turned his back to me and walked to the door.

I didn't want to accept that.

As we walked into the school and to our lockers, it became very apparent that Chase was right.

Kennedy was standing to the side of Lo, a distressed look in her eyes as she reached for Lo. But Lo flinched back, not letting her within an inch of touching her.

I looked to Chase, who shook his head.

"Well, that looks like a friendly conversation," Dieter commented as we quickened our pace to get to the girls.

Chapter 15

Kennedy

Lo's eyes accusingly glared at me.

I knew she had seen me with Bryan, but to have her look at me with so much disappointment and what I thought was disgust made me nervous for our friendship for the first time in my life. My best friend didn't even want me to explain. Wouldn't even let me explain.

"Lo…I'm sorry." I reached out to try and turn her toward me, to get her to just look at me.

She abruptly pulled back, evading my touch.

When she finally turned to me, her eyes were lit with contempt. "I can't even talk to you about this right now, Kennedy."

"Hey, girls." Dieter's voice came from behind me. He kept his distance though and didn't try to crack any jokes. Even he was hesitant to enter this conversation.

Lo reached for her books and slammed her locker closed with a violent push that vibrated through the surrounding lockers. I jolted back and stared at her with pleading eyes.

For a brief moment, I saw concern and compassion flare in her irises—like a flashlight with dying batteries, flickering to give me just enough hope before fading to black—but they quickly reverted to something unnamable. Resentment, repugnance. I wasn't sure what she was truly feeling.

"How could you even let him near you? You know what kind of damage he's capable of." Lo gripped the straps of her backpack like it was the only thing holding her back from slapping me.

Let's add on, pissed as hell.

Chase was now by her side, and even though we were all friends, the alliance was drawn. He wouldn't take his gaze off her face. I saw the worry flash in his hazel eyes, but a protective expression and stance overshadowed the fear.

I could feel Kyle beside me. And, even though I knew he was pissed with me, he still slipped his hand into mine and squeezed.

Looking over to him, I saw the steely expression that I knew was hiding a battle within him. He wanted to support me, but he wanted the same answers Lo did.

All I could do was let a single tear slip out.

I was going to lie to them. They wouldn't understand that, for one night, Bryan had made me forget—not what he had done to Lo, but what I had been going through. Even though everything was so much more complicated and *I* was so much more complicated, I was going to make it easier for them.

Lo released the straps of her backpack and waited with bated breath. Her arms were secured tightly over her middle, like I was going to rip out her heart from her belly button.

"He was just giving me condolences, Lo. I told him to leave."

A brief flicker of doubt crossed her face, her features showing all her emotions in her drawn eyebrows and pursed lips. Then, the switch to sad wide eyes told me she believed me.

Kyle instantly dropped my hand. I should have registered it as something significant, but I didn't take my eyes off Lo as she unwrapped her arms from herself, letting them fall limply to her sides.

"I still don't like it," she professed quietly, taking a small step toward me. "I don't want you to *ever* feel like I did that night and the days after. He's dangerous and manipulative; I know. He'll never change. And, if he's being nice to you now, knowing I'm your best friend…it just makes me worry. I don't want you to be a vulnerable target, something he likes, when you're emotionally fragile."

The silence stretched for a long moment after her words. I had nothing to say to that. She was probably right. About him. About my fragility. But he'd done nothing to me. And I knew that little three-letter word *yet* was in Lo's hand like a grenade. She just hadn't pulled the pin yet. But, for some reason, I didn't mind tempting fate.

Chase stiffened when Lo softened toward me.

"Why do I feel like I just missed a battle royale?" Talan's sprightly voice broke into the tense quiet.

Dieter laughed but then coughed to try and cover it. "Always late to the party, T." Then, he walked off to his own locker, immediately swallowed up by friends of his and a few girls.

All eyes were on me as I stood there with nothing more to say. *Honestly, what can I say?*

They were looking at me like they wanted this grand reaction, but I just didn't have it in me.

The bell rang, and everyone started to file in the direction of their classes.

"We'll see you guys later." Chase grabbed Lo's hand and pulled her toward the stairs.

She glanced back over her shoulder just once with an uneasy expression, trying to figure me out, before she followed Chase. As the hall started to clear out, I moved to my own locker to grab my notebook. I already knew Study Hall, my first class, with Lo was going to be awkward, and I was in no hurry to suffer through her intently staring at me, trying to figure out what the hell was wrong with me.

I don't know either, Lo.

"Why'd you lie?" Kyle's voice was gravelly and deep. I could hear the disbelieving tone in his question. "And don't lie to *me*, Kennedy."

I tightly squeezed my eyes shut. I didn't want to lie to him. The only good, pure thing in my life. "I ran into him at Dieter's party." I slowly turned to him, my back against the lockers.

His jaw clenched. I could hear his teeth grind before he took a deep breath.

"Is he why you were crying? Did he threaten you?" Kyle reached for my hand. Even though his words were laced with venom and hatred toward Bryan, he still managed to turn soft for me. "Is he threatening you now?"

Shaking my head, I explained why Bryan had been there in the first place and that he'd caught me crying. I left out the part where he'd grabbed me and tried to console me. I told him that Bryan had somehow gotten my number and started texting me and that I never engaged him first.

"But you didn't stop it?" Kyle's voice switched back to disbelief and confusion so quickly.

I could tell he was fighting to stay calm and not overreact, but I'd hidden something from him, and it hurt him. I could see it in the way he searched my eyes for the answers he wanted.

"He's been nice, Kyle. You know I'm not the kind of girl who's a bitch just to be a—"

"Don't do that, Kennedy!" he shouted as he slammed his hand into the locker right beside my shoulder.

I flinched, frightened, and he saw it. But that didn't deter his fury. Kyle crowded around me with his hands braced on either side of my head. My eyes widened.

"This is over. Him texting you. You talking to him. Over."

Tears gushed to my eyes, but his were filled with challenge.

"Block. And. Delete. His. Fucking. Number." He punctuated every word with a threatening, violent rasp.

In this moment, I was so incredibly terrified. Not of Kyle. But of what I had done. I'd betrayed his trust. I'd pushed him to be something else. I'd only ever seen him like this when he was on the field and that one time, freshman year, when he punched a kid for calling someone a terrible name.

"I mean it, Kennedy." His lips were a tight line of held back fury. "You're going to lose more than your best friend if you don't." He stared into my eyes, laying down a law and fact. "Don't make me this guy."

Then, he was walking away, shaking his head and turning to go down the Science hall. His hands were balled into fists by his sides.

I slumped back against the lockers and slid to the floor. My knees up to my chest, I wrapped my arms around them and cried.

Everything hit me at once. I was being stupid and childish, and I knew it. But I couldn't stop it.

I cried for my idiocy. I cried for my friendship with Lo. I cried for my heart that had just walked away with Kyle. I cried for my father. I cried for my mother.

And, even through all of that, I still felt numb.

Saved

When the final bell for classes rang and my tear ducts were all dried out, I stood on shaky, weak legs and walked out of the school.

Chapter 16

Kyle

"You all right?" Dieter whispered as I took my seat in Chemistry.

I shook my head once. No, I definitely wasn't okay. I was burning up with unprecedented rage. I was going to kill that fucking prick.

Kennedy had tried to defend that drug-dealing psychopath. It was more than just condolences he had offered, and I knew it.

"Is she all right?" he whispered.

I looked over to see the concern on his face.

"I think I fucked this up even more," I whispered back. I looked down at the desk where I'd placed my phone.

I should text her. Apologize.

Or, better yet, just go find her and apologize.

My reaction had been fueled by nothing but hate and anger and fear. Bryan could ruin her. In her fragile, vulnerable state that she couldn't seem to get out of, he could warp her and crush her like a bulldozer. And, as a result of that, he would ruin me, too.

After half an hour, D slid his phone over to me, so I could see the opened messages from Chase and his replies.

> *Chase: Did Kyle come to class?*

> *Dieter: He's sitting right next to me. Why?*

Chase: Because Lo was wondering why Kennedy wasn't in Study Hall. She thought they might have left together.

Fuck.

"Damn it," I said quietly. "Fuck. D, I gotta go."

"Is everything all right?"

"No."

I moved quickly, grabbing my backpack and phone. I ignored the teacher calling my name and asking me where I thought I was going. I was out the door in seconds, and when I cleared the front doors of the school, I jogged to my truck and was pulling out of the lot faster than what was considered safe.

I sped across town to her neighborhood, and when I screeched to a halt in front of her house, I saw her dad's old truck sitting in the driveway.

Jumping out of the truck and slamming the door, I readied the house key her dad had given me for emergencies and was rushing up to the door. Before I barged in, I knocked and rang the doorbell.

"Kennedy!" I shouted at the door. "I know you're in there. Let me in, babe."

When she didn't respond, I slipped the key in and turned the knob. Everything was quiet. I didn't find her anywhere downstairs, but when I started to climb the stairs to the bedrooms, I heard a door squeak. The older hinges in the house that groaned and whined gave this family home a personality you couldn't find anywhere else.

"Ken?"

I pushed her bedroom door open, but she wasn't in there. I'd expected to see her sitting on her bed or at her desk.

A quiet gasp sounded behind me.

Then, I knew.

God, I was such an ass to her. I knew I'd scared her. *But what other damage did I do?*

I let my head hang for a brief moment. *Fuck.* I'd messed up so bad.

Turning slowly, I took the few steps across the hall. I tapped softly. No sound came.

"Come on, Kennedy, let me in."

Finally, I could hear some sound. But it was nothing I really wanted to hear. Her crying was like me drowning. It hurt. It was like gasping for breath. I prayed it would become easier for her, for us. She was struggling, burying her emotions when we were in the company of our friends, even hiding her feelings from me. Consumed by the grief, Kennedy was letting it dwell within. She had to learn to live with the pain or fight it.

I needed her to fight.

Fight the pain.

Fight for us.

The faucet turned on. She was trying to hide the sounds of her crying, but I didn't want her to hide.

"*Kennedy*," I pleaded.

The water stopped. The door unlocked, and I immediately twisted the knob and pushed it open. She was standing there, facing me, with a yellow daisy shower curtain as the backdrop to her sadness. She still had tears racing down her cheeks and dripping off her chin.

I rushed to her and tightly embraced her small frame. Her arms stayed limp at her sides, prompting me to squeeze her even harder.

God, I'm such an idiot for treating her the way I did.

"Kyle..." she started to say but trailed off when her emotions got the best of her.

I slightly moved down and wrapped my arms securely around her to lift her. She wrapped her arms around my neck in a hesitant but strong grip. I carried her to her room and set her on the edge of her bed. Then, I knelt in front of her, constantly swiping my thumbs under her eyes to brush away her steady tears.

Kennedy kept her eyes sealed shut, sniffling the whole time.

After a few minutes, her hands reached up to fiercely clutch my wrists. She whispered, "I don't feel like myself anymore, Kyle. I...I just..."

She heaved out a strained breath, and I instantly recognized the overpowering scent of whiskey.

"Have you been drinking?" I asked quietly, concerned.

She broke out into a sob. Her chest heaved violently. "Everything...is so...messed up...Kyle." Her cries echoed through the room and through my bones.

"Shh," I tried to soothe her. "Baby, it's okay. I'm sorry, all right? I shouldn't have acted that way."

"It's not that, Kyle. It's more than that." Redness splotched her skin and tinted her eyes. Her grip on my wrists increased.

"We're going to get through this, Kennedy. Things are just going to be different."

I pushed myself up to kiss her sad pink lips. Her left hand immediately released my wrist and reached around to clutch my neck, keeping me close. Keeping my lips glued to hers. And, when she moved to pull me further up and fell back, taking me with her, I went willingly.

If this was how I had to fix us, to save us, I'd do it a thousand times over.

We became a tangle of limbs. Writhing and panting and begging for more. More kisses. More touches. More thrusts. Me on top of her. Her on top of me until I just couldn't handle the slow pace she'd set, and I roughly rolled her back beneath me.

When I finally moved off her, she was gasping for air.

I told her, "No one else gets this. *You*. Only me, Kennedy."

Something in me had snapped the day Lo called Chase.

I wasn't playing games.

Kennedy wasn't a game to me.

She was everything to me.

And, if I had to remind everyone, including *her*, I would.

Bryan wouldn't get any more of her time or attention.

Even though I was sorry for how I'd reacted, I wasn't apologizing for or taking back what I'd said. Whatever comfort he'd offered her was tainted, and if she continued to let it into her life, it would taint us as well.

While she lay on her back, I hovered over her on my side. My head was propped on my hand while my other hand slowly stroked the softness of her stomach. I watched as goose bumps appeared and then disappeared, chasing after my touch. I skimmed even lower, below her belly button, where the sheet teased and hid her core from me. I flipped my hand over and traced my nails higher, lightly teasing them over her ribs, a sensitive spot that made her squirm.

Her deep sigh caught me off guard. I glanced up to her still flushed face, and her storm-cloud gray eyes stared back at me. I couldn't see into her like I used to. There really was a darkness inside her. It was like driving through a torrential rainstorm— driving so slowly but not willing to stop while praying you would make it out on the other side of the storm safely and with no damage.

"What's wrong?" A frown took over my face.

Kennedy tried to smooth my lips into a smile with her thumb. "When I'm with just you, everything makes sense. Everything feels right."

"And when you're not with just me?"

"I can't stop thinking about all the things that have happened, that are happening, that *will* happen." Her voice was that deep, husky rasp that I loved so much, but her words felt so painful. Like a deep cut to my chest.

Her head fell to the side, away from me, and she sniffled again. "I know I told you to go…but I feel like, if you do, I'm going to lose you forever."

"To Texas?"

She nodded just once, tears glistening in her eyes once again.

I moved quickly and maneuvered myself, so I was on my hands and knees above her. I snaked my head over and down to catch her eyes. "You won't lose me. *Never.* You and me? We're forever, Kennedy. To heaven and back. The only way you are ever going to lose me is if you don't want me anymore."

When she rotated her head back to lay flat and stare up at me, she whispered, "I'm always going to want you, even when I don't deserve you. I need you."

I swooped down and nuzzled her soft neck. She had the sweetest smell, but now, it was tinged with our sweat and my saliva from me kissing and biting her earlier. Claiming—no, marking what was mine.

My phone started ringing from somewhere on the floor, breaking our moment.

"You should get back to school," she said quietly.

Her hands lightly pushed at my chest. I breathed in deeply, inhaling her scent and locking it away as one of the best scents ever.

I lifted my head and looked into those thunderstorm eyes. "Are you not coming back with me?"

Her head lightly shook from side to side.

"Why?" I moved my hand to stroke my thumb over her forehead that had a tiny crease in it from her frown. Then, I went down her temple and across her smooth, delicate jaw.

Her eyes flashed with trepidation. "I think I should give Lo a day to calm down. I texted her, and she never responded."

"She'll forgive you, babe."

I swiftly kissed her lips, but that wasn't enough. I started to devour her mouth. Kennedy lazily opened up to me, and when it was too slow, I forced her open with my own tongue. She moaned and tightly gripped my sides. I bit and nibbled at her lips before I pulled away completely, winded. Her kisses stole my breath. Every damn time.

Standing, I showed no shame as I walked naked over to my discarded clothes. I pulled my boxer briefs and jeans on, and then I sat on the edge of the bed to slip my shoes back on. I stood again and turned to look at her, smiling at her rumpled state.

"As long as he's out of your life for good," I deadpanned as I pulled my T-shirt over my head. When my head popped through, my eyes immediately sought out her expression.

She nodded and gave me a half-smile and nod. I walked back over and gave her one more kiss. This time, it was gentle. Her lips were swollen and bruised enough.

I leisurely backed up, preparing to leave but not completely ready to go, as I said, "I love you, okay? Just know that I'm *always* going to love you."

Then, I ducked out of her room, down the stairs, and back out to my truck. I would arrive back at school just in time for lunch.

I felt better than I had this morning. We were going to get through this. I just needed her to believe it.

Chapter 17

Kennedy

Chills had swept over me as soon as I heard the front door shut and lock.

Kyle had left me under the sheets, sated and breathless.

I'd driven home in a blurry fog of tears and sadness, rushed inside to my bedroom, grabbed the bottle of whiskey hidden in my dresser, and just stared. I could understand the lure of it for alcoholics. Everyone had their demons, and sometimes…the liquor was like holy water, expelling those demons to clear your mind for just a little while.

Then, the doorbell had rung, breaking me out of my staring contest with the damn bottle. I'd rushed to take a few swallows, and then I had hidden it before I slipped into my bathroom. Before I knew it, shoes had been rushing up the stairs, and I'd heard Kyle's voice calling out my name. The worry in his tone had brought instant tears to my eyes, and they'd gushed all over again. Nausea had taken over me, and I'd almost crashed to my knees before the toilet. I was losing myself and screwing everything up, and here he had come to check on me. Like the loving, caring boyfriend I knew he was. The way he would always be.

And I was being this selfish, ungrateful girl who didn't deserve him.

That was why I still couldn't believe I'd called *him*. I had known I was making a huge decision that could alter everything, especially with what this morning had been like. But, after all that I'd been through, Bryan was right; I just wanted not to think or feel for a little while longer. The only time I was free like that was when Kyle and I were together, consumed by each other. But that wasn't all the time, and when I was alone or even surrounded by people, I was suffocating. The silence was choking the life out of me, and the noise was like a tidal wave.

After Kyle had left and I'd gotten redressed, I'd sat on the bed and stared at the name and number, fingers poised to dial. My conscience had cursed me out, telling me I was such an idiot. But even the angel on my shoulder couldn't stop me from listening to the devil, the one that taunted me with whiskey and a clear head. The one that had me pressing Call and then walking out the door.

That was why I was here, at *his* house. I knew I was making a terrible mistake, but I was unable to stop myself.

"I knew you'd call," Bryan said smugly.

He was dressed in loose-fitting jeans and a black T-shirt with double red Xs on it and burn holes all over it. His hair was messy, like he'd just rolled out of bed. His eyes were bloodshot, and that devil's smirk was tilting his lips in a sinful kind of smile.

He looked over my shoulder, seeming paranoid. When he stepped back, he had a taunting grin on his face. "Did Kyle drop you off?" he mockingly asked. Then, he leaned onto the doorframe.

I rolled my eyes and turned to walk away. I was stupid to come here, thinking he wouldn't make me feel worse. It was just a one-time thing. I should never have assumed he'd be better than the past Bryan.

"Angel! Stop," his voice growled. "Shit. I was just kidding. Come on."

He grabbed my wrist, not my hand, just as I was about to step off the porch, and he pulled me into the house. He slammed the door shut and then reached behind me to flip the deadbolt, never letting go of my wrist.

"Come on." He pulled me past the stairs to a door behind it. "We're hanging out down here."

He pulled the door open and gestured for me to lead the way, and a burst of noise hit me—music and what sounded like a video game being played. Gunshots and grunts filled the silence between the changing songs.

I took tentative steps down until I could see what I was walking into.

Immediately seeing two other people, I turned and started to march back up the stairs, but I slammed right into Bryan's muscular but narrow chest, causing myself to bounce back and almost tumble down the remaining stairs. I would have if he hadn't reached out and grabbed on to my biceps, steadying me and pulling me close to him.

"Careful," he whispered, way too close to my face. His breath reeked of beer and cigarettes.

"Let. Go. Of me. I asked you if it would be just you, and you said *yes.* You *lied. Again,*" I hissed at him as quietly as possible, trying to stay unnoticed by the two guys sitting on the couches, facing the TV, playing some military game and cursing at each other.

He loosened his grip on my arms but didn't let me go, watching me with invasive eyes. "You wanted to hang out. They were already here." He carelessly shrugged his shoulders, acting like he hadn't done anything wrong.

"Seriously?" I whisper-hissed again. "That's your explanation for lying to me?" I rolled my eyes.

I stepped to go around him, but one of the guys stopped me.

"We can hear you, you know?"

My eyes widened at the sound of *that* voice.

"Dylan?" I growled at Bryan. "Now, I really *should* go."

I didn't like the way Dylan watched me. The way he tried to get under my skin—or worse, in my pants. He made me uncomfortable in a skin-burning, rash-building with bee stings everywhere kind of way.

"Quit being such a princess, Kennedy. It's not like we're going to gang-rape you. I like my women willing!" Dylan shouted over the music and the game, no emotion to his voice whatsoever.

But me? My eyes were wide with shock. *Who says something like that so casually?*

I hesitantly looked up at Bryan. His eyebrows were raised in a what's-it-going-to-be kind of way. Apparently, he was ignoring Dylan's little quip, as if bringing up gang-raping someone meant nothing.

Sighing, I made my decision. All along, I knew it was the dumbest decision I'd made today—second to calling Bryan in the first place.

I turned yet again to go back down the stairs. When I rounded the couch and was visible to Dylan, he briefly let go of the control with one hand to pat the middle cushion on the couch. I rolled my eyes at him, not even willing to give him an inch of acceptance, and strolled over to the love seat, passing in front of the TV.

Dylan shouted as his player was shot and killed. The other guy, who I didn't know and had never seen, cheered and fist-pumped the air, thanking me for distracting his friend. Dylan glared at me with an evil eye as he set the controller down. He got up, walked over to a mini fridge up against the wall, and pulled out three beers.

He handed one to Bryan and held out one for the other guy, but his face was buried in his phone. "Benji, you want this or not?"

Benji's head popped up. "Huh? What? Oh...no. I gotta head back to the city. Pops is getting pissed. I'm late for my internship." He stood and said his good-byes to Bryan and Dylan but didn't even once acknowledge me.

Bryan moved to take the vacated seat and leaned forward to slam the top of the bottle on the side of the coffee table, popping the cap off his beer bottle. Dylan pulled a bottle opener from his keys and popped the tops off the other two.

"Want one?" he asked me. He leaned closer, dangling a bottle between his fingers, holding it out to me for the taking.

My mind told me to say no, but my body reached forward for it anyway.

I caught his mischievous smirk and the dark twinkle in his eye. Suspiciously eyeing him, I brought the bottle to my lips and tipped it up, taking a deep pull. My mouth immediately wanted to revolt against the taste, but with what I was sure was a very unattractive face, I kept it in and swallowed it down. I preferred the burning liquor to the bitter beer.

When I pulled the bottle away, Bryan was eyeing me with his own devilish grin.

"Wanna play?" Dylan offered me the remote.

The TV displayed a military-style game I always saw Dieter and Chase play when we hung out at Chase's house.

"I'm really bad." I half-laughed, half-groaned at my terrible gaming skills.

"Sounds good. You can play under Benji's name. Screw up his ranks." He patted the middle cushion again.

I rolled my eyes, reluctantly moving over to sit between him and Bryan.

The game started.

I made it three steps before I was shot and killed. I glared over at Bryan, knowing it was him. "Was that really necessary?"

He just smiled and continued to play the game. I ducked around and shot stray bullets, never once hitting anyone. But that didn't stop them from killing me.

"This game is stupid," I whispered halfheartedly.

The comment made both guys laugh, and I just shrugged, sighed, and leaned forward to place the remote on the table.

I heard a hiss and then a, "Damn," groaned from Dylan.

I tilted my head toward him and caught him staring at my butt.

I quickly leaned back. "You're such a pig." I folded my arms and crossed my legs.

They both laughed again—of course, at my expense.

My idea to come here had not included Dylan. I felt awkward and out of place, which was exactly how I should feel, but Dylan had just made it worse. Made me more self-conscious, and I raised my guard. Although I probably should have felt more like that because of Bryan.

I messed with my nails and took sips of the beer Dylan had given me while they played their stupid game. I wouldn't look up unless Bryan cursed because he had been killed. Then, I'd shoot him a smug smile of my own, which he would sneer at.

Good times.

After some time, I found myself relaxing and burrowing further into the couch. I knew I shouldn't let myself get too comfortable around these two, but today's events were taking a toll on my psyche and body. I was tired from thinking about Lo. I was exhausted from arguing and doing *other things* with Kyle.

I let my mind shut off, not thinking about anything.

Soon, I was in that state of sleep where I was half-aware, half-unaware. I could still hear them cursing, the game and the music in the background. Yet I was so close to that dreamland. I willed myself to keep my eyes shut and just be in peace for a little while longer.

I had no idea how long I had been in that state, but suddenly, my phone was ringing with Kyle's ringtone, startling me fully awake. I was curled up on the couch against the armrest, my arms folded and tucked under my head. I jolted up, immediately wiping my mouth in case I'd drooled, and pulled my shirt down that'd ridden up while I slept. Then, I looked for my phone.

It was lying facedown on the coffee table in front of me. Apprehension took over my mind and body as the phone buzzed and rang across the table. I couldn't believe I was even contemplating not answering Kyle's call, but I was. The thought made my stomach sink with heavy guilt.

"You gonna get that?" Dylan came out of a room I assumed to be the bathroom.

I didn't miss the sarcastic tone he'd used.

The ringing stopped, and after a few silent seconds, I finally picked it up. A notification popped up, signaling the voice mail Kyle had just left. Then, a text popped up. I instantly opened it to read whatever he'd said.

Kyle: Dinner tonight with everyone?

Crap. I didn't even know what time it was, but a quick glance to the top of my phone told me it was after four in the afternoon. I'd been here for hours.

All the things I had been trying to forget swarmed my mind at once and took over. I shook my head from left to right multiple times, trying to get all the memories and feelings and the guilt to just *stop*.

The dinner was likely Kyle's idea. He was trying to create an olive branch for me and Lo to mend things, which I wanted. I did. I never wanted to betray my friend's trust. Just the thought of it stung my heart and made me incredibly sad.

And I knew what everyone was thinking. *I already betrayed her trust.*

A simple dinner with all our friends wasn't going to fix that. It would only cement the awkwardness and make it even harder for us…well, *me* to fix things. Especially in front of my closest friends.

I would fix things with Lo on my own terms. I had to. But, right now, I just needed a break from everything.

I looked around the room, finally taking notice that Bryan was nowhere to be seen.

"Where's Bryan?" I looked over to see Dylan texting on his phone, his thumbs moving at lightning speed.

His slightly overgrown eyebrows inched higher on his face when he looked up at me.

With a grin, he slid his phone into his pocket, leaned back on the love seat, and reached for the remote to flip through the channels. "He's on his way back."

"When did he leave?" *Why do I care?*

I should've already been gone.

You should never have been here in the first place. In my head, I could imagine exactly what Kyle would be saying. If he knew where I was. Who I was with. I could almost hear the actual disappointment. I could feel the fear pumping adrenaline in my veins, like when he'd banged his fists into the lockers and caged me in.

A door slammed upstairs, and I froze like a Popsicle. Door-slamming never led to good things. Then, the door to the basement opened. I turned to see heavy boots and jean-clad legs starting to descend the stairs. His feet moved so quickly, I'd think he wasn't even touching the steps, but the loud thud of his boots confirmed that he was.

When his head was visible and he could see me, Bryan's wicked smirk took over his lips. "Ah, she's awake." He stopped on the last step and reached up to the ceiling.

I took notice of his change of shirt. Instead of the shirt with burn holes from earlier, he was dressed in a crisp white oxford shirt with the top two buttons undone.

"You get a good nap in, Angel?"

I groaned. "Stop calling me that."

Dylan chortled. "But it suits you so well, Little Miss Innocent." He rolled his eyes, like he didn't buy into the label I'd been given.

They didn't know my dad had called me that. And they probably only taunted me with that nickname because of my upbringing. Maybe because of my good-girl reputation. But every time I heard it come from their mouths, it was a reminder of my father. I didn't want the reminders though. I had enough of my own.

Still flipping through channels, he asked Bryan, "You did drops?"

Shaking his head, Bryan responded, "Nah, just had some friendly conversations. Expansions and shit."

"Fuck, man, I thought you were keeping it small?" Dylan fired back with a shake of his own head. His lips thinned, like maybe he actually cared about his friend.

While they had their back-and-forth conversation that I wanted no details on, I finally looked back to my phone, rereading the text Kyle had sent me.

I should go, I thought.

With the end of school coming and all my friends leaving— and my own plans still up in the air, like a lost birthday balloon—I really should apologize for my weird and totally out-of-character behavior.

But am I really sorry?

Somewhere in the back of my mind, I heard the comment, *Not yet.*

I wasn't sorry now, but I would be. My own conscience was trying to warn me.

Bryan walked to stand in front of the couch and dropped a black backpack I hadn't noticed him carrying. My eyes glanced to the bag. Then, realization settled in, and the synapses in my brain finally started connecting dots.

"You went to pick up drugs," I accused immediately.

"Don't. You're *not* my girlfriend," Bryan snapped back as his eyes seared into me, daring me to lecture him.

I rolled my eyes, exactly like the brat I was becoming, but stayed silent. He was right. I wasn't his girlfriend.

And, even with him glaring at me and scolding me, I still didn't leave. I didn't want to face the reality outside of this dark basement.

The guys ignored me while they texted on their phones and flipped through channels. My own phone chirped with another text, and I nearly dropped it when I saw Kyle's name lighting up the screen, his message asking for an answer.

Bryan bent over to unzip the bag he'd brought in and started rummaging through it. He pulled out three Ziploc bags of different things. I'd been in enough drug awareness classes through school to recognize at least one. The first one was marijuana. Another bag had blue pills, and the other had a white powder.

My fear spiked, making my hands sweat, and my feet started tapping against the lush carpet. But that didn't stop my curiosity from overriding that fear.

"Looks like Angel wants a sample of your product, Endears."

My eyes briefly snapped to Bryan's, realizing he was watching me just as intently as I had been watching him pull out the drugs. Then, I looked over to Dylan and refused to let go of his taunting and amused blue eyes.

When I didn't respond, Dylan challenged, "Am I wrong?"

Chapter 18

Kyle

"So?" Chase was watching me clutch and squeeze my phone after reading my text from Kennedy.

"She's not coming. Said she just needs the day." I tossed my phone onto the kitchen counter at Chase's house.

We'd all come here after school with the intention of being diligent scholars and actually studying. So far, all we'd done was make dinner plans to try to get the group back to solid ground. I could tell that Lo was still worried about Kennedy. Maybe she was even a little frustrated and definitely a little hurt.

When I'd asked if she'd texted Kennedy or anything, Lo had just shaken her head, saying she didn't even know where to start.

Lo's fear of Bryan, Brent, and Cam was real. After the phone call she'd made to Chase when the girls were at the mall, I'd been paying more attention to her. Now, I could see the anxiety in her intense blue eyes every time Brent even passed her in the hallways. She'd get really tense and shy away, hiding into Chase's chest. A reaction I'd been totally blind to before.

I never wanted Kennedy to live with that fear. And if she did? Well, I would be just as protective and possessive of Kennedy as Chase was with Lo. If he could help it, Lo would never be out of his sight. That was how I was beginning to feel about Kennedy. But I couldn't very well make her be with me all the time. Her mom was already trying to keep us apart as much as possible.

In my opinion, it was weird how different David Kiblen had been from his wife, Sandra, where my relationship with Kennedy was concerned. He'd trusted us more, and she just despised me. Even as a pastor, he'd still let us cross some lines, like Kennedy and I staying at each other's houses. I had no doubt that he'd have been pissed and disappointed if he knew of what we sometimes did, but he'd still instilled enough trust in us to make the safe and right decisions, whereas Sandra had no faith in us at all, forcing us apart when she could.

She was an infuriating woman, especially after her affair had come to light. I still couldn't believe it, to be honest. A man like David only came along once in someone's love life—I was sure of that—and she had been willing to throw all of that away. And to move on so quickly, back to the guy she'd had an affair with, made me wonder if David was rolling over in his grave.

Whatever. It wasn't my place to judge, but David and Sandra had obviously worked through it enough to stay together. At least they had done that for Kennedy. I knew how much family meant to Kennedy. But, even with that knowledge, I couldn't help but think, if Kennedy had known about the affair before David passed, she would have been better for it. It would have been devastating, but at least she would have had her dad to help her work through her emotions. Now, she just had her mom and all the resentful feelings I knew she kept toward their strained relationship.

"Did you hear me?" Dieter loudly asked, his snapping fingers gaining my focus.

"What?"

"I said, we should just go get her. She can't hide from this forever. I mean, look at Lo…" Dieter trailed off and pointed to the sliding glass doors.

I looked out and saw Lo and Talan sitting on lawn chairs. They looked to be deep in thought.

"She misses her best friend. She told me she's worried sick about what Bryan's intentions are."

I tossed my pen down, and it skidded across the kitchen table. "I put a stop to it." Rubbing the stubble on my jaw, I pressed on, "It's over. Lo doesn't need to stress about him because Kennedy isn't going to be talking to him anymore."

"You sure?" Dieter asked skeptically.

"She's fucking done with him," I snapped. "She promised me this morning."

She wouldn't risk it anymore. She wouldn't risk *me* for whatever kind of solace Bryan had been trying to offer her.

Dieter accepted my nixing of the Bryan topic with a humph, and we resumed our work.

After leaving Kennedy's this morning, I'd felt this rush of adrenaline. A surge of power and domination. It was a wicked fascination, but she'd made me feel this crazy chemical intoxication. It still swarmed in my veins, like white rapids. I'd never been so alpha. And she'd never screamed my name louder.

I couldn't even stop smiling when I'd gotten back to school. Talan had kept making fun of me during lunch because she thought I was *smizing*, which I'd learned meant smiling with my eyes, as if the smile from my mouth wasn't enough of a dead giveaway. And, even though Dieter was unknowingly putting doubts in my head, I still *smized*, thinking about it.

But I made a mental note to get ahold of Kennedy's phone and make sure she'd truly cut ties. If I saw a text to her from him again…let's just say, I'd better not.

The drinking was bothering me, too, but I was keeping that knowledge and problem to myself. Our friends didn't need to know if she was hitting rock bottom. If she was already feeling like this, I doubted our friends knowing would help at all.

I didn't know if I was more concerned or angry about this new development. It was equal parts, I supposed. I didn't want her to feel like she needed to drown her sorrows, but I could understand her wanting to. But I was also pissed that she hadn't come to me before it got to that point. I'd have to keep a closer eye on her; that was for sure.

We spent an hour studying, not nearly enough to prepare for finals. And let's face it; I could barely concentrate on my studies with Kennedy taking over my thoughts.

We headed to one of Dieter's favorite restaurants. Some Asian-fusion place that I knew Kennedy would have hated if she had come with us.

Talan had ditched us, too, claiming she needed to watch her diet before some major audition she had coming up. I hated that she did that to herself, but she swore, it wasn't all that bad. That she enjoyed the challenges. She was too thin as it was, but I guessed that was a thing for serious dancers.

"So, did you ever find out if you had to live in the athletic dorms or a team house or whatever?" Chase asked me as our server refilled our drinks. "We finally picked a house, and I think it's perfect."

Shit. I'd completely spaced on living arrangements because I'd been so occupied with Kennedy.

I knew I didn't want to live in the dorms, and if it was between that and a team house, I'd choose the latter, but what I really wanted was to live with my friends and have my own space for when Kennedy came and visited. But, now, I was even rethinking that situation. I didn't want her to just come visit. I wanted her to be there—permanently.

That was an idea I knew her mother would never let fly without some serious grief, if at all.

Kennedy wouldn't even talk about her college plans, so there was no way to tell if she'd even considered my research.

I pulled out my phone and scrolled to an email that one of the coaching assistants had sent to me about training camp. There was no specific information on housing for players, so I quickly shot off an email to find out.

"Is it close to campus, or will we have to commute?" I asked while I read through a couple of more emails from the coaches.

Lo and Chase had some sort of conversation with their eyes, and then they looked to me.

Chase spoke first, "It's a fifteen-minute drive from the stadium and practice field. But, before we even tell you where or show you pictures, just know, we had zero say in the final decision." His eyes rolled dramatically, like a preteen girl who hadn't gotten her way. "And it's way more than what we wanted, but Lo's dad and mom kind of took our wants and turned them into their wants."

I chuckled and nodded my head. I knew Lo's mom and dad well, and I knew that anything Mrs. Grande wanted, she would get—no ifs, ands, or buts about it. And, even though we lived in the same neighborhood and came from equal financial classes, Lo's mom let her money show. My parents were much more understated. They didn't like flashy, but they still liked nice and respectable.

"Am I even going to be able to afford to rent a room in this house?"

Mrs. Grande's taste was not cheap. I shuddered to think of the rent this was going to cost.

Lo sighed. Her lips turned down into a frown, and she rubbed at her left bicep with her right hand. "You won't have to worry about rent unless you want to make arrangements with my dad."

"But how much are we talking? Like, four grand a month split between the three of us?" I knew Austin was expensive and if Chase was warning me about Lo's parents being involved, then I should expect the worse.

I knew my parents wouldn't complain. College towns typically had higher rent, as people liked to take advantage of college kids when they could. But I still didn't want that kind of expense.

"There is no rent." Lo didn't elaborate any further but instead picked up her phone from the table and stared at it.

My eyebrow quirked up, and I glanced over to Chase. He shook his head. Why? I didn't know. The housing situation must have been a sore spot for him and Lo.

Sighing, he clarified, "They bought the house for Lo. Said it was a good investment, that they might even consider retiring there. Weather's nice and all that. They wanted us to be in a secure neighborhood, and to be honest, it's older couples pretty much. But it's close enough to campus to still live the college life."

"Okay…so…hit me. What's the price tag? And when do I get to see pictures?"

Wordlessly, Lo pushed her phone across the table to me. My eyes nearly popped out of their sockets when I saw the first picture.

Houses certainly were not cheap in Austin, but this one? *Holy shit.* It had to be in the millions.

"Whoa." I quickly glanced up to see Lo dropping her chin to her chest, like she was embarrassed. "I mean…wow. This place is legit. You sure your parents aren't relocating now?"

The house looked like it was custom-built with high cathedral ceilings and dark hardwood floors. The pool and the awesome outside patio with a stone fireplace and kitchen area really sold me. I could definitely see calling this place home for four years. It kind of reminded me of a huge Tuscan villa.

"Dad said if you wanted to live with us, you're more than welcome. And Chase's dad is adamant that he'll be at every home game, so the size of the house kind of works out. That way, our parents will always have a place to stay when they come visit."

Lo constantly made me question how she'd come from a family like hers. She never flaunted her money, like her mom did. It was humbling to see, and the way she shyly talked about the house just cemented that modesty.

"So, do you think you'll live with us?" she asked.

"I just have to make sure it's not mandatory to live somewhere else. But hell yes! If I don't have to, then I'm definitely moving in with you guys. I'll talk to your dad about rent and stuff. It wouldn't feel right otherwise." And I was pretty sure my parents wouldn't be comfortable with us not paying at least some kind of rent either. "So, just out of curiosity, what's the price tag on a place like this?"

Chase instantly glared at me.

"Never mind. I don't want to know."

I motioned zipping my lips to appease him. He hated when Lo was uncomfortable.

Dieter slipped back onto his chair. I never even saw him getting up, but I immediately noticed the flushed look on his face and the flustered way he fidgeted with his phone.

"It's three million, almost four," Dieter answered me before taking a deep breath and slipping his phone into his pocket. "Lo's all self-conscious about it. Doesn't want people to think she's entitled, which she is. That's just the way old money works."

He shot her a pointed look, and from the way she stayed silent with narrowed eyebrows and violent eyes, I knew he'd hit a nerve.

"Stop it, D," Chase commanded quietly.

"It's fine," Lo grumbled, resuming her own fidgeting with her phone.

For a group of really close friends, we felt awfully disconnected. That only made me think of Kennedy more and what was going to happen come July.

The waiter came and took our orders and we chatted throughout the meal about classes and finals.

It was hard to believe we'd graduating and going to college soon. I'd felt like we'd just started high school and now it was over.

Kennedy and I had just gotten together a little over a year ago but somehow it felt like I'd known her my whole life.

After we finished our meals and paid the bill I spent the ride home trying to come up with a plan to convince Kennedy to come to Texas even if it wasn't right away. If I could just get her to commit to coming, I'd make things work until she got there.

I'd always known deep down that she was the only girl I wanted by my side. These rocky roads we were traveling were hell compared to the smooth paved ones we'd traveled before. And the thing that I'd realized through it so far was...I loved her so damn much. No matter how many times she'd pushed me away or retreated into her own world, it could never make my heart feel anything but the strongest need for her.

Wednesday was one of the quickest days I'd ever experienced. The whole day, I was busy with actual studying. I didn't think my brain could have handled any more studying, and when the day was over, I skipped a training session and went home for a nap.

Kennedy had been tied up with her own studying. She'd even opted to skip lunch. She and Lo had barely said two words to each other that morning, which had made Chase and me nervous with prom being in a few days and all of us going together. I just wanted Kennedy to have a good time, but I didn't see how she would if she wasn't talking to her best friend.

The whole reason Lo had even agreed to go to prom was because of Kennedy. She and Chase had wanted to skip out and do their own thing, heading to the city for a concert, but Kennedy wouldn't have that. She'd begged and pleaded for Lo to go, and when that hadn't been enough, she'd brought cupcakes and formally asked her to prom. Lo couldn't resist after that. It was kind of funny and a bit of an ego punch to us guys since none of us had done anything cutesy to ask our girls to prom.

I slept most of the afternoon and early evening away. When I finally woke up, it was eight o'clock, and Kennedy was getting herself ready for bed when I called, so we barely talked.

Thursday started pretty much the same, except for when I coaxed Kennedy back to my house for lunch. I didn't take my hands off her, my mouth off her, until two hours later, and we'd missed a class. Then, I took her back to school and walked her to her last class, still looking flushed and dazed from our afternoon fun. I sported the cockiest grin of all.

I couldn't get enough of her, and she seemed to feel the same way. We spent the whole afternoon in my pool after school. Flirting and kissing. I finally felt like we were becoming *us* again. She was happier, not as withdrawn.

We left the serious topics alone. Kennedy seemed to shut down otherwise, and I was finally getting my girlfriend back. The one who didn't let anything hold her down.

After a late dinner, she drove home, sated from one more session of me showing her how much I worshipped her body. I crashed the moment I'd gotten her text, telling me she'd made it home safely.

Now, it was Friday, and Kennedy had seemed off since this morning. Her mood had gone from happy and content to sad and annoyed, and we'd only made it through half the day. She was starting to engage a little more with the group again, but she was still quiet and seemed to be in her own little world, constantly burying her nose in a book and not paying much attention to anyone.

I was starting to feel an agitation deep in my bones that vibrated and constantly nagged at me to find out what was going on with her, why she was freezing our friends out.

Surrounded by laughter and shouting in the cafeteria, I tugged one of her earbuds out, and so the group wouldn't become suspicious like me, I whispered in her ear, "Why so quiet?"

Kennedy turned her face toward mine and caught my lips with a swift, soft kiss. I licked my lips and could taste her favorite strawberry lip gloss. When she pulled back and her eyes fluttered open, the usual light gray of her eyes was much darker.

What's going on in those storm-cloud eyes, Kennedy?

A small smile graced her lips when my stare lingered.

Her hair was down and around her shoulders, the golden blonde a tad messier than what I was used to. She usually had it perfectly straight or in fancy curls that spiraled down her back. This was more I-just-woke-up-like-this hair. She looked sexy as all hell like that. Her outfit was also on the slouchier side with a baggy off-the-shoulder top that showed her black bra strap. She kept tugging at the top to keep it covered, but every time she moved her slender arm, it would fall right back down and expose her delicate shoulder that sported one of my lighter love bites that was still noticeable.

What could I say? She'd turned me into a carnal beast. And I hadn't received any complaints yet.

Her kiss had wiped the question from my mind, and I lost my train of thought, staring into her eyes and eyeing her lips. Then, she gave me a quick smooch on the cheek and placed the earbud back in her ear.

"So…" Lo started to talk.

I turned my head back to the table and our surrounding friends.

Lo glanced my way before quickly looking to Kennedy and then back to me. "We decided that we're just going to take my car tomorrow."

From the corner of my eye, I caught Dieter's head whip up. Abandoning his lunch, he dropped his fork to his tray. The clash of the fork hitting the tray made everyone at our table turn to him. He then seemed to glare at me, burning my cheek with his laser eyes. When my head turned minimally to his and our eyes locked, he shifted his eyes toward Kennedy before coming back to glare at me.

I sat up straighter and draped my arm over the back of Kennedy's chair. She never bothered to look up.

"I thought we all decided to take my mom's Escalade?" I questioned hesitantly.

I watched Chase rub the back of Lo's hand, and then he exhaled deeply, his whole chest caving with the action. "We just think it'd be better."

"Yeah, sounds better to me," Dieter scoffed sarcastically as he pushed his tray across the table. "You guys just going to let this fester?"

Gross word, D.

His eyes darted to Kennedy again, but I could hear her music, so she was clueless to us as she looked down at her book.

I'd thought maybe she'd try to clear the air by now, but she was still avoiding the situation. I didn't understand girls and how they let stuff burrow under their skin, eating them alive, instead of just stepping up and fixing the problem. All guys were Mr. Fix Its compared to no-budge-on-the-grudge girls.

Kennedy was in her own world while we tried to keep it together for her. While I tried to save her from all the falling pieces.

"It's none of your business, Dieter." Talan was staring at him with daggers in her eyes and a snarl on her lips. Her hair was in a tight bun today. Her faded red T-shirt was a size too big.

I loved the way she had tuned into my protective state and was willing to back me up.

His eyes rolled severely, and a hollow pit formed in my stomach, but it quickly filled with uncertainty, not knowing what was about to happen.

"Where's Max, T? Shouldn't you be helping him rub one out?"

Talan sucked in a deep breath and pinned him with a hateful glare. I'd never seen her face contort with so much anger and disgust, especially toward Dieter. Recently, they'd done nothing but argue and make little jabs at each other, acting like ridiculous toddlers.

"You're such an asshole." She seethed. Then, she stood quickly, flipping him off as she left the table.

My eyes followed her as she quickly dashed through the cafeteria doors, and when she was gone, I looked back to Dieter. There was no remorse on his face, just a somber expression.

"Really, D?" I asked, scolding.

He'd never treated her like that before. And, if he had, it was never in front of all of us.

Now, I was pissed off at him. He couldn't treat her like that. She was like my little sister, and if that was how he treated my family, then we were going to have problems.

"I think it's best if we all drive separately," Lo commented quietly, trying to defuse a ticking bomb.

Chase leaned into her ear and whispered something. Her eyes shut tightly, and I looked away quickly. I didn't like seeing her struggle or be upset.

Lo was just like Talan was to me—family. And I hurt when they hurt.

"So, are we not all going to eat at my house before?" I hedged back into the topic that had started all the uncomfortable vibes. "My dad's already bought all the food, but if you guys don't want to…I guess I'll just let him know before he starts prepping tonight."

This time, Chase spoke, but his eyes stayed focused on Lo, "No, we're still gonna do everything the same, except for the rides."

I nodded, letting the conversation come to an end.

The bell signaling the end of lunch sounded, and we all stood to leave, the chairs sliding back and scraping against the linoleum all at once, amplifying the noise. Kennedy and I weaved through the students as I walked her to class. I carried her backpack and kept our hands laced as we dodged rowdy underclassmen.

"Is there a reason why you basically ignored everyone at lunch?" I tried not to sound too concerned about it, too tired of her shutting down on me when it came to serious topics.

Kennedy was usually the one to keep conversation flowing, and if there ever was confrontation, she was the one with the ability to calm everyone. My normal peacekeeper was suddenly Miss Passive. I didn't like it.

We stopped in front of the classroom, and Kennedy shrugged her shoulders, her top slipping off her shoulder yet again. "I'm sorry. I wanted to focus on studying. I've been really behind in Anatomy."

I edged in closer to her. "I just want prom to be a good time for you."

Her lips tipped up in a small smile. "It will be because I'll be with you. And I get to wear a pretty dress."

Laughing, I bent lower to kiss her strawberry-glossed lips. The one-minute warning bell rang just as I stepped closer, and she stepped back, breaking our contact and inhaling deeply.

"You'd better get to class." She lifted on to the tips of her toes and kissed my cheek. "I'll meet you after school." Then, she ducked into the room without a backward glance.

Chapter 19

Kennedy

I hissed out, air fiercely rushing between my teeth, as my back hit the side of Kyle's truck with a thump, and I cringed but didn't stop him. He was giving me exactly what I wanted from him. It was almost a punishment to myself for everything I continually screwed up in secret, behind his back.

He wouldn't understand, a voice whispered tauntingly in my head.

"Get out of your head," he commanded me with a whisper in my ear.

Little did he know, I was already out of my head. There was no way I could be in my right mind now because, every time I ventured back in, I was swarmed with anger. Sadness. And the worst one…guilt.

"Stay with me tonight." It was another command, but I didn't even get a chance to respond before he was pulling my face to his, nipping my lips and staring into my eyes with a savage desire, possessive and demanding. Then, he was kissing me mute.

Pushing me against his truck, his hips ground into me. My entire body heated up, my skin surely turning red with desire. His right hand skimmed down my neck, moving further down, until his hand was at the hem of my shirt and then under it. He moved up and up until he was cupping my breast in his hand and squeezing tenderly.

"This week has been crazy," Kyle said as he pulled away. Then, he dived into my neck to suck and bite.

He'd been marking my skin with his lips and teeth for two days. Something he'd never really done before.

I reached up with both hands and gingerly tugged his hair. "No more marks. Prom. My dress," I panted. "I'm already going to have to cover the ones you left yesterday."

"I like it." He smirked wickedly when he pulled back. "Mine."

He leaned back in and bit hard but quick. The sudden flood between my legs was turning me into mush. I was a puddle for him. Maybe I didn't want him to stop. My body sure as heck didn't.

"I can't stay tonight—" I gasped and lost my words when he thrust into me again, his jeans and my own keeping us separate.

"Why?" His hands grazed up and down my waist.

Even though I had an honest reason why I couldn't, it wasn't why I wouldn't.

"My mom's friend is in town and coming over for dinner."

His hands froze.

"What friend?" he asked cautiously.

I knew exactly what he thought because, when my mom had texted me earlier this morning, the same thought had crossed my own mind. Luckily, it really was just a friend. A female. Thank goodness.

I slightly pushed him back to calm my body. It was on fire and felt like it was zinging with untethered energy. Even my toes were tingling.

"Some woman she works with."

He placed his hand on the driver's window above me and leaned in.

"I've met her before. She's kind of rude and stuck-up, but she's nice…sometimes."

His other hand moved back to my waist, playing with the hem of my slouchy off-the-shoulder top.

"After, I want you in my bed."

"I'll try," I lied.

I was sitting on my bed with the door wide open.

Dinner had been an awkward fiasco of halfhearted compliments and sentiments. Shelly, the president of one of the nonprofits Mom worked for, was rude in a roundabout nice way— if that even made sense. The woman was impossible to get a grip on, I couldn't decide if she was someone to trust or someone to be wary of, and it was hard to tell if she was complimenting you or insulting you, but you'd still think she was being kind with her sparkling green eyes and wide smile. She'd never come around often before, but the way they'd talked over dinner was like they hung out every day.

They had drunk wine in copious amounts and giggled like everything was the funniest thing they'd ever heard.

I'd endured forty-five minutes of their high-pitched, highly annoying laughter and me being ignored for the most part. When Shelly had pointed out my hickeys and bite marks scattered across my bare shoulder, Mom had scowled and tsked, like she actually had a leg to stand on.

At least Kyle and I are faithful, I wanted to shout out.

Then, I'd excused myself to do some homework up in my room, which was where I was now, lying on my bed, blindly staring at my English notes.

I half-tuned into the clinking of dishes and the sound of the sink filling. It wasn't until Shelly asked a question that I zoned in completely.

"What does your daughter think of him?"

At the mention of me, I rolled off my bed and tiptoed to the top of the stairs. Dishes continued to clank and tinker. My mom never liked to leave dirty dishes for later, always making sure they were done and put away after every meal.

I heard Mom sigh. I imagined her hands swirling in the sink full of sudsy water while she hand-washed the plates and forks we'd used.

"She doesn't really know."

"Do you think that's smart?" Shelly asked softly, a slight shocked pitch in her voice.

"I don't want her to think I'm trying to replace him."

I rolled my eyes and snorted to myself. That was rich. She'd cheated. Jesus, she'd replaced Dad before he was even dead.

How could she think I would think anything other than that?

"She just needs time. I'll tell her when she's not grieving," Mom said dejectedly.

Am I still grieving?

I couldn't tell. I just knew I had to push all my emotions aside, or they would swallow me alive, like a Florida sinkhole.

And why isn't she still grieving?

"You're going to his lake house this weekend?"

"Yes. It's a good weekend to do it. We're going to leave after I take some pictures of Kennedy before her prom."

I could hear the smile in both of their voices.

My head instantly hurt from listening to her sound so damn happy. I tiptoed back to my room, strategically avoiding all the creaky floorboards. One of the plus sides of living here my entire life was, I knew where all the creaky boards were.

Grabbing my phone from the edge of my bed, I pulled up the messages that Bryan had sent me earlier, trying to talk me into coming to a party at Dylan's. I'd originally told him I'd think about it. Then, with Kyle and my guilt, I'd texted him back and told him no. He'd been texting me every hour since, trying to talk me into it. I sent him one last text to tell him I needed to forget about him and everything that'd been going on.

I closed out of my messages, feeling overwhelmed again, and tossed my phone behind myself. Just as I heard it hit the pillows, it pinged with a message. I had a feeling it was Bryan again, so I ignored it and went to the bathroom to brush my teeth. When I came back, it pinged again. Letting curiosity overtake me, I went and checked it.

But, instead of Bryan, it was Kyle.

Kyle: You coming over tonight?

I texted him back, a pinch to my heart as I pulled further away from him.

Me: Mom wants me to stay in.

His response was quick but had nothing to do with me coming over.

Kyle: Call Lo. Fix it. She's worried about you.

I couldn't do that though. She was the one person who would see right through me.

And who the hell is he to command me to fix something?

I loved that he cared so much, but lately, he had been a tad suffocating to me. Like with the constant texting and trying to control how and when I dealt with things. It made my brain ache with frustration. My temple pulsed with the oncoming anxiety, and a sharp pain probed behind my right eye.

I didn't bother with a response. Before I even had a chance to put my phone down though, it was ringing and vibrating in my hand. An unknown number flashed across the screen, and even though I usually ignored those calls, something told me to just answer it, so I did.

"Meet us around the corner," was all the deep voice said before he hung up.

I frowned at my phone. I didn't recognize that voice at all, but it was definitely male. It could have been Dieter or maybe Chase. *But whose unrecognized number would either have been calling me on?*

Against my better judgment, I slipped on a pair of black flats, grabbed my phone, and then stealthily crept down the stairs. Mom and Shelly were still chatting away in the kitchen, half-hushed and half-slurring their words and jokes from the wine. I carefully opened the front door, cringing when it groaned, and then the screen door squeaked. Mom hushed Shelly, trying to see if she heard anything else, but Shelly cracked up for some reason, causing Mom to laugh, too.

I quickly slipped out of the door as silently as I could. I made sure to keep the knob twisted until the door was all the way closed to keep it from latching back too loudly. I took light steps down the porch and then jogged across the front yard to the sidewalk.

The grass in our front yard was slightly overgrown, another effect of my father not being here. He'd never let the yard work go untouched. Dad had loved to be outside and working.

I remembered the time he'd decided to plant flowers along our front porch. The day was crystal clear in my memory, as if I were still living the moment.

"Do you know what I love most about today?" Dad questioned as he dug at the flower bed he'd just spent the whole morning on.

I lay on my stomach on a porch step, shading in Belle's dress in my new princess coloring book. My hair was in a French braid that Mom had done earlier while she sat inside at the bay window, looking out, and I sat on the newly painted white floorboards.

"What do you love most about today, Daddy?" My voice was squeaky and distracted. I was more concerned about staying in the lines of Belle's dress.

When he didn't answer, I looked up, and our identical eyes locked. He stuck his tongue out as he crossed his eyes, and I giggled at his silly face. My laughter and his deep chuckle floated through the warm air.

"I love that I get to see the most beautiful angel and hear her laugh." He gazed at me like I was that most beautiful angel, but I knew it was Mommy.

He went back to planting the flowers Mom had picked out last week. I looked up to the bay window, realizing Mom was no longer sitting there, reading her book, but standing and watching us closely. A bright smile lit her face when she noticed me watching her. Then, she turned away from the window and went farther into the house.

Before I got stuck in the happy memory, I looked both ways down the road, not sure which way to go, before I decided to head to the right. When I turned the corner, I spotted a red sedan idling by the curb, the lights off. I walked up to the passenger window that was way too tinted to see through. The window rolled down, making a humming noise, and Bryan's smug face came into view.

"Oh," I said, confused. Then, when Dylan leaned over the console and into Bryan's space, it clicked. "You were the unknown caller."

"Get in," Dylan demanded.

"Why?"

"Because I said so."

"I thought you were someone else."

"But it didn't stop you from showing up, now did it? And you knew, deep down, chances were, it was going to be one of us showing up, didn't you? So, just get in." Dylan was too cocky for his own good. His demanding tone only succeeded in pissing me off.

"No."

"Come on, Angel. You told me you needed to forget about everything, so just get in. I'm here to help you have a good time." Bryan propped his head and arms out the window, trying to lure me in.

He looked like a stranger who was trying to get me to take his lollipop before he kidnapped me. It wasn't a funny scenario, but the image of him holding a lollipop almost made me laugh.

"I think you misinterpreted my text. I said, I needed to forget *you*." I shoved my finger into his forehead.

Shrugging, he said, "I can help you with both then."

"Kiblen, just get in the fucking car before I get out and *make* you." Dylan was becoming frustrated. His constant rev of the engine made sure I knew it, too.

"That's kidnapping."

Just as I was going to walk away, my phone pinged with another text.

Kyle: I know it will help if you just talk to her.

I sighed at his text.

Then, I made my decision. I slid into the backseat of Dylan's red sedan. The plush, vented leather seat enveloped me, and I sat back as I sighed, annoyed, because I was such an idiot for getting in this car.

Dylan turned around as the door shut, smirking and then winking. His hat sat low on the back of his head, the flat bill almost sticking straight up off his head. When he turned back around and started to drive off, I leaned forward and thumped his hat down over his face.

"You look stupid, wearing a hat at night," I said spitefully as I settled back into my seat and slid the seat belt across my body.

"Oh! She's feisty at night." He chuckled darkly. "Careful, Kiblen. You just might turn me on."

"You're disgusting."

Silence took over the vehicle as we drove. Bryan continued to skip through music during the thirty-minute drive to Dylan's house. I quietly looked out the window, watching signs go by and trees blur into one fluid blob. The sky was overcast and ominous.

As we pulled into Dylan's large circle driveway, I took quick notice of the fact that only a small number of cars were here, nothing like the last party, and all the cars were expensive. Most of them, I didn't even know what they were. Dylan parked right in front of the entrance door and got out. Bryan pulled my door open as soon as he was standing.

"Why do I get the feeling, this isn't a high school party?" I asked, following them up to the door.

When Dylan opened the door, a wave of sound hit me. Clinking glasses, light piano music, and cheerful laughter and conversations were taking place as we entered the dramatic foyer with the massive, sparkling chandelier above that always caught my attention.

"Hope Masters knows you like big, shiny things," Bryan whispered by my ear.

I placed my hand on his face and shoved him to the side. He was always so unfiltered with me. Always flirtatious and in my face about things. And, even though he was this sketchy human being with a drug business and questionable morals, he was so easy to be around. He never made me feel...well...anything.

A few men in business suits and women in cocktail dresses stood and fluttered around the house with glasses of champagne and tumblers full of amber liquor. Immediately feeling out of place in my jeans and flats with my hair not even brushed today, I tried to pull Bryan back.

"What are we doing here?" I whisper-hissed.

He just laughed and walked off. I didn't know anyone here, obviously, so I followed him to the same door that led to the basement.

I walked down the dimly lit stairs and into the large room that I'd only been in one other time. That same feeling I'd had the first time I was here immediately took over my mind and body—uneasiness yet the desire to not care.

Just like last time, there was a handful of what I assumed to be high school or college kids lounging around and talking. The same projection screen was on with music playing through the speakers. I looked over to the bar to see Bryan mixing a few drinks.

Slowly making my way over, I pulled out a black leather barstool with a high back and took a seat. "When you said there was a party at Dylan's, I didn't think you meant his parents were having a fancy soiree."

He pushed over a glass with a murky mix in it. I raised the glass to my lips and took a tentative sip, just like the last time. My mind always told me to second-guess his drink-making, but scarily enough, I had only done so for a brief second before taking my first swallow. He eyed me the whole time, eyes roving over me, from head to chest, the rest of my body hidden below the bar.

There was a fog in his eyes, something I'd never seen before, but it wasn't his normal mischievous, devilish glint. It was more playful.

"Hey, Kiblen." Dylan's voice was starting to grate on my nerves.

I rotated my body to look over at him lounging on the couch. His body was spread out, relaxed, and taking more space than necessary. My eyebrow rose, my silent acknowledgment to him.

His finger crooked at me, beckoning me to come over to where he sat. I looked back to Bryan, and he slightly scowled at Dylan, but as soon as his eyes switched back to me, noticing my eyes on him, he schooled his features and smirked.

He was being exceptionally quiet tonight, and I wasn't sure how I was supposed to interpret that. He usually had plenty of things to say even if I didn't. I found myself observing him and his friends more than I engaged.

I slid off the barstool and went to take a seat on the couch. "What's with the fancy party?" I asked Dylan as I sat.

His grin put me on edge.

"My dad works in investments. He likes to have fancy parties for rich people looking to get richer."

"And I'm here because…"

"Because Bryan has a thing for lost souls and corrupting good little girls like you."

My jaw dropped open and then snapped shut. I glowered at his arrogant smile. Then, I chastised myself because, in all reality, I'd already known that. I knew exactly what Bryan was like. I knew what lengths he would go to if he never got what he wanted. That small bit of knowledge put my danger sensors on high alert. Because, when all of this was over—and it would end—he wouldn't get what he was after. Not from me. And that just might piss him off.

"How do you know him?" I checked over my shoulder to catch Bryan talking to a petite redhead.

When I shifted back around, Dylan's lips tilted wickedly, like he knew a secret. "We go to school together."

"Why aren't you guys at school now?" It suddenly occurred to me that most universities were still in session, yet they were home when most college students were preparing for finals.

His smirk died a little as he reached for the iPad to mess with the music. "We got into some trouble. My dad arranged for us both to be able to finish our finals at home and online."

"What kind of trouble?"

"Need-to-know trouble."

He changed the songs without even letting a full song finish, seeming irritated. I stopped asking questions and just silently shrank back, letting the oversize couch swallow me up. I watched as the younger crowd—I assumed, sons and daughters of the parents upstairs—milled around and talked. Some were smoking cigarettes and what I was sure was more than just a tobacco-filled stick.

It felt like I'd been sitting and staring aimlessly for ages. Bryan had disappeared. Dylan was talking to some guy sitting next to him. A girl in a short black tube dress and sky-high purple heels was dancing around with her other friend who was dressed almost identically, but her dress was red, and her shoes were black. They seemed to be in another world as they danced and ground into each other. Their eyes rolled, and their heads lolled. The way they danced was like they were hearing a different song than the rest of us, completely off beat and sluggish.

I sat there for only a few more minutes before I couldn't take it anymore. Even Dylan had disappeared while I was gawking at the girls. I stood and started to head to what I hoped was the bathroom.

I flicked the light switch up. One lone lamp in the corner gave off a dim light. In the adjacent corner were two chairs, one occupied by Bryan. It was a bedroom. A large chaise lounge was at the end of the bed. Paintings of forests and old cabins adorned the olive walls.

My eyes swept back to Bryan, who was fidgeting with things on a low table in front of him.

"Ah, she's come to find us."

My head whipped back toward the bed. Dylan was sprawled out on the bed with his neck at an awkward angle as he gazed at his phone.

"What are you guys doing in here, in the dark?" I asked as I veered closer.

"Shut the door," was all Bryan replied. His head never rose. He stayed completely focused on whatever was in front of him.

I carefully pushed the door closed, hesitating to be alone with them.

When it latched shut, I moved to the chaise and perched my butt on the edge.

"Doesn't it make you nervous to be in a room with two guys you don't really know, the door shut, and a loud party going on beyond?" Dylan questioned with an unreadable tone.

I couldn't tell if he was being sarcastic, curious, devious, or plotting, but he'd read my mind exactly.

I didn't say anything because, yes, it did make me nervous. It was written all over my face. My body language. My lack of response. The way I shifted stiffly, teetering on the edge of the chaise, wondering if I should book it the heck out of there.

My gaze trailed back over to Bryan as he stopped messing with all the little baggies on the table and started to count the cash that sat in a pile next to them. His eyes latched on to mine as he folded and put a rubber band around the money before he placed it in his backpack on the floor. He leaned back up. His hand lifted to his mouth, and he popped something in, washing whatever it was down with a tumbler full of amber liquid.

"Are you taking whatever those girls are on out there?" I asked cautiously.

He smirked, his head shaking faintly, as he leaned back and continued to take large swallows of his drink.

In the silence that followed, I tried not to focus on the bags he had on the table before him.

I walked over and sat in the chair angled to the side of him. "What's this?" I picked up a bag with two blue pills in it.

"X."

I picked up a bag with white powder. "Cocaine?"

"Yeah, blow."

"Why blow? Don't you sniff it?"

All he did was nod, his eyes narrowing slightly.

"Marijuana?" I asked as I picked up the last bag.

He only nodded.

"And those?" I pointed to the last bag with three little orange pills.

"Xanax."

"What did you take?"

"Ibuprofen."

I tossed the bag down and rolled my eyes. "Liar." My arms crossed under my chest, as I was instantly annoyed with his lies. I wished people would stop treating me as if I were so fragile and just be *honest* with me.

Dylan laughed at my expense. "You're so sheltered."

"I'm serious," Bryan said.

Dylan dramatically rolled off the bed. "He only smokes weed. Don't you know, dealers don't do the products? That could become a problem, an addiction, a death sentence by the boss." The way he spoke as he crept calmly over to the table was taunting and aggressive and full of sarcasm. He picked up the bag of white powder and threw a hundred-dollar bill down. "Luckily, I'm not the dealer."

"Obviously not," I scoffed, rolling my eyes to high heaven.

"Those girls out there"—Dylan pointed to the little blue pills—"this is what they're on." He pointed to a bag of orange pills. "Those? That's what half of the middle-aged women upstairs are on because half of their husbands are cheating on them, and they can't handle being around their mistresses." He held up the white powder. "And this? This is what every rich fucker with a God complex is on."

His serious expression, the way his eyes narrowed, and his looming posture sent chills up my spine. I could feel the goose bumps scattering across my arms.

Bryan stiffened in his chair, his spine straightening. His eyes focused on Dylan, who'd stepped back and walked over to the side of the bed. He took a credit card out of his wallet.

I turned away and focused on Bryan. My mind was trying to come to terms with everything that was happening.

"Do those pills really make you feel better?" I quietly asked him, a mere whisper.

"It's not about feeling better. It's about feeling less. You came here with me, saying you just wanted to forget. Forget how shitty you discovered your life really is. Maybe even forget how controlling your boyfriend is becoming. Or does he not know?"

No emotion showed on his face as he kept talking, "I bet, after he found out you'd been talking to me, he became possessive and rough, making sure you knew who you belonged to. All the while, he's been pissing his pants, terrified you just might see a different light than the one he shines on you." He leaned forward, his elbows resting on his knees. "So, do you want me to help you with that pressure and those thoughts you're trying to forget? Or are you going to sit there and judge my methods?"

"My life isn't shitty. It's…complicated."

He reached for his phone when it vibrated on the table.

"I didn't think this was your method," I whispered. Hearing about his reputation and witnessing it were two totally different things. I had a hard time seeing the bad.

"Oh, come on, Kennedy. Yes, you did. Stop fucking with me. What do you want me to do to help you forget?"

I stood up and paced. This was so fucked up. I was so screwed up for being here.

God, what would Kyle think of me?

He wouldn't understand me for considering this. He'd always thought of me as the happiest girl, the one with the glass half-full all the time. He didn't understand that I was breaking apart at the seams. Every meticulous stitch in my perfectly normal life was stretching and unraveling completely.

I couldn't grasp reality because everything felt so nightmarish. No one understood. I didn't even understand. I just needed the edge to be sanded down. I needed the stark reality to fog a little, so I could simply cope for a little while longer. I never thought I'd let grief take me down like this. It would have happened eventually. I'd thought I would have years before I lost my dad.

It wasn't only that though. I thought I had been grieving okay. Getting through the days. Letting the good memories overshadow the recent bad memories of losing him. Then, Mom had brought home a new man, invited him into our home, and crapped all over that progress. I'd started to resent her and fear that she was the cause of me losing the person I had been closest to on this earth.

Realizing that made me shake and tremble with anxiety of the truth. My throat tightened with the effort to fight off my tears.

Bryan stood and took one step to get closer to me. He reached for my hip and pulled me in. Backing up, his knees hit the back of the chair, and he leisurely sat down, pulling me with him the whole time. I stood firmly between his legs even though he tugged a little more. His intent was clear, but I wouldn't give him the satisfaction.

He sighed and rolled his neck. Popping noises made me cringe.

"Kennedy, look at me. Let me see your eyes when you try to lie to me." His eyes dropped from mine, scaling my body and gleaming with lust.

As he tilted his head up to catch my eyes again, his hands stayed on my hips, and I stupidly let them stay there, guilt worming its way through my heart and soul. I knew this was so, so wrong.

"This isn't right." I pulled back and went to sit on the chaise lounge.

My head was absolute chaos. It was a classic cliché of devil and angel on my shoulders.

Bryan didn't hesitate to follow me. He towered over me before he squatted down. His hands moved to my knees. I locked them together tightly, and his lips tilted up deviously. One hand slid higher, testing me. He kept sliding it up, putting the slightest pressure down. He started to trail back down but moved inward, teasing the line where my legs connected. I gasped. I was shocked that he'd make such a bold move, but then again, I wasn't shocked at all. Let's face it; this was bad-boy Bryan. No limits. No rules. No fucks given.

"I'm not having sex with you." I found my bravado and made sure he knew that was a line I would never cross.

His hand stilled, the pressure easing.

I started to shake from nerves.

He noticed and grinned. "I can make you feel less. Or I can make you feel more."

He casually stood, and I leaned back to avoid being level with his crotch, but he followed, leaning forward while I went backward. He moved swiftly, roughly planting his hands on either side of my shoulders, one knee propped up by my hip, and his lips came into contact with my ear. The cage he put me in made my heart pound relentlessly with frightened adrenaline.

My breath hitched, and I shook even harder. Nerves took over. I didn't want this.

His breath was hot and searing, fanning against my cheek like a hot summer breeze. Then, he whispered, "Tell me, Kennedy, what do you want more?"

My eyes closed.

God, I wanted it all. But not like this and not with him.

I moved my arms up and shoved hard at his chest, but he didn't budge. I locked eyes with him, giving him a silent warning that I wasn't okay with this and not to fuck with me like this. He gradually inched back and then stood on his own. A cocky, daring smirk was on his thin lips.

"I need a drink." I stood and walked out.

I'd chosen my own destruction. And, while I wanted to escape, I didn't want to ruin my damn life.

Chapter 20

Kyle

Chase, Dieter, and Max were all at my house. We were playing Xbox to pass the day. They'd come over right after breakfast with their garment bags over their shoulders, looking like they'd just rolled out of bed. Just like me.

"So, she actually kicked you out?" I asked as I messed with my phone, playing Crossy Road and dying every five seconds while they played against each other on the Xbox. This simple fucking iPhone game was addictive.

Chase nodded while stuffing his face with chips between kills. He talked around his food, "Told me to consider it a practice run."

"Isn't that something you do for your wedding?" Max laughed. "You guys are already playing house."

"For real," Dieter commented over the TV, music, and us laughing. "You guys have lived together for, like, a year. I'd have been tapping it on the daily."

A chip flew through the air and nailed Dieter on the cheek. "Shut up," Chase groaned.

After dying for the millionth time on my game, I switched back over to browsing classes at UT. Chase was going in as undecided. Lo was going for Graphic Design. Dieter had told me he was going for a degree in Women's Studies. I'd laughed at that one and told him he didn't need a degree. I was still undecided myself. I couldn't really pinpoint what I wanted, outside of Kennedy and football.

"What are you concentrating so hard on?" Chase asked.

"Majors and classes."

"Did you decide on what you wanted to do about housing?"

"During training, I have to stay with the team. After that…if you guys still don't mind, I wanna move in."

"Dude, yes. We still don't mind. This is going to be an epic four years!"

I grinned at one of my best friends. I couldn't fucking wait.

How cliché would it be if I said we were on the precipice of greatness? Too cliché?

Yeah, I thought so.

"Is Kennedy still going to Wheaton?" Chase hammered his thumbs against the remote, arms shifting around wildly, trying to take out Max's soldier.

I shrugged and stood up. "I don't want her to."

"Where else would she go?"

I shrugged again. "I tried to talk her into deferring for a semester and moving to Austin with me. She could apply to Texas Christian University for the spring semester if she really wanted to go to a Christian school. I know it's important. And TCU is a hell of a lot closer than Wheaton. She shot me down. And, when I briefly brought up other schools in Austin or even just going to UT, she just wasn't having it."

"You guys going to do the distance thing then?" Chase grimaced. He hated being away from Lo.

I just nodded. I wasn't going to give Kennedy up. No fucking way. So, that was our only option if she didn't come with me.

"I'm gonna hit the shower first." I pulled my shirt up from the back of my neck and whipped it off, throwing it to the corner of my room. "We'll need to go pick up the girls by five for pictures."

I shut myself into my bathroom where I finished stripping and stepped into the shower.

I stood under the hot water for longer than necessary to be clean, letting it beat down on my back, as my mind flitted through all the shit I had to figure out.

I could hear the metaphorical clock ticking in the background, counting down to my inevitable departure for training camp. And with that ticking clock came the struggle of leaving Kennedy behind. I didn't want her to fall deeper into that quiet depression she was trying to climb all the way out of.

Stepping out of the shower, I wrapped a large towel around my waist and tucked the edge in to keep it up. I shaved the stubble I'd been letting grow, only because, a week ago, Kennedy had told me she loved the feel of it. But Mom would have fussed if I hadn't gotten rid of it for pictures.

My face, smooth as silk, made me look like a little kid, but whatever. I grabbed another towel to dry my hair and walked back into my room, roughly scrubbing the towel over my head. The guys were still in the same spots in front of the TV, and Dieter sat at my desk. I grabbed a pair of boxers and basketball shorts and slipped them on before I whipped the towel at Dieter.

"How's Shay getting here?" I asked.

His prom date was from Rivers, so I wasn't sure if he had to go pick her up or if she was driving down.

"She's at Chase's already."

My head whipped to Chase. He was looking over at me, too.

"Uh, how did I not know about that?" Chase asked, switching his gaze over to Dieter.

Dieter pushed up from the chair and walked toward my bathroom. "Because Lo set it up. I didn't know until this morning. She didn't want Shay to feel left out since we were all coming here for dinner."

"Oh. Well, yeah, that makes sense. My girl knows her shit." Chase laughed it off but looked at me with wide eyes and a weird frown on his face. When Dieter disappeared into the bathroom and we heard the shower start, he grinned and tried to stifle his laugh. "Bet T is *loving* that." Chase said under his breath.

"That girl was so weird at his party. I don't think she said ten words. She just grinned awkwardly and laughed at the most random shit." Walking over to the chair Dieter vacated, I took a seat and pulled up some music. "Have you talked to Lo?"

He shook his head as he grabbed his phone off the floor. "Not since this morning."

"Hey, Kyle?"

I heard my mom shout over the music, and then there was a soft knock on the door. I turned the music down and told her to come in.

She partially stepped in and then leaned against the doorframe. "Oh, good, you boys are getting ready. I want to do some pictures of just you and the guys before you go get the girls and are all starstruck. Chase, your mom sent me some pictures of their hair and makeup, and they are stunning." Mom was smiling so wide, happy as could be.

"Mom, seriously? Are you about to cry?"

Her eyes were glistening just a little, but her smile was taking over her entire face.

Clearing her throat, she shook her head. "No, I just can't believe it's my baby boy's senior prom. And the girls have been over so often, they feel like my own now, too." Her hands clapped, and she shook her hair out behind her. "Okay, so thirty minutes." She pointed at me and then the guys. "Be dressed and downstairs." Then, she was slipping back through the door and down the hallway.

"She was totally about to cry," Max commented from the couch with a cheesy smile on his face.

I grabbed a mini foam football from my desk and tossed it at him, but he dodged before it could hit him.

"Can you guys go shower in the guest room and the bathroom down the hall?" I swiveled back around and turned the music back up. I was amped up for the night and to see Kennedy all dressed up and gorgeous.

I sent her a text.

Me: Send me a pic of your beautiful face.

She sent me a picture of her hair all puffed out. I hoped it wasn't staying like that. Her gray eyes were lined with a fierce black, making her eyes almost look sinister, and her long lashes made her eyes look huge. Another one came through, and she was half-pouting in the picture, her lips shiny and glossed, someone behind her clearly pulling on her hair.

I sent her a picture of my abs, feeling vain and wanting to show off what I knew she loved. She sent back a heart emoji, and I told her I couldn't wait to see her all dressed up and gorgeous.

We'd been doing this flirty-texting thing for a while, but as we had grown closer and started spending more time together, I realized we'd let that taper off. I never wanted her to feel like I didn't want her, so I'd been texting her more, especially when we were apart, making sure she knew I loved her so much and that I thought about her all the time. Maybe I had a little bit of a hidden agenda behind all the texts, but I couldn't help it. I only wanted her fixated on me. Not anyone else. And certainly not Bryan fucking Endears.

As "Female Robbery" by The Neighbourhood played, I thought about how I was going to tell Kennedy that I would be leaving the day after Fourth of July. I was still trying to figure out a way I could persuade her to come with me. Even though I'd be busy with training and practices, we could still finish up the summer and get our bearings in the city. Maybe that would convince her enough to stay in Austin for good.

I could only hope.

I couldn't dwell on it all too much. Mom would start shouting soon if I didn't get my ass in gear, so I stood and walked into my closet, grabbing the tux bag. I hated dressing up like this, but I couldn't deny how suave a tux could make me feel.

Hanging it on the door, I started to unzip it when I heard my bathroom door open.

"Dude, what is this pussy-ass girl music, Kyle?"

I glanced over my shoulder to see Dieter walk over to my laptop. He switched it to Jay Z's "99 Problems."

"Much better!" he shouted over the blaring music.

I just nodded my head. Only Lo got my eclectic taste in music, but it wasn't like I didn't listen to rap. One of my best friends apparently thought he was a young Slim Shady.

We dressed in our tuxes. I let my tie hang around my neck and left my vest open, slinging my jacket over my shoulder. Dieter did the same with his bow tie and jacket.

"Do you think your mom can help me tie this thing?" he asked.

I almost died of laughter. "Seriously, man? Maybe you should have gone with the clip-on."

I swung my bedroom door open and walked into the hallway just as Chase opened the guest bedroom, completely dressed, with his red tie already in place. Everything else was black—shirt, vest, jacket, pants, and shoes.

Dieter stepped up behind me and groaned, "Now, I know why she's always trying to dress you. She's got you all GQed up."

Chase just chuckled and sauntered off down the hall, tossing a few parting words as he went, "If it gets me laid, like it did when we went shopping for this fucking tux, then she can GQ me all fucking day."

"Lo has him so whipped." Dieter laughed quietly before walking down the hall after Chase.

I waited for Max by my bedroom door while they made their way downstairs. The bathroom door down the hall swung open, and Max stepped out, looking sharp as well. His vest and tie were a dark gray.

"Looking sophisticated, Maximillion." I said, fidgeting with my phone in my pocket.

His grin was instantaneous. Seeing him out of jeans and a hoodie was almost unbelievable.

"Ready to smile until our cheeks are numb?" he asked as he met me in the middle of the hallway.

I heard Mom squeal, and I internally grimaced but plastered a wide smile on my face for her benefit. Before Max and I even made it halfway down the stairs, she was snapping away photos, like a paparazzo-crazed lady. Her expensive camera with the huge lens and bright flash was constantly clicking photos and blinding us while I put my hand up to block the intrusion.

After she made sure we were all put together—meaning our ties weren't crooked, our jackets were lint-free, and Dieter's bow tie was flawless—we all stood in awkward poses, smiling like fools, as she danced around the room, directing us so that she could get the best shots. We started out on the stairs, hands gripping the banister, hands clasped in front of us, and then she was ushering us to the front door. But she couldn't forget about getting individual pictures, too, so she shooed us back to the stairs, one by one.

I remembered her acting just like this when Leighton had gone to prom three years ago, fluttering about and all excited, but she'd been too damn busy with taking pictures of everyone else to breathe and have a picture taken with her in it, until Dad stepped in and told her to get her ass in a picture with Leighton.

Dad took a deep breath before he walked over and grabbed ahold of the camera, just like he had done when it was Leighton. "Your turn, honey. Let's not forget to get my beautiful wife in a picture with our boy."

She blushed deeply and smacked his chest. "Stop it, Jeff. He doesn't want to take a picture with his mom. This is his night."

Dad nodded toward me, and I took my cue to walk to the kitchen. I pulled out the corsage I'd bought just for her from the fridge. She'd never admit it, but she loved the attention. Walking out, I held the clear container behind my back and went over to her with a smirk on my face.

She asked what I was hiding, and I grinned even bigger.

I brought the corsage up to my chest.

She laughed. "Stop it. That's for Kennedy."

"Kennedy's favorite flower isn't a white calla lily. It's yours." I opened the container and slipped out the corsage, which was a white calla lily with blue and silver ribbons and some pearly things, all creatively bunched together.

Mom tried to hide her smile with a glare, refusing to accept my gesture. She put her hand up to her mouth, physically forcing her smile away, as she glanced all around the room. I took her hand and slipped the pearled corsage on. Before I could pull away, she grabbed my hand and squeezed. Tears were shining in her eyes, but a scowl was still marring her face, especially since I'd managed to make her cry. She was such a softy.

"I don't know how I got so lucky with the best husband and kids ever."

All the while, Dad was continually snapping pictures of our moment, just like Mom had done with all us guys. When she cleared her emotions from her face even though they stayed in her eyes, she gestured for Max, Dieter, and Chase to join us for the last group pictures—one on the stairs and one outside.

Then, we all climbed into our vehicles.

We were picking up the girls from Chase's and then meeting our parents down the road from my house at the lake to take even more pictures before coming back here for dinner. I didn't know why the heck were we wasting so much gas, going back and forth.

Dad was staying behind to start grilling, and Mom had already prepared desserts for us.

I turned up my "pussy-ass girl music," as Dieter liked to call it, and drove straight to Chase's house. I pulled up right behind Dieter's Audi. I stepped out of the truck and walked over to the concrete driveway, buttoning up my jacket. Chase's dad came walking out with a grin on his face and a beer in his hand when he saw us all huddled around, waiting.

"Man, am I glad to see you boys. It's been nothing but high-pitched squealing and glitter. I think I'll be able to smell hairspray and perfume until the day I die. I can even taste it." Mr. Carter took a long chug of his beer, nearly finishing it, before he pulled it away from his lips. "And, boys?" He paused as we all turned our attention fully to him. "Brace yourselves. And *behave* yourselves."

I thought we all smiled a little deviously for the briefest moment before he pinned us each with a hard stare, ending on Chase.

"*You* especially." He pointed the long neck of his beer bottle at his son, not letting the warning glare in his eyes disappear, until the front door opened wide.

All our heads swiveled to the door, one by one, waiting to see who would step out first. Mrs. Carter, Chase's mom, enthusiastically hopped out the door with her arms out, doing jazz hands, making us all laugh. I glanced at Chase and laughed when he smothered his face in his hand, shaking his head in embarrassment.

Then, Mrs. Carter stepped to the side, and the first girl to come out was Shay, dressed in a fancy short red tutu kind of skirt and a jeweled red crop top. Her smile widened when she caught sight of Dieter. I looked over to see him fidgeting with his bow tie and not making direct eye contact with her. I didn't know why he'd asked her to prom if he wasn't into her.

Mrs. Carter had her own big camera snapping away pictures as he walked over to Shay and offered her the daisy corsage he'd gotten her. Shay frowned slightly, but when Dieter took her hand and pulled her to him for a brief kiss, she shrilly laughed, and the frown was forgotten.

I looked back up to the door to see Talan standing there. A scandalous dress made even my eyes pop.

"Holy shit," Max whispered under his breath before he walked up toward her. "You look incredible, Talan."

Her cheeks tinged pink. She said something quietly to him and accepted his hand. Mrs. Carter clicked photos of them, like she was going to miss a historical moment.

I took in her dress while Max fastened a flower-and-feather corsage to her wrist. Then, she secured a similar boutonniere to his tuxedo lapel. Her dress was almost indecent but totally her with a deep V on her chest, crazy low cut in the back that ran almost to the base of her spine, and a high split up her right leg. It was gray from the chest to mid-thigh but covered with a sheer black lace all the way down to her ankle.

"How do I look, wannabe big bro?" She smirked when she caught me practically glaring.

"Like you need a poncho." I laughed lightheartedly.

If she really were my sister, there'd be tons of broken noses and broken dicks walking around our school. She was smart, but it was her confidence that would get her in trouble. It made guys want to challenge it. And she had to have a lot of confidence to wear a dress like that. She was her dad's worst nightmare. That was why he always looked to me to protect his only daughter.

Next, it was Lo. Her long brown hair was in a fancy updo, completely out of her face. Her dress was long black lace that hugged her figure all the way to her knees before flaring out. Chase hissed and then smirked as he walked up to her. He kissed her cheek, looking like a love-struck puppy. She turned to the side, so Chase could slip her fancy, expensive, imported corsage on, and Claire could snap pictures.

Blonde hair caught my eye, and my head quickly turned back to the door to catch Kennedy—*beautiful, striking, so fucking gorgeous Kennedy*—stepping out the door. Her wild gray eyes locked on mine, lined with thick black liner. Even from where I stood, I could see her crazy long eyelashes flutter. The picture she'd sent had done her no justice. She was the embodiment of pure beauty. Piercing eyes and lips lured me in and made me want to drop to my knees and worship God for creating such a stunning angel.

Her dress, a bright shade of coral that really made her glow, had a flowery bust and a sheer waist before the flowery design began again. My vest and tie perfectly matched her dress. A golden collar-like necklace shone and dragged my attention back to her delicate neck.

I smiled wide, and she granted me with one of her own smiles, teeth white and lips shining from her gloss. I slowly walked over, taking the cymbidium orchid corsage out of its plastic case. I didn't even have to reach for her wrist, as she was already holding her hand out. My eyes flashed to hers before I looked down to fasten the corsage to her wrist, and I waited for her to pin the matching boutonniere to my lapel.

"You're so fucking gorgeous, Ken," I whispered quietly in her ear.

Chase's mom squealed. "That was the cutest damn picture I'd ever taken." She pointed to Chase and Lo. "Do something sweet and romantic, so I can take a picture like that."

"Mom," Chase groaned.

"Yeah, Claire. Don't encourage that shit. Lo's dad will lose his mind," Mr. Carter said with a puff of hot air. Then, he swigged back the rest of his beer.

"Oh, hush," she said with a devious smile. "Come on! This is your only prom!" Her head nodded toward her son and Lo.

Lo laughed loudly before she gripped Chase's lapels and pulled him in tight.

Oh, jeez, I thought.

She certainly wasn't afraid of making a scene anymore.

Chase moved swiftly, dramatically dipping her back. Lo's high squeal made Claire laugh and squeal, too, as she snapped pictures, like my mom had done at the house. I was pretty sure her index finger was getting the workout of its life right then.

"They're showing us up," Kennedy joked lightly.

"It doesn't matter," I whispered into her ear as I stood behind her, my chin resting on her shoulder and my arms wrapped firmly around her waist. "Our love isn't flashy. But it sure as hell feels like bright stadium lights with a roaring crowd."

She squeezed my hands that rested on her stomach, letting me know she felt it, too.

Chapter 21

Kennedy

"I don't ever want to take my hands off you," Kyle roughly growled down at me.

We swayed to the music, my dress swishing and flowing with us. My hands were locked tight around Kyle's neck, and his hands were gripped firmly around my hips.

I lifted my cheek off his chest and stared up at him. His perfect nose. His chiseled jaw. His deep brown eyes that stared back at me with an intensity capable of sending shivers throughout my entire body, shaking me to the core like an earthquake. My whole body trembled all the way to the tips of my fingers, and I clenched my hands harder together.

"Then, don't," I said softly. My voice was a scratchy rasp, and it'd been like that since this morning. After Bryan and Dylan had dropped me off at my house. After too many drinks and not enough water and only four hours of sleep.

Getting ready had been a struggle. I'd had to really push through. Lo had barely said anything to me. Talan had kept asking why my eyes were so dark, if I'd gotten enough sleep, if I was feeling okay. I'd only made it through with lots of coffee. And I didn't even like coffee, so that was something. But Chase's mom had made sure to load it with cream and sugar. I was bloated, but at least I wasn't falling asleep at prom.

Mrs. Carter had kept a watchful eye on me that made me slightly nervous. All throughout pictures and dinner, I'd felt like eyes were constantly on me. Like they knew I was hiding something.

My self-consciousness had taken over, and I'd retreated back into the quiet persona that I'd recently adopted, not really knowing how to deal with all the stares.

And who knew? Maybe I was just being incredibly paranoid, but as I watched Talan and Lo sitting at a table by the dance floor, heads together and sneaky glances catching my eye, I felt justified.

Their eyes on me made my skin itch, my mind race, my heartbeat quicken.

I could see the questions behind Lo's worried ocean blues.

"I'm glad they decided to rent out this place instead of that old, musty hotel that had a noise ordinance."

Kyle was gazing around the ballroom decorated with a blue, gray, and black color scheme. Light projectors aimed at the ceiling made it look like it was covered in stars. Black, gray, and midnight blue drapery covered the walls, giving that true midnight feel.

"Hey"—Kyle's hand touched my cheek, his thumb tracing back and forth under my lip—"you feeling okay?"

I nodded and gave a soft smile. "Yeah, I'm fine. Why?" I took his hand from my face and laced our fingers together.

"You just kind of stopped dancing, and you had this faraway look on your face." He grinned and started to pull me toward the table with all our friends. "I wanna get you home." He glanced down at me and grinned.

"What? No way! We're going to that party after this." Dieter had apparently been walking behind us. He slapped Kyle on the back, pivoted to stand in front of us, and then pointed at me. "No backing out. Free booze, better music at a big-ass house, and no chaperones. We're all going, and we're all going to have a fucking good time."

His eyes squinted past my shoulders. I turned to see his date, Shay—who was really weird and giggly—talking to some guy from the basketball team.

"Is Shay coming?" I asked when I turned back around.

He scowled and shrugged. "We haven't even danced. She's been bitching about her hair all night." Pulling his phone out, he sent what I assumed was a text and then glanced back up to Kyle.

"You ready to be announced Prom King and Queen? Then, we can fucking bail."

Kyle smiled widely. "Sure, man. We'll drop all the cars back at my place and change. Then, we can ride together. I have a feeling, I'm going to need to be your DD."

"Damn straight, bro. After the fucking night I'm currently having with pissy girls and bad attitudes, I'm going to need more than a few drinks."

I heard a scoff and looked around Dieter to see Talan practically fuming. Her eyes had a wild look in them as they were pinned to the back of Dieter's head. She was a freaking bombshell tonight. The dress and hair. And let's face it; she had that dancer's body. But, right now, she was ticking. And Dieter was about to detonate her.

The school principal took the stage at the end of the dance floor and tapped the mic, causing a loud thump and then a high-pitched whine. Everyone groaned and covered their ears. He took the mic and walked toward one of the DJ speakers, making the shrill noise escalate.

I sat down in one of the chairs at our table and grabbed my coral clutch hidden under the little black sweater my mom had forced me to bring. It held my phone, ID, a little bit of cash, and three little baggies that stayed hidden underneath it all. I had been obsessing over the clutch the entire evening. Terrified to even open it and check my phone. Too scared someone might see the drugs Bryan had made me take before I got out of the car.

"Just in case," Bryan had said.

And I'd stupidly let him shove them in my pocket. As soon as I'd walked into my room, I'd grabbed the empty clutch and shoved them in. I couldn't just leave them in my room where my mom could find them.

Now, they were the only things my mind could focus on.

I briefly registered my name being called as one of the Prom Queen nominations along with two other girls, and then Kyle's name was called for one of the Prom King nominations, followed by a loud rumble of football players chanting and stomping their feet. He was standing behind my chair, his hands braced on my shoulders, softly kneading and squeezing, as we awaited the announcement of the winners. I leaned back into Kyle's abs and took a deep breath. Some might have thought I was worried Kyle would be chosen as Prom King and another girl as Queen, but I wasn't. My only distress was on how this night would end.

Principal Scott coughed and cleared his throat to get everyone's attention and quiet the shouting. "Ladies first," he said as he ripped open a silver envelope and pulled out a black card. "And your nominated Prom Queen is…Kennedy Kiblen!"

Kyle squeezed my shoulders even tighter and leaned down to kiss my cheek. "You're definitely my queen, baby. Go get your crown."

I breathed in deeply, not excited about the spotlight, but I still plastered on my winning smile. Kyle helped me stand and walked me over to the stage steps. I stumbled and tripped over my dress a little on the first step. Kyle immediately gripped my hips and steadied me.

"You all right?" he murmured quietly.

I nodded and took a shallow breath, stiffening my back. I finished going up the last two steps to accept the shiny golden crown covered in sparkly rhinestones.

The spotlights and the students surrounding the stage made my body break out in a fever. All eyes on me weren't my cup of tea. I started to feel faint and nervous while everyone clapped as I adjusted the crown that Casey Sneider had awkwardly placed on my head.

Principal Scott waited for the applause to die down and then pulled out the Prom King envelope. With lots of flourish and definite pride, he quickly announced it, shouting Kyle's name. I wasn't surprised in the least. Our classmates went crazy for Kyle.

The other football team members were howling and shouting out, "Number twenty-four!"

I smiled my overdone radiant smile, trying to keep Kyle from noticing my sudden unease from all the attention. Kyle took the stage with relaxed exuberance. Beaming his megawatt smile with his white teeth, his chiseled chin, and his twinkling eyes, he turned to face me. And, for the briefest moment, when our eyes connected as he dramatically knelt down for Casey to place the matching golden crown on his head, I saw his eyes narrow at me. It could have been for a number of reasons, but deep down, I knew he had seen me faking it.

He just knew me too well. A gift and a curse.

Bryan's *gifts* were making me more and more nervous. I didn't know why I'd thought keeping them close to me would be any smarter than just hiding them in my room somewhere. I wish I'd had the brilliant idea to sneak in my just-in-case flask to help me take the edge off. If it were with me, I bet I'd practically feel the pull to my clutch like a ball and chain. A neon sign beckoning me like a barfly. But, with Bryan's little baggies hiding in there, I had the urge to toss the clutch in the trash.

I pushed down all my thoughts and took Kyle's offered elbow, following him back down the steps and to the middle of the dance floor. Our friends and classmates created a wide circle around us and watched as we danced as King and Queen. Then, they took their own partners and joined us to the slow dance. "Little Things" by One Direction played throughout the room, and in the distance, I heard Lo groan and Talan squeal. I just listened to the soft song and swayed with Kyle.

If it weren't for Kyle, I knew that I'd never have won the title of Prom Queen. If I were honest, I'd thought it would have gone to Lo, but she hadn't even been nominated. Hell, I wasn't even sure if it hadn't been a pity vote for me after all I'd been going through and who my boyfriend was. That made my win feel tainted even if it wasn't true. I berated myself for thinking like that.

I used to be Miss Optimistic, who Kyle had been trying to steer me back toward, trying to get me to come out of this shell and not be this negative, quiet, selfish girl I'd been acting like. He'd been giving me all the incentive, all the attention, all the *love* that I could possibly need to coax me out of my dark depression.

Is it possible to feel happy and content yet angry and disconnected, all at the same time? I was sure I wasn't the first to feel this way with a contradiction of emotions.

But, for some reason, I'd found some kind of solace in the pit of despair. It might be the furthest thing from what my father and my Savior would want for me, but as far as I was concerned…I finally felt a smidgen of relief from the role of being the perpetual good girl, the pastor's daughter.

People change, right?

Especially after something that affected their lives forever. It forced you to accept things you didn't want to. It shed light on things that had once been hidden from you. It made you move on.

So, this was me changing. Moving on.

Forgive me, Lord, because even though my way of moving on was wrong and against everything I knew, I wasn't willing to give it up just yet. No matter how dark and sinister the road was. No matter the damage it would cause.

And, tonight, I made the decision to take full advantage.

After our dance and official photo for the yearbook, Kyle, I, and our friends grabbed our things and made our way back to Kyle's house. The plan was to change, eat a snack, and then head to an after-party that Dieter knew about.

Before we left Kyle's house, I rushed back up to his room and grabbed my satchel purse, dumped the contents of my clutch into it, and then secured it over my shoulder.

I should have seen red flags as we made our way to the freeway and drove in the direction of Fielding City.

I should have seen enemy flags as we entered Dylan's gated neighborhood.

I should have feigned illness when we parked at the end of Dylan's driveway.

Instead, I acted like nothing was wrong, like nothing would go wrong, like I wasn't one hundred ten percent freaking out.

"Who do you know at this party, Dieter?" I hedged cautiously.

If he knew Dylan, did he know that Dylan and Bryan were friends? I doubted we'd have come here if he did.

Keeping his eyes on Talan, who'd piggybacked on to Max. Dieter barely spared me a glance as he answered me, "The kid who lives here has been throwing parties like crazy, I guess. Everyone's been talking about them. I don't really know him that well, just in passing."

As we walked up the long driveway, I wiped my sweaty palms up and down the cutoff jean shorts I'd slipped on. The nerve-racking emotions flowing through my body made me jittery and paranoid. Kyle's arm wrapping around my waist proved that much when I nearly jumped a foot in the air.

He chuckled lightly and squeezed me to him. "We'll just stay for a little while, okay?" he said. "I know this isn't really your thing, but you can relax. I'll drive home, so if you want to drink, you can. Just don't take drinks from anyone but us."

His voice should have calmed and soothed my sudden anxiety, but the closer we got to the front door, the harder I had to concentrate on not breaking down.

I only prayed with my deepest hope that Dylan would act like he didn't even know me and that Bryan wasn't here.

But, of course, only fools hoped for things to go smoothly when you'd weaved a web of deceit.

Dieter rang the doorbell as soon as he reached the opulent entrance. It only took a few seconds before the grand wrought iron and glass double doors opened. Those custom doors led into the marbled floor foyer with the shiny chandelier that always dazzled and stole my attention. I could barely see it from where Kyle and I stood behind our group of friends.

I shrank into Kyle's side, trying to hide from who I knew was at the door.

Dylan's loud but laid-back tone sounded above the chatter of our group. "Well, well, well."

As he swung the doors wide open, we slipped inside, and I continued trying to stay hidden, small, and unnoticeable against Kyle's broad chest. A lump formed in my throat. I just wanted to avoid conflict as much as possible. My life was already complicated enough. I didn't need to add Kyle getting into a fight and risking his scholarship for me.

"I can see you brought your whole crew with you. Didn't think you'd actually show, Dieter." There was an edge to Dylan's voice as our group spread out, and Dylan and I caught each other's eyes. He knew I was within the circle, and he was being absolutely smug about it when he grinned wide. "Masters, long time no see. Heard you got recruited?" He hadn't heard from me, but the way he eyed me made it seem like it could have been from me.

I tried not to focus on Dylan. Instead, I ignored him and gazed around the house. My eyes darted to all the people who were standing around and mingling. I didn't think this kid knew how to do a single thing subtly or with moderation. His parties were always jam-packed full of people. A combination of high school and college kids. Dieter wasn't wrong when he'd said Dylan had been throwing parties like crazy. It was like an every-other-night thing. It made me wonder if his parents were ever even home or if they cared in the slightest what their kid was up to.

"How do you know Kennedy?"

My name being said brought me back to the situation I'd so stupidly gotten myself into. Kyle's body had stiffened, his hand squeezing my side to the point of pain, and I was just now noticing.

"Mutual acquaintances. Right, Kiblen?"

I could have killed Dylan. I nodded lightly, not willing to give him my voice. It would shake and betray me.

Please…keep your mouth shut, Dylan.

Dylan's eyes were shining with untold secrets. That scared me.

I glared at him and hugged myself closer to Kyle, which prompted him to loosen his grip on my side. I subconsciously rubbed at the spot his fingers had gripped to ebb the throb away.

"Where are the drinks, Dylan? I came to party." Dieter unknowingly took the attention off me.

I let my shoulders drop and inhaled a deep breath, clearing the lump in my throat.

Dylan led us through the house, waving and saying hi to people as we went. I'd never been anywhere in this house but down in the finished basement that he always led me to. The grandiose of this house was too much to believe. It was similar to Lo's mom's interior-design tastes. Everything looked expensive and pristine. Some older pieces, like the artwork on the walls, and some of the furniture looked antique but still luxurious.

We slipped out the French doors that led out onto a tiled patio. The huge lagoon pool with all its rock designs was the main attraction. Some girls were lounging on the side of the pool with their feet in the water, and others were splashing around with a few guys in the pool.

Kyle released his possessive grip on me and started chatting with Chase.

"This bar's fully stocked. Help yourselves." Dylan walked by me and lowered his head to mine as he quietly spoke, "We're downstairs if you find yourself looking for a break."

And then he walked away, grabbing a girl by the hips and pushing her backward into the house, his lips going to her neck.

Shameless as ever.

I turned back to my group of friends and sighed with unsure relief. Their conversations turned to talk about Texas and school and classes—something I wasn't a part of.

Over the next hour, Kyle stood between my legs as I perched on the bar, talking and joking with our friends. I'd finally had enough when they continued to talk about their living arrangements for next year. I told Kyle I was going to use the bathroom. I slipped away and went into the mansion where I found a bathroom off the foyer. Alone, I took deep breaths, unable to look at myself in the mirror.

I was considering the unthinkable.

And then I was *doing* the unthinkable.

Slipping out of the bathroom, I only checked over my shoulder once to see if anyone I knew was close by. The door to the basement was unlocked this time.

How many people does Dylan actually let down here?

Considering the size of his parties, there was never more than a dozen people in his little den of debauchery.

As I began descending the stairs, Dylan came into view when he started to come up them. A grin instantly painted his face. The dim lighting gave him that shadowy rogue look, making him all the more intimidating.

"Hey, Bryan!" he shouted over his shoulder.

"Fuck off, man! I'm busy."

I heard a growled rumble.

"You bring our gifts?" he asked me as I took the final steps toward the basement.

I stopped short with a couple of steps between us. Our eyes were level, and Dylan must not have liked it because he took an extra step up. I pulled the three little baggies out of my bag. Not saying a word, I held them on my palm between us.

He eyed my hand and then chuckled before he glanced back up. "I think we both know that they've been in the back of your mind since we gave them to you. They're paid for, Kennedy. Just keep them. Use them. We'll keep your secret. Scout's honor." He closed my hand to keep the paraphernalia in my possession.

"You paid for these?"

"No sweat." He shrugged and moved to the side, so I could finish my descent.

As soon as I could see the couch, my face froze in shocked surprise. I immediately turned around and slammed into Dylan's chest. Public displays of affection were definitely not my kink, but holy hell was it Bryan's and the girl who barely had any clothes on, her bra pushed down and breasts hanging out.

"Hey, Bryan," Dylan called out.

"Fuck *off*, Dylan." His words came out muffled since his face was buried in her chest.

"Okay, fine. Come on, Kennedy. We can hang out in the office." He smiled down at me as I took a slow step back, and then he threw his arm around my neck, rotating me slightly to lead me toward the office.

"I thought you said no one was supposed to go in here," I commented quietly as I was pulled along.

"Bryan!" the girl shrieked.

I glanced over my shoulder just in time to see Bryan adjusting himself in his jeans and stalking toward us.

He thrust his hands into his hair to smooth it back and winked at me. "Funny seeing you here."

I faced forward, ignoring his comment.

I could feel Bryan quickly closing the distance between us. As Dylan and I stepped through the door, I walked over and sat on one of the leather chairs that looked like it'd been sat in more than any piece of furniture in this designer house. Closing the door after Bryan, Dylan flicked the lock and took a seat at his dad's opulent desk.

"You still have them?" Bryan asked.

"Oh, she's got them. Clutched in her fist."

I shot a glare at Dylan.

"What? You know, you could have stayed upstairs with your perfect all-American football player and his straight-edge friends. *Your BFFs for life.* But you didn't. You came down *here*. Now, let's have a good time. Your choice. What kind of fun do you want to have?"

"I'll make a recommendation." Bryan smirked as he leaned his back up against the wall, one foot up against it, bending his knee. His arms were crossed over his chest, like he couldn't care less. "You pussed out last night."

I cringed at his crass word.

"Alcohol's not gonna do it for you, Kennedy," Bryan said.

"This oughta be good." Dylan snickered.

I once again glared at him with my icy-gray eyes.

He and Dieter were so similar; they could've been best friends if they went to the same school. Although, knowing the little I did about Dylan and the plethora of information I knew about Dieter, I wasn't sure if their extracurricular activities would be the same, outside of girls. But those personalities? The I-don't-give-a-flip attitude? Yeah, they were the same. Even the way they always cracked crude jokes.

"No," I said forcefully.

But, when I was with these two, my curiosity would override my knowledge of wrong and right. I did wonder what kinds of things I'd feel with the highs they knew so much about.

"Blue," Bryan said.

I looked to him, confused. *Blue?*

"The blue pill, Angel. That's what I'm recommending."

"I just said no."

"I don't really care what you just said. Peer pressure and all. I wanna see what kind of girl you are when your inhibitions are lowered." He pushed off the wall and came toward me. "Give me the bags."

I thrust my arm out and placed them in his waiting palm. He took the bag with the blue pills and then shoved the other two back at me.

"I don't want them," I whispered heatedly.

Ignoring me, he shoved them back into my purse himself.

He took the two pills out and walked over to Dylan, placing one on the desk in front of him. "I've gotta deal tonight. You cool?"

"I'm straight." Dylan's answer came with that dreadful smirk. He picked up the pill, winked at me, tossed it in the air, and caught it with his tongue. He twisted the cap off a water bottle he had sitting on the desk, took a quick sip, placed the cap back on, and then chucked the bottle to Bryan.

"Your turn," Dylan chimed in as he jumped up from the chair and started to walk toward me.

"Kyle's here."

"So?" Bryan asked. He stood only a foot from me with the little blue pill in his palm, waiting for me to take it. "He'll thank me later."

This isn't you, that inner voice whispered in my ear. I knew whose voice it was, but it didn't matter.

You left me, was my only response to it.

I stood and paced away from them hovering over me. I didn't like how they always felt the need to tower over me.

My purse started buzzing. I hadn't been gone long, but that wasn't the point. Kyle didn't know how well I knew Dylan even though I barely did. And Kyle definitely didn't know that Bryan and Dylan were chummy; otherwise, there was no way we'd even be here. Especially with Lo and Chase.

"Better answer that," they both said in unison.

I turned my back to them, needing to think without being able to see their coercive faces.

"You had fun last night, didn't you?" Bryan came up behind me so silently that I never even heard him. I hated when he did that.

His breath crept up my neck, and I shivered. Not in an appealing way though. He could be so sweet sometimes with me, but then he'd become crass and overwhelming till I feared what he would say or do next. With him, I never knew who was standing before me. The guy who tried to console a crying girl at a party or the guy who thought drugging a girl was okay, just to get a little revenge.

"You didn't think about all the shit on your plate. You just drank and had fun. This will be ten times better than that. And you'll feel amazing. We took care of you last night, and we'll take care of you tonight." He paused, like he was going to say more, but instead, he breathed in deeply behind me.

It was true, too. He had given me exactly what I wanted. But it killed me that I was going against everything I had been raised to believe. I was breaking the promise to my father that I would never seek a high that wasn't natural and that could harm me.

Kyle gave me that natural high. Kyle was my constant. And I loved Kyle. That would never change. I would never cheat on him. Even though Bryan and Dylan were ruggedly handsome and didn't hide their attraction to me, I wasn't attracted to them. They were simply a way for me to forget, to get out of my head.

"How do you even know what it's like if you don't do the things you deal?" I whispered, shaking my head from side to side.

My hands fidgeted with the hem of my T-shirt. I didn't understand Bryan at all.

"I don't do them now. Doesn't mean I haven't done them." His voice softened.

"Just try it, Kennedy. You'll like it, I promise." Dylan came closer to me this time. His eyes were already dilating. He was bouncing on the balls of his feet, making me jittery, nervous, and uneasy.

Could it really be that bad?

I'd heard classmates gossip about their wild weekends and the drugs they'd tried. They'd seemed to find it an experience worth having.

Besides, Kyle was here. If anything really did go wrong, he'd fix it. Even though he'd be so angry with me.

With all those thoughts, I made my decision. I turned and took the pill from Bryan's hand. He smirked as he untwisted the cap from the water bottle and handed it over to me. I stared at the little blue pill with a weird design on it before placing it on my tongue and washing it down with warm water.

"Don't let her drink with this. Got it?" Bryan addressed Dylan with authority but never took his eyes off mine.

For some reason, it made me nod my own head. Like some scared little girl.

"Yeah, man."

"Chase and Lo are here. If Chase sees you...or even Dieter and Kyle, they'll freak out," I said to Bryan. I didn't know why I continually tried to save him. It was ironic really. Me, the girl who didn't want to be saved, saving the guy who was trying to corrupt me.

"You act like you care, Angel. Be careful with those mixed signals you like to send."

"I don't like to see people get hurt."

His haughty smirk made me want to slap him, and even though my palm twitched and started to rise, I refrained.

My phone that incessantly buzzed in my purse stole my attention. "I should get back."

"Remember to drink water. And *don't* mix alcohol with this. Especially for a newbie," Bryan said sternly before he backed away, unlocked the office door, and walked out.

"Aw, you act like you care, Devil," I threw back at him with as much sarcasm as I could gather.

"Overdosing is bad for business!" he shouted back but kept going without so much as a glance back.

My eyes widened in fear and realization of how stupid I was actually being. *What if I did overdose?* It would be exactly what Lo had been trying to prevent. I was such a freaking idiot. A naive freaking idiot and a terrible friend.

I should have been staying far away from Bryan and his drugs after what he had done to her. She'd almost died, and here I was, not giving a damn, taking a little blue pill. I briefly considered forcing myself to throw up. *Because really? What. In. The. Hell. Am. I. Doing?*

"He's just being an ass, Kiblen. Quit freaking out. Come on, let's get you back to that boyfriend of yours before he starts tearing my house apart, looking for you."

I quickly followed Dylan as he walked out and toward the stairs. It was too late now to back out. The little blue pill was already in my system.

"What is this supposed to feel like? Am I gonna be like a zombie trying to dance to dubstep, like those girls last night?"

He laughed hysterically and had to stop halfway up the stairs to catch his breath. "Holy fuck, Kennedy. That was…too…fucking funny. You painted the…funniest image in my…head!" he said it all through a laugh, breaking the words up and making it hard to understand him.

As he continued to try and control his kid-like giggles, I shrugged. "That's what it looked like."

We stepped out of the basement, and I was immediately hit with loud music.

At least it's not dubstep, I thought.

Rap music overtook the house, and shouting and laughing could be heard from every room.

"Seriously, Dylan, how long does this stuff take to affect me?" I whisper-hissed at his back.

He cheerfully greeted everyone who offered him the time of day—which was *everyone*—as we walked through the rooms on the main floor.

Paranoia is definitely one of the side effects, right? What about rambling? Jesus, I am stupid.

Stupid to trust these guys. Stupid to befriend them. Stupid all around.

"Kennedy!"

I whipped around at the bellow of my name to see Kyle and every one of our friends charging toward me.

"Where the fuck *were* you?" Kyle asked as soon as he reached me. His hand took immediate hold of my elbow and pulled me off to the side of the large living room we were standing in.

"I was talking to Dylan," I explained. My voice shook with worry. *Can he see a difference? Am I being obvious?*

The possessive look in Kyle's eyes made me tremble in more ways than one. God, he was so gorgeous and broad and muscular. A sudden rush of dizziness hit me, and I swayed. Unexpectedly, my mind felt splintered and distant. Kyle swiftly reached for my waist to steady me. Tingles spread from where his hands gripped me and throughout my body. Electric currents zinged through my body and all because of one touch. His touch.

"Did you drink anything?" His concern was written all over his face. The way his sculpted eyebrows pinched together and his lips thinned were a dead giveaway. But he was still stunning.

I'd take any emotion he gave me. They were all sexy.

I thought back to the day he'd followed me home, after I'd tried to talk to Lo about what she saw at the mall. And, even though the memory was filled with shame and guilt for deceiving my best friend and seeking solace in a bottle, the only thing I could remember was his relentless touch. Rough yet still so tender with me. I could almost feel the grip of his hands around my wrists as he—

"Kennedy…" Kyle's worried voice and perplexed eyes bored into me.

I slowly shook my head from side to side because I was afraid I'd make myself dizzy. I felt so dizzy and I didn't want him to ask more questions. I simply wanted to have a good time now.

"Are you sure?" He pushed in closer.

When I exhaled a soft, "I'm sure," I could have sworn I heard him sniff.

He kept a tight grip on my hip, exerting that alpha dominance he'd recently taken on.

Sexy.

"I promise," I declared with a nod of my head and a smile causing my cheeks to ache.

He searched my eyes. I watched his shift back and forth as he examined mine.

"How do you even know Dylan?"

"He knows someone who used to go to Dad's church."

At least I wasn't entirely lying. Dylan knew Bryan, whose mom attended my dad's church.

I took in Kyle's casual jeans and T-shirt. His chest protruded, his torso tapering off at his sexy oblique muscles.

I knew Kyle was going to push for more questions, but right now, I didn't want to feel barraged with them. To stop him, I kissed him. And didn't stop. My lips on his was the best feeling in the entire universe. A fire lit up within me. It was like time had stopped.

I moaned. And it must have been a loud moan because Kyle pulled back and shushed me. His face lit up with an adorable smile that made me grin. He swooped back in and kissed my lips with more force, but right as I started to feel the need burn hotter, my head dizzy, he swiftly pulled back.

"Later," he whispered in my ear. Then, he softly kissed my cheek. His lips seared my skin, even with the lightest touch.

Is this what ecstasy does to you?

My skin tingled and burned with every touch to my body.

"Kennedy! It's my song! Come on! Come dance with me!"

I turned in time to see Talan running toward me. She tore me away from Kyle without apology, tugging on my arm and swaying her body.

"Ugh, Talan, really? I can't dance. Especially to this…"

But she ignored me as an upbeat and melodic song blared through the speakers. It wasn't really the type of song that everyone else danced to, the grinding rap that you heard at most parties. But Talan loved it. She sang and danced around with me, circling around me, grabbing my hands, and twirling me. She bounced on her tiptoes, shaking her butt and rolling her hips, doing her thing. And let's face it; the girl had moves. It didn't matter that she was mostly classically trained. On a dance floor, the girl owned it, no matter what the music was.

"What is this?"

She tossed her hair back and grinned. "'Strange Love' by Halsey, my anthem."

"For Dieter?" I grinned.

She scowled, her eyes darkening with the mention of his name. "Fuck Dieter."

She ended the conversation by dropping my hands and doing some moves on her own before she went to pull Max out to dance with her. He only hesitated for a second before he was grinning and following her without protest.

I heard him ask if she ever tired.

She laughed as she replied with, "Wouldn't you like to know?" A cheeky smirk lit up her face with mastered mischief.

Soon, I was feeling the bass, as if it were my own heartbeat. The lyrics spilled from my lips as I lost myself. When Talan touched my arms or spun me around, I shuddered. I couldn't explain the feelings. It was…something…wild. More. *The best.* I liked this high. This toxic chemical blur of touch and sensory overload. It was different than the numb I got from alcohol.

If this was how I felt when Talan touched me, well…then I wanted Kyle's touch. *Everywhere.*

I could feel his eyes following my every move, so I moved more. Trying to be fluid and hypnotic, my muscles melting. Loose and free and blissful. And, deep down, I prayed it translated, and I wasn't a dubstepping zombie. It was weird, but I loved it.

I could feel the sweat building on my skin from so much dancing, which only added to the weird sensations I was experiencing. Every drop of sweat that dripped off my forehead or raced down my spine captivated me. My mind ached from all the overpowering sensations.

And, when I shut my eyes…it was like staring at the sun. Blinding and all too much.

When I opened my eyes, Dylan was suddenly close to me, dancing with a girl I didn't know.

"High looks good on you, Kiblen."

Dylan's lazy smile could kill a girl from swooning so hard but not nearly as deadly as Kyle's glare as Dylan inched closer to me. I could feel the heat of his stare, and for a brief moment, I shivered from fear, wondering if Kyle was about to pounce on Dylan for being too close.

But then I basked in the dominance he radiated, like he would knock out anyone who dared to get near me, because I knew the fierce way his eyes narrowed and his eyebrows furrowed wasn't at me…but for me.

My skin tingled with impatience. I begged him with my eyes to come and get me.

Chapter 22

Kyle

"Ken's acting weird, right? It's not just me?" I asked the guys as the girls danced in the center of the living room.

Lo kept a distance from Kennedy, always letting Talan dance between them or doing her own thing off to the side. When Talan and Lo partnered off to do their girl-grinding that was just plain weird for me to watch, Kennedy was fine in her own little world, her movement fluid and almost uncaring.

Dieter chugged on his beer before responding, "If I'm being honest, she's been weird for the last few days. I didn't want to say anything. And, now, I feel like we're total pussies, talking like fucking chicks." He half-laughed, half-groaned at his own statement before taking another deep pull from his beer.

"Lo said she was looking rough when she came to the house this morning," Chase commented, like he didn't really want to say anything at all. But, you know, bro code. He shoved his hands in his pockets, never taking his eyes off Lo.

"Did she say anything about she and Kennedy talking?" I asked, watching Kennedy with the same intensity as he did with Lo.

Kennedy's cutoff shorts were tight, hugging her ass and showing off her thighs. I didn't like the way other guys stared at her.

When Chase didn't say anything, I swiveled my head toward him.

He shook his head from side to side. "From what I've seen, they haven't said much more than five words to each other the whole night."

From a distance, Kennedy looked just like all the other girls having fun. She was dancing at a party and hanging with her friends. But, from my point of view—the protective, aggressive point of view—I knew something was off.

When I'd first found her after she left to use the bathroom, she'd been too nervous. That was why I'd thought maybe she'd accepted a drink from someone. She had been quiet and distracted. Her cheeks had looked flushed, and when she'd swayed, I'd immediately thought something was wrong.

"She looks wired." I looked to Dieter and then back to Kennedy, watching her throw her arms up in the air and then lower them to her neck. I could see her sweat sparkling off her skin. And, if I wasn't mistaken, her own touch was arousing her something wicked. She was making it damn near impossible to focus on anything but her.

"How much do you know about Dylan?" I asked.

Not only was I keeping a sharp eye on Kennedy, but I was also keeping a keen eye on Dylan. He seemed too fucking wired himself, bobbing to the music and constantly touching whatever girl danced with him, like no one was even around to see.

And he was never far from Kennedy. He kept moving closer to her throughout the songs, but other girls were keeping him occupied for the most part. It bugged me, and I kept clenching and unclenching my fists.

The bastard never touched her. At least, he hadn't yet, which was good because I didn't want to have to kick the dickhead's ass because he was getting too handsy with my girlfriend. I didn't fucking care if it was his house.

"You would know more about him than me, don't you think? Football camps and all that." Somehow, Dieter had another beer in his hand even though he never left to get one. He popped the tab and chugged.

"We only went to one camp together. His dad always bought his way into the exclusive camps. I just went to the ones I'd been invited to." I'd never really thought that exclusivity was worth it. If you were good, you were good.

Shrugging, he said, "I just know he came home early from school and has been throwing parties for weeks. Everyone from the private school has been talking about them."

I watched as Dylan edged closer to Kennedy. He'd been getting on my nerves the entire night, and I'd finally had enough. He acted like he knew her way better than what he'd claimed.

"I'm over this. Ready to head out?" I asked the guys.

Their responding nods gave me the go-ahead to grab my girl and get the hell out of there.

I walked up to Kennedy, who was lost in her own little world of dance. Damn, did she look good. She'd never seemed more free and careless with her dancing. She'd always been a little self-conscious but never enough to let it completely hold her back. Now though, it was like she was tossing her inhibitions in the fire, letting the smoke from them cloud the space, like it was a veil to hide behind and do all the things she dared.

She'd only ever danced like this in front of me a couple of times before—at Dieter's cabin last year before all the bad shit with Lo had happened and when I'd gotten home from Texas. She'd expressed that same carefree attitude and just let herself have fun. But, even then, she was still reserved. Now, it looked like she just didn't give a fuck.

I didn't want to crush her good mood, but I was done with this fuckhead's party and with him staring at my girl, hovering, like she was the one he wanted grinding on his dick.

Her eyes widened as I made my way to her from across the room. She had a smile on her face that made my heart soar. I reached for her, wrapping my arms around her and pulling her in close.

I whispered in her ear, "I want to get you home." I kissed her neck, slick with sweat and tasting salty, and then punctuated the sentiment with a hard squeeze to her hips. "Now."

Her head bobbed up and down, and her arms that had wrapped around me trailed lower and lower until she reached the hem of my shirt and slid her fingers underneath to touch my lower back. Her hands felt like burning coal on my skin. The thin sheen of sweat that had built on her skin made her aroma tangy but also sweet, as it mixed in with her perfume. She smelled sinful, and I couldn't stop breathing her in deeply. Into my soul.

I wanted her all to myself. I fought the needy urges building in my body and hustled her toward our friends before I decided to find a vacant room upstairs.

"Good?" I asked our friends, who were all huddled in a circle.

"Yep. We headed to your house?" Chase asked, hooking his arm around Lo's neck.

"Yeah, if you guys still want to. Let's get out of here." I led our group out to our cars.

Lo, Chase, and Talan climbed into Lo's Camaro while I helped Ken up into the front seat of my truck, and Dieter jumped into the backseat.

We set off toward the highway, listening to the music on the Sirius Top 40 station because that was Kennedy's favorite station.

I kept glancing over to Kennedy. She had her eyes closed as her head bobbed to the music, and she kept rubbing on her biceps and then her thighs.

"You all right?" I asked for what seemed like the millionth time today.

She never opened her eyes. She just hummed before saying, "I just feel so good tonight." And that was it.

Kennedy's response should have worried me, but instead, it sparked a deep need for her. It was always there, simmering beneath all the other thoughts about her, but lately, I'd become insatiable, and she was just as eager and willing to forget everything else, so we could be together in our own little world.

I wanted to tell her I'd make her feel even better later, but with Dieter in the backseat, I figured it'd be awkward, so I just reached over, placed my hand on her upper thigh, and squeezed. She jolted for a second before she moaned quietly and pressed her head against the headrest, like the caress was just too much for her.

It was like my thoughts were passed to her with just a simple touch. There was no need for words. We could communicate with as much as a look or brush. It'd always been like that with her. I guessed that was why I'd fallen so quickly for her. We just got each other.

I pulled into my driveway with Lo's car close behind, and we climbed out of the truck.

"What do you guys wanna do? Swim? Movie? Just crash?" I asked everyone as we walked in through the front door.

I tossed my keys on the entry table and wandered into the kitchen to grab a water. Dieter pushed me out of the way to grab a beer from the bottom shelf and then waltzed away with it already cracked open and pressed to his lips.

"You want something, Ken?" I asked.

Talan and she were dancing together and laughing.

"I need water, Your Majesty!" she exclaimed as she picked up her crown that she'd discarded on the counter when we came home earlier to change.

She squealed when Talan dramatically spun her out and back in. It was nice to see her laughing and having fun with her friends. This was the girl I had fallen in love with. The happy and bright smiles that lit up her whole face. She was so beautiful and enchanting when she let loose.

"He said I needed to drink water!" she shouted as Talan dipped her back.

Wait…what? I shook my head. *Who said she needed to drink water?*

"What is with her?" Lo whispered quietly when she came up to my side.

I shelved my confusion for another time.

I shrugged as I twisted the cap off a water bottle, not as concerned as I had been earlier in a house that I wasn't familiar with and a guy who seemed to be getting too close to her.

"She's just having fun." But, still, I knew something was off. I could see it in her eyes, the way they had darkened. I just didn't want to give a voice to my suspicions. Maybe I was being naive or even scared, but I didn't want to ruin a good night—Kennedy's good night.

So, maybe she'd snuck off to drink something on her own without us watching. She'd drunk the other day when she was sad and depressed and we were fighting. And that was a definite red flag. But we had been together all night. Nothing would go wrong.

"Yeah, okay." Lo rolled her eyes and pursed her lips.

I didn't see Lo as the unforgiving kind, but then again, she'd been a lot different since that whole thing with Bryan, Brent, and Cam last year. It didn't take a mind reader to see how hurt she was on the inside from Kennedy letting Bryan into her life, even the slightest bit.

Kennedy danced her way over to me and wrapped her arms around my neck. She kneaded and pulled at my hair, forcing my head to fall back. "I want to go swimming," she whispered. "Naked." Then, she boldly and sloppily pressed her lips against mine.

I pulled away a fraction and shook my head at her, trying to suppress the images of that activity from my mind. "Not tonight, babe."

She dramatically pouted her bottom lip and thrust her hips into me.

"We have guests, Kennedy. No way." I tightly gripped her hips.

She wasn't into PDA, so what the hell was going on?

The look in her eyes was unfamiliar but still gorgeous. Anything and everything about her was stunning, but those gray eyes were the epitome of beauty. Even if they were slightly darker tonight. They completely stole my attention as she frowned up at me. I couldn't take my eyes off hers.

"You guys sure you don't just want to go to bed?" Dieter snickered at us.

I looked over Kennedy's shoulder and grinned. They were all watching us, each with a different expression. Chase's face was etched with curiosity. Lo's was marred with a passive-aggressive worried look. Dieter smirked at us but then buried his face in his phone. It took me a second to realize Talan was missing.

"Kennedy actually wants to do some night swimming. Anyone else?" I asked.

"Yeah, we'll join," Chase responded while rushing toward Lo, dipping down and throwing her over his shoulder.

Lo squealed and squirmed, trying to get down.

I walked Kennedy backward to the foyer with her arms still wrapped around me, mine guiding her by the waist. When we got to the stairs, I followed Chase's move and dipped down, tossing her over my shoulder.

Kennedy kicked and smacked at my back as she screamed, "Kyle!"

Her protests were pointless though. I had her in a tight embrace and was halfway up the stairs. Her hands clutched my sides as she giggled softly after I told her to hush. That gravelly rasp I was so attracted to came out to play, and I fought back a deep groan.

That fucking voice.

I roughly shoved my bedroom door open and walked toward my closet. When we were just outside of it, I swung her back upright and grinned at her wobbly stance and her twinkling wide eyes. I swooped down for a kiss, quickly and softly touching my lips to hers, thrusting my tongue out to trace her lips. My hands were on her waist, clenching the material of her shirt, ready to tear it off.

She suddenly pushed me back and held her stomach. Her face paled before she rushed toward my bathroom.

"Babe?" I questioned as I chased after her.

She slammed the door shut right as I reached it. I heard the toilet seat slam open before the obvious sounds of her retching came. I slowly opened the door and peeked in to see her face buried in the toilet.

"Kennedy?" I stepped up beside her. I took the hair she had been holding with her left hand and pulled the pieces she'd missed up into a makeshift ponytail. "It's okay; I've got you," I said.

She groaned and then braced herself for another round.

I knelt and waited for her to pull away. I rubbed her back as she calmed down from a third round of retching. Blindly reaching up to flush the toilet again, she slumped over into my side.

"I wonder if anyone else is feeling sick," I mused as I continued to stroke her back.

She only groaned, still clutching at her stomach. "Can you give me a second? I need to brush my teeth."

I swiped my hand over her forehead before standing and helping her up. "Did you feel sick earlier? You're burning up."

"No. I'm fine. I promise." Her weak smile wasn't much of a comfort though.

I moved to the door and leaned my shoulder against it as she grabbed her yellow toothbrush and my toothpaste. I watched as her hand shook slightly as she squeezed the paste out. I scanned her movements and then looked up to her face—pale and gaunt with slightly blue lips and rosy-red cheeks.

I slipped out into the hallway just as Chase was coming up the stairs, walking toward me.

"What's taking you guys so long?" He was already dressed in his board shorts, shirt discarded.

I glanced over my shoulder to the bathroom. "Is anyone feeling sick?"

He shook his head. "Not that I know of. Why?"

"Because Kennedy just threw up."

"Did she drink anything at the party?" He leaned up against the wall, and I did the same.

Shaking my head, I thrust my hand through my hair. "She said no earlier, but now, I'm not too sure. Maybe she did, and she just didn't want me to know..." I trailed off, thinking about all the weird behavior and the way Lo had been worried about her. How Dieter had said she'd been acting weird. How I'd caught her drinking in the morning after all the drama at school the other day.

She definitely had to have had a drink, maybe more than one.

"Is she all right now?"

I nodded, and when I heard the bathroom door shut, I gestured to show I was going back in and told him I'd be down in a few minutes.

Kennedy had stripped off her shorts and shirt and was standing in her tank top and little boy-shorts underwear. She walked over to my dresser and opened the third drawer to pull out a pair of my sweats. She started to slip on my team sweats that had *Eagle*—our school mascot—written down the side when she looked up and saw me. Her eyes were red with tears building up.

"Better?" I asked as I edged closer to her.

When I was near enough, I took in her flushed face and sad eyes. She'd been sick a few times around me, but this time, she looked like she'd been through hell.

She fiddled with her hands and nodded, licking her lips that looked chapped compared to the smooth, glossy ones I'd kissed earlier.

"I think I just want to lie down. This day really took it out of me, I guess."

"Sure." I moved over to the bed and started to pull the covers down for her to slip beneath.

She settled slowly on her side, keeping her right arm wrapped around her stomach, and her left came up to rest under her head. I covered her up with the sheet and comforter and sat on the edge, stroking back the hair that'd fallen in her face, before I leaned down to kiss her forehead. She was hot but not enough to be too worried of her having a fever. Her eyes drifted shut.

"I'm going to get you some water, okay?"

She kept her eyes shut and hummed her response. I slipped back out of the room and walked down the long hallway to the stairs. I could hear quiet murmuring as I descended, but who was speaking wasn't clear. When I rounded the corner to the living room, Lo was sitting on the floor with Chase behind her on the couch.

"Hey," she greeted me. She gave a weak smile. "Is she okay?"

"Just sick. She's pretty exhausted, so she's lying down."

I fell back against the wall and folded my arms across my chest. When I took a deep breath, I swelled up and held it. I always felt like I was waiting with bated breath when she swung from having such a good time back to a quiet and reserved role.

When Lo sighed loudly, Chase tensed.

"What?" I asked.

"Nothing," she said as she shook her head and pulled her knees up before wrapping her arms around them.

"Just say whatever you want to say."

She took her time in deciding whether she was going to talk or not, so I pushed off the wall and headed for the kitchen. I wasn't just going to stand around for her to spit out whatever she was holding in.

I grabbed a water bottle from the fridge, shouted that I'd see everyone in the morning and to help themselves to whatever they wanted, and went back up to my room. Kennedy was already asleep, rolled over onto her left side, her hair all over her face and my pillows.

I sat up in bed for a couple of hours, just watching her rest. Her eyes twitched from side to side, and I wondered if she was dreaming of me. Of the past. Of the future. I wanted inside her mind, but she'd locked me out. I couldn't break through her invisible walls or her shifting emotions.

The only times I felt like I'd made an emotional breakthrough was when she wanted me physically.

I can keep giving her everything I have, but how long will it be before it isn't enough? What if it already isn't enough?

Chapter 23

Kennedy

I ached. My stomach felt tied up in intricate knots, ones only sailors knew. My head pounded a beat that was too swift and loud. And how I'd felt last night, the freedom and the rapture, was gone. I was down. Disappointed. Guilty. I was *sad*.

I felt dead and disgusting.

I rolled over, reaching my hand out to search for my phone that I assumed was lost in the sheets. When I couldn't find it, I opened my eyes to see Kyle's room. The sunny day outside was visible through the open curtains.

"Hey."

I jolted up when I heard Kyle's voice behind me. He walked out of his bathroom, wiping his hands on a towel, while his dark chocolate eyes roved over me. I noticed his forehead was creased, and his lips were thinned, like they would do when he was worried or angry.

"Hi," I said quietly. "What time is it?"

He glanced down to the black watch on his wrist, the Rolex his grandfather had gotten him for his eighteenth birthday. "Just after two." He walked over to his desk and sat down. "Everyone went home after Dad made breakfast. I tried waking you." His voice was even with no inflections, making it hard to nail down his mood.

His back was to me, and I couldn't see his face anymore, so I wasn't able to read if he was upset or annoyed.

Those knots in my stomach seemed to constrict to an unbearable tightness, bringing the nausea from last night back tenfold.

"I'm sorry," I said in a timid voice.

He shuffled some papers on his desk until he found the one he had been looking for. "Your mom called a couple of times."

"Oh."

"You never talked to Lo, did you?" His voice dipped low. That was the only tell he gave me to his inner emotions. He was miffed, and he was keeping something inside.

My best friend and my boyfriend were much more alike than they'd ever know. They both kept their emotions bottled up with little physical clues as to what they were feeling.

I shook my head even though I knew he couldn't see me. I still didn't know what to say to Lo. The truth was so much darker now. She'd never understand, and the trauma she had gone through last year would only make her angrier at the decisions I had been making. There was no lying to Lo though. She had a way of seeing beyond the bullcrap.

And that scared me. Everything scared me really. Last night had scared me, especially after I'd gotten sick. The past few weeks had scared me. Kyle scared me. Not in a dangerous way but in a I-might-lose-him way. And, if he knew what I'd been doing and who I'd been spending my time with, over him and my friends, he'd leave me. Kyle was loyal to the death. A betrayal from me? And with Bryan and Dylan involved? There wasn't a greater one.

That was the most terrifying thing of all. And it was all in my hands. All that terror could go away if I wanted it to.

But, even with that fear, I couldn't chase away the feeling to forget everything, to stop feeling so sad, to stop thinking.

"Kennedy!"

My shouted name tore me away from my thoughts. I had done it to myself. I'd gotten lost in my head, the pain, the memories, the need to move on from my father's death, and I'd made crap decisions with how to cope.

"Did you hear a word I just said?" Kyle had moved to the bed and was now bracing himself over me.

I'd been so caught up in all of my stuff that, even with my eyes open, I never even noticed him move. Never felt his weight press into the bed as he caged me in.

"I'm sorry," I apologized. *Again*. "I was just thinking." *Truth*.

He sighed but didn't comment on it. He just moved back to the topic of my best friend.

"Look, I get it. Everything is still really weird, and the whole Bryan thing threw everyone off. But don't push away your best friend. She's worried about you, just like I am and everyone else who cares about you." His lips landed against my forehead. "I love you so damn much, and I don't want you to hide away in your head and not talk about things. It's not healthy."

He sounded like the school counselor and the grief counselor who had been brought in to help me deal with my father's death.

My head nodded but only out of muscle memory. I hadn't made it move. It just had because that was what I had been used to doing lately. It was the kind of acceptance that pacified everyone's questions and concerns.

He pulled back and stared into my eyes. I stayed unblinking, letting him look for whatever it was he needed to see. I didn't know if he'd ever found it, but he swooped down to kiss my lips.

And then it was a tangle of tongues. His dominating mine. Hands pulling at clothes. His knee slipping between mine to spread my legs.

And all those thoughts? They just slipped away. Because this was the natural high that made me forget everything.

That took my breath away.

This was the only high I needed. And I vowed to let it be the only one from now on.

Days passed where the only high I sought was with Kyle. Getting lost in him was the easiest thing I could ever do. The only thing that I knew was right.

But the problem was, I couldn't be with him twenty-four/seven. I couldn't be with him all day because of our opposite classes and because of the obvious—it being school and all. I couldn't stay at his house every night, or my mother would constantly call—pretending to be the caring mother she had been when Dad was alive, demanding I come home, and preaching to me about what my father would have wanted.

She'd tried in vain to get me to go to church for the evening service on Sunday, the day after prom. She'd come home that afternoon from Cole's lake house. Thankfully, alone. I'd immediately refused. I couldn't walk back into that church. Not yet. Probably not ever. It hurt too much to even think about going in there and not seeing my dad standing in front of the congregation, giving one of his inspiring sermons. It hurt even more, picturing the junior pastor, who was now the senior pastor, standing in his place.

Even thinking about it brought tears to my eyes. Change was inevitable. I knew that. But I wanted to keep a place in my mind that he never left. If I went and saw someone else doing his job, his passion, it would shatter the memory.

I avoided Mom for the rest of the week, only talking to her when we would have dinner or in a brief text to let her know I was at Kyle's.

She invited Cole over for dinner a couple of nights. I ate in my room on those nights. I couldn't stomach seeing him sitting at our kitchen table with a smile on his face and love shining in his eyes. So, I sought refuge in my room, hiding from what I knew was coming. Craving a reprieve from all the weird, crazy feelings coursing through my body.

And then it was Friday again. Finals would start on Monday, and then the senior class would have a week off before graduation, and summer would officially begin. I was supposed to be preparing and studying, but I couldn't even concentrate long enough to review my notes.

My email had been pinging daily with notices from Wheaton. They wanted to know what my plans were, if I was still coming, and they reminded me to send my final transcript after graduation, so I could still be considered for the honor classes my admissions advisor and I had discussed months ago.

The pressure was on and building, and I didn't even know what I wanted anymore. I didn't know if Wheaton was right for me. But it was the only college Dad and I'd talked about. It was his alma mater, and that had been really important to him. And to me.

I had backups, of course, but I'd never intended to use them. One was in St. Louis, but I never envisioned myself there. It'd always been only Wheaton.

But I also always thought Kyle would choose a school close to home, too. Now, he was going to be hundreds of miles away from me. I didn't want to think about the distance.

Studying was pointless. I couldn't stay focused on a single subject to actually learn anything. Not wanting to be cooped up in the house any longer, I sent a text to Kyle. I needed to escape everything that was barreling down on me, choking me until I couldn't breathe. I had to leave it all behind just for a little while. And I wanted to do that with him.

When thirty minutes had passed while I'd done nothing but stare at my ceiling and he hadn't responded, I called him. It was only eight p.m., but he had said that he was going to get a workout in.

The phone rang and rang until finally his generic, "Hey, this is Kyle. Leave a message," voice mail picked up.

I left a quick message, asking him to call me. There wasn't much else I could say without freaking him out and making him worry, so I kept my voice steady and cheery.

I glared at the walls in my room, covered with old picture frames that I hadn't dusted in weeks. I was usually much neater than the disarray my room was in now. I'd stopped putting my laundry away and quit sweeping every other day. Obviously, I'd let the dusting go, too. If something had a specific place to go, it was no longer there.

My dresser and the little pullout couch in my room had become cluttered and piled high with clean but unfolded or unhung clothes. Mom had gotten fed up, and I'd come home from school to see it all back in their rightful places, only for me to repeat the process over the next few days.

The silence was starting to get to me. Mom was still at some planning meeting for the nonprofit she worked for, and I'd been home alone all afternoon and evening. I paced the hardwood floor in my room, clutching my phone in my hand. I could hear the old grandfather clock downstairs ticking as the pendulum swayed. It was a gift from my dad's dad. We'd had it in the house for as long as I could remember. When Lo used to sleep over, she would complain about the loud gonging in the middle of the night.

"Now, I know what she felt like," I said out loud. Then, I shook my head for talking to myself.

The quiet was making me lose my mind. All the little sounds I'd known were there but never really paid any attention to were suddenly so noticeable. Aggravating and taunting.

I moved over to my laptop sitting on my bed and pulled up some music on Spotify. It was linked to my Facebook account, and the sidebar would show any of my friends who also had it. Dylan, who'd added me after his first party I'd gone to, popped up, and the sidebar showed what he was now playing. I clicked on the song and the playlist, and then I clicked to follow it.

Tove Lo was the artist. A song I'd never heard started to come out of the speakers. "Habits" was the title, but it was a remix. It was slow and almost annoying in the beginning. I waited for the lyrics to start, and I groaned when I heard them.

Leave it to Dylan to listen to some song about staying high.

But isn't that what I've been doing? Seeking highs to distract me all the time?

The world kept moving forward, but all I wanted to do was rewind and pause at a time before my dad was gone.

I was deeply curious about Dylan and Bryan. As confusing as they were, I wanted to know why they acted like they did. They both came from well-off families. Obviously, Dylan came from money—if his house was any indication. And Bryan's dad was rich. Or at least that was what I'd heard. From what Bryan had told me, his dad was never around though because of some important job with an important title that kept him in New York City.

Perhaps it was nosiness or my self-sabotage that had kept me going back to them those few days. I couldn't nail Dylan down, but the night his parents had had their fancy party and I'd walked into the room, he'd seemed on edge, and the way he'd described the drugs and the people who took them was angry. Like he resented them but couldn't help himself from being one of them. Bryan was even harder to pin down. If what Dylan had said was true, then Bryan didn't take any of the drugs he sold.

But why does he need to sell them in the first place?

And me?

I had been looking for a high to keep everything off my mind. But, now, to forget my pain and frustration, I sought out physical highs with Kyle. No more alcohol and drugs. I had been stupid to even take that route. And, afterward, my conscience had beaten me black and blue with guilt for being *that* girl. It wasn't worth it. But, when Kyle had first denied me on the night of my father's funeral, I'd sunk deeper into depression. Letting myself feel unwanted and lonely and sad. And, sometimes, the anxiety would just get to me, and the things Bryan had offered were right in line with what I wanted.

Before I could delve into more of my thoughts, I heard the front door open and close. I wasn't expecting anyone. Fear rushed through my veins as I crept to my door. I listened for any telling sounds or for someone to call out, but nothing came.

Did I leave the door unlocked?

I tiptoed closer to the stairs, straining my ears to catch any sounds. Papers rustled, and a drawer slammed. I flinched. Someone could be robbing us, and I was home alone. I ran back to my room, tripping over my own two feet, as I grappled for my phone on the dresser.

As soon as I had my fingers poised to dial 911, my name being shrieked was the only thing that stopped my trembling hands. Taking a deep breath, I walked to the stairs as my mom called out again.

"Kennedy Grace!" She sounded furious. Not the kind of tone that would have me skipping down the stairs with delight.

Instead, I took slow steps, descending the stairs, and even slower steps as I followed the sound of a slamming drawer.

She was in Dad's office. A place she hadn't been for weeks. It felt eerie and smelled stale and dusty compared to the smell of fresh coffee. Mom even used to sit in here and read as Dad worked. But, now that I thought of it, she hadn't done that in months.

I stepped into the doorway, and my eyes immediately glanced toward the liquor cabinet.

It was open, and the bottles that I'd stuck back in, either empty or almost empty, had been pulled out and placed on the desk.

"Care to explain this? Imagine the shock I got when I noticed the key to the cabinet wasn't under all the papers but sitting on top. Your father never drank these, Kennedy. So, why are there two empty bottles and two nearly empty ones?" Mom reached for one of the bottles with only a few drinks left in it, tipping it one way and then the other, the clear liquid sloshing around, before sighing and placing it back down. "Kennedy?" Her voice softened fractionally. "Is this a cry for help?"

I scoffed. My anger rose back up, surfacing like hot lava, even though I tried to keep it in.

"Please tell me you didn't drink these by yourself."

"What difference would it make?"

"Are you being pressured?"

Of course she wouldn't answer a question, simply moving on and looking for someone else to blame.

"Why are you in Dad's office? You haven't been in here for *weeks*," I hissed as I moved further into the office.

She huffed, her back stiffening and her shoulders held back. "Right now, I want to know what's going on with you. This isn't like you." Her eyes begged me to give her an answer worthy of her precious little angel daughter, who had been raised to do no wrong.

"How would you know what I'm like now? You haven't been around." I wondered who this brazen, disrespectful girl was. I'd never been so insolent toward my mom or toward anyone.

"Because you don't want me around. And, even when I am, you're running off to the Masters' house like this house is on fire. Tell me what I'm doing wrong, Kennedy. Talk to me."

She moved around the desk to come closer to me. I could see the pain in her eyes.

Or is it guilt?

And, as I took her in, I saw the black cocktail dress. One that hinted to an evening out. Not business as usual.

If I wondered who I was, then who the hell was my mother?

We were both hiding and lying. Keeping secrets.

What would Dad, her husband, think of us now?

My head shook. I didn't want to feel all this resentment toward her, and if I told her, if I let the hate out, I wouldn't ever be able to take the words back. And I knew they'd hurt her. Because they hurt me. They singed me up from the inside.

"Kennedy, you're shaking. Just talk to me. I'm not going to be mad. We need to get through this as a family." Her soft words didn't calm the flames at all.

I snapped. "But we're not a family, are we? Don't you get it? Do you even feel the guilt? Because I feel the pain! You ruined this family, and he's gone because of *you*!" My words shook, but they were loud, so powerful that they became like hammers and nails.

Pounding in the points for her to realize. And if that wasn't enough, I'd give her more. I'd show her my pain.

My conscience begged me to stop. To breathe. But I couldn't. Wouldn't.

My body moved before I knew what was happening, and with strength I hadn't known I had, I forcefully swiped my arm across the desk. All the papers and glass bottles and picture frames that sat on the desk flew across the room and hit the wall with an echoing bang. Glass shattered and splintered, raining down like my tears. Tears of anger and sadness and guilt. And I screamed. I screamed so deafening that my own ears ached with the pitch.

And, when I stopped screaming to breathe, I took notice of Mom's teary eyes as she held her hand over her mouth. Truly shocked at what I'd just done.

I'd missed a bottle. The one with the vodka that I couldn't ever bring myself to finish.

"And drinking this," I murmured quietly as I picked it up, "blurred the thoughts and the anger enough for me not to act like *that*." I gestured to the chaotic mess I'd just created. "It's been weeks since you've been in here, Mom. It's taken you that long to notice these bottles are empty. Where do you think I got the bottle of Crown Royal, Mom? I didn't get it from Kyle. I got it from that cabinet. You were so wrapped up in whatever the hell you were doing, you didn't even notice."

"I didn't know you were in so much pain still. I thought you were doing okay," she whispered through her sniffles.

"Still?" I asked incredulously.

She didn't *get* it.

The bottle felt like it weighed a hundred pounds in my hand. I wanted to throw it as hard as I could at the wall where there was now chipped paint. I set it down with a thud though. Not having the energy to do much more.

"How can I fix this?" Mom rushed toward me again, not letting me back away, before her hands were grappling with mine as I tried to evade the touch. "You can't do this to yourself. It's dangerous. We'll go to counseling. I'll call the pastor, and we can do this together." Her tears flowed freely now, taking the thick mascara on her lashes with it.

She never put so much effort into her looks before. The hateful thought quickly crossed my mind, but I stomped it out and took in her sadness, seeing that it matched mine. And, for the first time, I felt like she could see me and the hell I'd been going through, putting myself through.

I reluctantly let her pull me into a hug. My body shook from the emotions—the longing for my father's hugs, the grief of realizing that would never happen again—that swirled inside me, threatening to drag me under and keep me submerged.

"Your father wouldn't have wanted this, Angel. I love you so much, and I don't want to lose you, too. We'll get through this. *Together.* I promise."

Mom squeezed me so tightly. It should have been comforting, a safety zone, but all I could do was stay apprehensive and stiff, unsure of how to breathe easier. She'd finally seen the anger, but I still held back so much, and it felt like it was killing me inside. Slicing me up. Bleeding me dry.

And there was that little voice that told me to numb that pain, the burden of my emotions. My new weakness. Maybe I *was* dependent. *Addicted.*

I started to pull away. Needing some space and a chance to breathe. As my eyes unclenched and I looked down to the mess of shattered glass, broken picture frames, and scattered papers, I only felt a smidgen of relief before I was overwhelmed with guilt. I looked at the picture of Dad holding me when I was only a few minutes old, blissfully ignorant to how cruel the world would be when God snatched up my father. His smile was wide, eyes teary, as he cradled me in his large hands. Love was the only thing that could be seen in that picture.

I couldn't feel that love anymore, and it hurt.

"Don't worry about it, Kennedy. I'll clean it—" She was cut off by the doorbell ringing.

It had to be Kyle. If he'd called me back or texted and I hadn't responded, then he'd be worried. It wouldn't be the first time he came over without announcing himself. He always just knew when I needed him the most. And right now? Yeah, I desperately needed him.

"I'll be right back to help."

But, before I could move, Mom pulled me into another crushing hug. I thought her body trembled, but I couldn't be sure. She had been so stoic lately, and even though she'd finally just shed tears for my breakdown—probably from fear more than sadness—

I still wasn't one hundred percent okay with her. We weren't back to normal mother-daughter standards for us. I could still feel the distance and the negative energy saturating the air, like a humidifier was pumping caution into the atmosphere. I couldn't help but inhale it deeply.

There was a loud knock on the door this time. Pulling away from me, Mom swiped under her eyes to remove the smeared mascara. She tried for a smile, but it was forced.

Another pounding knock made my legs move out the doorway and to the front of the house. Kyle had a key, so I was surprised he hadn't used it already. But Mom's car was in the driveway, so he was presumably being cautious.

My hand went to the knob, and I readied myself to jump into his arms. I wanted his comfort more than anything. The constant battle of thoughts and emotions were draining me, and the only way I wanted to be drained now was underneath him.

I swung the door open with a rush, creating a gust of wind to smack my hot skin and burning cheeks, the only signs of my bottled feelings.

But who greeted me wasn't Kyle.

No, of course it wouldn't be.

"Hi, Kennedy."

Cole.

"Kennedy, maybe you should call Lo. We can do a girls' night—" When I didn't answer her because I was too busy staring at another cause of all my emotional wreckage and anger, she came around the corner from the kitchen and stopped midway down the hall. "Cole." She didn't sound as surprised as I had expected. But her hands clenched around the broom and dustpan she'd procured from the closet.

"A little spring cleaning, honey?" Cole's voice dripped with adoration, his own form of honey.

How fantastic and nauseating.

Anger flared again. And I thought Cole saw it in my eyes, as he stepped back an inch.

"Don't. Call. Her. That."

The clipped and edged way I'd sneered through my teeth at him caused my mother to grip my upper arm.

"Kennedy," she scolded.

I yanked away from her. "Looks like you already have plans for tonight, *honey*." I glared at her, my eyes burning with more tears. "Dad called you honey. Is Cole your replacement? Or, when Dad called you that, did you always wish it was your home-wrecking boyfriend?"

"I won't be spoken to like that, Kennedy Grace."

I almost expected her to wag her finger in my face. But she didn't. She just stared at me, like she didn't recognize me or the one-eighty my emotions had just taken.

Cole marched to her side and leaned in to press a kiss to my mother's forehead, but she at least had the decency to push him back with her hand to his chest and a subtle shake of her head.

How conservative of her, I thought.

She had the balls to cheat but not to flaunt her rebound.

The whole thing made me sick.

"Fuck your *girls'* night," I growled at her.

Even though I wanted to scream bloody murder and tear my hair out, I turned and headed for the stairs as quickly as I could, needing to be far away from her and her *lover*, texting Kyle as I went.

Me: Please come and get me.

My phone finally rang. I picked it up from the bed and sighed when I didn't see Kyle's name. Bryan's name flashed across the screen instead.

Last weekend was one of my weakest weekends.

"Hi," I answered right before I knew it was going to go to voice mail. My hesitation should have told me that answering was a bad idea.

"You disappeared, Angel."

"Why do you always call me that?" I asked, exasperated with the nickname.

"Because that's what you are. Fallen or not, you'll always be an angel in my eyes." His voice was scratchy, like he'd been smoking for hours.

"Do you like me? Is that why you keep texting and calling?" Asking him was stupid because I didn't really want the answer. Things were complicated enough.

I fidgeted with the bottom of my gray-and-yellow-chevron bedspread. A gift from Kyle because I'd wanted a comforter that was as fluffy as his, so he had gotten me this one, saying that the gray would remind me of his bed and that the yellow reminded him of me and the sun and how I smiled so brightly. He was full of cheesy lines like that when he talked to me. With me, he didn't use that serious demeanor, his calm and collected attitude, that he always dominated the room with. He would joke and laugh and say silly things to make me smile.

I felt like a traitor as I sat on one of Kyle's gifts and talked to Bryan, so I stood from my bed and paced again.

"That's a stupid question, Kennedy."

"Why?"

"Because I know commitment when I see it. And you? You're so committed to Kyle, it almost makes me sick."

I stayed quiet. *If I make him so sick, then why does he continue to talk to me?*

"Did you call for something other than to insult me?" I hissed. I wasn't in the mood for this kind of conversation.

His laugh was rougher than his speech. He should really consider quitting smoking. "Yeah, come over. Bring what I know you haven't used."

I rolled my eyes and rubbed at my forehead. Of course that was what he wanted.

I still hadn't heard back from Kyle. I pulled the phone away from my ear and went to my messages just to be sure. There wasn't anything, and that empty feeling started to come back.

Sometimes, I worried I was too dependent on Kyle. That made me feel even worse because he was about to go to Texas, and if he realized how much I needed him, he'd never go. I couldn't let that happen. I would never hold him back from leaving to conquer the world. He deserved to be recognized for his achievements. He was one of the best football players in the state. That was why he had been offered full rides to all the colleges that expressed interest in him.

Kyle had told me that, when he had gone to Texas for his visit, a couple of the players told him that the previous quarterback the team had recruited was injured and wouldn't ever be playing football again and that Kyle's name was at the top of the list for recruits. It didn't matter that it had taken another kid's injury for him to get the offer from Texas. He had still been on their radar.

I looked at my phone one more time, willing a response to come through. I shouldn't have been disappointed when my ability to force a text had failed. The silence pushed me to make my decision.

"All right," I sighed softly. "I'll be there in a few minutes."

I grabbed my over-the-shoulder Coach purse and threw it on before shutting down my laptop and flipping the lights off. Phone in hand, I braced myself to ignore Mom's and Cole's whispers. I jogged down the stairs and out the door, quietly shutting it before I set off down the sidewalk and toward Bryan's house.

When I came up on the two-story home that was lit up in every window, I slowed. Two girls were sitting on the driveway, hair in messy ponytails, wearing high-waisted shorts and crop-top tanks. Music played from one of their phones while they were hunched over, painting each other's toenails.

"Can we help you?"

I recognized the girl from one of my classes and the picture that Bryan had shown me that night at Dieter's bonfire.

Bevin, Bryan's new stepsister.

"Is Bryan here?"

"He and his stoner friends are down in the basement." She looked back down to her friend's foot. Then, her head promptly popped up, and she studied me closely. Her eyes narrowed to a squint, eyebrows arching in confusion. "Hey...aren't you Kyle Masters's girlfriend?" she asked with a hint of disbelief.

I nodded hesitantly. *How does she know Kyle?* I knew she was new to our school. From what Bryan had told me, she used to live with her mom a few towns over, but she didn't get along with her mom's boyfriend, so she'd moved in with her dad, who was now married to Bryan's mom.

"He must really trust you."

I was taken aback by her comment and took immediate offense. I stiffened up, straightening my spine and narrowing my eyes. "Excuse me?"

"Kiblen!"

I spun around to see Bryan and Dylan on the front step, cigarettes in their mouths, with laid-back postures, each leaning against the doorframe on either side.

"Come on." Bryan gestured into the house with a backward head toss. He pulled a deep drag on his cigarette, the end of it glowing bright red. When he was done, he flicked the cigarette toward Bevin and her friend.

Bevin screeched before yelling, "You're such a fucking asshole, Bryan!"

I glanced back over my shoulder at the friend to see her eyes glued intensely on the two bad boys.

"Maybe you should mind your own fucking business and stay out of everyone else's," Bryan said to Bevin.

"I was just asking her about her boyfriend, dickhead. You know she has a boyfriend, right? Oh, wait. Of course you do. You love chasing after what you can't have."

"Shut up, slut."

"Hey!" I shouted, breaking up their sibling dispute.

I hated hearing guys putting down girls like that. Lo used to get called a slut all the time from girls and guys who didn't even know her in any way other than her name. I didn't know Bevin, but it sure as hell pissed me off, hearing her being degraded like that even if she had been a brat to me before.

I stomped across the grass and up to the guys. Taking out the baggies as discreetly as I could, I slapped them against Bryan's chest. He swiftly put his hand over mine just as I started to pull mine away. I ripped my hand out from under his and spun around to leave when Dylan gripped my elbow, roughly halting me.

I glared at him over my shoulder with narrowed eyes and pursed lips until he released my arm. My face burned with contempt as he stared into my eyes.

"Oh, come on. Don't leave all pissed off." Dylan pulled another cigarette out and lit it with a match, carelessly shaking it to rid the flame.

"Why do guys put girls down like that?" I questioned even though I knew they couldn't give me an answer worth justification.

These guys were the womanizers with double standards that Mom had warned me about.

Dylan leaned down and whispered in my ear, "Time for some fun, *Angel*. This one is the best yet."

Wrapping his arm around my back, he guided me inside, and I didn't protest. I had no intention of doing drugs they had, but that didn't stop me from going down to the basement.

Chapter 24

Kyle

"I'm telling you—" Chase grunted and breathed out heavily through his final rep.

I spotted him, holding the barbell out from his chest, while he lay on the bench. Even though I was entirely too distracted to be any good for this.

"Moving down to Austin at the same time will just be easier. So, if you leave after the Fourth of July, we will, too."

"Your parents already closed on the house?" I directed my question to Lo, who was lying on the floor of her basement gym.

We'd come here every Friday to work out when Jacob, her dad, was home. They only came back to Davidson on the weekends they he had off. Her parents would stay in the city when her dad wasn't traveling for work and her mom wasn't following him like a detective. They needed to be closer to the airport because he'd often have to fly out at a moment's notice, and her mom preferred the city to our smaller community.

Her dad had spared no expense for his home gym. It boasted all new equipment and weights, and it certainly didn't smell like the rank high school or local gym we would use when Jacob wasn't home.

Lo sat up and leaned back on her hands. "Yeah, they closed last week. Mom just wants to get the interior decorator in and everything set up before we get there." Her eyes rolled dramatically, and she made a choking noise before flopping back to lie down.

"Are you sure your parents aren't relocating down there, too? I mean, that's a lot for a bunch of college kids," I mused.

She harshly scoffed and then sat back up to look me dead in the eye. "You know my mom, Kyle. When has she not thrown her money around like it's fucking confetti?" She pushed herself up to stand and then walked over toward us.

Chase was counting down from twenty, and as he got lower in numbers, she decided to push down harder on the barbell.

"Fuck, babe. I'm struggling here already." He tried to keep his breathing steady and not laugh at her devious little smirk. "I'm. Not. Freaking. Kyle. The Hulk." He paused at every word before pushing up harder. The veins in his neck were popping out.

I laughed out loud. "Thanks, man. I like that compliment. You little pussy."

"Gross."

"What?" I raised my brows at Lo with a smirk of my own.

"Do you guys always have to refer to a weaker man as a *pussy*? It's such a fucking insult." Her hand was still pressing down on the barbell.

Struggling to fight off her extra weight, Chase grunted out in agreement to Lo's comment, "Yeah, you dick."

"Not helping, babe." Lo glared down at her mouthy boyfriend.

"Exactly, it's an insult. But not toward you. Just your girlie boyfriend." I grinned at her before winking.

"Fuck! Okay, I'm done!" Chase shouted before roughly pushing the bar up one more time.

Lo and I helped him guide it back to its rack, seeing the slight tremble in his arms. He quickly sat up and pulled his shirt up to wipe the sweat from his face and temples.

"I seriously hate how fucking flirty you two always sound. And really? A fucking *wink*, Kyle?" He shook his head as he stood, shaking out his arms and then stretching them over his head.

I shrugged. That was just how Lo and I were. She was one of the guys to me.

"It's just weird. You're one of my best friends, and she's my fucking girlfriend. No talk of pussies and no fucking cutesy winks. Please?" He held his hands up, like he was praying and begging us to stop.

It only made us wink at each other and burst into laughter.

Lo glanced down at her phone when it chimed. "Well, this has been entertaining, but unlike what you two consumed earlier, I don't have to burn off three-thousand calories. I've got plans. You two have fun." Lo marched over to Chase, stretched up on her toes, and kissed his jaw before walking past him. "Bye, Kyle!" She winked at me over her shoulder.

Before she could get too far away, Chase reached for her hand and pulled her back, saying, "Wait, where are you going?"

"Dieter is here to pick me up." That was her only explanation.

"Uh, okay. But where are you going? And why is Dieter here to pick you up? You drove here."

She pulled him in close by the hips. I bent over to pluck my phone off the floor, giving them a moment.

I heard her whisper, "We're on a mission. I'll tell you about the results later. Beckon told me something and I just want to see if it's true."

The word *results* completely caught my attention. *Fuck, is she pregnant?* And, before I could stop my big fucking mouth, the question, "Are you pregnant?" was blurted out.

Chase turned to me with wide fucking eyes, and a crease in his forehead that said, *What. The. Fuck?*

"What? No!" Lo shouted. "Jesus, Kyle. What the fuck?" She took in Chase's worried expression and grabbed his face, her palms on his cheeks. "I promise, I'm not fucking pregnant."

He slowly dipped his head, blowing out a deep breath.

"I'll see you later, okay?"

Chase nodded stiffly, and she kissed him good-bye, strutting up the stairs.

We waited till we heard her shout to her dad that she'd be back later, and then the front door opened and slammed closed.

"Holy shit. Don't ever say something like that to me again."

"Paralyzed you a little bit, huh? Guess you should have stuck with the condoms, so you wouldn't have had that momentary doubt." I laughed as I took my seat on the bench and leaned back.

"We *are* using condoms. But shit happens, bro." He moved behind the bench to help spot me.

I lifted the barbell as he half-assed spotted and tapped on his phone.

"You're already playing house. It's not like things would change all that much." I adjusted my grip and started silently counting my reps.

He grunted before quietly commenting, "You're one to talk. And, *yes*, actually, a baby would fucking change things. *Everything.*"

Neither one of us said anything after that.

I hastily pushed the weight up and then brought it down slower. I was exerting way too much force to keep lifting this amount of weight, but I had a lot of bottled up emotions to get out.

Kennedy had been killing me lately. With her body. With her silence. We'd been together a lot in the past few days. Skipping lunches at school to go back to my house. She'd been slipping out of her house late at night to creep into my bedroom before sneaking back to her house before her mom would wake. I'd been picking her up before school and dropping her off right before her mom would start hounding us with phone calls. We were inseparable.

But, even with all that time spent together, we hadn't really talked. Not about her. Not about college. And definitely not about me leaving for Texas. Very freaking soon. The older we got, the faster time seemed to go by.

"We should follow them."

I strained to hear Chase through my own thoughts.

"What?" I pushed through another five lifts.

"Let's go." He took the barbell from me before I could even lift it again. "We're gonna follow Dieter and Lo. They've been whispering all fucking week, and I want to know what their 'mission' is." He air-quoted her description of what she and Dieter were about to get up to.

I smelled trouble, but I didn't want to raise his suspicions any more than they were.

I sat up, shaking my head. "Dude, don't you think you should have said that, like...I don't know...ten minutes ago? They're already gone." I swiped my hand across my sweaty forehead.

"I'll just ask D where they're going. He's not gonna lie to us."

He paced behind the bench while the phone rang throughout the room on speaker.

"He's not going to an—"

"What's up, man?" Dieter's voice cut me off.

"What's this I hear about a mission? And why the fuck weren't we invited, you dick?" Chase tried to keep his tone light and humorous but failed epically, instead sounding more pissed than anything.

"Don't fucking worry about it, you little bitch. I've got Lo and T with me. We're grabbing a bite to eat at Buffalo Wild Wings. I'll have your girl back to you in a couple of hours."

"Just fucking tell me what you guys are up to. I don't want to have to pick up Lo from jail because she let you talk her into doing something fucking stupid."

I waved my hands at him and mouthed at him to hang up the phone. He was so caught up in figuring out what they were doing that he didn't even realize Dieter had just given us enough information to find out on our own.

Chase scrunched up his face at me, looking all sorts of confused. He mouthed back at me, *Why?*

"Look, I know you worry, Chase. But don't worry. And, if anyone goes to jail tonight, it'll be *because* of Lo. This was all her fucking idea. So, have some peace of mind."

The background noise got louder, and I heard a hostess ask if they were ready to go to their table.

"Great. That gives me *so* much peace of mind, you dick. I want a fucking update every thirty minutes, so I know your dumbasses haven't gotten arrested. And tell Lo she owes me now."

Talan shouted in the background, "You're not getting a blow job, Chase! No one fucking likes that!"

Dieter sputtered, and I imagined he'd tripped over his own feet with shock.

"Lies. *I* fucking like that," Dieter said.

Both of the girls groaned and gagged.

"Exactly what you'd be doing if—"

"Stop!" Talan yelled, cutting off Dieter's tangent.

"So, we'll be back at Lo's later."

Then, the line went dead.

"Ugh, that fucking dick. He always does this. He's been more of a friend to Lo than us lately. It fucking drives me insane. What the fuck happened to the bro code?" He clenched his phone, looking like he was considering throwing it but thought better of it. Glass mirrors lined the wall he was facing. The veins in his neck betrayed his attempt to seem calm, frustration clearly taking over.

Moving toward the stairs, I told him, "Come on. I'm going to take a quick shower, and then we can go."

"Go? Go where. He didn't tell us what they were doing!"

I kept going up the stairs. "No, he didn't. But he did tell us where they were, and they were just sitting down. So, we can go stake out the restaurant and follow them. We'll go pick up my mom's Escalade. Should be discreet enough for them not to catch us."

"Fuck, you're right. How the hell did I miss that? Let's go!" He raced up the stairs behind me, passing me and rushing to Lo's bathroom.

I quickly used the one on the main floor.

If we were going to do this, we couldn't waste a bunch of time.

Earlier, I had missed a phone call from Kennedy. She knew we were working out, so I wasn't too worried about calling her back. As I showered, I missed another. Then, the moment I was dressed and primed to call her back, Chase banged on the door.

"Quit jerkin' it, Kyle. Let's go!"

Fuck. And he said Dieter was the dick?

"All right," I sighed, slipping my phone into my back pocket.

Kennedy could wait. She'd told me she was going to be studying all night, so she probably just wanted to talk during a study break.

We drove to my house and switched out my truck for my mom's SUV.

Then, we were incognito, staking out the restaurant, waiting for Dieter, Lo, and Talan to exit.

I checked my messages while we waited. Kennedy had left one, but it didn't sound urgent. I started to send her a text message when Chase smacked my chest with the back of his hand.

"Dude, there they are."

I turned my head to glare at him. He just glared back.

Dick.

"I'm going to start calling you Dieter, you prick. Seriously."

"Wait…why the fuck is Beckon picking them up?"

I quickly looked out my window to see Beckon jumping out of his lifted truck. Lo skipped around the back of the truck, trailing her finger across the tailgate.

I cracked the window in hopes of hearing what they were saying, but we were too far away to hear anything but mumbling.

"I've known him and hung out with him for a year, and I still get fucking twitchy with anger toward him," Chase said lowly. I had no problem with the guy and I'd thought Chase was cool with him but apparently not as cool as he led everyone to believe.

I rolled my eyes. "Anger or jealousy?"

"Fuck off. Like you wouldn't get jealous if your girlfriend were friends with a guy like Beckon. He's cool but he's such a fucking player."

Little did he know that I did feel that way about Kennedy and Bryan. Beckon was child's play compared to Bryan. Beckon had a reputation for one-night stands. Bryan was a drug dealer. I'd rather Kennedy want to be friends with Beckon, the playboy, instead of the criminal Bryan, who I know has no limits and would tempt her into doing drugs—or worse, overdose her out of revenge.

Beckon held the driver's door open for Lo, and she climbed up behind the wheel.

Apparently, she was driving his truck. My eyes bulged out of my head when I watched Dieter's keys fly through the air, and Beckon snatched them before they hit the ground.

"I don't think we have to worry about Beckon going with them," I mumbled.

Starting the Escalade, I waited, my eyes trained on the truck, while Dieter and Talan climbed in.

"You know what's funny?" I asked, chuckling a little to myself. I answered my own question, "The fact that Dieter trusts Beckon to drive his precious Audi. But Beckon only trusts Lo to drive all of his vehicles."

Chase mumbled, "She's a really good driver." It sounded like it almost pained him to say it.

Taunting him couldn't be helped. "And definitely better than you. Remember that time you decided to park at the front of the—"

"They're leaving! Follow them!" Chase cut me off with an exaggerated shout, his finger pointing toward the moving truck.

Doing as he'd said, I cautiously pulled out of my parking spot and started to follow the borrowed truck. Once we were on the road, Lo was heavy on the gas, so I had to maneuver through cars that had pulled out in front of me.

Chase stayed focused on the truck that I kept a considerable distance from.

Worry was stamped on his face. "I don't know what kind of mission they're on, but...why the heck did they need to switch vehicles with Beckon?"

Shrugging my shoulders, I concentrated on driving. My phone vibrated in the cup holder. When we came to a stop at a red light, I glanced down to see Kennedy's name flashing on the screen with a text notification.

Fuck. I'd forgotten to call her back.

The light turned green, and I had to ignore the urge to check my phone. I weaved in and out of traffic and followed closely behind Lo but not too close, always keeping a car or two between us. Lo made a hasty turn into a neighborhood that I almost missed because I was in the left lane.

Cursing, I sped up and cut off a small sedan before making a quick turn down the same street.

"Fuck, do you think they saw us?" Chase cursed.

I shrugged. If they had, they weren't trying to shake us because they slowed down, making it easy to follow them. We weaved in and out of neighborhoods before we finally made it to a neighborhood I recognized.

Because it was Kennedy's.

Chase broke the quiet silence with his own bewilderment. "Kennedy lives in here, right?"

"Yeah," I answered back, confusion evident in my tone.

The lifted truck pulled off to the curb in front of a random house up ahead, and I rolled to a stop on the block before, not wanting to risk getting too close or passing by them.

"Do you know anyone who lives in here besides Ken?" I asked, bracing my hands against the steering wheel and pushing myself deeper into the seat.

His head shook once. "Nope. Not that I know of."

We waited for Lo to drive off, but after five minutes, they turned off the truck. I did the same.

And then we sat and waited. And waited some more.

Chapter 25

Kennedy

On the couch, Benji sat with a beer in one hand and a cigar in the other. Sweet-smelling smoke clouded the room, and I waved it away, my hands flailing in front of me, coughing when I inhaled too quickly.

Music played semi loudly but not overbearing, like Dylan's parties usually were. An angry song blared through the speakers, something Lo would probably know.

I took a seat on the edge of the single chair in the room. Bryan and Dylan took the rest of the space on the couch. I kept my eyes focused on everything but them. The finished basement was nice. The walls were painted dark gray, giving it a movie-theater kind of feel.

Pulling the coffee table closer to him, Dylan held his hand out to Bryan. The baggie full of white powder was placed in his hand, and when he glanced over to me, he winked and then began his process of separating lines with a credit card. Then, he took out something from a metal case that was the size of his wallet. He pulled out what looked like a mini straw. Leaning over, he placed the plastic little tube up to his separated lines. In quick succession, he snorted three lines. Sniffing hard and holding the bridge of his nose, he leaned back.

I watched as he visibly shuddered.

"You want a drink, Kennedy?" Benji held out a beer.

I looked down and eyed the bottle of amber liquor at his feet.

He noticed where my eyes had drifted and chuckled. "Or you can have some Johnnie Walker. Ladies' choice."

"You sure you don't want to try *this*, Angel?" Dylan's voice was clear and deep as he fidgeted with the last line, straightening it on one side and then the other. He was mocking and taunting me in his speedy high. Almost instantly, his eyes turned dark and demented.

"Don't let this loser pressure you." Benji smirked.

I just stared, wide-eyed, at Benji as he took a deep breath, his cheeks puffing and rounding, like he was about to blow the white powder off the glass coffee table. But, before he could, Dylan roughly shoved him and then pulled back to punch him in the arm.

"Ouch! You dick. I was just messing with you." Benji rubbed at the spot on his arm.

"And I'm just messing with her." He smiled at me, but his eyes flickered from the powder to me a couple of times.

I shook my head once. That was the kind of thing that could ruin my life for good, and while I'd tried their stupid ecstasy, it'd ended with me being sick and regretting it. I wasn't going to make that mistake twice.

All the lies and secrets were enough to keep me down and surrounded by a pool of guilt. I didn't need to add life-threatening addiction to the mix.

Johnnie Walker was suddenly being dangled in front of my face. I'd told myself I wasn't going to use this vice anymore. Wasn't going to be the weak girl. I'd just wanted to get out of the house, and that was the only reason I was here.

Kyle never returned my calls or texts. I wasn't mad. But I couldn't sit in that house and hear Mom and Cole whispering. Hear my mom's nonchalant giggles. Or the sound of her new boy toy's deep chuckle.

And who in hell did he think he was, coming to our house? Even stepping foot in our house.

He was scum. A man who had preyed on my mom's emotions and weaseled his way into her life. Her bed!

I knew all the fault couldn't be put on just Cole, but it was so much easier, blaming him and *hating* him.

My mom was still my mom. I would never wish differently. But I could not forgive her for being the catalyst to all this destruction.

Before I could stop myself, I was holding the bottle, unscrewing the cap, and drinking down whiskey that was too smooth. Too soothing.

And then more. And again.

The guys watched but said nothing.

The music was turned up.

A cup with different whiskey and some Dr. Pepper was shoved into my hand. Benji wanted his whiskey back.

I was lost in my own head.

My phone vibrated in my pocket.

I ignored it.

The cup was constantly filled without my notice. I just simply drank down the smooth liquid, like it was water.

I tried to stand, but the moment I was on two feet, I felt like I was on a boat. Unsteady, rocking, I reached for something sturdy to grasp, so I wouldn't face-plant on the rug. It just so happened that the something sturdy was Bryan's shoulder.

His hands went to my waist to stable me as he said something. A big grin was on his face, laughter in his eyes. His touch almost burned me. And not a good kind of burn. The kind that ate you up, swallowed you whole. The wildfire kind. Engulfing any and everything in its path.

I couldn't comprehend his words. I just knew I needed air, or I was going to throw up. I tried to pull away from him and his grip on my hips, pushing at his chest to get him to let me go.

There was laughter, and looking to the side, I finally heard the words clearly enough to understand.

"Think she's finally ready for you, Bry."

More laughter.

Wrenching myself away from Bryan, I quickly moved to the stairs. Tripping over the air. Nothing really blocking my path.

Air.

I need air.

Air that wasn't smothered in sweet yet pungent smoke. Air free of testosterone and spilled beer and whiskey.

Breathable fresh air.

This alcohol was hitting harder, quicker than I'd ever experienced. But then again, they had been filling up my cup. Bryan and Dylan had made sure Benji kept my cup filled to the brim at all times.

Stairs.

I had to get up the dang stairs. When I lifted my foot for the first step, I underestimated the height of the stair and almost smashed my face into the higher stairs.

Hands halted my crash, pulling me flush against a chest. A chest that made me nauseous.

"I need air." I was panicking. I didn't like anyone against me. I didn't like feeling breath that wasn't Kyle's. It caressed my neck like the sharpest razor blade. It made me queasy. Made me shiver with fear.

I shook my head, pushed forward, and stumbled up the stairs. All the while, I could feel the heat radiating off Bryan as he trailed behind me.

And, when I burst through the front door and took a few steps off the front porch, I never expected to look left and see what I did. Who I did.

A familiar truck.

A familiar face.

My best friend stepped out of the lifted truck. Followed by the opening of the passenger door. One of our other friends. Then, another one, a newer friend that had become family.

Three faces. Staring at me, wide-eyed, with shock. Not believing their eyes.

Then, all the shame and guilt and pain and memories swarmed me. Took over my body like a nasty virus. And the feeling in my stomach was suddenly too much.

Everything came up.

All the deception.

All the sadness.

All the fear that I would lose more than I already had became reality.

While I was throwing up the alcohol, Bryan tried to help me. Tried to hold my hair back with his hand on my back as I braced myself over the grass.

Neither of us saw the punch coming.

Chapter 26

Kyle

I called Kennedy's cell over and over. Her text was cryptic. While I wanted to abandon this stakeout, courtesy of Lo and Dieter not telling us what the fuck was so important and why it had to be secret, Chase argued.

"She's fucking fine!" he yelled at me when I told him I needed to go.

Kennedy needed me. I wasn't the type of boyfriend who ignored texts and phone calls. I didn't know what was wrong. I needed to know what was wrong.

"Chase, just fucking get out of the car and go talk to Lo. There's nothing happening here."

The phone stayed connected to my ear. It was ringing, but Kennedy wouldn't pick up. She'd wanted me to come get her, but now, I couldn't even get ahold of her. My stomach twisted with knots formed by fear and guilt. Fear for not knowing what the fuck was going on and guilt for not rushing to Kennedy.

Kennedy: Please come and get me.

I read the text sent an hour ago over and over. No other details. Just a simple request.

But why did it make my heart race with anxiety?

The phone still rang and rang as I continuously called and hung up. The first two times I'd called, I'd left concerned voice mails, asking, "Baby, are you okay?"

Shit, what if her mom took her phone?

Cursing, I gripped the steering wheel tighter, the muscles in my arms constricting.

Kennedy could have tried to drink again.

Fuck! What if she got wasted and passed out? All the shit scenarios I could think of started rushing through my mind. Each image got scarier as I thought of the depression she couldn't seem to get herself out of, no matter what.

"They're getting out," Chase murmured under his breath.

I held mine.

Finally, something is fucking happening.

Tonight was dark, the sky ink black, with little stars out and the moon covered with clouds.

Where we'd parked didn't give us much visual as to what was going on. I watched as Lo slid out of the driver's seat first, followed by the passenger door opening and Dieter stepping out. Then, Talan slid out of the backseat.

I looked to Chase. He looked to me. And then we were both out of the Escalade and jogging down the street with quick, quiet steps. We held back a bit, crouched behind the truck Lo, Dieter, and Talan had climbed out of. Chase and I scoped out the surroundings before making a grand entrance.

Lo's gasp made us both pop up with fear-infused limbs. She wasn't moving, but even from where we were, I could still see her body shaking. And then she was moving forward, and that was when I looked up the random driveway we were standing by.

Except it wasn't random. And the long blonde hair was familiar. So familiar, I could smell the phantom scent of her just-washed hair. The coconut scent wafting around me.

Then, I was moving forward. Because I realized who was holding the silky smooth, fruit-scented hair back as her small frame bent over at the waist while she vomited into the grass.

I noticed the hand planted so low on her back, his fingertips almost curved around her ass.

Red.

I saw red.

But Lo beat me to it, shoving Bryan away from my fucking girlfriend, as she lost her insides on freshly cut grass.

Bryan didn't even have a chance to realize what was happening. His movements were slow, probably from all the drugs he'd no doubt used. His eyes widened a second before the impact.

I saw the wind back, the weight Lo put into her upcoming punch. Her whole body moved forward with wicked fast momentum. He had no time to react before her fist connected with his nose, and the crack of bone was heard over the sound of Kennedy dry-heaving. Lo always did pack a mean punch. I almost felt sorry for Bryan as I heard the snap of his nose.

"Shit!" Chase cursed, rushing toward Lo.

His arms wrapped around her, pinning her own down, before she could get in a second swing. But that didn't stop her from spitting at Bryan's face, her saliva mixing with the blood pouring out of his nose. She even kicked out, trying to inflict more damage.

Talan was by Kennedy's side before I could even grasp what the fuck was going on.

I thought I was in shock.

She fucking lied to me.

She promised me. Told me she'd deleted his number. Sworn she'd never talk to him again. Yet here she was. Puking up her guts with his hands groping all over her.

Who is this girl and how the fuck am I supposed to be okay with this? I am not fucking okay with this.

I was pushed over the edge. The final straw dropped. Camel's back broke. End of forever. All the fucking clichés.

I saw our past, present, and future evaporate before my eyes.

I couldn't fix her. Couldn't seem to fucking make her happy anymore. She had been keeping secrets. Sneaking around behind my back.

I didn't even know who she was anymore.

All the chaos swarmed my mind, like bees stinging me, and I couldn't fucking deal. I wanted to throw my hands up and swat away the irritation. Then, my eyes moved to Bryan, honing in like fucking lasers. I glared at him. Slaughtered him with my narrowed eyes.

Before I knew what I was doing, I sprinted toward him with my fists clenched, ready to fucking give him what he deserved. Dieter was in front of me. His hands shoved at my chest, bringing me to a halt. I batted his hands away, but they came right back up, pushing me harder and further back.

"Your fucking scholarship, man," he growled lowly, trying to be my voice of reason.

All the while, in the background, Lo was screaming at Chase, demanding he let her go and swearing a million curses.

My eyes stayed focused on Bryan.

Bryan, being the major piece of shit he truly was, overheard the low warning and smiled at me through bloody teeth and a crooked nose. "Yeah, All-Star, your fucking scholarship. Don't think they'd be too happy with trespassing and assault charges for their brand-new golden boy."

The threat was there. Layered with goading and cockiness. He thought I wouldn't jeopardize my scholarship, but he was wrong.

Dodging Dieter's hands, I started to back up. When D thought I'd gathered my senses, I faked left and sprinted around him quicker than he could comprehend. His curse was loud and worried as he tried to grip my shirt, the material stretching but not halting me the slightest bit.

I was in Bryan's face before another word slipped out. His doped-up eyes focused on me with veiled boredom. But I could smell his fear and disdain as well as the whiskey and beer seeping from his sweaty pores. It was so strong, I wanted to vomit.

I could see the smirk Bryan wanted to unleash, but instead, he stood there, stoic, waiting for my next move.

"Didn't we warn you last year, Endears?" I brought up our past encounter, the one where Chase had beaten the shit out of him and Dieter had threatened to sic his detective father on him. We'd advised him to stay the fuck out of our sights and town. And especially away from Lo. Little had I known, I'd need to worry about *my* girlfriend.

He swallowed slowly but didn't back away. No, not away but forward. Bringing us chest-to-chest.

"You know what's bothering you the most, Masters?" He pushed forward some more, trying to unbalance me. To intimidate me.

All it really made me do was tense up. Breathe harder. Clench my fists tighter.

"The fact that, even after you fucked her, she came running to me."

I lost it. I fucking lost it.

I shoved him back, and as he stumbled and almost crashed against the steps, I charged forward, fist raised. Ready to knock his fucking lights out. Just as I was about to connect, an elbow hooked around mine, and I was being dragged back again.

"GET THE FUCK OFF ME!" I shouted with pure venom.

My vision blurred with rage. I was going to black out from the overwhelming adrenaline and fury. Bryan knew exactly what to say to unhinge me.

As I struggled against the person holding me back, Dieter stood in front of Bryan and uppercut him in the stomach. Bryan groaned, leaning forward in a protective stance, bracing for more. He was outnumbered and outmatched.

Then, the front door opened. Two guys walked out. I recognized one as the guy who'd let us into his house party after prom.

Dylan, the douche bag I'd played football against.

Before Dylan or the other guy could do anything rash, Dieter shoved Bryan back, and he finally crashed down against the stairs. I would have felt sorry for him had he been better than the dog shit in the grass.

Fuck him.

I struggled harder to get free. I wanted his face black and blue.

"You just signed your own death certificate in this town," Dieter spit at him.

He spun to walk toward me, as I was still being held back by who I knew was Chase now. One of his arms locked over my right shoulder, and his other arm was locked across my chest. I hadn't expected Chase to be that strong, but he was. His grip kept me secured.

"Let's go."

I was tugged back. Chase refused to release me. When he rotated me and our backs were to the scumbag's house, he shoved me forward. I didn't stumble though. I just charged ahead. My muscles ached. I was fighting to not fight, and somehow, that took more energy than simply going back and letting Bryan feel a world of pain.

We reached Beckon's truck parked on the street.

Talan had Kennedy propped up against it.

She looked green. Sick and sweaty and reeking of smoke and whiskey.

I didn't even recognize her. She wasn't Kennedy anymore. She was a liar.

The fury within me swelled to an astronomical amount.

My hands slapped against the door panel on either side of her head, caging her in. Kennedy's drunk eyes flitted up to mine. I saw her fear. Her *regret*.

"*Why?*" I begged her to answer me. To give me something to make this all seem okay, but deep down, I knew there wasn't an answer in the world that would make me see her as the Kennedy I knew.

Kennedy's eyes, usually a smoky gray but almost black that night, flooded with tears. She shook her head before croaking out, "I don't know."

My right hand lifted and slammed back down. "BULLSHIT!"

She flinched so hard, it was almost like I'd physically assaulted her. She tried to stifle her sobs, but I could tell she was scared and overwhelmed.

I'd never been so angry with her. Never physically reacted violently toward her until recent weeks. But, right now, I could have squeezed her until the truth finally came out of her pouty lips.

Even with all the animosity, I saw her turmoil. We'd always been so connected, never really needing to use words. That ability had been severed since her father passed, but as I glared into those storm-cloud eyes, I could finally feel that connection again.

Beyond the truck, a voice from one of The Three Stooges carried over to us.

"You should have fucked her when you had the chance."

Overwhelming fury prompted my hands to fist, and my vision blurred, turning black, as adrenaline flooded my system. I almost sprinted to get back to the front porch. To finally fucking land a blow to that cocksucker's face.

"He's not worth it, Kyle." Kennedy's voice was meek, but it had enough of a punch to stop me as I moved closer to Bryan's house.

I paused.

In the middle of the driveway, I just stopped. The three guys stood by the front door and just watched. Waited. Their stances widened, and their eyes narrowed.

My breathing was labored and rushed. Chest rising so high and collapsing even further. My heart rose in my throat as I dropped my chin to my chest and released my clenched hands.

I couldn't do this anymore. I didn't know what I could do to fix this, her. To ease her struggles and pain.

Turning slowly, I met my friends' eyes. Each of them wore an expression of pity and sadness. Watching the girl we all knew fall apart in front of us wasn't easy. And it tore me up even more. But I just couldn't figure out how to make this work.

Lo's eyes were the saddest. She clutched her hand to her chest. I could already see the swelling in her hand from the fierce strike she'd landed.

"You know what, Kennedy?" My voice was harsher than I wanted it to be, but I still had all this hatred coursing through my veins. I scratched at the back of my neck.

Dylan's words were taunting me, trying to get me to turn my back on her and charge toward Bryan, the asshole who had made this all ten times worse. If he would have just stayed away, none of this would be happening.

I rushed back to her. Her back was against the grill of the truck. She must have tried to follow me as I charged to the front porch, but she'd used her words to stop me instead. She looked weak and wasted.

"I can't do it anymore. I can't sit back and just watch you self-destruct. You won't let me in. You won't talk to me."

I buried my face into her neck as I whispered low, words only for us, "But you'll let me fuck you till you pass out. And I don't even know if it's real anymore. I don't know if you wanted it because you loved me or because your guilt for *lying* to me was eating you up."

My hands went to her waist, and I squeezed tightly, hearing her gasp from the punishing grip.

"So, you're right, Kennedy. He's not worth it. But neither are you. We're fucking done." I inhaled deeply, taking in the scent that wasn't hers. Then, I exhaled, letting go of all the bad memories that had accumulated these past few weeks.

My hands relinquished her, like they were burning. I couldn't even look at her tear-stained face as I stepped to the side and continued to take steps away from the girl I'd thought was my forever.

I heard her break down. A gut-wrenching sob piercing the night. The rush of shoes running on gravel behind me. I prayed it wasn't her because, if it were, I'd push her away, and I didn't think I could do it twice in a matter of minutes.

Dieter was by my side in seconds.

I slid back into my mom's Escalade, jammed the key in the ignition, and put it in drive. Dieter sat silently beside me.

I didn't want to be this guy, the one that was cruel and violent, but I clearly wasn't what she needed.

A lump formed in my throat, threatening to choke me.

I hit the gas. Never looking back.

Chapter 27

Kennedy

Graduation Day

"After the ceremony, Cole wants to take us to dinner to celebrate. Think you'll be up for it?" Mom asked as she finished curling the ends of her hair in her bathroom.

I was sitting at her vanity, applying one last layer of X-Rated mascara.

My eyes were much darker than I usually did them, but they matched my mood.

I hadn't seen or heard from any of my friends in days. It was all expected. I'd royally screwed up. I'd broken their trust, and I'd broken their hearts.

I looked down at the necklace Kyle had given me, hanging low between my breasts. It hurt to look at the charms, but I couldn't stop. I needed the reminder. The reminder of who I had been and whom I'd lost.

My vision fogged until I was lost in my mistakes, remembering the weekend with vivid clarity. Even when it had all been happening, it'd felt so surreal. Like an out-of-body experience. A nightmare I didn't want any part of. All the while, I'd known I was the catalyst to my own destruction.

"You know what, Kennedy?" Kyle scratched at the back of his neck.

I was weak and sick from throwing up. The alcohol still muddled my brain, but I could see his muscles and veins twitching with rage. I'd moved from the side of the truck to the front with staggered steps, never taking my hand off the truck, trying to avoid face-planting. But, in all honesty, I probably deserved a face full of concrete.

With speed and brute force, Kyle rushed at me, coming back to the truck and where I stood. I tried to keep my flinch minimal, squeezing my eyes shut, as he gripped my hips punishingly.

"I can't do it anymore. I can't sit back and just watch you self-destruct. You won't let me in. You won't talk to me." He wanted to shout, but he tempered his voice, trying to be soft with me, even when I knew he probably wanted to turn around and kill Bryan.

He buried his face in my neck and hair, his voice dipping to a sinister whisper. "But you'll let me fuck you till you pass out. And I don't even know if it's real anymore. I don't know if you wanted it because you loved me or because your guilt for lying to me was eating you up."

Breathing felt impossible. I didn't deserve air. So, I held my breath, waiting for the killing blow I knew he would deliver.

His hands gripped my hips so tightly, I knew they'd bruise. But I didn't care. I deserved his pain. I prayed for it.

"So, you're right, Kennedy." My name was venom on his tongue. "He's not worth it. But neither are you. We're fucking done."

My heart incinerated. The flames licked at half of my soul as the other half held the match.

Kyle's deep inhale stole the last bit of breath I had.

When his exhale warmed my cold, clammy neck, I finally blinked and let the tears of my demolition fall.

His punishing touch was gone, like a flash of lightning. I was blinded by the striking contrast. There and then gone before I even knew what had happened, but it felt so close, I could almost grasp it. Then…like thunder, I heard him walking away from me. I crumbled to the ground, like the earth was shaking. Because my earth, my world, was shaking.

A sob ripped out of me, tearing me up from the inside. It was unbearable.

Hands were on my arms and my face, encouraging me to calm down. Soothing words sounded like nonstop screaming. I recoiled away from the soft hands that squeezed my biceps.

"Kennedy. Please…calm down. Breathe." Lo's voice tried in vain to calm my hysteria.

But why was she? I'd lied to her, betrayed her. I'd befriended one of the people she feared most.

It only made me that much more upset. She was my best friend. The best friend. And I'd betrayed her trust. I wasn't deserving of her help or her sympathy. She should be throwing punches at me, just as much as she had with Bryan.

I shook with remorse at what I'd done. I'd ruined everything, and I had no one to blame but myself.

Shoving at her hands to get them off me, I stood quickly. But the alcohol still hindered my body and movements. I swayed left and nearly fell again. My head was light, and the contents of my stomach rolled, if that was even possible. I'd pretty much lost maybe five days of food.

Stronger, larger hands gripped my shoulders to keep me from falling back to the ground. For a moment, I prayed and wished and hoped that Kyle had come back. Forgiving me for my crappy decisions and realizing that I needed him. Loved him. Wouldn't survive without him.

"Let's get you home, Ken."

Severe disappointment hit me like Lo's fist to Bryan's nose. I almost expected my nose to bleed. Chase's voice wasn't the one I wanted.

Then, it really hit me. Kyle had just ended us with a finality that was irreversible. I could still feel the hate radiating off him, like Chernobyl.

I continued crying as they helped me up into the insanely lifted truck.

Once I was buckled in, I mumbled, "You guys shouldn't help me."

"No, we shouldn't. But we are," Lo sneered.

"Babe," Chase chastised.

My head was a fishbowl of whiskey. Even though the drive to my house was only a couple of blocks down, I felt like I was in and out of consciousness for hours.

Then, I was held up by my best friend's and her boyfriend's shoulders under my arms as they helped me up my porch steps. The porch light switched on, illuminating us in a yellow glow. The front door swung open and then the screen door. My mother's gasp pulled my lolled head up to attention.

As if my fall from grace hadn't been far enough.

"What happened?" Mom's shrill voice interrogated us as soon as we were by the door. She propped it open and ushered us in.

I was so out of it that, when they finally got me up the stairs and to my bed, I could barely comprehend what was being said.

Mom was frantic, but I just wanted to tune everything out. I closed my eyes and felt the room spinning.

"I think I'm going to be sick," I groaned as I started to roll over to the side of the bed.

"Maybe you all should go," Mom shooed Lo and Chase from the room and told them to come back tomorrow.

After throwing up one more time, Mom helped me brush my teeth and change my clothes.

I cried when I lay back down. Kyle was gone, and he'd basically sent me off with a big eff you. One that I no doubt deserved. But that didn't stop the pain from consuming me even more.

Mom sat at the foot of my bed. Her hand rested on my calf as I curled up on my side. "Angel, what is going on with you? I never thought I'd see you like this." Her soft voice was full of fear and concern.

"Please don't call me that." My voice was gravelly and tired, hitching at the end with another sob.

Everyone who called me that eventually left me. I wasn't that Angel anymore. I wasn't that Kennedy anymore. Tonight had proven that. So, I didn't deserve that nickname any longer.

She sighed as she stood from the bed, but she didn't say anything, nor did she speak before she left the room, leaving the door cracked just slightly. But I could almost hear the devastated disappointment she kept within her.

I cried myself to sleep that night.

When I woke, the sun shining through my curtains, I burrowed further into my bed, wrapping the comforter tighter around me. It was all just a bad, terrible dream. I tried to convince myself that was true. Tried to sleep away reality.

Mom came to wake me in the late afternoon with soup and Advil.

We didn't talk as she sat at the end of my bed and waited for me to eat. The hot soup settled in my empty stomach like a brick. It almost made me sick again, but I fought the urge to throw up.

Pushing away the tray, I settled back on my side. My knees pulled up, and my arms wrapped around them.

Mom's heavy sigh made me clench my eyes shut. "Kennedy..." Her tone reeked of frustration and concern. "Last night...baby girl, I never thought I'd have to see you like that." She moved up the bed to get closer to me, but she still didn't touch me. "Lo told me you've been off. That you haven't been acting like you. What do I need to do to fix this? You cannot let this be your path. Your father would have been beside himself if he saw you like this, honey."

Words kept pouring out of her mouth, and the whole time I sat there and listened silently. I didn't interrupt her because I knew it was the truth. I couldn't let Bryan, alcohol, and drugs be my coping mechanism. I couldn't let sex with Kyle be my distraction from all the pain.

I coughed to clear my throat, but it was raspy, no matter how many times I'd cleared it.

"I just want to move on," I said in a soft whisper. "I promise, I won't fall like that again. I know Daddy would have hated what I'd done, who I'd become. But I can't talk about it anymore. I've ruined everything. My friends hate me. Kyle broke up with me. I just want to move on, Mom."

"Kennedy."

I focused back on my mirror image. My eyes, tinged with red, shone with unshed tears. I shook my head and took a deep breath.

I was moving on.

"Dinner? Cole? He really wants to celebrate with us." Her voice was hopeful as she focused on putting the finishing touches on her makeup.

My heart raced with the idea of letting someone else in. Someone who might try to replace my dad.

But, again, I was moving on, and that meant I had to let go of my hatred of Cole, of my mother's infidelity, that festered within me.

I nodded my acceptance. "Sure, Mom. Sounds fine."

I smoothed my hands down the skirt of my dress. The navy color made my skin look even paler than I was. My blonde hair was pin straight.

"You look so beautiful, Kennedy Grace." Mom finally stepped out of her bathroom to stand beside me as I looked at myself in the floor-length mirror. She reached over to the vanity to pick up my cap and then helped me secure it in place with bobby pins. "You're so grown-up. It almost breaks my heart."

I walked over to the bed where my white graduation gown lay, ironed and crisp.

After I slipped it on, Mom bent low to help me zip it up. I made sure Kyle's necklace was tucked underneath.

"Your father would be so proud."

The reminder that he wasn't here broke my heart all over again, but I couldn't let that pain consume me.

We smiled as we hugged. Mom squeezed me tighter. Her sniffle tugged at my heartstrings, and for the millionth time that day, I was seconds from bursting into tears.

Kyle was originally supposed to pick me up before the ceremony, but instead, I rode with Mom. It was easier that way now that we'd made plans to go to dinner with Cole. I wasn't going to the combined graduation party that we'd all planned at Dieter's godparents' farm. There wasn't a point in making a scene. I knew I wasn't welcome, and I would never expect to be forgiven so easily.

As Mom pulled into the parking lot, I fought the urge to search for my friends. For Kyle. They were nowhere in sight though.

I climbed out of the car and kept my gaze down, watching my steps as we walked into the school.

"I'll meet you out here after the ceremony." Mom kissed my cheek before she left me standing by the entrance of the gym.

All the seniors were instructed to meet in the auditorium to get lined up by their last name. I hesitated walking in. My heart raced. The fear of seeing Kyle and him not embracing me, holding me, touching me…it was devastating.

I had to face my demons though. So, I steeled my spine and walked through the auditorium doors. The large space was filled with excitement coming from the girls' loud screams and guys' howls. It was the normal chaos for our graduating class. Loud and cheery like when we'd won the basketball state championship.

Being here only made me more anxious. I'd figured, if I just walked in, got it over with, I'd finally calm. That wasn't the case though.

Talan saw me before I saw her. Her shouting my name made me spin in a couple of circles before the aisle cleared for her to walk up to me. She was wearing a red sundress and strappy red wedges.

"Hey!"

I was pulled in for a tight hug before I was ready.

"You look so pretty, girl. You ready for this?"

I wanted to say no, but when we separated, I just nodded softly.

"You're coming to Dieter's, right?"

I shook my head, biting my cheek to stop myself from crying. I wanted to go, but I wouldn't put my friends through that. And I'd already promised my mom I would go to dinner.

Talan's eyes were sad when I finally gained the courage to look directly at her. She reached for my hand, but I clasped my own together. Hurt from my recoil marred her face like a slap.

"I'm sorry."

She didn't need to be, and I told her that, "There's nothing for you to be sorry about, T. I'm the one who messed up. I just...I don't know."

"You don't have to explain it to me, Kennedy. I probably know more than Lo, Dieter, and even Kyle, what it's like to lose yourself. And, hey...even if you burn down bridges, it's not like you can't rebuild." Her smile at the end of her words of wisdom was contagious.

My own smile, albeit small, made my heart feel lighter. My chest felt fuller with much-needed air.

She hugged me one more time, and this time, I embraced her just as tightly as she did me.

"I'd better get back to my parents. I just wanted to come down before you all walked and tell you congratulations."

I wished she were a senior with us, but unfortunately, she was a year younger.

She walked gracefully up the aisle, disappearing through the doors.

A teacher shouted for everyone to settle and start lining up to head to the gymnasium.

From that moment on, it was fast-paced with a whirlwind of speeches and names, smiles and handshakes.

When my name was called, I walked up the stage steps, shook the principal's hand, and accepted my diploma. As I walked down the exit steps, I couldn't fight my gaze from wandering, from seeking out the only eyes I wanted to see. But, when I found Kyle seated three rows behind my own empty row, his head was down.

He never looked up.

I slid back onto my seat and kept my head down as I realized I was sending up a prayer. A prayer that I never thought I would ask for.

I prayed he would find happiness. Even though I knew it would be without me.

We met Cole at the expensive restaurant in Fielding City. I'd wanted to back out when Mom told me where we were going, but I couldn't bring myself to disappoint her anymore. She had been so elated when I agreed earlier. I might not agree with the decisions my mom made, but if she was willing to forgive me for mine, I'd have to forgive her for hers.

Dishes clanked, and waiters refilled glasses all around us as Cole, Mom, and I sat at a square table covered in a crisp white tablecloth. Conversation was sparse, but Mom tried her best to fill the awkward silence and cut the tension.

I had to admit, Cole was trying. It was just hard to respond to questions I didn't have answers for.

"So, you'll be at Wheaton next year?" Cole continued cutting into his medium rare steak that I couldn't really bear to look at.

When I glanced to my mom, her eyes were sharply watching me. I nodded my head. I had no reason not to go there. It was always my number one, but that didn't stop me from thinking about Kyle and the research he'd done for me when he found out he might go to Texas.

"Sandra told me you're going to study Christian Formation and Ministry along with Psychology?" My nod encouraged him to continue. "So, you'll be double-majoring?"

That was the plan, but I was already struggling with my faith and my future, and suddenly, all the work and responsibility felt entirely too overwhelming.

I could feel my eyes widening, and my breath became labored. Thankfully, Mom stopped the questioning about all that and changed the topic.

I appreciated Cole's kindness and effort to get to know me. I told him as much when we finished our desserts before vacating our seats to leave the restaurant.

They kissed as he held the driver's door open for Mom. I quickly glanced away. I had to look away from the display of affection because of the resentment it stirred inside me. No matter how hard I'd tried to stomp in out, it still lingered like a hot coal.

Thankfully, they kept it short, and soon, Mom and I were back on the road and on our way home. I checked my phone for any messages even though I knew it was in vain. Everyone should be at Dieter's by now. I considered texting Talan just to feel a connection to someone but decided against it. I didn't want her to feel like she was in the middle or had to choose a side.

When we arrived home, I said my good night and slipped upstairs. Mom didn't question my quiet demeanor or early bedtime or why I wasn't going out to be with my friends. I knew she wanted to know all the details of what had happened, but our short conversation the morning after what I liked to call The Biggest Mistake Ever kept her at bay.

I lay in bed for almost an hour when I decided I needed fresh air.

It wasn't until I was in Dad's old pickup truck, windows down, pulling into the church's parking lot, that I realized where I was going.

Chapter 28

Kyle

Kennedy Grace Kiblen. A name that held so much value to me yet made me ache and anxious.

I'd felt her eyes on me as soon as the name after hers was called. I still couldn't bring myself to look at her. She'd been sitting just three rows ahead, but I'd kept my head down, too scared of what would happen if our eyes connected. If she felt my gaze on her.

Would my eyes convey how much I wished she'd just sprint into my arms and apologize for all this pain she was causing me?

Because I was in pain. Devastating, heart-failing, soul-crushing pain. My heart had been left on the asphalt road in a neighborhood I couldn't bring myself to drive through.

After I'd gotten ready for graduation this afternoon, I'd found myself in my truck, heading to Kennedy's, to pick her up, so we could ride together for our final drive to school. That'd been the plan, but it wasn't anymore.

I had sat at a stop sign, in silence, debating if I should turn left toward Kennedy's, or right, toward the school. I couldn't break myself away. Kennedy had been ingrained into my life, and cutting her out so quickly, so forcefully, had felt like cutting out a lung for a transplant. Except there was no transplant, and I'd forever be left gasping for air that just wasn't there.

And, now, I was sitting in a lawn chair, holding a bottle of water, and staring into the fire. Friends surrounded me. All slightly tipsy on alcohol or just floating on the natural high of *finally* being done with high school.

Some girls were more on the drunk side. They were crying into each other's shoulders as they realized high school was really over and that the small pond they'd ruled was about to be the big sea that had bigger fish ready to chew them up and spit them out.

I, for one, couldn't wait till I could get away from high school. From all the reminders of a love found and lost.

A kick to my chair jolted me out of my head. When I glanced up, I saw Dieter was holding a beer out to me. I shook my head as my only answer, and he shrugged and popped the cap off for himself.

Now that I wasn't staring off into space and everyone had calmed down for the most part, I felt claustrophobic. Ironic, considering we were out in an open field and the sky was clear, stars shining. I could remember countless nights when it had been just Dieter and whatever girl he was dating that night, Chase and Lo, Talan, and Kennedy and me sitting around a fire, just like this, and never being happier. The only thing that rivaled my happiness with Kennedy was football.

I suddenly wished with everything I had that David hadn't passed away. That Kennedy still had her father and that she was still my girlfriend.

I wondered what the pastor would say. What quote he would use from the Bible to help guide me. Or if he would go rogue and just tell me to follow my heart.

But my heart was torn in two. One half pined for Kennedy and begged me to run to her. The other half threatened to stop beating altogether if I even considered putting that muscle through that kind of strain again.

Before I knew what I was doing, I was standing.

Then, walking.

Then, driving.

Windows down. Radio off.

My phone rang three or four times, but I silenced it.

Then, I was at the Christian church, walking up the steps and slipping inside. This wasn't any normal church. It was more like a theater with a stage, comfy seats, and large projection screens.

Kennedy's father had made this church—"with the help of the Lord," he had always said—into a local gem. People from four towns over would drive here just to hear his sermons. He'd created a safe haven. And, even though he was gone, I could still feel his presence.

I slowly walked up to the front row and sat down in the first seat. Kennedy's mom usually sat in this seat with Ken right beside her and me next to her.

Praying wasn't ever really my thing, but I found myself praying, hoping David could hear my prayers, too. I prayed that Kennedy would forgive my harsh words. I'd lost all my cool when I saw her getting sick with Bryan's hands on her. I prayed his nose would heal crooked and his face was permanently swelled. Then, I prayed for my own forgiveness because I had a feeling God was shaking his head at my vengeful prayer.

Above all that, I prayed Kennedy would find herself again. Because I didn't want her to be lost and alone.

When I stood to leave, I noticed a new portrait hung at the back of the room.

David.

He was still here. I could almost hear his voice as he told us all to have a blessed day after one of his sermons.

I stood, rooted, underneath it, staring up at the lifelike portrait of him smiling down at me. The large picture of her father hung on the wall, proudly displayed. Underneath were his name and his favorite Bible quote.

Jeremiah 29:11
"For I know the plans I have for you," declares the Lord,
"plans for welfare and not for evil, to give you a future and
a hope."

Kennedy would be fine. She had the best guardian angel there was—if the chills I got from staring at the portrait meant anything.

My parents and friends and I had changed the moving date for Texas to Monday instead of the day after Fourth of July. I hadn't even had a chance to tell Kennedy when I was leaving, but now, it didn't even matter.

I was sure Dieter and Chase were now worried and wanted me to come back to the party, but instead, I decided to go home and get started packing. I needed to keep moving forward and not standing idle, waiting for shit to get better.

I skipped down the steps with my head down. When I looked up, I saw a familiar truck parked in front of the steps, and it brought me to a dead stop.

Kennedy's dad's old F-150 idled by the curb. The windows were up, and her head was resting against the steering wheel. Even from a distance and not being able to see her face, I could tell how beaten down she was.

I struggled with whether I should go to her or just move on. This was the first time I laid eyes on her since I'd left her crying on the road. My chest tightened, a lump forming in my throat. I wanted to hate her and leave without ever feeling anything, but I couldn't, so I moved to the driver's window and rapped my knuckles on it.

She jerked back and brought her hands to her face, covering her eyes before wiping underneath them. It took her a minute to gather herself before she finally glanced to the side and quickly looked away.

Tapping against the window again, I waited, tucking my hands into my front jeans pockets.

It took her another moment, but when she took a deep breath, her chest heaving with the action, she finally rolled the window down.

At first, there was nothing but silence, the idling truck the only noise.

Kennedy fidgeted with the seat belt before muttering a quiet, "Hi."

I could only nod at her, my own voice running for the hills.

"What are you doing here?"

God, that rasp. I missed her scratchy voice that could bring me to my knees.

This time, I offered a shrug. The motion lifted my shirt, and she glanced down to my waist.

I almost smirked but spoke instead, "Talking to your dad, I guess."

Her brows rose in shock and confusion before her eyes were glistening with more tears. It only took her nod to get them to fall. I wanted to reach out and wipe them away, but I couldn't bear touching her.

"I really miss him." The levee broke, and suddenly, she looked like she was drowning. Her perfect face twisted in pain as she held her hand to her chest, covering her heart.

"I know, ba—" I cut myself off. Instead, I said, "I know you do."

Her head fell into her hands, and she cried softly.

"I think you should come in. You haven't been inside since he passed, right?"

Through muffled sobs, she nodded her head.

I opened her door, leaned over her to turn the key, and then motioned for her to get out of the truck. "You need to see something."

I hoped what I showed her would change her opinion of this place. This sanctuary.

I escorted her up the steps into the church, but I never touched her even though my fingers itched to feel her soft skin. Usually, when we came here, I would hold her hand, and she'd be the one to pull and guide me in through the front doors. In the past, she'd loved being here, and she had told me it was her second home. A place where she knew she could always turn. But, when David had passed away, it was like she'd lost all faith.

I hoped and prayed, when she saw his portrait, she could feel his presence, like I had.

We came to a stop just inside the auditorium doors. I turned around and pointed, so Kennedy rotated. She gasped, her hands shooting up to cover her mouth.

Then, she whispered, "He's still here."

Kennedy could feel his spirit. If I did one good thing for her, I was glad this was it. I was glad I could reunite her with something she'd truly felt was completely gone. She stared at the portrait with tears still streaming down her eyes, taking the dark eye makeup she'd apparently done for graduation with it.

"I can almost hear his voice. His sermons captivated a roomful of believers in the ultimate higher power, the almighty Lord." She smiled before coughing on a sob.

"I know losing him changed you, Kennedy."

She shook her head. Not feeling like hearing this again. Not wanting to feel me breaking her heart again.

"I still love you. You have to know that," I said.

She turned away from me. Her arms hugged her middle, and I feared she was going to collapse when she hunched over slightly.

I didn't let her get far though. My arms quickly wrapped around her, pulling her back to my chest and squeezing tighter than ever before, even if it almost killed me to touch her. When she trembled, I shook with her. I hadn't touched her in days, but I knew I had to hold her together. Her fragile, broken heart, mind, and soul.

Kennedy held her breath until it was all too much. A horrid cry ripped from her throat and nearly shattered my eardrums when it turned into a scream.

This was the first time I saw her truly letting her emotions free instead of burying them so deep that she was numb to everything.

Nails bit into my forearms. I could feel the slice of skin as she dug in harder. I'd take her pain though, no matter what. I still loved her.

God, I love her.

I loved her so much, it hurt.

But this…this hurt so much worse. Holding her and knowing I had to let her go. Knowing I wasn't going to be here in three days. Knowing I would be hundreds of miles away.

This was the last time I'd hold her in my arms.

I'd ended it.

And, now, I had to accept it.

"I'm so sorry," she cried. "I messed up." Her nails finally loosened, but her hands still gripped tight. "You didn't deserve what I did. The lies and the silence. You only tried to help me, and I messed it all up, Kyle."

"Shh…" I soothed. "It's over, Kennedy."

My words only made her cry harder.

I loosened my arms from around her chest. She rotated slowly, but I kept my arms hugged around her.

"I should let you go." Kennedy's face was flooded with misery, her eyes huge and silently begging me not to walk away from her.

The two torn pieces of my heart exploded, like they had been hit by a grenade.

Nodding, I released her, knowing she meant more than just letting me go right now.

"Do you want me to walk you to your truck? It's late." I didn't know what to do with my hands, so I shoved them back into my front pockets.

"No. I'll be fine. I think I'm going to stay for a little bit."

I jerked my chin in a subtle acknowledgment. "Yeah, all right. Well…I'll see you around, Ken."

Chapter 29

Kennedy

Radio silence from everyone was what I deserved, but after two weeks of it, I thought I might actually go insane. I missed my friends something fierce.

Mom had talked me into going to counseling. We'd only been twice, and I always felt worse about my decisions leading up to this point, but deep down, I knew I needed to recognize my mistakes out loud. Knew I needed to ask for forgiveness and a second chance.

I wanted that second chance more than anything.

That was why I was at Lo's house, standing on the front step, debating if I was going to ring the doorbell or knock. I'd already been to Chase's with no luck. All the cars that were usually in the driveway were gone.

Just ring the dang doorbell, Kennedy. It's not going to bite you.

But the girl who answered the door might.

Muffled chimes rang out on the other side of the door, but no footsteps followed. I waited for less than a minute before pressing the doorbell again. Gathering up the courage to come here was hard enough. I couldn't just walk away now.

Even though she still might hate me in the end, I needed to get this out. Apologize for betraying her trust, for not caring enough about her feelings, and for not thinking about any of the consequences.

"Lo!" I shouted up at the window I knew was hers after the third doorbell ring had gone unanswered.

"Crap," I muttered.

Taking out my phone, I dialed her instead. Nothing but unanswered rings.

Then, I called Chase, but he didn't answer either.

I couldn't call Kyle. I wasn't ready for that yet.

So, instead, I called Talan, hoping she could point me in the right direction. Maybe they'd gone to the gym.

"Kennedy?" Her questioning tone was drowned out by wind.

"T, are you at home?"

"No. I'm on my way to a dance thing in Indianapolis. What's up?" She had to shout over all the background noise.

"I'm trying to find Lo."

"Oh...um, she's not home."

I groaned, "Yeah, I know. But I've been to Chase's and her parents', and I don't really know where to look from here."

The scratchy interference ceased.

She must have rolled the windows up because I could finally hear her clearly, and she wasn't shouting as she said, "I thought she was going to tell you."

"Tell me what?" My blood pumped faster as I waited for her response. A lump uncomfortably lodged in my throat.

"God, I hate being in the middle of this, but you were going to find out one way or another. Kennedy...they left for Austin already. The Monday after graduation."

My heart plummeted to the ground. As did my body.

They left? Already?

All of them?

"I'm really sorry."

There was no need for her to be sorry. This was all my fault anyway.

"It's not your fault." I coughed, trying to hide the fact that I was about to break down. "Good luck at your dance thing, okay? Call me if you want to hang out soon."

I ended the call before she could respond.

Sympathy wasn't something I wanted.

I wanted Kyle.

I needed Kyle.

But I couldn't have him.

I was supposed to ask for a second chance.

He didn't know it because I hadn't had the opportunity to tell him yet, but he'd saved me in my father's church, showing me I hadn't truly lost my dad forever.

I'd forever be grateful for that.

Thankful for him.

After everything I'd done, everything I'd lost, I was saved by the only person who knew how to save me.

Chapter 30

Kyle

Three Months Later

Texas heat and humidity was new to me, even after three months of training in it. Sweat poured down my face, the back of my neck, my chest. Everywhere.

Cursing like a sailor helped with the frustration of the sweat stinging my eyes.

I hadn't completed a pass all practice, and Coach was getting more and more pissed by the second. If I threw another interception, I'd be doing sprints until the end of days.

"Get your shit together, Masters! Before I bench your ass for the game!"

"Fuck!" I cursed again. Not that it was helping my game any. Just made my tension ease a little.

Dante Clemmons, a beast of a linebacker, slapped my back so hard, I stumbled forward. "You need to get laid, Masters. You're focusing on all the wrong things. Don't worry about your fucking three or nine. Get the ball to the running back before *I* lose my damn mind."

My game had been off since I got here. I'd been training harder and harder to improve, but I couldn't get it fucking right. At first,

I'd thought it was training with a new team. We hadn't ever played together. Hadn't built the connections yet. Hadn't gained the trust that they had my back and wouldn't let me get taken the fuck out.

After six weeks of nonstop bonding with stinky, farting, burping slobs, I was ready to be done with it and get back into my own room at Chase and Lo's house. Rooming with a three-hundred-forty-pound Southern Bama boy with the worst hygiene and thickest accent had been a treat, but it was definitely time to get back to my comfort zone.

We broke the huddle and set the play. Before I knew it, I snapped the ball. I thought of Kennedy instead of the ball soaring through the air, and it didn't connect with my wide receiver's hands. He stumbled, trying to catch my short throw.

A roar ripped from my throat as I dropped my head back and threw a fist into my own helmet. "What the fuck? Come on!"

Shrieking whistles blew, and Coach called practice but not before his clipboard flew through the air.

"Everyone, shower up." He kept his back to us, his shoulders dramatically rising and falling.

Shit. I just fucked myself.

"Masters."

I hadn't expected Coach's tone to be as light as it was, but I didn't hesitate when I responded, "Yes, sir?"

He waited till the team was headed to the locker room before turning and glaring at me. "I didn't give you a full-ride scholarship and a starting position, so you could fuck around and drop balls all over the field. You throw interceptions like that during a real game, and you can kiss your scholarship fucking good-bye." Pulling a towel from his back pocket, he wiped at his own perspiring forehead. "You were all-American and would have won your state championship had you had a stronger defense. We've got the strongest defense in the Big Twelve, and your offensive line is with you every step of the way. Something tells me it isn't the team. It isn't the plays; you've got those down pat. So, what the fuck is going on in your head that's making you throw away my fucking ball?"

I thought about the phone call I'd answered earlier.

Talan had called to check in before she walked into dance practice.

We'd FaceTime once a week. She'd been traveling the entire summer, going to different dance recitals, competitions, and auditions. Even though I knew she was used to that lifestyle, I could still tell she was missing us.

But this call was different. She hadn't FaceTimed, and she'd seemed to be all over the place with the topics of conversation.

Finally, after hearing her ramble for twenty minutes, I'd asked her point blank what was wrong.

What she'd told me nearly knocked me off my feet.

"Spit it out, T. I have to get to practice."

A doorbell chimed in the background. I knew that bell like I knew my text tone. She was getting ready to walk into the dance studio.

"I don't know if you'll want to hear it."

"Come on, Talan. I don't have all day. Is it about Max? Or that French or British douche bag that you told me about?"

"Neither of them. It's about Kennedy."

I stopped breathing at the mention of her name.

It must have been enough for Talan to question whether or not I'd hung up.

When I finally did breathe in, my mind immediately thought of the worst-case scenarios. "Is she okay? Did something happen?"

"Yeah, yeah. She's fine. I guess. I mean, I haven't really seen her all too much, but I finally got ahold of her today. I knew she was supposed to be moving into the dorms. But, when I offered to help today, she kind of blew me off."

Memories of the Kennedy right after her dad had passed came to the forefront of my mind.

Did she fall back into that depression? Fuck! Is she involved with Bryan again? Are they a thing now?

"You're going to have to get to the point, T, or I'm going to be on the next flight home."

"She's not at Wheaton, Kyle. And she's not going to Wheaton. She wouldn't tell me where she was, but I know she's not at home. And her mom's gone, too."

"What do you mean? Are they selling their house?"

"Not that I know of. There's no for-sale sign." She huffed out a breath. "I just thought you'd want to know. I mean, I would want to know." There was a hint of accusation in her tone.

I hadn't told Kennedy when I was leaving. I'd just left, thinking it would be easier. But I couldn't tell you how many times I'd almost turned around to go back and get her. Every fifty miles had felt like five thousand.

It was too fucking far.

"When's the last time you saw her, T?"

It was hard to mask my concern. Talan would be the first one to recognize my distress.

"I've been on the road a lot. It's probably been four weeks or so."

"Shit. And she didn't tell you where she was or where she was going?"

"She's safe. I begged her to tell me at least that." She stopped talking, and I heard someone hollering her name in the background. When she focused back on me, she was short and in a hurry. "I'll call you later, okay? I have to get back to rehearsal."

Then, she was gone while I was left hundreds of miles away with too many racing thoughts and terrible nightmares trying to morph into reality.

I almost did book a flight back home. I even went as far as looking up flights that would leave within a couple of hours.

But it wasn't my place anymore. I'd given Kennedy up.

And I'd been regretting it every single day since.

"Girlfriend troubles? New school? Worried about classes? I can't let you fuck up the first game of the season, Masters. You'll play next Friday, but damn it, kid, if you're not on your A game by halftime, expect to be benched for the first half of the season. I've got a senior with a shot shoulder hitting targets better than you right now."

Coach gave us the weekend off, and I took advantage of the opportunity to head back to my shared house with Lo and Chase.

Dieter had decided to do the dorm thing for the first year, but he had been staying with us more often than not. Classes had started this past Monday, but it was nothing but syllabi and introductions. So, there was that saving grace.

When I walked through the huge double-door entrance to our new home, the tension ebbed from my shoulders. And, when I smelled the taco aroma wafting out from the kitchen, my stomach was nothing but grumbles and impatience.

"Holy shit, tell me you made enough for me, too?" I shouted through the foyer before making my way into the spicy-smelling kitchen.

Lo's light laugh was a heavenly sound as she waltzed around the kitchen island in her tank top and cutoff shorts, preparing all sorts of yummy goodness. "Yes, there's enough. Kind of assumed you'd be home tonight."

"Mmm, you're the best cook in town, Lo."

She winked at me just as Chase walked in.

Groaning, he went to the fridge and buried his head in there. "Again with the fucking winks?"

"Relax, man. She's like my sister," I tossed over my shoulder, retreating from the kitchen to go up to my room to shower before dinner.

My phone lit up, and for a brief moment, I prayed it was Kennedy.

When I knew she was back home, safe, and somewhere I could find her, I could manage the urge to abandon everything I'd worked for to be by her side.

Now though, with her MIA...

I felt like an addict who had just found out my drug of choice no longer existed.

Chapter 31

Kennedy

I missed Kyle's arms around me.

I missed his kisses to my temple. My lips.

I just missed him.

Driving down the road, I blasted Halsey's new album as loud as the truck would let me without blowing the old speakers.

With the windows down, my long blonde hair blew all over the place, constantly trying to strangle me. Sometimes, I wanted to just chop it all off, but then I remembered how much I hated short hair. And how much Kyle had loved running his fingers through the silky strands. How it'd made me shiver and tingle and beg for more. How he'd massaged my scalp before moving on to my shoulders, my back, and eventually much more intimate parts of me that would steal my breath and curl my toes.

Just thinking about it made me burn up, and my stomach tightened with need.

If I could just feel him again…

I realized I'd accelerated a little too much with that train of thought and let off the gas just a bit. Cruise control would be nice during a trip like this.

I'd been on the road for what felt like days.

Mom had tried to talk me into flying or at least letting her drive me down. But I wanted this time to myself.

Twelve hours on the road was surely enough time to reflect and gain my courage back. Enough time to make this all seem like a brilliant plan that would not blow up in my face. I expected minimal shrapnel, but that was probably wishful thinking.

My phone rang once again. Every hour on the hour, Mom would call to check on my status. It'd pause my music every time I got to a lyric that I wanted to belt out on the freeway. But I didn't dare ignore her calls. She'd send out a search party if I missed even one check-in.

"Yes, Mom?" I tried not to sound too exasperated.

"There's an accident on thirty-five. Has all the lanes shut down. If I estimated right, you should just about be there."

Checking the time on the dash, I groaned. I was already running late and was afraid I wouldn't make it in time. An accident with shutdown lanes was exactly what I didn't need.

"Just don't be in a rush, Kennedy. Drive safe, and keep your eyes open."

"I know, Mom."

"Okay, Angel. Cole's telling me to just let you drive, so I'm going to *try* to give it a rest and let you actually do that. *Please* don't forget to call me when you get there, sweetie."

After I promised I would definitely call her the moment I parked the truck, we each said, "I love you," before hanging up. Hopefully for the last time before I arrived.

Just as I hit I-35 and picked up speed, not twenty miles in, I hit traffic. Slower, turtle-speed traffic. Until I wasn't even a turtle. Traffic was at a dead stop. I clenched the wheel and pushed my sore back into the seat with extended arms.

As if I haven't been in this truck long enough.

I threw the truck in park and waited. I sent up a quick prayer for whoever had the accident, hoping that they were okay. Then, I prayed the authorities got everyone rolling soon.

The sea of people I tried to weave through was getting harder and harder to maneuver. Somehow, it felt like, for every step I took forward, I would be knocked back three, especially when a bulky, rude guy who didn't even bat an eye at me bruised my chest and stomped on my toes.

As luck would have it, I'd missed the game by five minutes. Not only had there been a bad accident on the highway, but of course, I had also gotten lost in a big city I'd never once been to. I'd probably circled the city twice, continually missing my exit.

So, now, instead of following the crowd out of the stadium like I should have been, I was trying to get in the stadium, fighting against the crowd.

If I was right, I'd made the right decision by going in against the grain to get to the field.

Kyle had this thing he would do after every game he won.

He'd make his way into the stands and sit directly in front of the fifty-yard line.

For all I knew, I'd come in on the wrong side of the stadium, so my first sighting of him would be of his back.

As I finally made it through the crowd and into a tunnel that led to the middle of the stadium, I stopped to take a deep breath.

This was the moment I'd built myself up to for twelve hours.

The stadium lights were insanely bright as I followed their guidance through the tunnel. My eyes shut as I exited, too afraid to actually look and see him there.

What if he doesn't want me here? What if he's moved on?

God, did he already move on?

After I scanned the stadium all the way around, disappointment washed over me like ice water.

He wasn't here.

I wasn't from here. Didn't know anyone besides Kyle, Lo, Dieter, and Chase. But they had no clue I was in town. No one did, except for my mom.

As many times as I'd considered just picking up the phone, I'd needed the space just as much as they all did. And, unfortunately, none of them probably knew my number.

Bryan had forced my hand, and I'd had to get a new one. Even after blocking his number, he'd still found ways to call and text me. It wasn't too much of a problem anymore with his phone calls being monitored and limited.

Dieter's dad had apparently launched an investigation and gone after Bryan and whomever his boss was to get him and his drugs off the streets. The last call I'd received from him was from the county jail.

Looking around the stadium one last time, not seeing Kyle, I'd have to give in and call someone.

I came here for a reason.

I wasn't leaving until I saw my plan through.

My truck was parked so far back at the stadium that I'd sprinted here, hoping the game might have gone into overtime. Now, walking back to it felt like a million miles with the weight of disappointment on my shoulders.

"Kennedy?"

The deep voice almost shocked me numb, but I turned eagerly.

"What are you doing here?"

Dieter was in a white T-shirt with an orange Longhorns logo on the front. He didn't look happy to see me, and he pulled out his phone and started to text someone.

Quickly, I blurted out, "He doesn't know I'm here. I wanted to…I don't know. Surprise him, I guess."

"Well, this is gonna be one hell of a surprise."

"He wasn't in the stands, like he usually is. Or I was too late maybe." I kicked at the gravel under my shoes. Tiny rocks rolled to Dieter.

I got the impression that he didn't want to be around me. His hands flew over the screen of his phone before he finally pocketed it. I stayed silent, staring past him just so that I wouldn't have to look him in the eyes.

He was usually the jokester, but right now, he had a frown on his face as he assessed my frazzled state. I was sweaty from sprinting to the stadium and then being smothered in a sea of Longhorns fans, excited they'd won the first game of the season. My jean shorts and T-shirt wore the remnants of my road trip, wrinkles and coffee spills giving me away.

"You drive here from home?" Dieter asked me.

I continued to avoid eye contact as I shook my head.

Cole had invited Mom and me to his lake house again, and this time, instead of declining, I'd accepted. I'd needed the time away from a place that held a lot of overwhelming memories, some that I would get lost in and buried under. Feeling old urges surface until I spun back into a depression. Not just with my dad but with Kyle. And even Lo.

After a few weeks at the lake house, Cole had invited us to St. Louis. At first, I'd only gone because I wanted to look at another school, not entirely sure if Wheaton was still where I wanted to be. But then I'd realized I felt ten times better in a city that had very few bad memories, and I couldn't bring myself to go home just yet.

"You're not gonna talk to me or look me in the eye?" He laughed gruffly, but I still looked away. "I'm not mad at you, Kennedy. I know you were going through some shit. But you really fucked our group up. Fucked Lo and Kyle up."

Tears pricked my eyes. "I know." I tried to keep my voice sturdy, but it quivered with remorse.

"At least you know. Come on. Where's your truck? You can give me a ride to the after-party."

I led the way to the farthest part of the parking lot back to my truck. When we got there, Dieter took my keys. It was better he drove us anyway. I had no clue where we were going or how to get there.

We both climbed in to the cab of the truck and buckled our seat belts.

"How's Talan?" he asked me expectantly.

Unfortunately, I hadn't kept in touch with her as much as I wished. She was always on the road, and I was trying to keep it easy for her by keeping her out of the middle.

"I talked to her last week. She was busy with dance. We didn't really hang out this summer." I was sad that I hadn't seen her more, but she was so busy, and then I'd left town.

Dieter hummed as he maneuvered through the heavy stadium traffic. I was glad I didn't have to deal with this. Driving by myself for twelve hours and through this hectic city traffic had been enough for my nervous system today.

"I think it's good you're here, Ken." It was the first time he sounded sincere since he'd found me.

"I'm really scared," I admitted as I gazed out my window while we drove down a street filled with bars and restaurants.

He whipped into a parking spot and turned to me. "What you did was fucked. I don't think you know what you did to Lo. She was tormented by that guy, and you befriended him." Even he sounded pained by my stupid decisions.

"I know, Dieter. I really messed up. And I'm really sorry it all came crashing down like that. But I'm here to fix it."

"Good. Better bring your A game."

The street was packed with college kids out to celebrate the big win. Dieter led us to a patio bar. He'd been here all summer, so it shouldn't have been a surprise that he knew all the best spots to celebrate and hang out. He only introduced me to a couple of people, mainly girls. The guys all leered and whistled, effectively making Dieter switch to protection mode.

Jackass might have been one of his many nicknames and personalities, but he was one of the best protectors I'd ever had.

"Dieter!" my best friend's voice shouted over the crowd.

I could hear her, but I couldn't see her as Dieter pulled me along behind him, weaving in and out of tables and then over toward an outdoor bar.

"Brought a little surprise with me, guys."

Chase's deep laugh sounded before Dieter could pull me forward. "Yeah, Dieter? Another brunette we'll have to entertain when you decide to ditch her at our house?"

"Oh, fuck off. That happened *one* time." Even though I couldn't see the evil smirk on Dieter's face, I knew him and his reputation with girls well enough to know it was there. "No, I found a stunning familiar face."

With that, he jerked my arm around, and I came face-to-face with my best friend.

Lo.

Her eyes were still insanely blue, the color almost calming to my anxious, shaky body. She could slap me right here, and I'd take it with no problem.

Those eyes widened in shock before softening with sadness.

Every time I turned around lately, tears were forming in my eyes. I hated all the crying I'd done in the past few months, but seeing my best friend and the soft smile tipping her frown up made me want to weep all over again.

"I'm sorr—"

She was hugging me before I could even get the words out. Her arms so strong around my neck, she cut off my oxygen. I took it with no argument. I'd let her squeeze the life out of me, but first, I had to get my apology out.

Squeezing her back, I tried to clear my throat to get her to loosen her grip. She laughed into a cry before letting me go. Her hands wiped frantically at her eyes and cheeks before she pulled me back in for a softer hug.

My voice cracked as I pushed out my hoarse apology, "I'm really, really sorry. I never should have betrayed your trust like that. I just wasn't myself, and I let him manipulate me. I'll never forgive myself for the pain I caused you."

She slowly pushed me away and took in my features. She didn't comment on how hellish I looked. But she did make my heart stop with her next words.

"I'm still really, really mad, Kennedy." Her serious face with her drawn eyebrows, pursed lips, and sharp cheeks terrified me as she blew out a deep breath. Then, her lips gave way to a tiny smirk, but I didn't dare follow suit yet. "But I did get to break his nose because of it, and believe it or not, my therapist agrees that did a world of wonder for me."

"Are we okay then?" I asked hesitantly. I didn't want to get my hopes up for a quick repair or push her into something she wasn't ready for.

I could feel the curious stares locked on our embrace as she thought out her next response.

Releasing a huge sigh, she whispered, "You're my best friend, Ken. I've still got to work on fully getting over this. Him. But, yeah…yeah, we're okay."

Embracing her in a fierce hug this time only seemed natural. We each wrapped our arms around the other so tight, I feared we'd pass out from lack of oxygen.

"All right! All right! Enough with the waterworks, you two. I'm getting misty-eyed over here." Dieter tried to pry our bodies apart.

With laughs filled with raining tears, we finally let go. But our smiles stayed.

A huge weight lifted from my shoulders after that hug. God, I'd missed my best friend. That hug was exactly what I needed before I braced the next challenge. The one where I gave my all to Kyle. And prayed he gave me a chance.

Dieter guided us to our seats before heading off to get us drinks. I was thankful when he came back with all waters.

Chase and Dieter teased each other back and forth and rehashed the game.

Apparently, Kyle had struggled early on during the game and had almost been benched before he pulled off a huge pass and got the team a touchdown. That pass had kept him in the game.

I wished I could have been there, but I would just have to be at the next one.

Not wanting to pester but feeling the day's travel catching up to me, I asked how long we'd be here and if anyone else was joining us. Three sets of eyes were heavy weights on me as they watched me fidget with the straw wrappers on the table, folding and tearing them into smaller and smaller shreds.

No one actually answered my question. Probably because I refused to make eye contact.

They all knew what I wanted an answer to.

I needed to know if Kyle was going to be here or if I needed to just chuck it up in the air and call it a day.

Through all the silence though, I heard a dull hum. I looked around the table, expecting my friends to hear it, too, but it was just me. The magnetic pull from my eyes to Kyle was always there. This time was no different. I scanned all the faces that were coming toward us until the crowd split, clearing a path like parting waters.

Two really buff African American guys who looked like they could eat not only me, but Lo and Dieter as well were the first to come through. And, as they headed to the inside bar, the best damn sight I'd ever seen finally made an appearance.

"Kyle…" I thought I'd barely whispered it, but apparently, it was loud enough for his dipped head to hear and jerk up, searching for the source of his name.

It was then that I realized there was a girl walking beside him.

She was much taller and much thinner than I was. Her hair was blonde but had black and red highlights throughout. I wanted to be despicable and tell her to get her trashy hands off his arm. She kept tugging on his arm to get his attention, but he still scanned the crowd to find whoever had called his name out.

To save me just a little bit of embarrassment, Dieter shouted over the howls that welcomed the football team, "MASTERS!"

Kyle's head whipped up and straight ahead. His eyes went right to Dieter as he stood on his chair. The crowd that had parted started to close off again, and Kyle had to bob and weave through people to reach us.

Soft, slender fingers wrapped around my clenched fist.

I hadn't seen Kyle in months. Hadn't heard his voice. Hadn't smelled his perfect scent. All man. Some spice. And so darn intoxicating.

"I don't know if I'm ready for this," I whispered to Lo.

She squeezed my hand tighter.

"Thank God you guys got a table. My feet are killing me," the blonde girl whined as she lifted her foot, decorated by a spiky heel that was definitely made to kill. She seductively rotated her leg. The way she kept lifting her leg was about to become like the moment when Britney Spears had stepped out of the limo, flashing her bits. Before we got the money shot, she spun quickly, so her back was to the table, and she wrapped her hands around Kyle's neck.

Her red lips were at his ear. Whispering dirty things, I was sure. She seemed like the type.

And, dang it, I was terrible. I shouldn't judge her. I didn't know her. She could have been a really nice—

Okay, no.

Her leg was lifting.

I started to stand, my hand still covered by Lo's. "I'll just catch up with you guys later."

Clearly, I'd made a mistake.

I shouldn't have expected him to stay single. *He's the starting quarterback, for God's sake!* I was nobody to him now, and this moment only solidified the terrible fear that coming here was a mistake.

When I looked back toward Kyle, I realized his eyes were on me. His lips were parted in a shocked O.

I noticed his hands weren't even on the girl until he was gripping her waist to push her to the side.

"Ken?" The disbelief on his face was hard to decipher.

Is he happy or mad that I'm here?

Water droplets dripped from his hair that was a little shorter than I last remembered it. They splattered on his orange polo shirt, darkening the material.

"Ky," the blonde whined the shortened version of his name that I knew he hated as he discarded her completely.

I wanted to jump with joy and shout a snotty cheer that she had just been dumped, but I knew what it felt like to be cast aside by him. It wasn't easy, and it left you reeling for weeks. Months. I still wasn't over it.

"What are you doing here?"
I wanted to say, *I'm here to get you back.*
Instead, I said…nothing.

Chapter 32

Kyle

Kennedy was within reaching distance. I could practically feel the heat of her body, like it was against mine. Goose bumps rose all over her arms as she stood there and silently stared at me.

She was beautifully disheveled.

Hair high on her head in a messy bun.

Stains on her light-blue shirt and cutoff jeans shorts.

"Ken, baby…what are you doing here?" The term of endearment had just slipped out.

I saw her lips twitch when she heard it.

God, I missed you, Kennedy.

Her gray eyes sparkled under the patio lights. I couldn't help but take in her curves and light skin.

"She came to apologize," Lo spoke quietly. Proudly.

When I looked over to her, she smiled softly, and I could see the wetness still on her cheeks. She could have masked it for sweat on this humid night, but the mascara mixed in with the streaks told me she'd shed some hefty tears tonight. Her eyes started to shine more, and she looked at me with pleading eyes.

Hear her out, Lo mouthed to me.

I nodded.

Of course I'd hear Kennedy out. I'd been trying to find her for a full week.

She'd never been very active on social media, so it was no surprise that had ended up being a cold trail. From there, it was just her phone number. I'd pulled her number up for the first time in weeks, and instead of hovering over her name, debating if I should call, I'd just done it. Pressing down and waiting for the other line to pick up.

The automated voice letting me know the number had been disconnected was like being charged by a five-hundred-pound defensive tackle. I almost couldn't breathe as I'd blankly stared at my phone. That had been my last opportunity.

Talan had sworn that she'd just spoken to Kennedy on that number. I'd freaked even more when I started to think about all the wrongs out there.

She could have disconnected the number because she didn't want to be found.

She could be hurting herself.

She could be with...

No. I hadn't allowed myself to think about that.

But, now, she was here. In front of me. Looking stunning even though I knew she felt grungy.

Her eyes kept glancing to the side. To the blonde who had attached herself to me as soon as I'd stepped out of Clemmons's truck.

I didn't even know her name, and she certainly wasn't my type. She was the kind to spritz copious amounts of cheap perfume all over her body in the hopes that it would mask the scent of her cigarettes. She chomped on gum when she whispered in my ear, and I almost lost my mind with how irritating it was.

But, now, the girl I was still in love with, the girl I never should have walked away from, was standing like a mirage right in front of me.

I reached for her, but the blonde intercepted my hand. I almost knocked her off-balance when I wrenched it away.

"I'm sorry. I'm not interested." I didn't even look at her. Just kept my gaze on Kennedy.

The blonde huffed out a breath before calling me a dick extra loud, so the crowd would hear. I rolled my eyes but focused back on Kennedy.

Stepping closer, I breathed in deeply. She smelled like the road and Bubble Yum gum.

"I tried to make it to your game, but there was an accident," she finally spoke.

Her raspy voice nearly made me drop to my knees.

Then, what she'd said registered, and my hands were frantic as they reached for her face before skimming her arms and gripping her waist and hips. "An accident? Were you hurt?"

"No. No, I wasn't in the accident. There just was one. It blocked off all the lanes, and then I got lost downtown. I meant to be here sooner."

I squeezed my eyes shut as I fully accepted that she was okay. She wasn't hurt, and she was here.

My lips pressed to her forehead and whispered that same sentiment, "It's okay. You're here now."

Kennedy was hesitant to touch me but finally placed her hands on my hips. She was tentative and light with her touch. Probably afraid I'd push her away. But I was done with that.

"I know you just won your first game and want to celebrate, but is it okay if I say good night and we meet up tomorrow to talk? I just drove all day and would love a shower."

No.

I didn't want to let her go.

I squeezed her arms tighter. "Where are you staying?"

"All the hotels were booked because of the game. I have to drive back north an hour to my hotel."

My head shook. No way. She wasn't going anywhere. "You can come back to the house." I looked to Lo for confirmation.

"Wouldn't have it any other way," Lo agreed.

"I don't want you to leave. You should celebrate with your team," Kennedy said.

One of my teammates slammed into my back, and I stumbled into Kennedy, trying like hell to keep us upright and from me crushing her. We ended up against another table, her caged between my legs and my hands now on her waist.

"Let's get out of here," I whispered for only her to hear.

God, I wanted nothing more than to kiss her lips. Squeeze her thighs. Bite her shoulders.

Claim her as mine once again.

Three months apart wasn't that long, but it felt like an eternity.

Dieter, Lo, and Chase decided to stay behind for the celebration.

After going back through the crowd and being slapped one too many times on the ass, we finally made it back to her truck.

Kennedy and I rode in silence back to the house. At every red light, I'd glance over just to confirm she was still there. That this wasn't a dream. Because I'd had this dream before. The one where she finally made her way back to me, and we tasted a lick of happiness before she was suddenly gone again. Where she was gone like smoke, but I could still smell her lingering in the air.

She must have seen my disbelief at her actually being here because she reached over for my hand.

Our fingers laced together, like they'd never been separated for three long months.

The house was dark when we pulled into the driveway. We walked up the path to the front door, and before I could even get the door open, I had to kiss her. Pulling her in front of me, I pressed her back to the door, and my lips hit hers in a smashing-teeth kind of kiss.

Gasping for breath but unwilling to separate, I lifted her legs, and she wrapped them around my waist, locking her ankles to keep herself from slipping.

"We should…" she said.

No, I didn't want to talk yet.

"Kyle…"

That fucking gravelly voice.

My dick couldn't handle it, instantly standing to attention.

"Kennedy." I ground up and forward, pressing her harder to the door.

Her hand against my chest fisted my shirt before she released it, and her flat palm shoved me back with all her might, but I had seventy pounds on her. I only pursued her harder.

"Stop, stop. Please," she begged.

I groaned. I growled and thrust forward.

I missed her so much. I was turning into a savage.

"Can we please just go inside and talk? I really need to get this out and in the open."

Her legs unlocked, and I guided her body back down to solid ground. I finally slid the key in and swung the door open after taking a few calming breaths. She still breathed heavily as she walked in. As we went, I flipped switches to illuminate the rooms until we ended up in the living room.

"You drove from Davidson?" I asked.

"No, St. Louis."

My brows furrowed. "St. Louis? What were you doing there?"

"Mom and I stayed with Cole for the summer."

Well…this is news. And completely unexpected.

Apparently, Kennedy and I really did need to talk. This was a development I never saw coming.

"You disconnected your number?"

I had so many questions, but I couldn't stop staring at her legs.

"Is your room upstairs?" she asked instead of answering.

I nodded.

"Do you have your own bathroom, like at home?" she asked.

At least she still considered my parents' house home.

"Mmhmm. You want to shower? I'll make us something to eat really quick."

"That sounds great."

I showed her my room and the bathroom, motioning to her where the extra towels were and laying out some of my old sweats and a T-shirt for her, before I went back to the kitchen.

I scrambled some eggs, cut up some strawberries, and made her a hot cocoa. Everything was random but all things I knew she loved. When I walked back into my room with a dinner tray and the food, she was standing by my window, looking out at the pool glistening an aqua blue.

Motioning to the bed with a jut of my chin, I waited for her to get situated before placing the tray over her lap.

"Eat. Then, we'll talk." I swooped in for another quick kiss to her lips.

Slowly, she devoured all the eggs and strawberries. Then, she sat with her hot cocoa mug clutched to her chest.

My hand rested by her foot. I'd watched her eat, only stealing small bites every once in a while.

Chewing wasn't supposed to be so damn sexy, but everything she did was turning me on.

Maybe Clemmons was right. Maybe I did need to get laid. And the only girl I wanted to get laid by was sitting right in front of me, wearing my baggy sweats and T-shirt and slowly chewing her last strawberry with a whipped-cream mustache that she was none the wiser about.

"I really missed you." I just needed her to know that.

I was over all my anger and hatred. I just wanted her back by my side, and if her driving twelve hours to see my first game wasn't proof that she wanted the same thing, I didn't know what else was.

She smiled delicately. I had to lean forward and suck the whipped cream from her top lip. It had been taunting me, so I had to get rid of it.

She set the mug on the nightstand and moved the dinner tray to the floor.

"I should probably start from the beginning." Her chin dipped down to her chest, her cheeks reddening with embarrassment. It took her several deep breaths and the wringing of her hands to get her to continue. "When Dad died, I was terrified and lost. So incomplete. And this pain"—she rubbed at her chest, like she was about to experience a heart attack—"it wouldn't go away. At first, you wouldn't touch me, Kyle. And I don't blame you because the things I said...the things I did...I should have known I was losing it."

"It's okay to lose it sometimes, Kennedy."

Her head shook, and tears trickled down her cheeks again. "When you got back from Texas and told me how excited you were, how much you liked it down here...I felt that pain quadruple. Suddenly, it wasn't just in my chest anymore. It was everywhere, and I could feel you slipping away even if I was the one pushing you to go."

My hands reached for hers, and she let me hold them in my own.

"I would have stayed if that was what you wanted, Ken. Baby, I would have stayed."

"I didn't want you to have to choose between what I wanted and what you wanted." Her hands were shaking. "You'd already sacrificed so much for me, and I wasn't going to let you do it anymore. Texas was where you wanted to go. They wanted you, Kyle. Who was I to take that opportunity away from you?"

Now, my head shook. "You wouldn't have taken it away if it was my choice."

"Stop!" Crying out, she snatched her hands away from me. "When you got back from Texas, Bryan was at that bonfire to pick up his stepsister. He found me crying because Mom and I had been fighting. We weren't even really fighting. I was just so mad at her for cheating on Dad. For letting Cole ruin our family.

"I convinced myself that Dad had been so stressed out, his heart broke. That the stress of his wife choosing another man over him had stolen his life. The doctor had told me it could have been stress-induced. It only made my belief stronger. Made me hate her that much more."

She sniffled, but she held off the waterworks. "You remember the day my mom wanted me to come home for lunch after I had been staying with you for a while? I fought with Mom. She finally admitted she'd cheated on Dad and gave me some bullshit excuses as to why. After, I trashed my room and passed out on my bed. I even packed my bags, and I was going to call you, but Mom told me I couldn't go.

"I was so drained. I didn't fight her, but I wish I had. I wish I had just let you come get me when you called. Because then maybe none of this would have happened. I wouldn't have run in to Bryan when he randomly walked by my house. Or at least, I think it was random, but I know how manipulative he was to me.

"I wish I'd never gotten in Bryan's car and gone to Dylan's. Maybe I wouldn't have kept sneaking alcohol out of my parents' liquor cabinet or your closet. Maybe I wouldn't have drunk and found comfort in their brand of letting go."

She twisted around until she could climb off the bed. I sat and listened to her, all while trying to understand her hurried thoughts and veil my anger.

Bryan had sucked her into his shitty life when she was vulnerable. He'd preyed on the weak and emotional. That was his high more than his drugs.

Pacing the room, she went on. Telling me about the ecstasy. The coke they'd tried to get her to do. How Dylan always hinted about Bryan wanting to fuck her. How that final night, when everything had come to light, that she felt like they were getting her so drunk so that she would black out.

Thank God she hadn't.

If they would have...

They could have.

That was all I could focus on. It had been three to one. She was nothing compared to the weight of three grown men.

The fear almost choked me to death until I remembered she had gotten out of there. Only to be destroyed by me instead.

"Bryan wouldn't stop calling and messaging me. Then, he called from jail. So, Mom and I went and got my number changed."

Bryan is in jail?

"Wait, he called you from jail? What did he want?"

She shook her head. From the look in her eyes, I understood that she hadn't answered because she didn't know, but because she didn't want *me* to know.

"Kennedy," I growled her name, punctuating it with a fierce scowl.

"At first, he just wanted me to come see him. Then, he got angry when I told him to stop calling. He's pissed at Dieter and all of you. I told him you guys had nothing to do with him going to jail, but he wouldn't listen."

The more we talked about it, I could tell it was upsetting her, so I let the topic go for the moment. I made a mental note to talk to Dieter about all this. I wondered if he'd actually talked to his dad about investigating Bryan like we'd threatened last year.

Kennedy stood by the window, staring out at the pool again. I sidled up behind her but kept my hands to myself. If I touched her, I wouldn't stop. I'd strip her of *my* clothes and throw her on *my* bed.

And we wouldn't leave till Monday morning.

"When do you have to go back?" The question had been bugging me the whole drive here.

She spun to meet my eyes. "I guess it just depends on when you want me to leave."

"Never."

"Kyle, I don't know how many times I can say I'm sorry, but you have to know I am. I don't want your forgiveness because I know I betrayed you and all our friends. But I love you, and—"

"Stop talking. Now."

My hands were in her hair, pulling softly to maneuver her head to the angle I wanted. My tongue was in her mouth in seconds, her moan granting me unhindered access.

She bit my lip and pulled back, making me wince but spurring me on. I surged forward, harder. If she wanted to play dirty, I could play dirty.

"Wait." She tossed her head back and gasped.

"No, not this time." I slid my hands down her back, keeping our bodies together as close as possible, until I could grip the backs of her thighs and lift her back up.

I was burning up. I wanted to fuck her so bad, but I didn't want to be rough with her, like I had been during those final weeks. Where I'd bruised her pelvis because she wanted it harder. Where she'd had bite marks all over her neck and chest because she'd sworn it was what she wanted.

"My phone's ringing."

A distant ring could definitely be heard, probably buried under her clothes on the bathroom floor, but that wasn't important right now.

Right now, the only thing that was important was her being laid out on my bed, beneath me. Taking me all in. My hands caressing the smoothest, silkiest skin. Her hands gripping my biceps. Urging me to just love her.

And I would.

I'd love her until love was all she felt.

No more sadness.

No more self-destruction.

"Kyle."

I softly laid her on the edge of the bed. She scooted up the bed and lay back, arching her back and clenching the comforter.

Damn it!

She made it so hard to not pounce and fuck.

"I'm burning up," she moaned. "Get these clothes off."

She wasn't talking about hers because her hands were already frantically pushing her sweats off and not even bothering to take the T-shirt off. Just shoving it up and baring her small breasts for me. Her nipples were peaked and begging for me to show them my undying attention.

"This is real, right?" Her voice was nothing but heavy breaths and sighed words as I licked and sucked all over her chest and stomach.

"So real, Angel." I licked one tight peak, and she bucked her hips.

"You never answered my question…"

I struggled to remember what question she wanted an answer to.

"My dick's so hard, it has to be real, Kennedy."

"No…" she sighed.

"What, Ken? No what?"

My hands were shoving my unbuttoned, unzipped jeans down my thighs. She took the free moment to catch her breath, slowly sitting up.

She smoothed the fallen strands from her bun back. "When do you want me to leave?"

I had a face full of shirt when she asked that question for the second time. I ripped it away and chucked it across the room.

"Maybe you didn't hear me the first time." I yanked her ankle to flatten her back to the bed.

That breath she'd just caught was already lost. I straddled her hips and leaned down to cage her head in with my arms.

My lips hovered over her right cheek. "N"—kiss on the left cheek—"E"—kiss, lips—"V"—kiss, left breast—"E"—nibbling her neck, right where her pulse hammered, and her full-body shudder made my cock twitch—"R"—bite, right breast.

She groaned, and I nearly came.

Chapter 33

Kennedy

Kyle's mouth was doing very wicked things to my body. We never had a problem being intimate, but my body was going to combust from the heat swirling deep within and through every vein.

I tried to roll us, so I could be on top. I wanted to torture him just as much as he was tormenting me.

My phone continued to buzz in the bathroom, but Kyle refused to let me focus on that as he slid lower down my body. His tongue worshipped every inch of my waist as he tried to shift further and further down. We'd never done oral, and although I was feeling adventurous, I wasn't ready for him to be that intimate with my downstairs.

I tugged at his hair, gently pulling him back up. His chest rumbled against me as he chuckled.

"Still not ready for me to go down on you?" His eyes held a challenge, but I offered one of my own.

"I just want you so deep inside me, I see stars."

"Oh God, Kennedy. Keep talking like that." He leaned over the side of the bed and reached for a condom. "You haven't been—"

"No, Kyle. Never."

His question was warranted, but I didn't even want to know if he had. Kyle had been down here for months, and if the girl from earlier was a sign of what went after him...well, she spoke for herself.

He slid the condom on with expert precision. "Don't worry, Angel. No one. I've only wanted you. Thought of you every time I needed a release."

He slid the head of his cock over my clit. My stomach tightened with anticipation. He made me so wet, I could barely handle it, but his words made my eyes prick with tears.

Jesus, I am a water well of epic proportions. Everything is making me cry.

"I love you," I breathed out.

I loved him so much, it hurt. But he soothed the pain as much as he caused it.

"When I saw you sitting at that table tonight..." He started to slip inside slowly, so slow that I almost dug my nails into his insanely muscled back to urge him further. Before I could even get the leverage though, he was thrusting in and out, moving just a little deeper with each drive forward. "I thought I might have gotten tackled on the field and knocked out cold."

A hiss made my spine tingle when he bent down to whisper in my ear, "Baby, if I wake up from this moment and you're not here...you'd better be ready. Because I'll be coming for you."

But he didn't wake up.

In fact, we never went to sleep.

My phone beeped with voice-mail notification after voice-mail notification. "I have to get those."

"Uh-uh." Relentless python arms held me down.

Giggles bubbled up but were cut off short when those python arms squeezed me to silence.

I strained out just one question, "So, they're making you bulk up?" Then, air returned to my lungs, and blood flow began its normal cycle.

Maneuvering to sit against his headboard, Kyle pulled me up with him. His T-shirt dwarfed my body, so my modesty was intact.

Not that it mattered too much. He'd managed to defile me all night and once this morning. I was in dire need of a shower, but he refused to let me out of the bed.

"Just tone up." He flexed his muscles for me.

I could see that each muscle had become more and more defined since I last saw him. Three months could really change a person.

My phone buzzed one more time. I couldn't take it anymore. I'd ignored it enough and I knew my mom was probably losing her mind.

I'd meant to call my mom the moment I arrived back at my hotel. I'd called her right as I parked at the stadium, but I hadn't had the chance to call her again when arriving at the hotel for the night. Because I hadn't made it to the hotel last night. And I was thanking the Lord that I hadn't. Because this bed...Kyle...this was where I belonged.

When I started to crawl over Kyle's legs, he growled and tossed me back on my ass.

"I told you no." His bared teeth went directly for my neck as he straddled my hips and caged me in with those huge arms.

I shrieked. He could be so intimidating even if I knew he was playing. My body's natural instinct was to flail and kick out.

I kicked his shin with my foot but caught his groin with my knee. He wheezed out a tight breath.

"Are you okay?" I tried to come off concerned, but it came out surrounded with stifled laughter.

"Ugh. Go get your phone, Kennedy. I need a moment to recover."

I cringed at the high-pitched, pain-filled tone he had.

I whispered as I slid off the bed, "I'm really sorry."

When I picked up my phone, notifications lit up the screen. All from my mom. Instead of scanning the messages, I just dialed her number.

Her frantic voice, followed by the calming voice of Cole, filled the line before I could say anything.

"If anything's happened to her, I'll kill you!" she screamed into the phone.

"Jesus, Mom. This isn't *Taken*, and you're definitely no Liam Neeson."

"It's probably just her calling you back, Sandra." Cole sounded far off in the background.

"It is." I waited for her to stop her theatrics. "I'm fine, Mom. Dieter found me at the stadium, and then we all met up at a little restaurant." It was best to leave out the fact that it was a bar. I'd promised Mom I wouldn't drink and that I'd stay away from that kind of environment. "I'm with Kyle now, at Lo and Chase's house."

"So, everything is okay?"

I tried to appease her worrying mind as best as I could.

We chatted for almost an hour while Kyle recovered from his *accident.*

But, before I could hang up, she asked to speak with Kyle.

He slipped into the bathroom and turned the water on in the shower and the sink to muffle out his voice. I knocked in vain, trying to get in there to hear what they were talking about—I mean, to take a shower.

On the impatient fifth knock, he swung the door open and held the phone out to me, a smirk lighting up his whole face.

You're an ass, I mouthed.

Mom's muttering was still going strong.

I suspiciously eyed him before putting the phone to my ear. "Mom?"

"So, you're happy? This is what you want?"

Her question made me narrow my eyes even more at Kyle. They were unclear squints now. His smirk was now distorted from the shadows of my eyelashes.

"I'm happy," I agreed. "As far as what I want...I just want to be with Kyle."

"All right then."

I loved the happiness that I could hear in her voice. She was genuinely happy for me.

"It's too late to enroll in a school for this semester, so find a job. You can't just sit around. Find a school you like that you want to go to down there. And we'll get everything ready for the spring semester."

Kyle pulled me back against his chest as I stared into the mirror. With his knees bent, he was low enough to rest his chin on my shoulder.

I love you, he mouthed.

To heaven and back, I mouthed back.

"Kennedy Grace Kiblen, did you hear me?"

I focused back on the phone call, shaking my head, trying not to smile so hard. At this rate, my cheeks were going to be sore. "What'd you say, Mom?"

"I love you, okay? I know you're making the right decision. I just want you to know you can always come back home. And Cole says St. Louis is your home just as much."

It was still hard to accept the fact that my mom had moved on. It was hard to accept that it was with the man who had nearly wrecked my entire family. He wasn't the only one at fault; I knew that. I recognized that. I was just as much to blame in the end as anyone else.

And that was why I had forgiven him. Just as he'd forgiven me for my crappy teenager attitude. He'd accepted me as much as I had accepted him.

For now, that was good enough.

Kyle had run down to my truck to get my suitcase late last night, so I could brush my teeth. I pulled out a modest tankini, so we could join our friends outside. The others had been up for a while. Their splashes and shouts from the pool and patio echoed up to Kyle's window.

Kyle and I showered and made ourselves decent before heading downstairs. Slow claps embraced us as we made our way outside.

Red splotches marred my skin as the embarrassment kicked in. Dieter's girlie moans and Chase's grunts made it ten times worse as they aired our activities like a dirty rated R play.

Kyle flipped them all off, and I just buried my too-hot face into his chest.

This was our normal.

It felt so good to be back to my old self.

The Kennedy who loved her faith, family, and friends.

The Kennedy who didn't need to be saved.

Because I already was.

EPilogue

Kyle

Sprints could kiss my ass.

Coach had us running because Alex Wright had fumbled the football four times at Friday's game. We'd all kick his ass if he wasn't the assistant defense coach's son. He was already getting his ask kicked with his own brand of punishment. The assistant coach was giving Wright a verbal ass-beating that made even me pucker up. I almost felt bad for the kid before I remembered what the fuck I was doing.

Suicide. Sprints. That. Never. Ended.

If we won our next game, we'd be going to a bowl game. As a starting freshman quarterback, I needed that bowl game, so we could take it on to the championship game. I wouldn't be able to do that if Wright kept fumbling my fucking football.

The whistle blew, and I dropped to the ground like dead weight. The fatigue settled into my muscles almost instantly. I couldn't decide if I was just in pain or already dead.

"Hit the showers, boys. And don't drop my fucking football in a game next time."

It took me longer than usual to get up.

I blamed Kennedy for that.

We'd made up for lost time, sure, but that hadn't seemed to satiate her. For such an innocent little angel, she certainly did like to tempt me like the devil. Her teasing never lasted long. She almost always got herself so worked up, I'd have to finish the job.

I wasn't complaining, but after the pleasurable workout she had given me last night and the punishing workout I'd just completed—thanks to Sir Drops the Ball A Lot—I didn't know if I'd be able to walk to my truck.

"We're still hitting up your girl's work tonight, right?"

I squinted up at one of my teammates, not sure who it was until I sat up.

Gabe Rollins was a six-foot-six beast built with enough muscle to feed a Third World country.

He held his hand out to me to help me up.

I took it, knowing I was about to be yanked up from the ground like an unwanted weed. "Easy. Last time, you nearly dislocated my shoulder."

His laugh was his only response before he was pulling me up. "Yeah, and when's that spitfire brunette coming back to town?"

I hadn't noticed all the players that had stuck around outside, too caught up in my head, planning what I wanted to do to Kennedy later tonight.

"Masters!" Rollins shouted.

"Huh? Who? T? She's off-limits. That's my little sister you're talking about."

A couple of guys laughed before throwing out a few crude comments.

I shook my head before anything else was said, and I sliced my hand through the air, like a guillotine. "If I find out anyone on this team gets near her, heads will roll. Just fucking know that." My words were final, and anyone who contested it would find out firsthand.

"Aw, come one, Masters. At camp, you said you only had an older brother." Drew Lawrence, one of the seniors, elbowed the guy next to him. "Can't be keeping all the hot pussy to yourself. Share the—"

He was clocked across the jaw before he knew what was coming. His body hit the ground like a sack of potatoes.

Clemmons shook out his hand and squatted down to where Lawrence held his jaw like a little bitch. "No one talks about Little T like that. She's my little sister, too, you punk ass. So, watch your motherfuckin' mouth before you don't have one."

I couldn't help but grin. I'd told them. They should have known better.

"I'll see you all at the bar." I left them all standing around Lawrence, cracking jokes about how he'd better not be that easy to take down on a game day.

I drove home faster than necessary, ready to see my girl again.

When I got home, I showered quickly and changed into jeans and a button-down. Kennedy had a thing for gripping the collar of my shirt when she kissed me. I was tired of her stretching out all the necks of my T-shirts, so I wore button-downs to avoid it.

Then, I was out the door, honking my horn to hurry Chase.

Chase hopped in my truck, so we could pick up Dieter at the dorms.

When Dieter slipped into the backseat, he was muttering under his breath. All I could catch was *motherfucker* and *stupid whine-ass*.

"Problem, D?" Chase twisted around to see our friend.

I just glanced in my rearview mirror to catch him looking up and glaring some murderous vibes at us.

He pointed to the dorms he'd just walked out of. Three floors up and the second window from the furthest out, there was a guy waving down at us with one hand and flipping us off with the other.

"He fucking wiped his ass on one of my T-shirts and then threw it on my bed. He's lucky I only punched him once and walked out."

Chase and I both gagged at the thought.

"You should just move in with us. Like we told you to do from the beginning." Chase threw a mini hand sanitizer bottle back that Dieter didn't even hesitate to use. "And, now, we need to come up with a good plan for retribution. You don't fuck with us."

As they schemed and discussed revenge, I drove us downtown to the bar where Kennedy and Lo had found jobs.

Lord, help us all.

Kennedy's mom had told her to get a job, but when she'd found out it was at a bar, she'd demanded Kennedy quit right then.

I hadn't thought it was a good idea at first either. But she was under twenty-one, and the owner absolutely loved her. She ran the mechanical bull and sometimes stepped in to help bus tables.

The first time I'd met Savannah, the owner, I'd thought I was going to get my ass kicked. She was the buffest damn woman I'd ever seen. And she took an instant liking to our girls, even threatened to castrate us like the bulls she had on her ranch if we ever hurt *her* girls.

She paid them well and worked around their schedules. Kennedy and Lo never worked a game night, and when the crowds got rowdy, security was right beside them. That was a major plus for Chase and me. It was hard enough to know they were here, being hit on every night, and not lose our minds.

It was a Thursday, so we could expect the crowds to be big but nothing like a Saturday.

Some of the football guys were already there, taking up the tables with their massive bodies. Clemmons was sitting at the bar, chatting with Lo and Savannah.

I didn't see Kennedy anywhere, so I walked over to ask Lo where she was. Before I even made it that far, Kennedy's voice was loud and clear on the bullhorn.

She flipped the siren switch and got the bar to quiet down.

When it was silent, she brought the bullhorn back to her mouth. Her cutoff jeans shorts were sexy as all hell. They were just short enough to torment me but not so short that they were obscene. Her sleeveless lace top was a deep red with a high neck. Her custom cowboy boots that I'd had made for her with angel wings, a cross, and our initials made her look like the queen of Texas.

I was so busy taking in her body that I didn't realize she was waiting for *my* attention to be on her.

When our eyes connected, she winked and blew me a kiss. "A little birdy told me a quarterback was here to catch himself a mustang."

A chorus of oohs and aahs rang out.

I shook my head, my grin taking over my face.

"Who's this little birdy?" I shouted back at her.

She stood up at a podium that housed the controls for her mechanical bull.

Kennedy pointed to Talan, who jumped into the mechanical bullring. A big cowboy hat that I could tell wasn't hers was flopped down onto her head. She was wearing a similar outfit to Kennedy's, but her tank was lower cut. I shook my head. She was going to be trouble tonight.

I cupped my hands around my mouth while shouting back, "She got it wrong! I'm not here to catch a mustang."

Kennedy raised an inquisitive eyebrow and waited, her pouty lips puckered.

"I'm here to be saved by an angel!"

This time, a very feminine chorus of awes rang out, and before I knew it, Kennedy was down from the podium, across the cushioned mechanical bull pit, and jumping off the barrier, so I could catch her. Her legs wrapped around my waist, and her watery smile made me chuckle a little.

I wiped at her mascara that threatened to run with her emotions. "Catching that mustang was easier than I thought it'd be." I was aware of how cheesy I sounded. That was why I couldn't stop smiling and laughing.

"I love you, Kyle."

The softest lips touched mine, effectively shutting me up. We stayed just like that, embracing one another, as music started, and we faded to the background of everyone's night.

"To heaven and back, Kennedy. Even through a little bit of hell."

The End

Playlist

"Fader" by The Temper Trap
"7/11" by Beyoncé
"Worth It" by Fifth Harmony
"GDFR" by Flo Rida
"Simple Desire" by All Mankind
"Sugar" by Maroon 5
"Ride" by Twenty One Pilots
"Bitch Better Have My Money" by Rihanna
"I Mean It" by G-Eazy
"Female Robbery" by The Neighbourhood
"99 Problems" by Jay Z
"Little Things" by One Direction
"Strange Love" by Halsey
"Habits" by Tove Lo
"Love Songs Drug Songs" by X Ambassadors

Acknowledgments

I honestly have to thank the readers first, especially the ones who checked my Facebook page every week—commenting, messaging me, and wanting this story as badly as I wanted to write it. You were all so patient, and I can't thank you enough. *Saved* was supposed to be published in early 2016, but life kept getting in the way, and family became my number one priority. But you guys never stopped wanting this story. And that means the world to me.

I laid to rest three family members this year, and as hard as that was, I found *Saved* saving me. I've always kept my emotions buried even though I know that isn't a healthy way to deal. Writing gave me an outlet, something to look forward to, and a way to express all my bottled-up emotions. So, thank you again, readers, for giving me this opportunity.

To my parents—You support every crazy idea I come up with. I can't thank you enough. You make every dream attainable, and even when I crash and burn, you're there for me, picking me up and loving me through it. I love you.

Juice-tin—Bro, I'm still the funniest person in this family.

My cousin, Brandi—Your unwavering support and cheerleading makes me believe anything is possible. P.S. Can we please go back to Lake Wylie?

Jennifer— Thank you for always being a message away.

Jovana— My goodness, you are my editing savior! I'm so lucky to have gotten the chance to work with you. Thank you for taking on a newbie!

Colleen, the best damn beta reader in the world—You make me love writing even more, especially when I make you cry. ;) I can't wait to attend more reader events, which let us share our joy for books.

About The Author

Krista Holly is a writer currently living in the most humid state ever—aka Florida. Originally from the City of Sin, she's the youngest of two. She's traveled the country, going from coast to coast, for as long as she can remember, only fueling her gypsy heart. She's a Namast'ay-in-bed kind of girl and an ambivert, only because her day job refuses to let her be an introvert. She studied all sorts of things in college before settling on business. Krista loves the color orange and the fall season, which only enforces her need to move out of the forever sunny and warm-as-hell state of Florida.

Wanted is her debut novel, published in April 2015.

Saved can be read as a stand-alone, but recommended to be read after *Wanted*.

Connect Online!

www.kristahollyauthor.com

www.facebook.com/KristaHollyAuthor

www.twitter.com/Krista_Holly

www.instagram.com/kristahollyauthor